WITCHES
of
BROOKLYN
WHAT THE HEX?!

Also by Sophie Escabasse

Witches of Brooklyn

Sophie Escabasse

Witches of Brooklyn
What the Hex?!

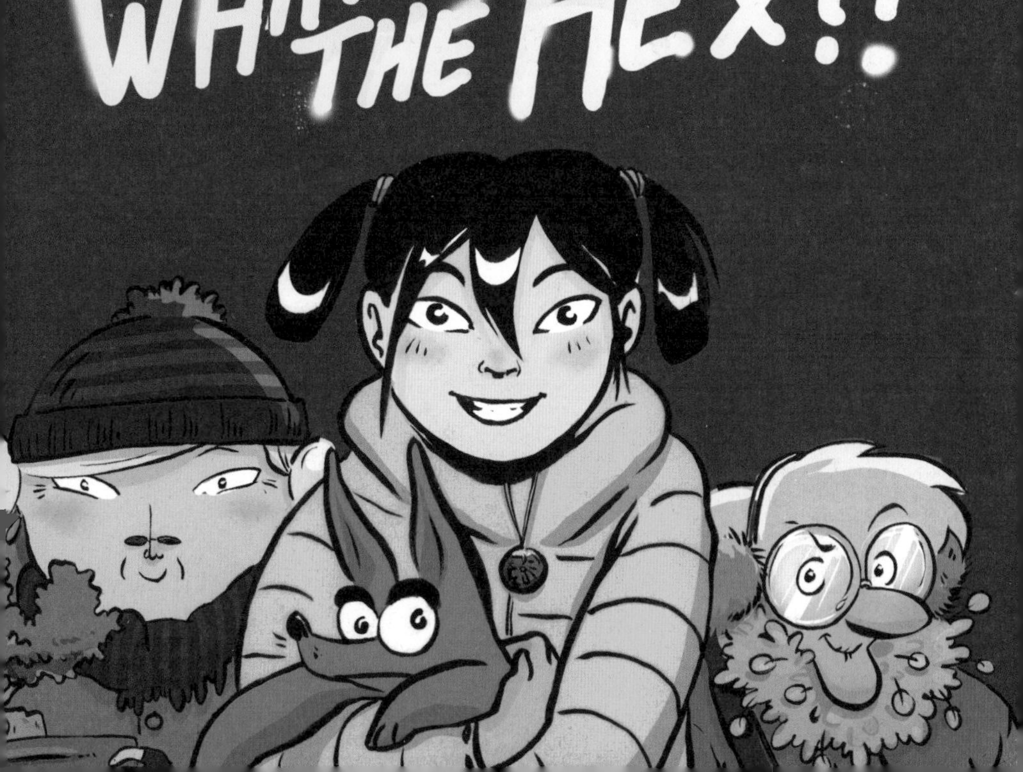

What the Hex?! was drawn with red pencils of all sorts, until they were two and a half inches long. Book 1 was sketched in blue and I wanted to easily differentiate the sketches of book 2. Then all the pages were scanned. Inking and coloring were done with Procreate and Photoshop.

Text, cover art, and interior illustrations copyright © 2021 by Sophie Escabasse
Case art used under license from Shutterstock.com

All rights reserved. Published in the United States by RH Graphic, an imprint of Random House Children's Books, a division of Penguin Random House LLC, New York.

RH Graphic with the book design is a trademark of Penguin Random House LLC.

Visit us on the Web! RHKidsGraphic.com • @RHKidsGraphic

Educators and librarians, for a variety of teaching tools, visit us at RHTeachersLibrarians.com

Library of Congress Cataloging-in-Publication Data is available upon request.
ISBN 978-0-593-11930-3 (pbk.) — ISBN 978-0-593-12544-1 (trade)
ISBN 978-0-593-11931-0 (lib. bdg.) — ISBN 978-0-593-11932-7 (ebk)

Designed by Patrick Crotty

MANUFACTURED IN CHINA
10 9 8 7 6 5 4 3 2 1
First Edition

A comic on every bookshelf.

For Brooklyn and all my friends over there

Chapter 1

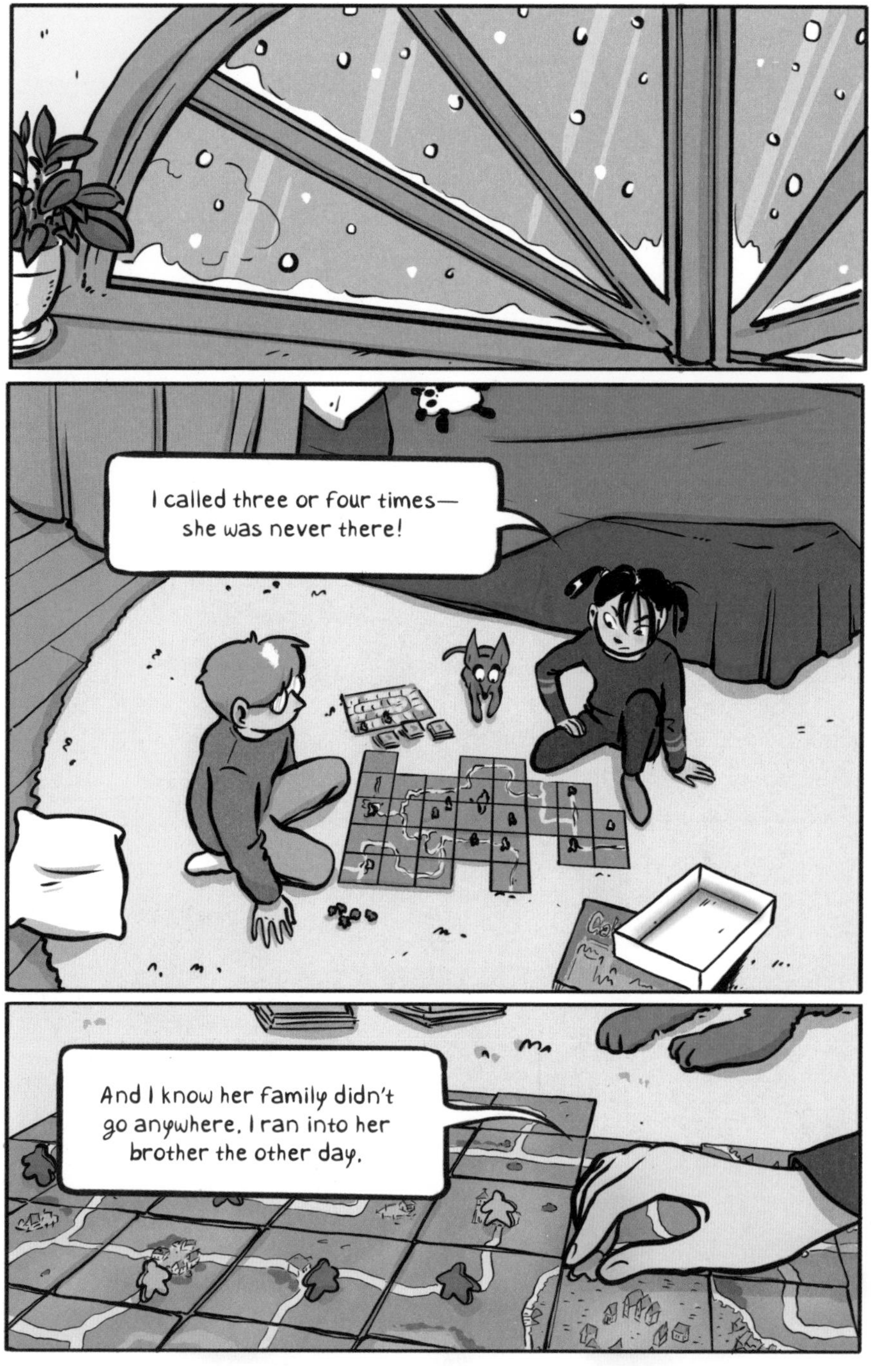
I called three or four times—
she was never there!
And I know her family didn't go anywhere. I ran into her brother the other day.

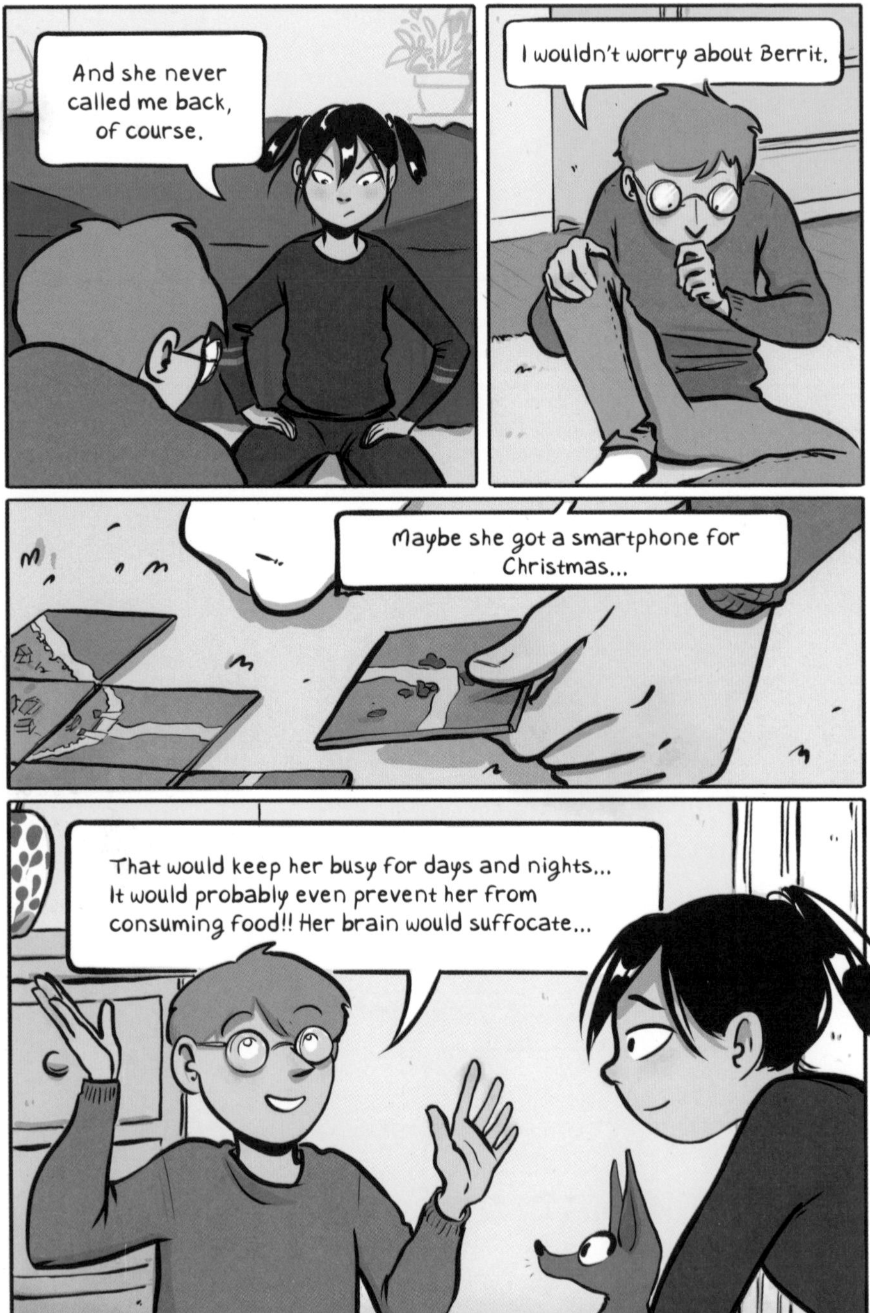
And she never called me back, of course.
I wouldn't worry about Berrit.
Maybe she got a smartphone for Christmas...
That would keep her busy for days and nights... It would probably even prevent her from consuming food!! Her brain would suffocate...

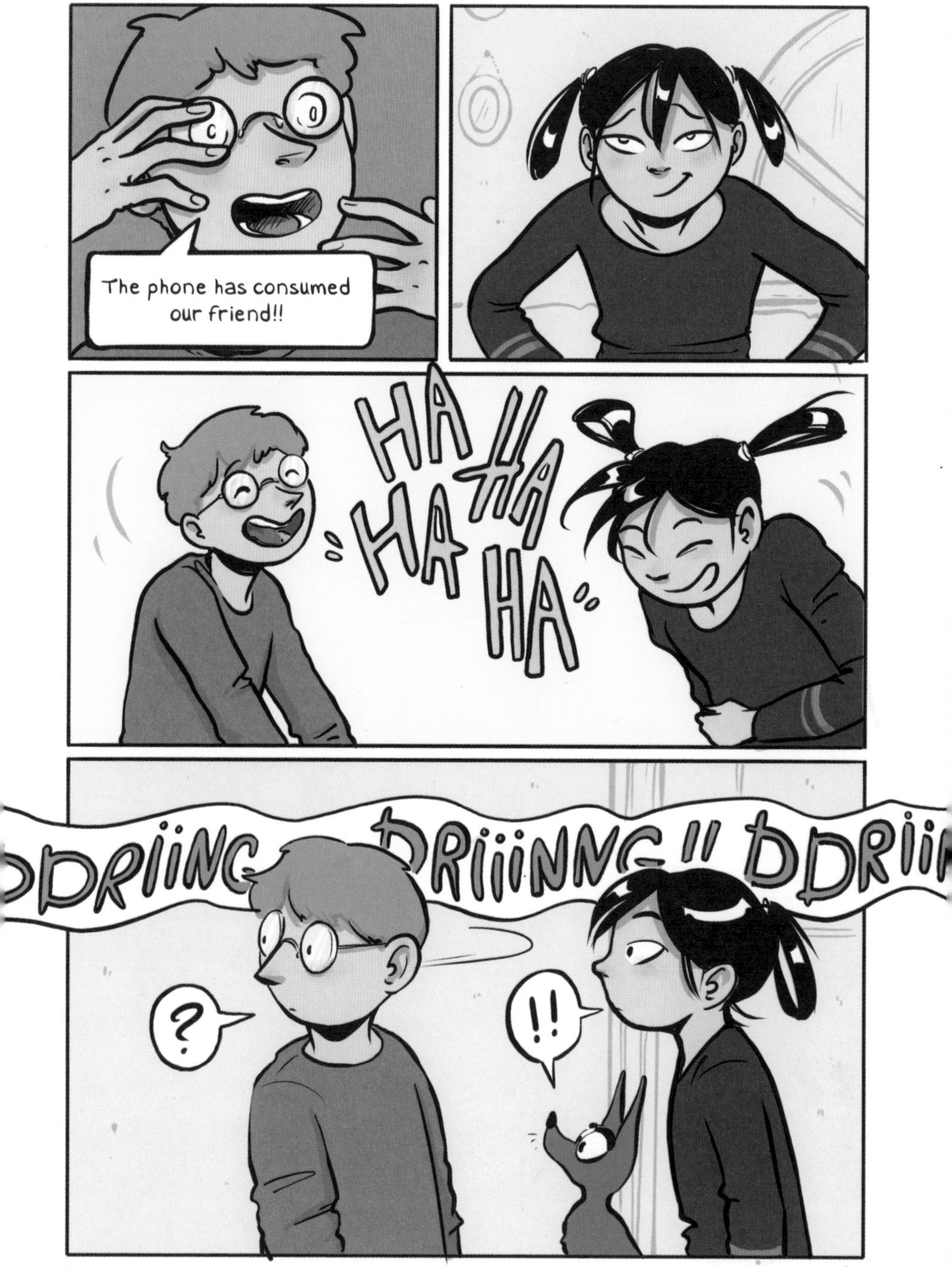
The phone has consumed our friend!!
HA HA HA HA HA
DRIING DRIIINNG!! DRII
?
!!

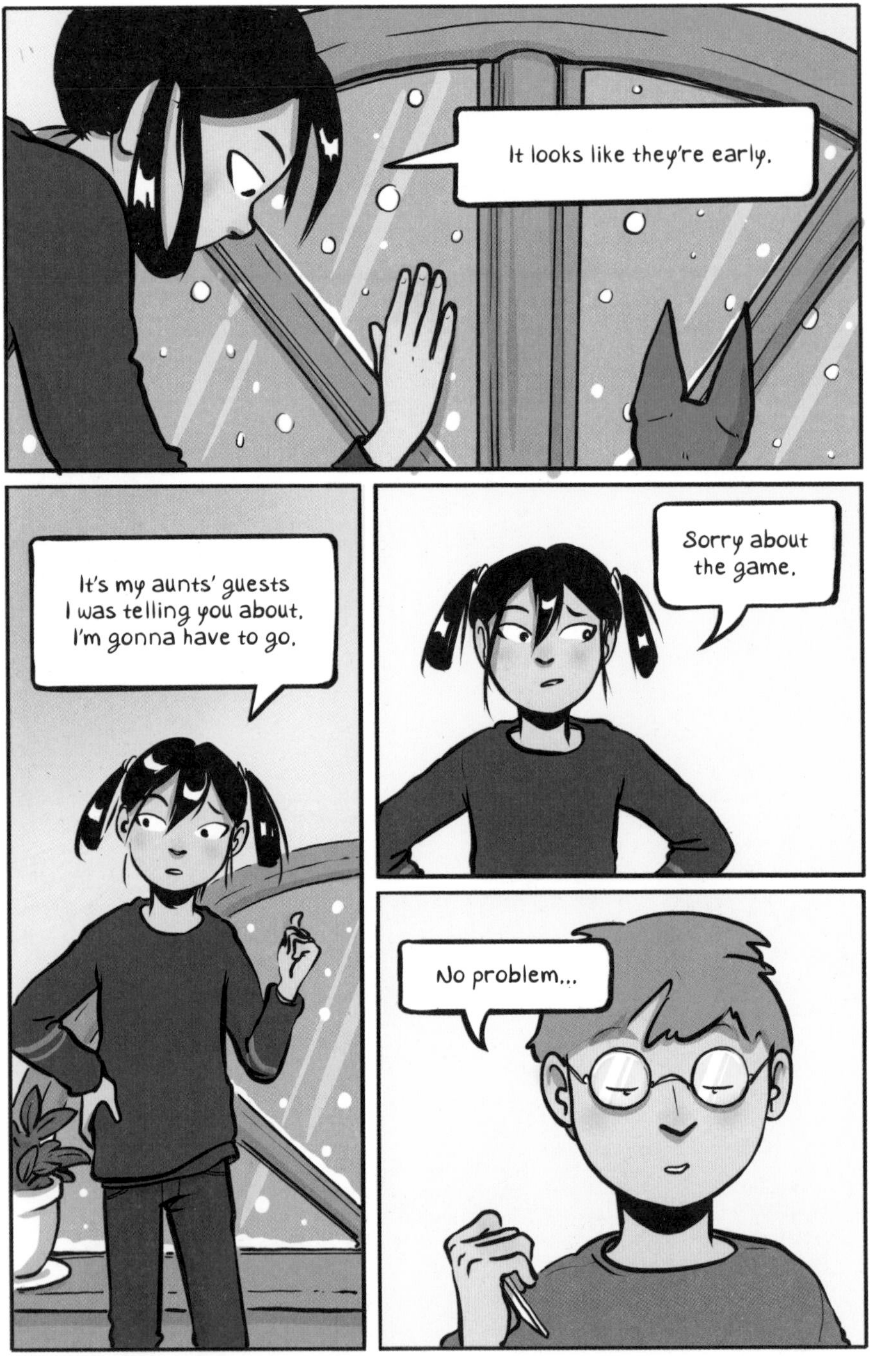
It looks like they're early.
It's my aunts' guests I was telling you about. I'm gonna have to go.
Sorry about the game.
No problem...

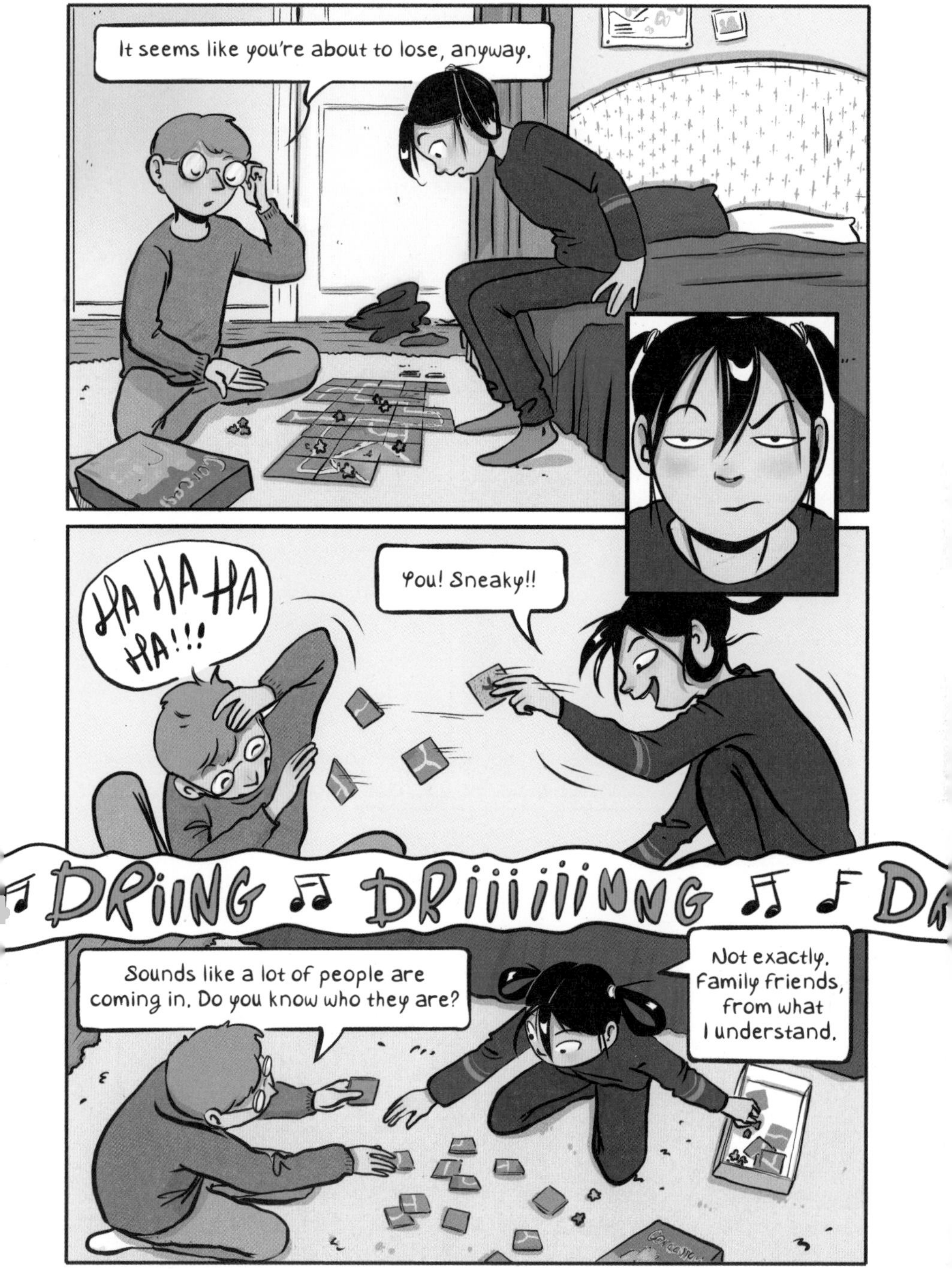
It seems like you're about to lose, anyway.
HA HA HA HA!!!
You! Sneaky!!
DRIING DRiiiiiiNNG DR
Sounds like a lot of people are coming in. Do you know who they are?
Not exactly. Family friends, from what I understand.

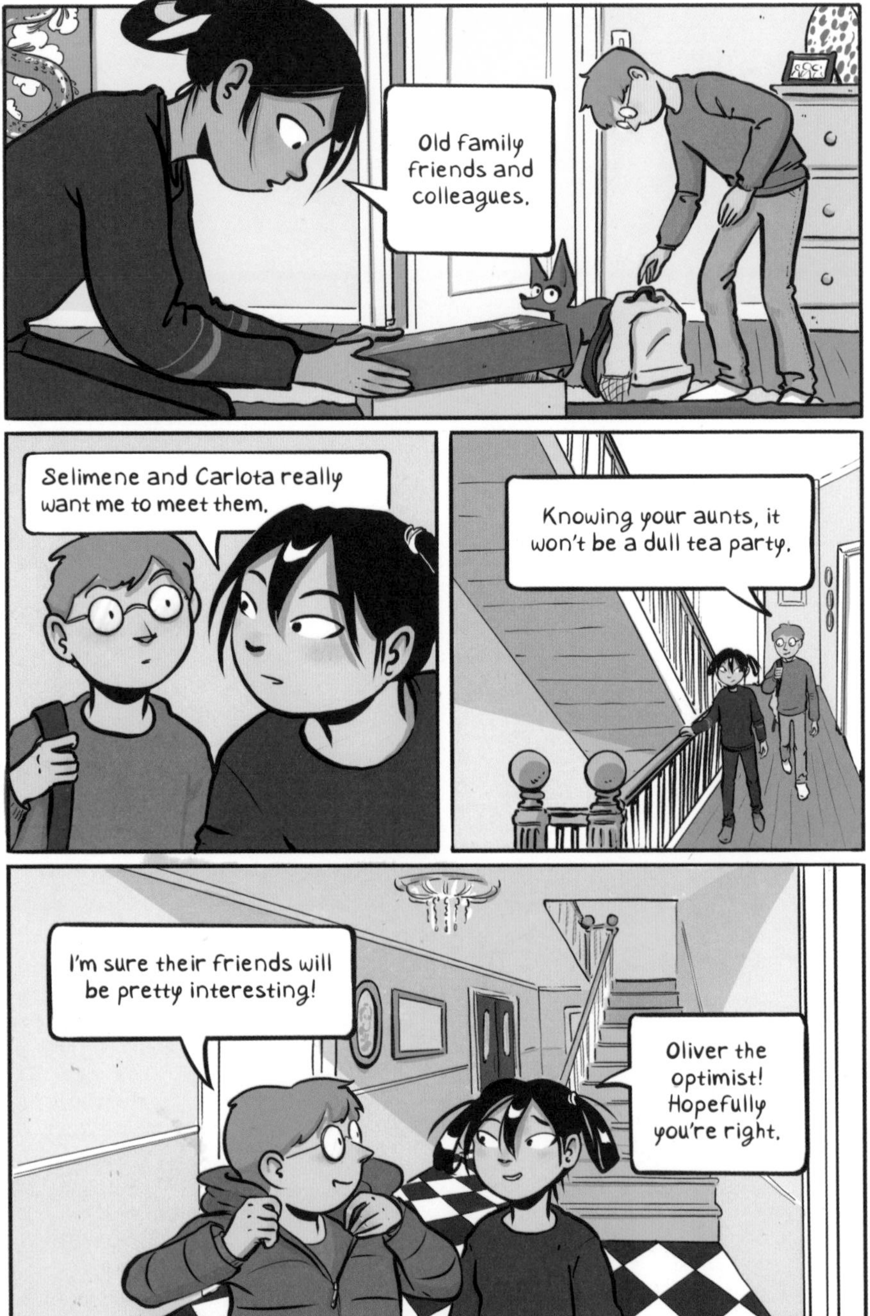
Old family friends and colleagues.
Selimene and Carlota really want me to meet them.
Knowing your aunts, it won't be a dull tea party.
I'm sure their friends will be pretty interesting!
Oliver the optimist! Hopefully you're right.

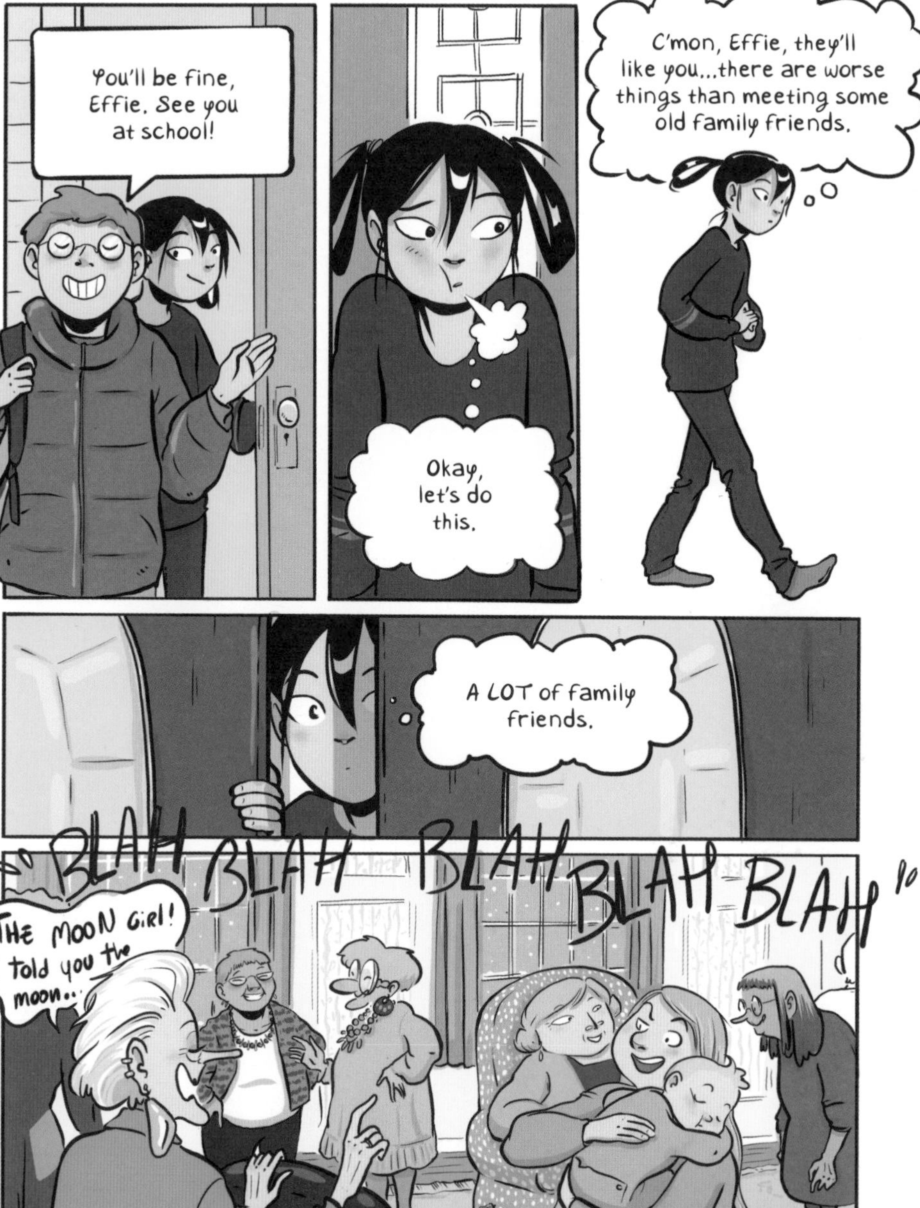
You'll be fine, Effie. See you at school!
Okay, let's do this.
C'mon, Effie, they'll like you...there are worse things than meeting some old family friends.
A LOT of family friends.
"BLAH BLAH BLAH BLAH BLAH"
THE MOON GIRL! I told you the moon...

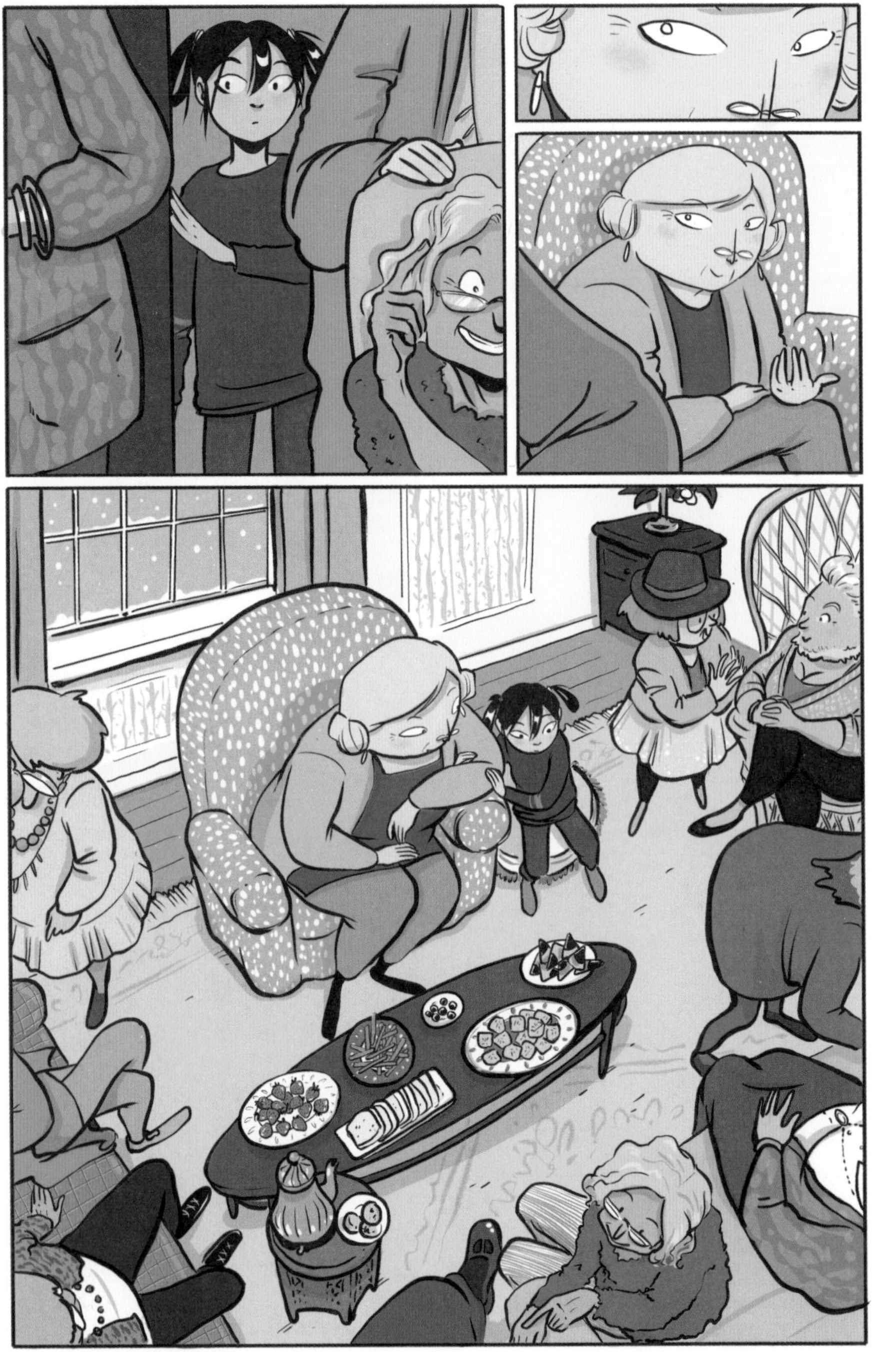

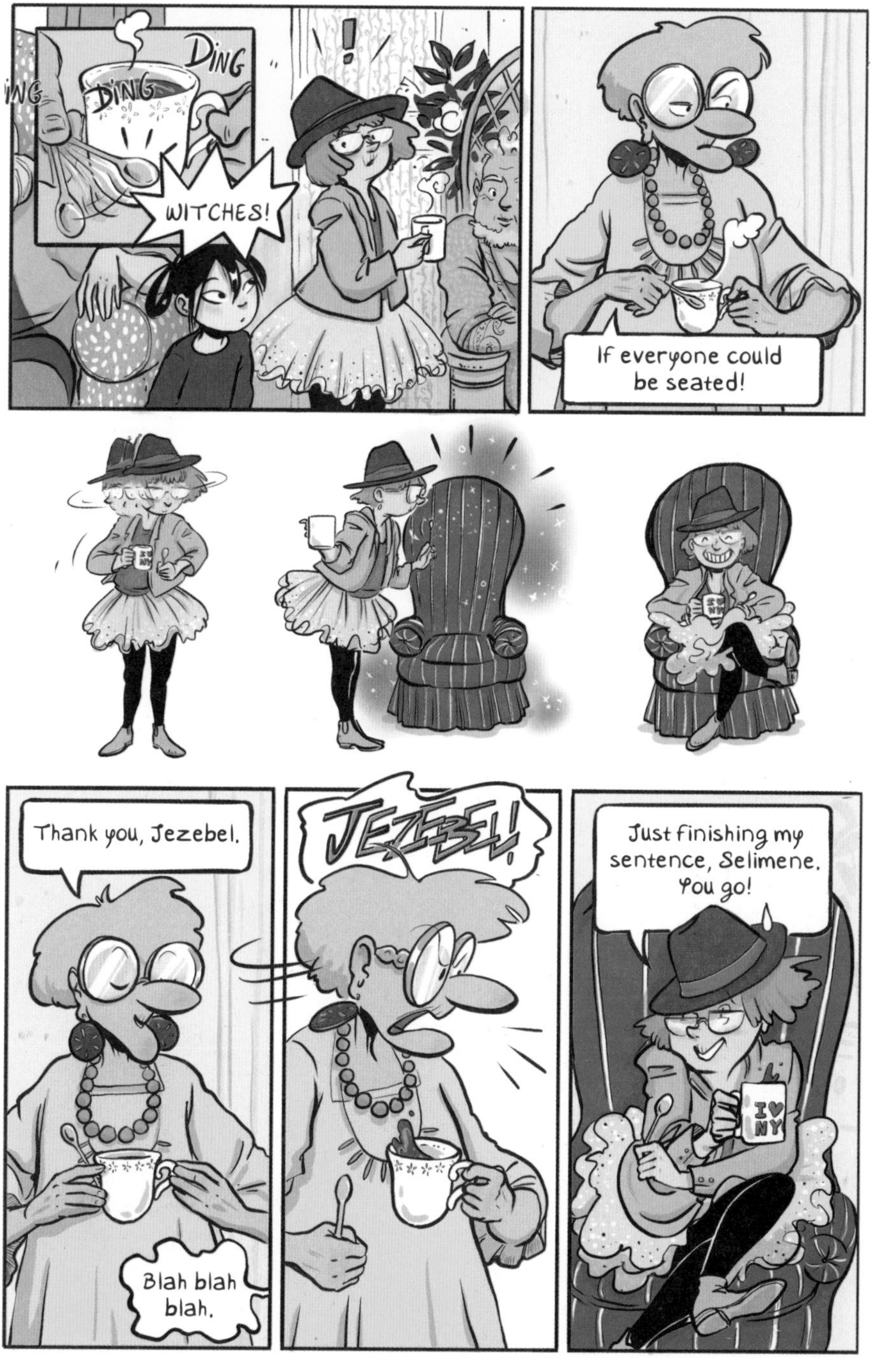
ING
DING
DING
WITCHES!
!
If everyone could be seated!
Thank you, Jezebel.
Blah blah blah.
JEZEBEL!
Just finishing my sentence, Selimene. You go!

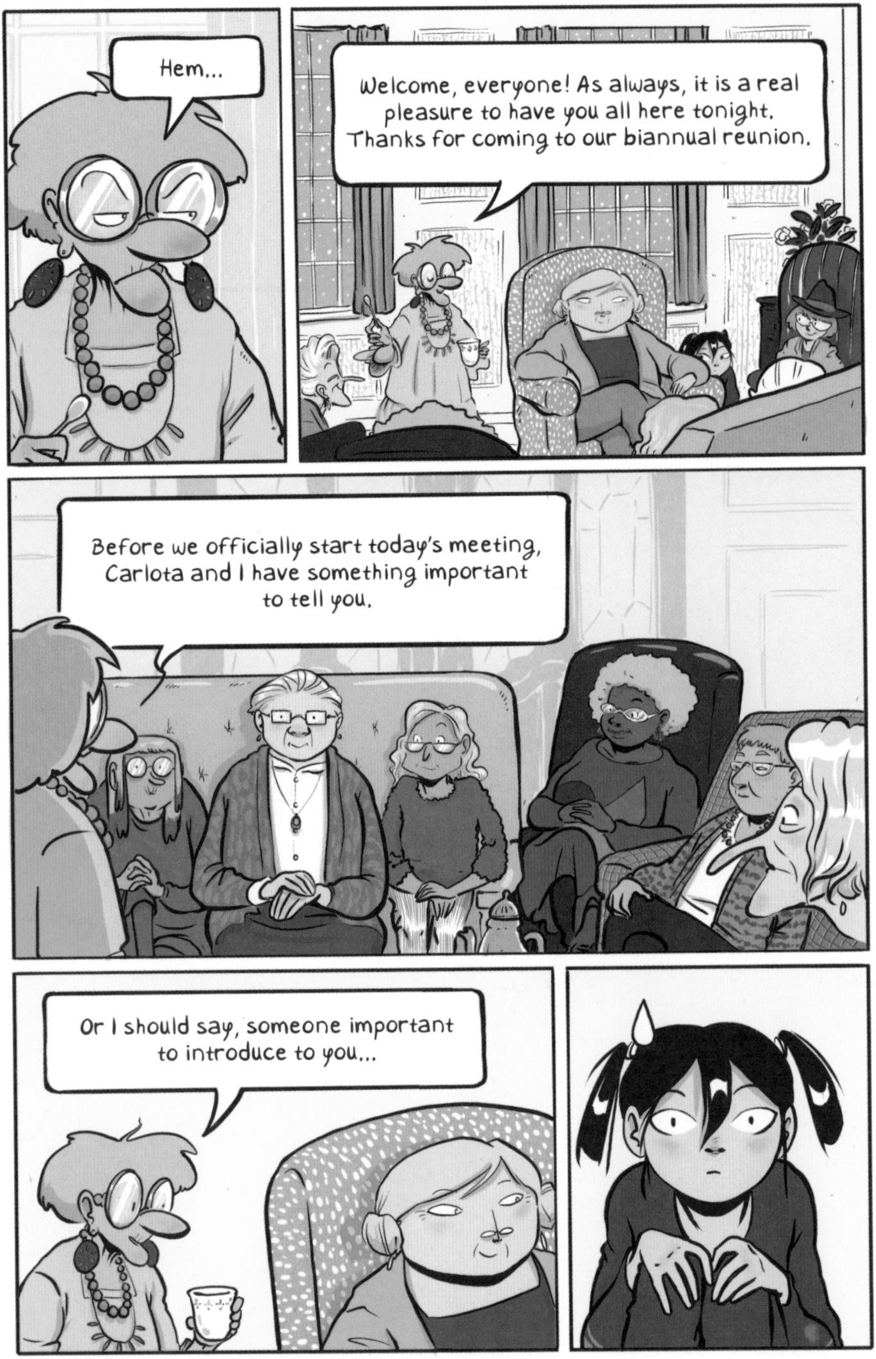
Hem...
Welcome, everyone! As always, it is a real pleasure to have you all here tonight. Thanks for coming to our biannual reunion.
Before we officially start today's meeting, Carlota and I have something important to tell you.
Or I should say, someone important to introduce to you...

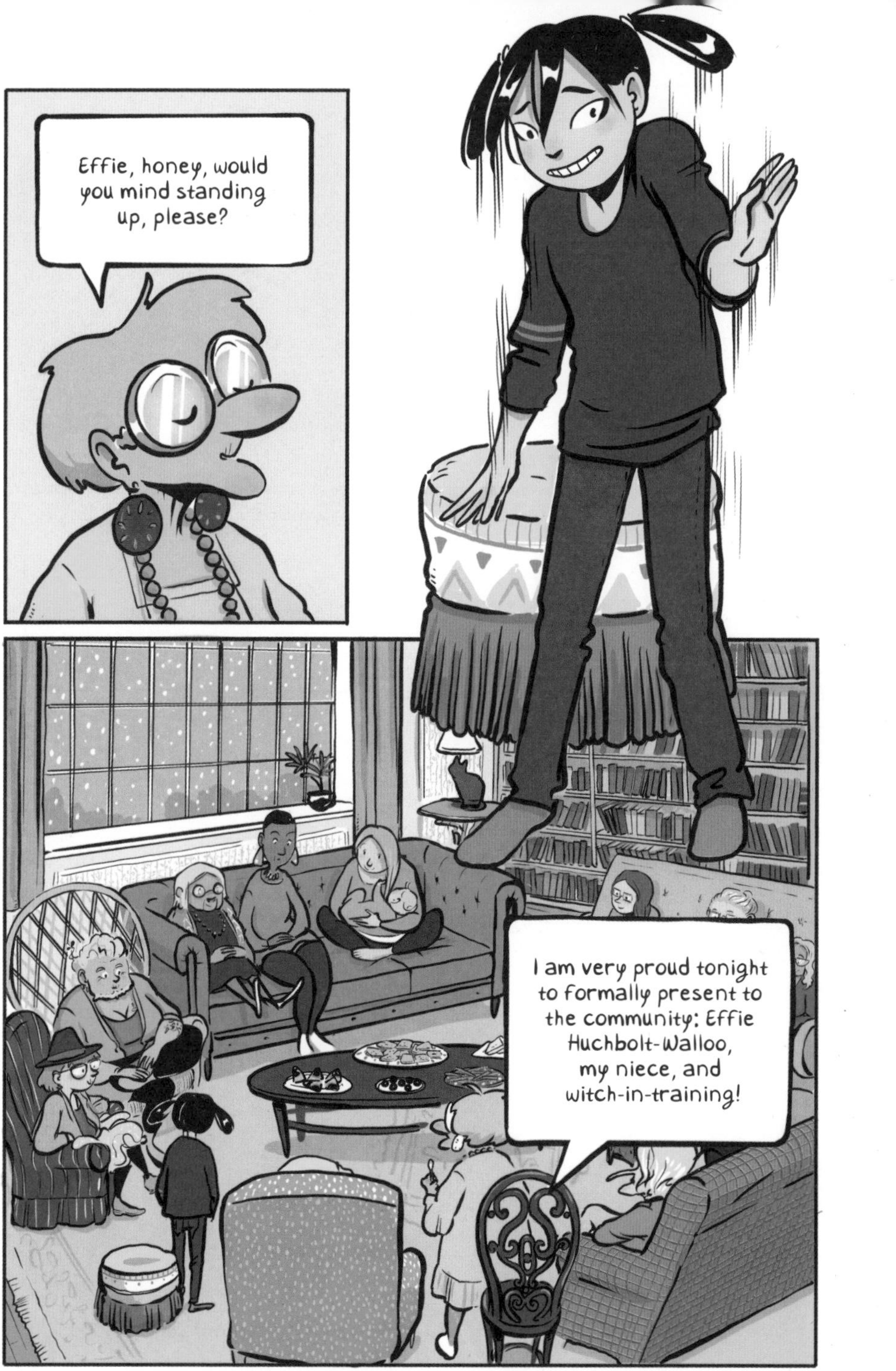
Effie, honey, would you mind standing up, please?
I am very proud tonight to formally present to the community: Effie Huchbolt-Walloo, my niece, and witch-in-training!

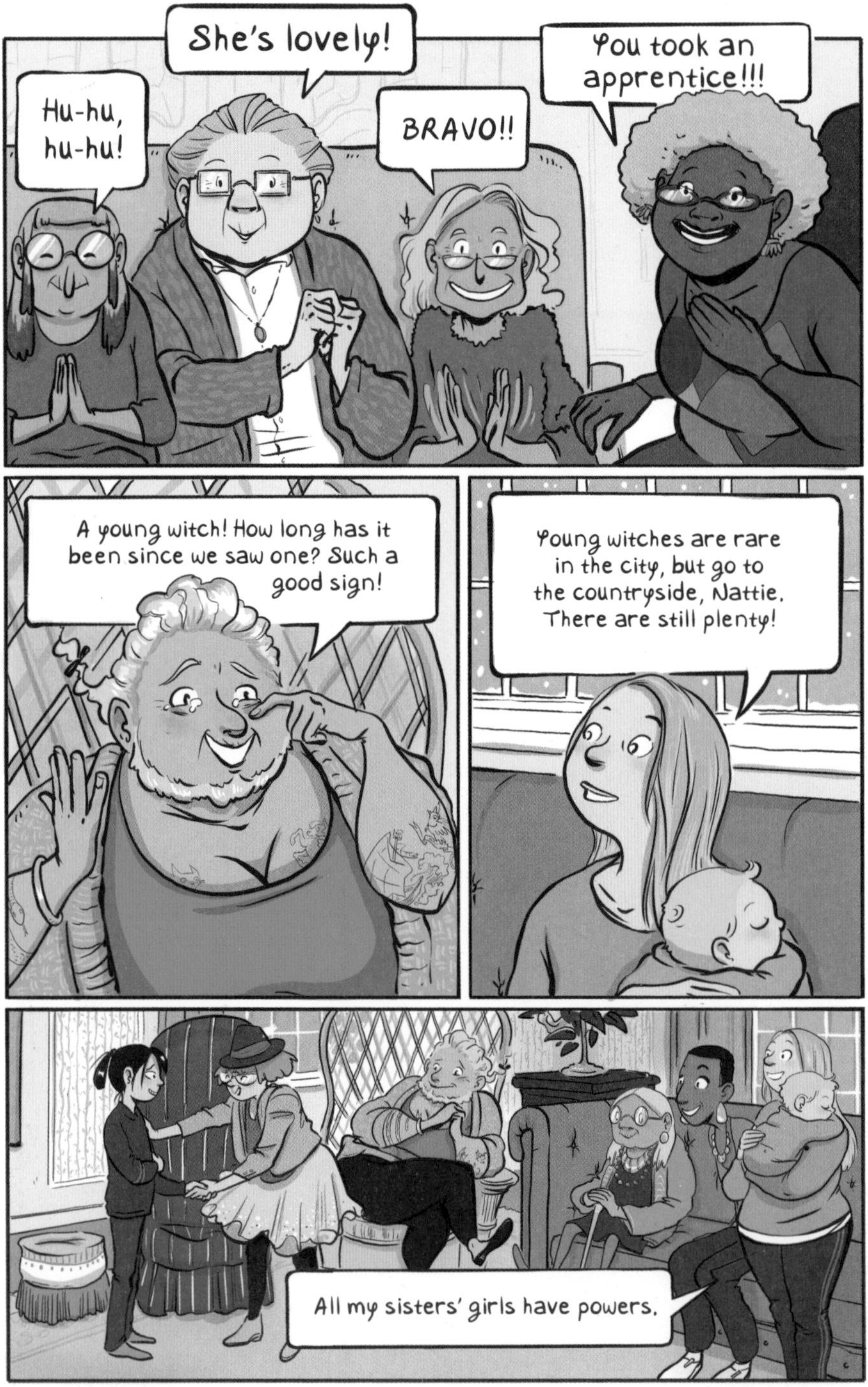

Hu-hu, hu-hu!
She's lovely!
BRAVO!!
You took an apprentice!!!
A young witch! How long has it been since we saw one? Such a good sign!
Young witches are rare in the city, but go to the countryside, Nattie. There are still plenty!
All my sisters' girls have powers.

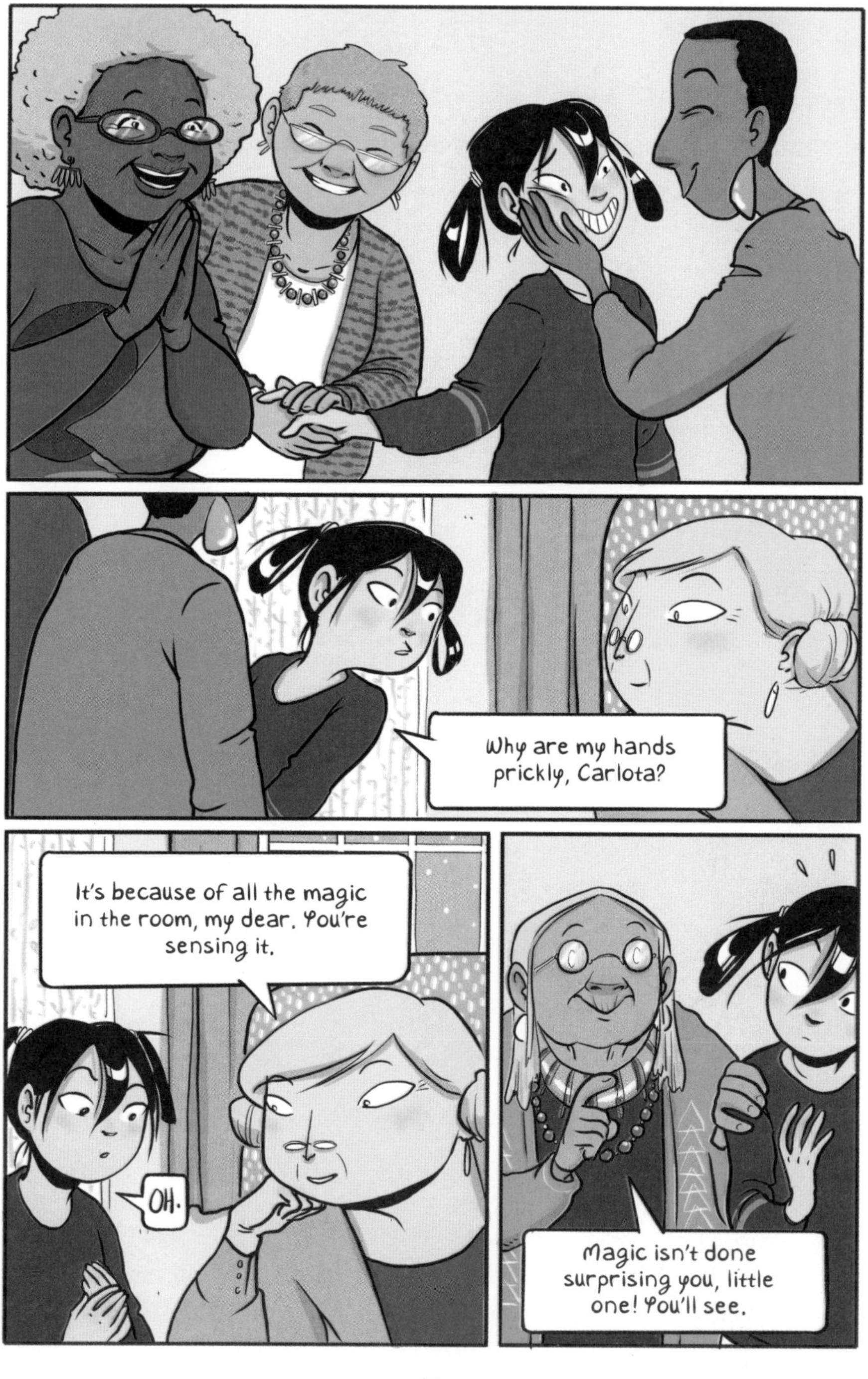
Why are my hands prickly, Carlota?
It's because of all the magic in the room, my dear. You're sensing it.
OH.
Magic isn't done surprising you, little one! You'll see.

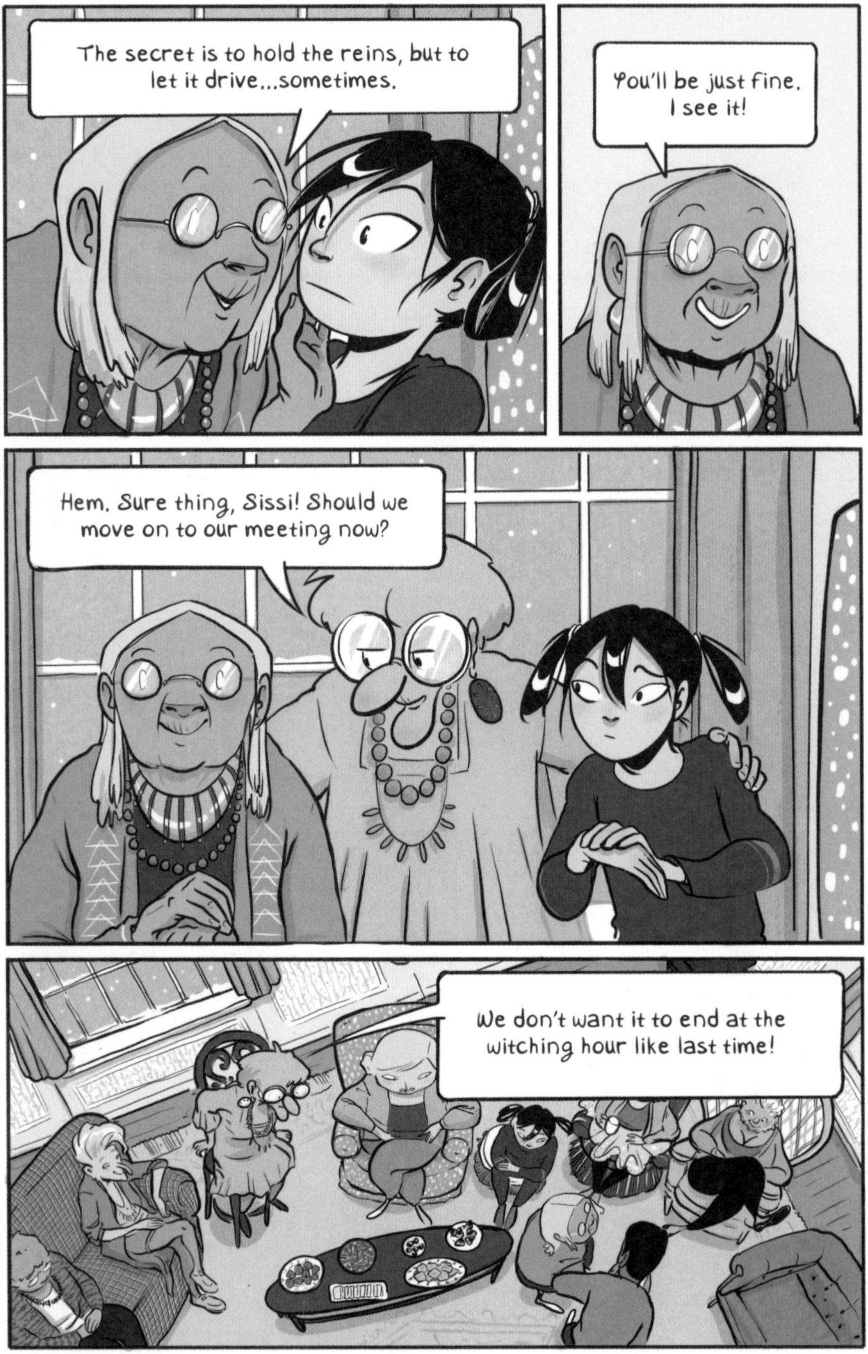
The secret is to hold the reins, but to let it drive...sometimes.
You'll be just fine. I see it!
Hem. Sure thing, Sissi! Should we move on to our meeting now?
We don't want it to end at the witching hour like last time!

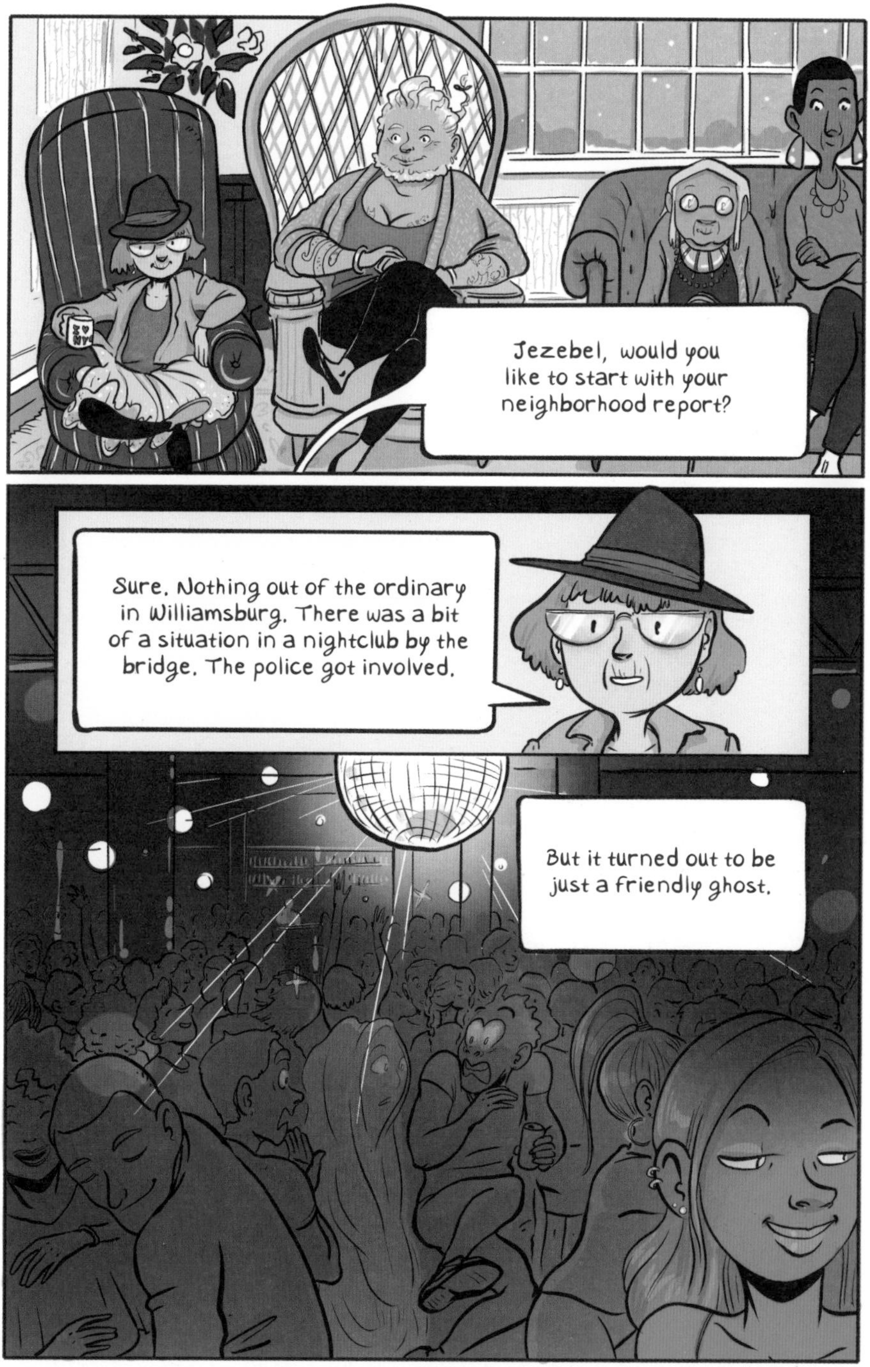
Jezebel, would you like to start with your neighborhood report?
Sure. Nothing out of the ordinary in Williamsburg. There was a bit of a situation in a nightclub by the bridge. The police got involved.
But it turned out to be just a friendly ghost.

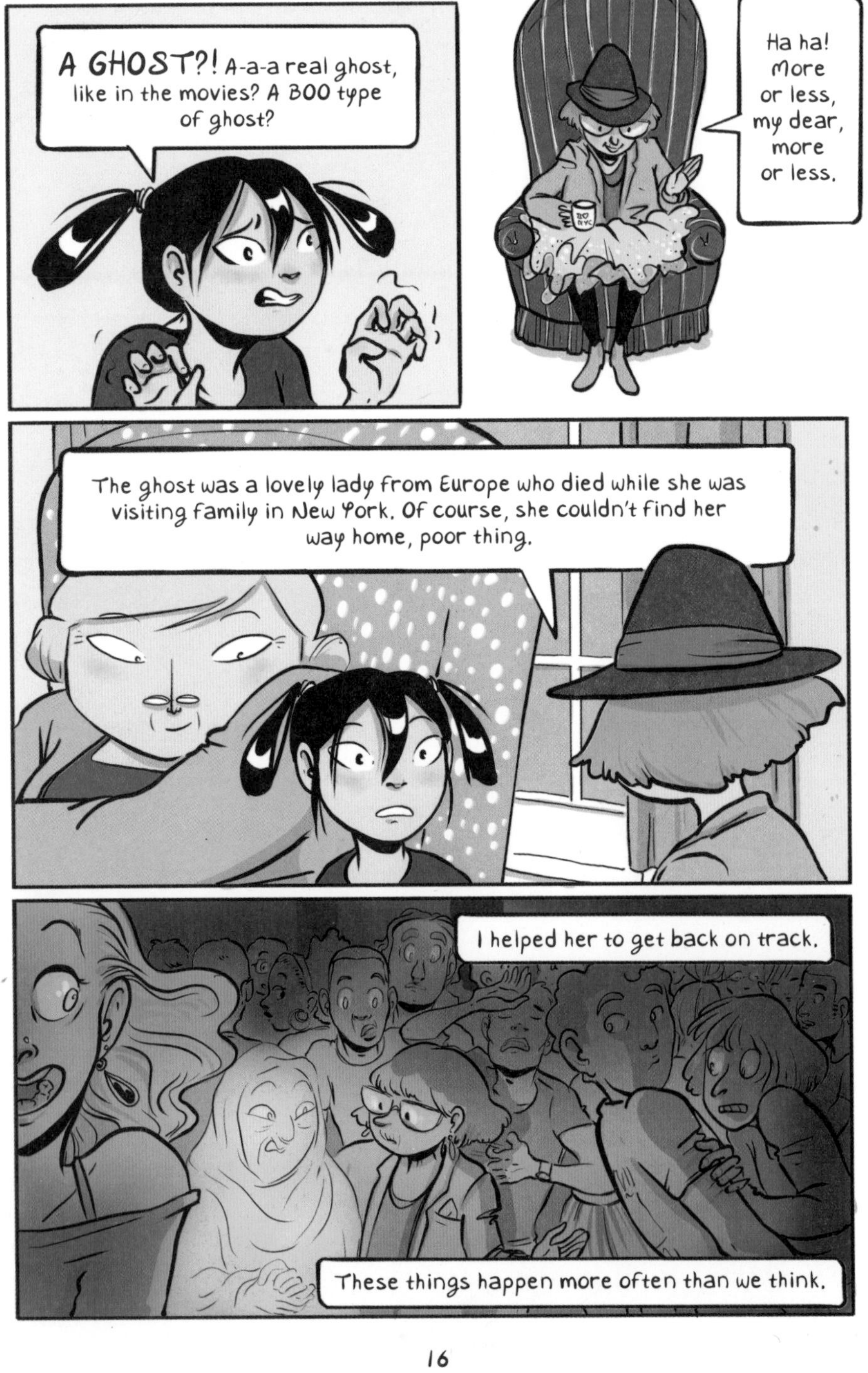
A GHOST?! A-a-a real ghost, like in the movies? A BOO type of ghost?
Ha ha! More or less, my dear, more or less.
The ghost was a lovely lady from Europe who died while she was visiting family in New York. Of course, she couldn't find her way home, poor thing.
I helped her to get back on track.
These things happen more often than we think.

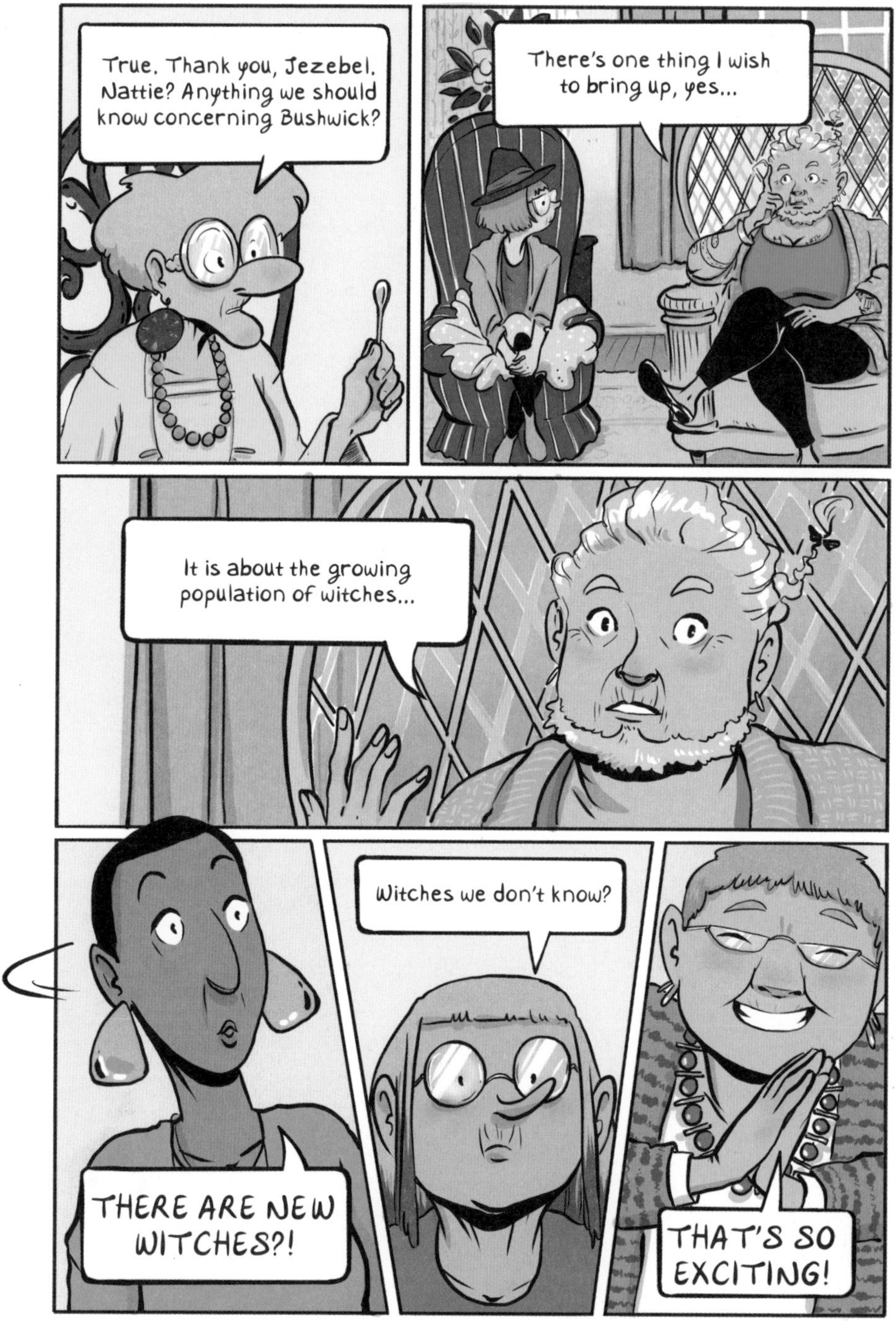
True. Thank you, Jezebel. Nattie? Anything we should know concerning Bushwick?
There's one thing I wish to bring up, yes...
It is about the growing population of witches...
THERE ARE NEW WITCHES?!
Witches we don't know?
THAT'S SO EXCITING!

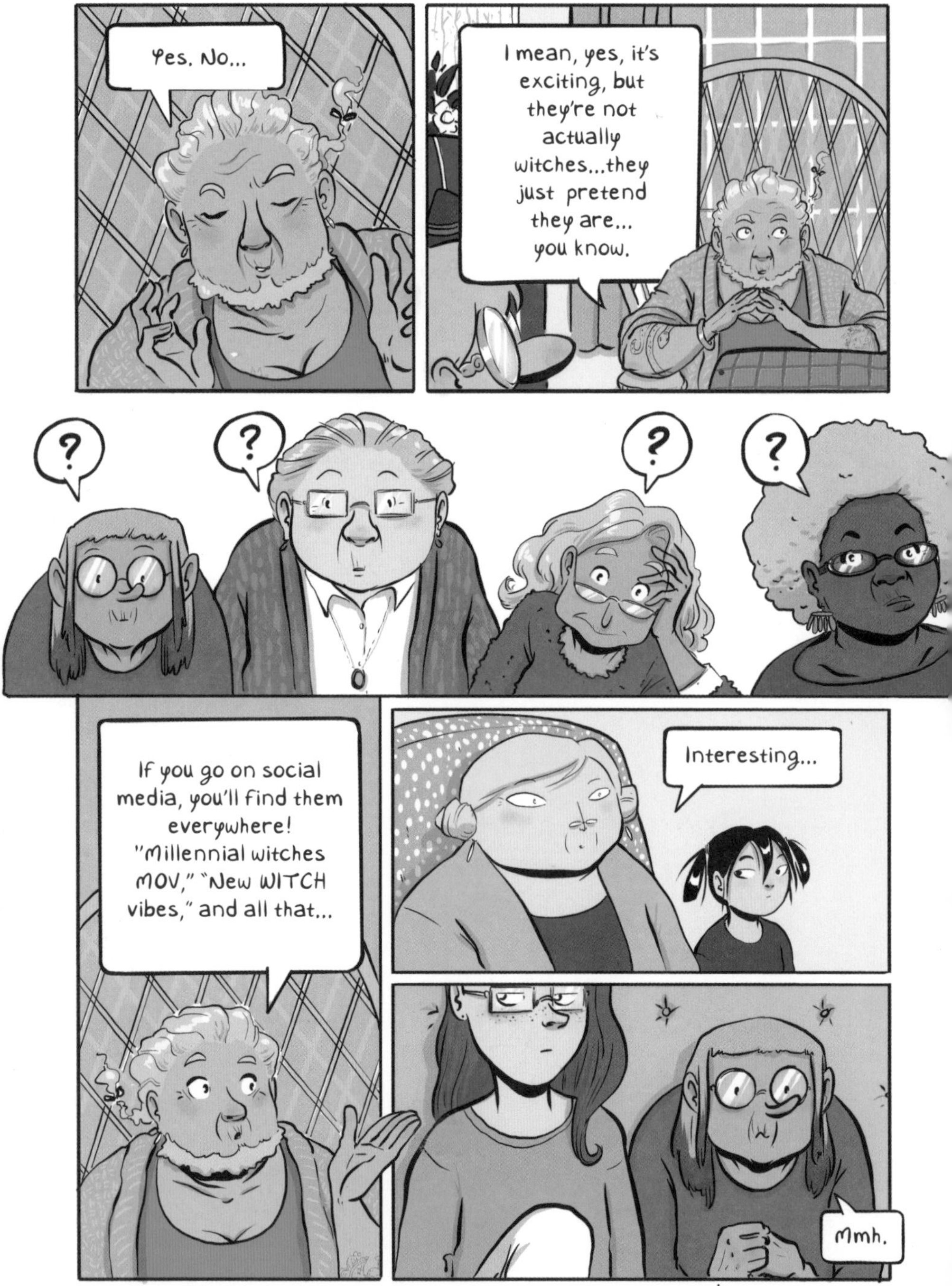
Yes. No...
I mean, yes, it's exciting, but they're not actually witches...they just pretend they are... you know.
?
?
?
?
If you go on social media, you'll find them everywhere! "Millennial witches MOV," "New WITCH vibes," and all that...
Interesting...
Mmh.

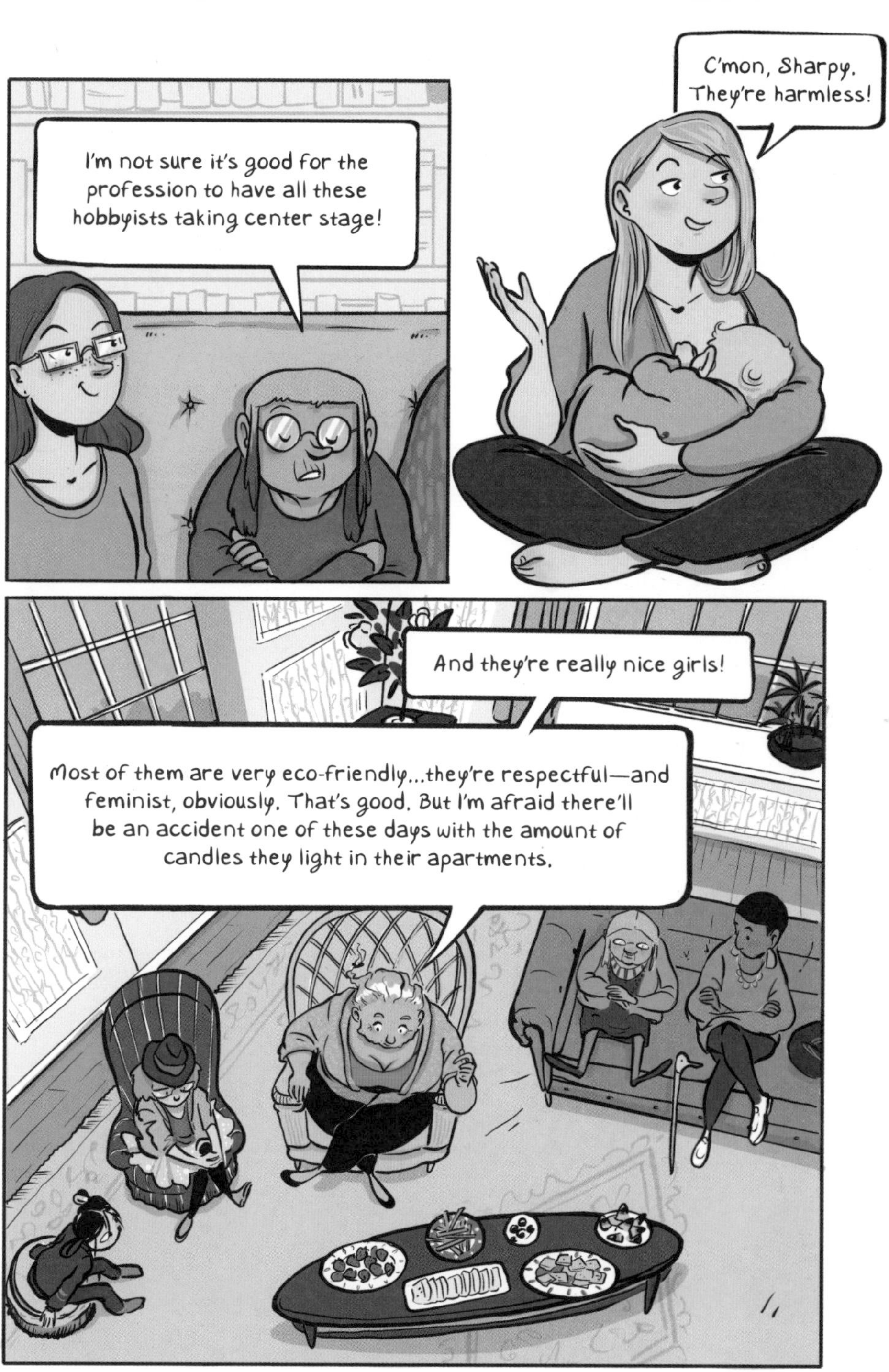
I'm not sure it's good for the profession to have all these hobbyists taking center stage!
C'mon, Sharpy. They're harmless!
And they're really nice girls!
Most of them are very eco-friendly...they're respectful—and feminist, obviously. That's good. But I'm afraid there'll be an accident one of these days with the amount of candles they light in their apartments.

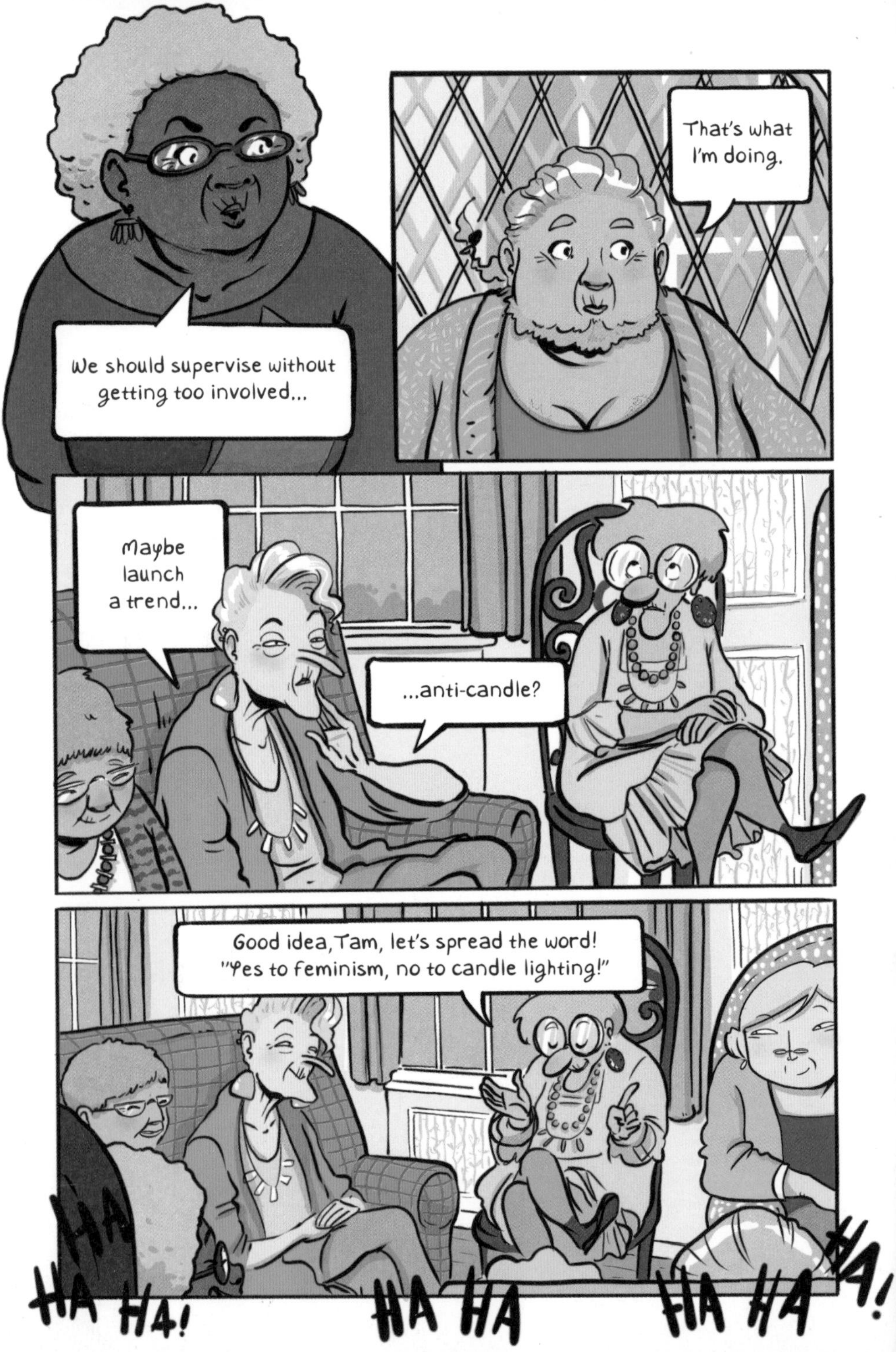
We should supervise without getting too involved...
That's what I'm doing.
Maybe launch a trend...
...anti-candle?
Good idea, Tam, let's spread the word! "Yes to feminism, no to candle lighting!"
HA HA HA!
HA HA
HA HA HA!

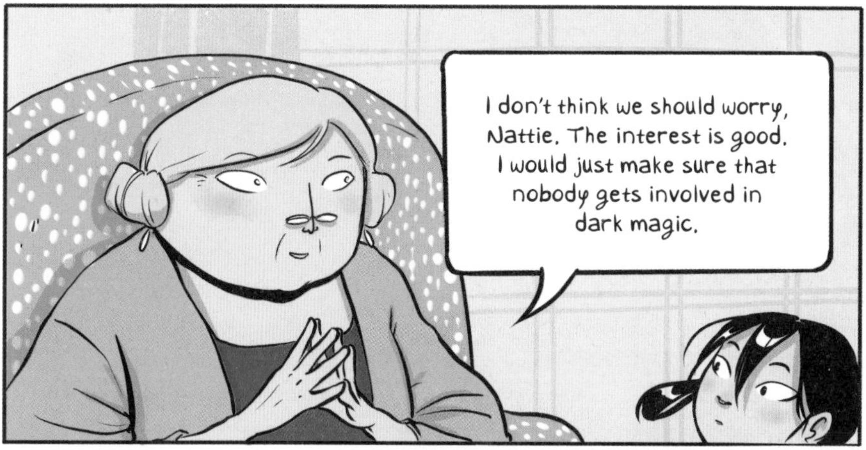
I don't think we should worry, Nattie. The interest is good. I would just make sure that nobody gets involved in dark magic.

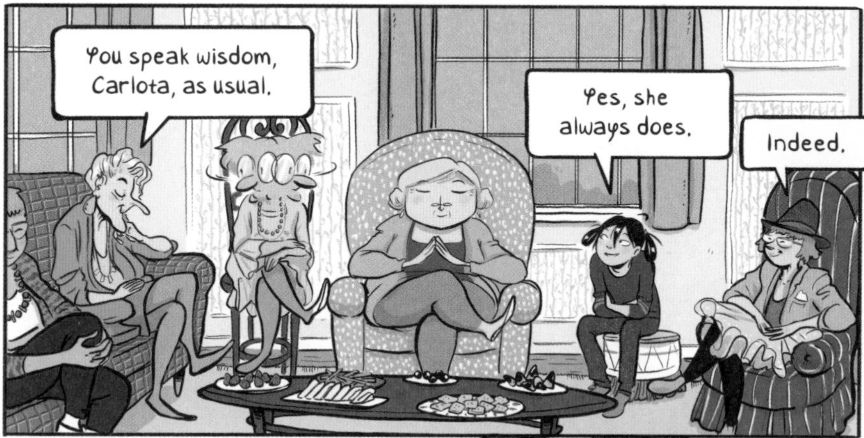
You speak wisdom, Carlota, as usual.
Yes, she always does.
Indeed.

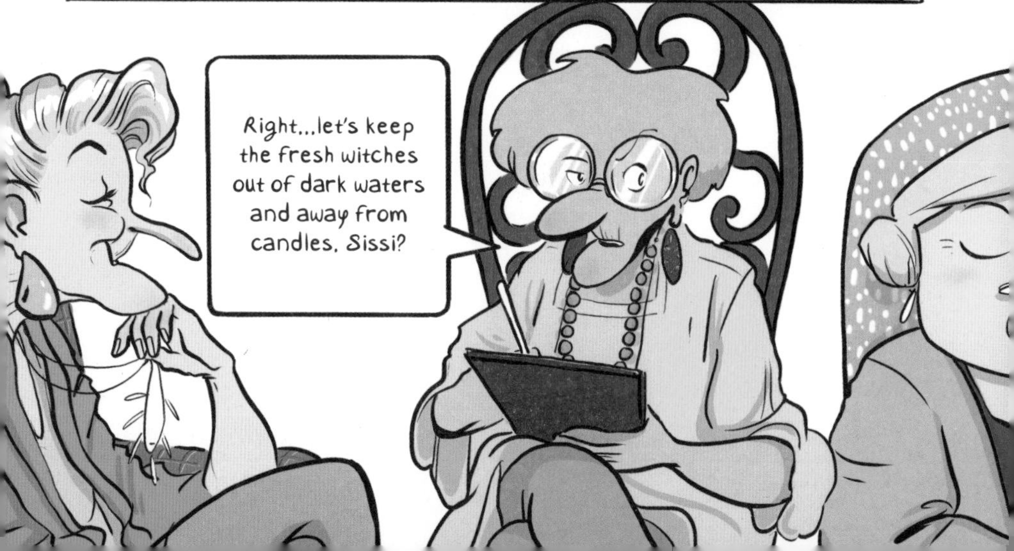
Right...let's keep the fresh witches out of dark waters and away from candles, Sissi?

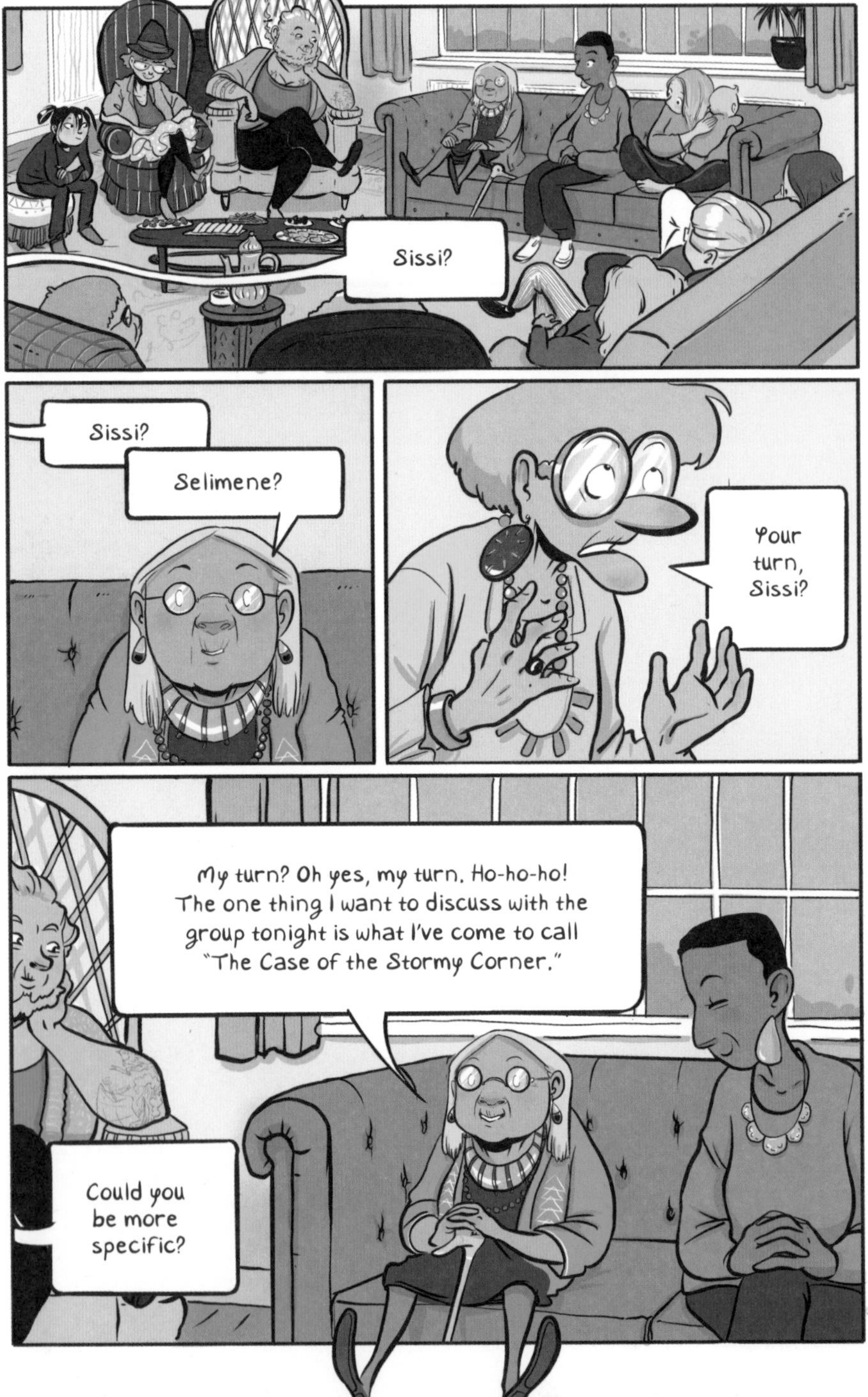

Sissi?
Sissi?
Selimene?
Your turn, Sissi?
My turn? Oh yes, my turn. Ho-ho-ho! The one thing I want to discuss with the group tonight is what I've come to call "The Case of the Stormy Corner."
Could you be more specific?

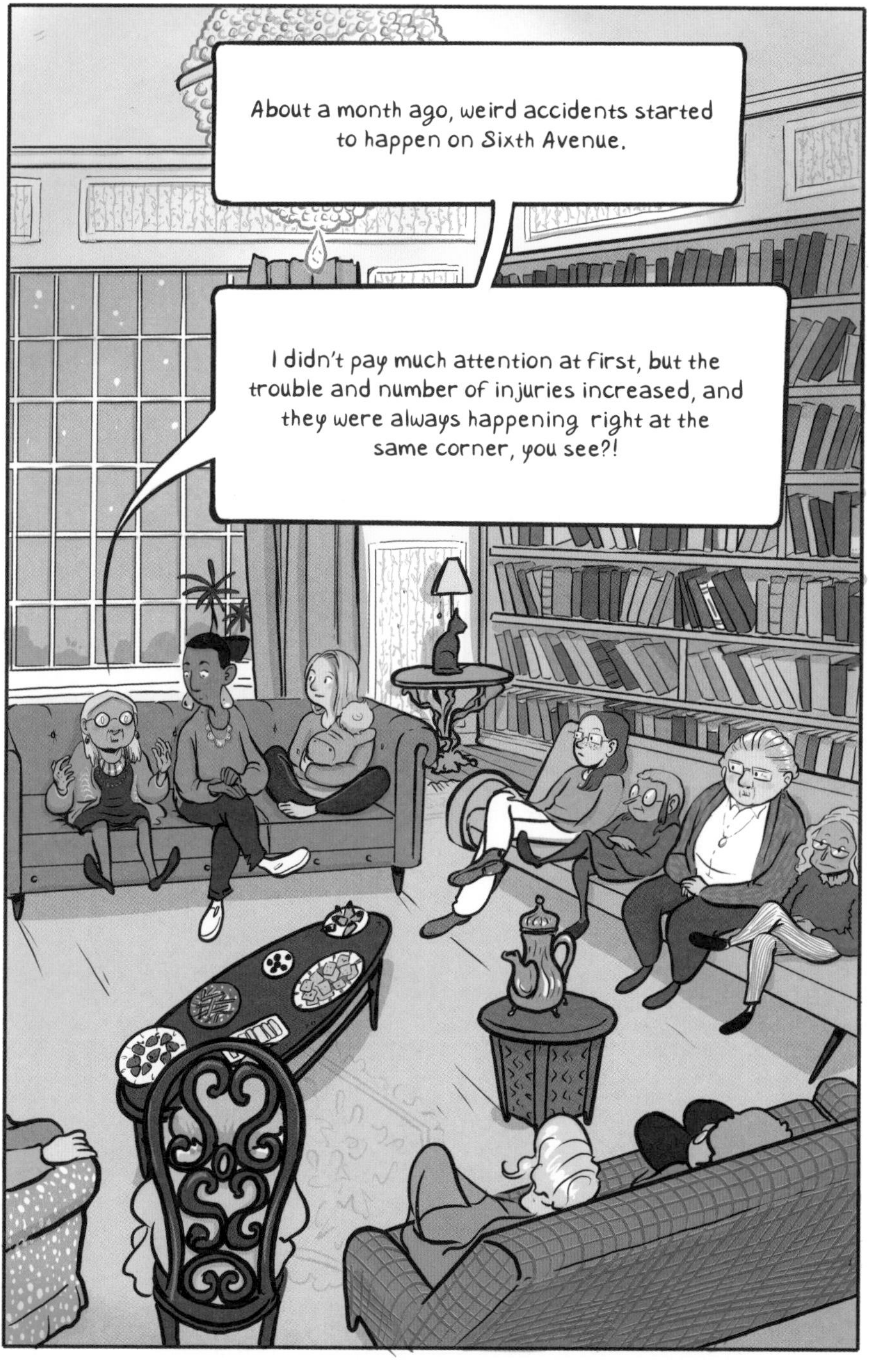
About a month ago, weird accidents started to happen on Sixth Avenue.
I didn't pay much attention at first, but the trouble and number of injuries increased, and they were always happening right at the same corner, you see?!

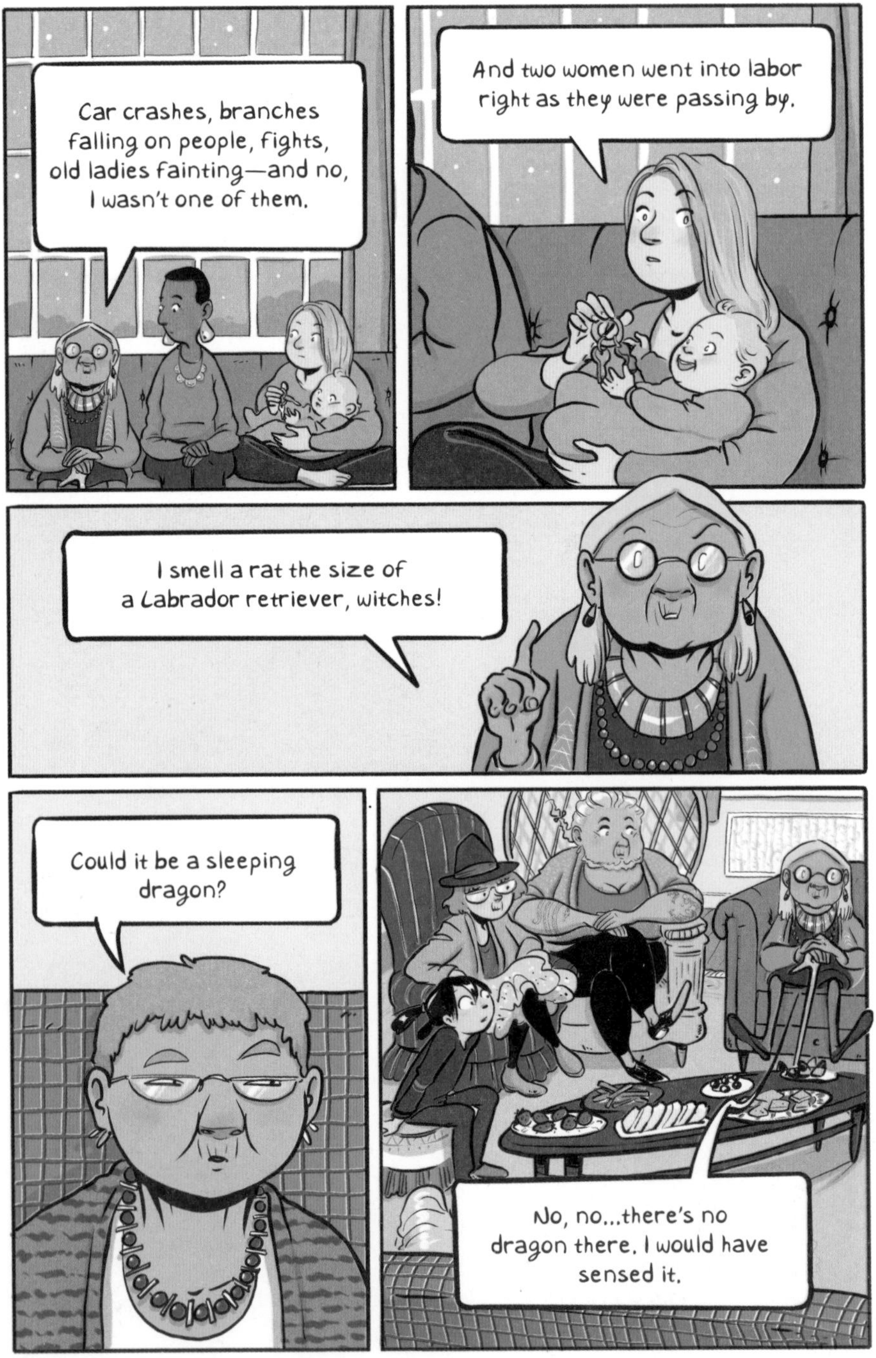
Car crashes, branches falling on people, fights, old ladies fainting—and no, I wasn't one of them.
And two women went into labor right as they were passing by.
I smell a rat the size of a Labrador retriever, witches!
Could it be a sleeping dragon?
No, no...there's no dragon there. I would have sensed it.

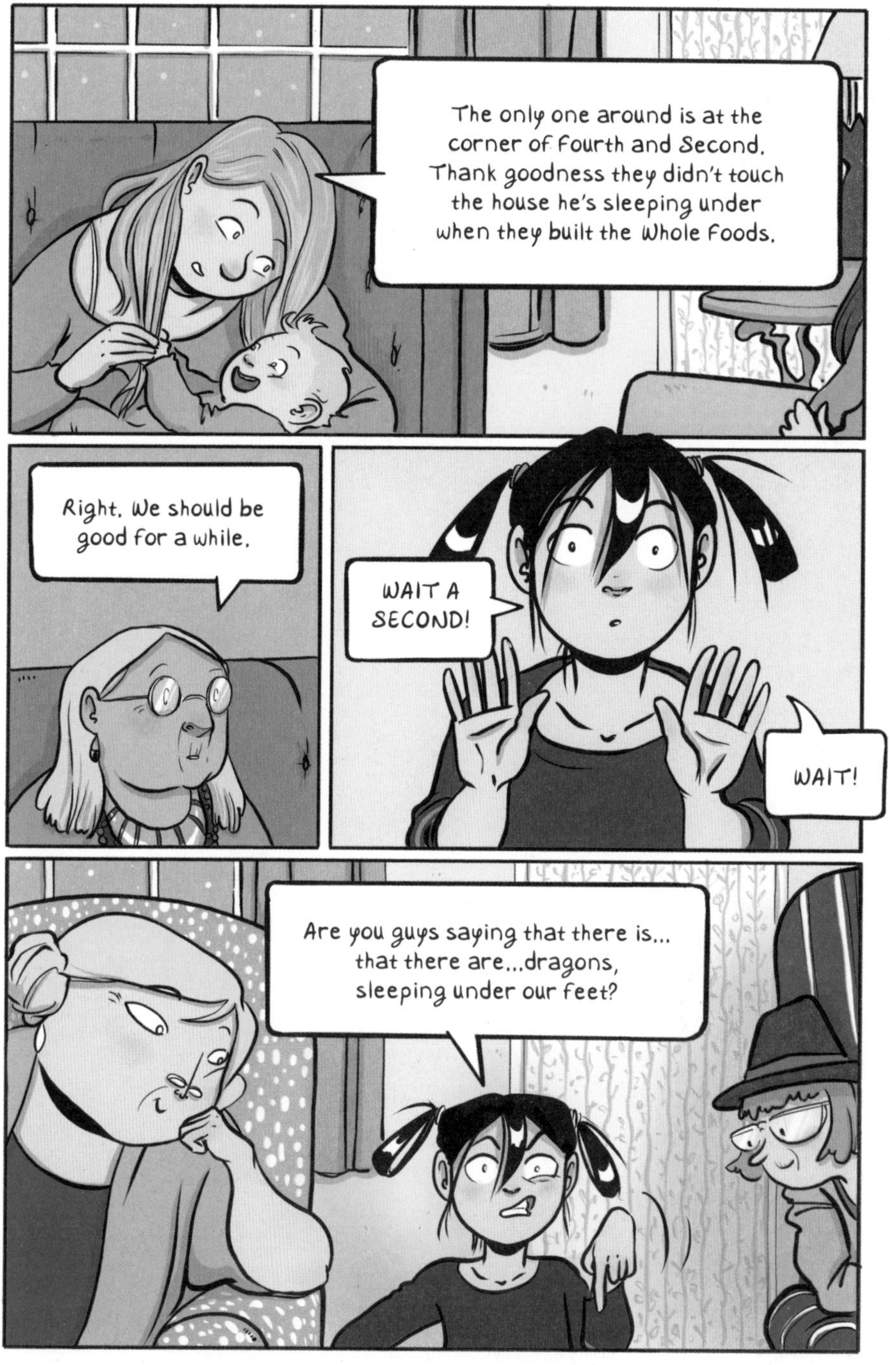
The only one around is at the corner of Fourth and Second. Thank goodness they didn't touch the house he's sleeping under when they built the Whole Foods.
Right. We should be good for a while.
WAIT A SECOND!
WAIT!
Are you guys saying that there is... that there are...dragons, sleeping under our feet?

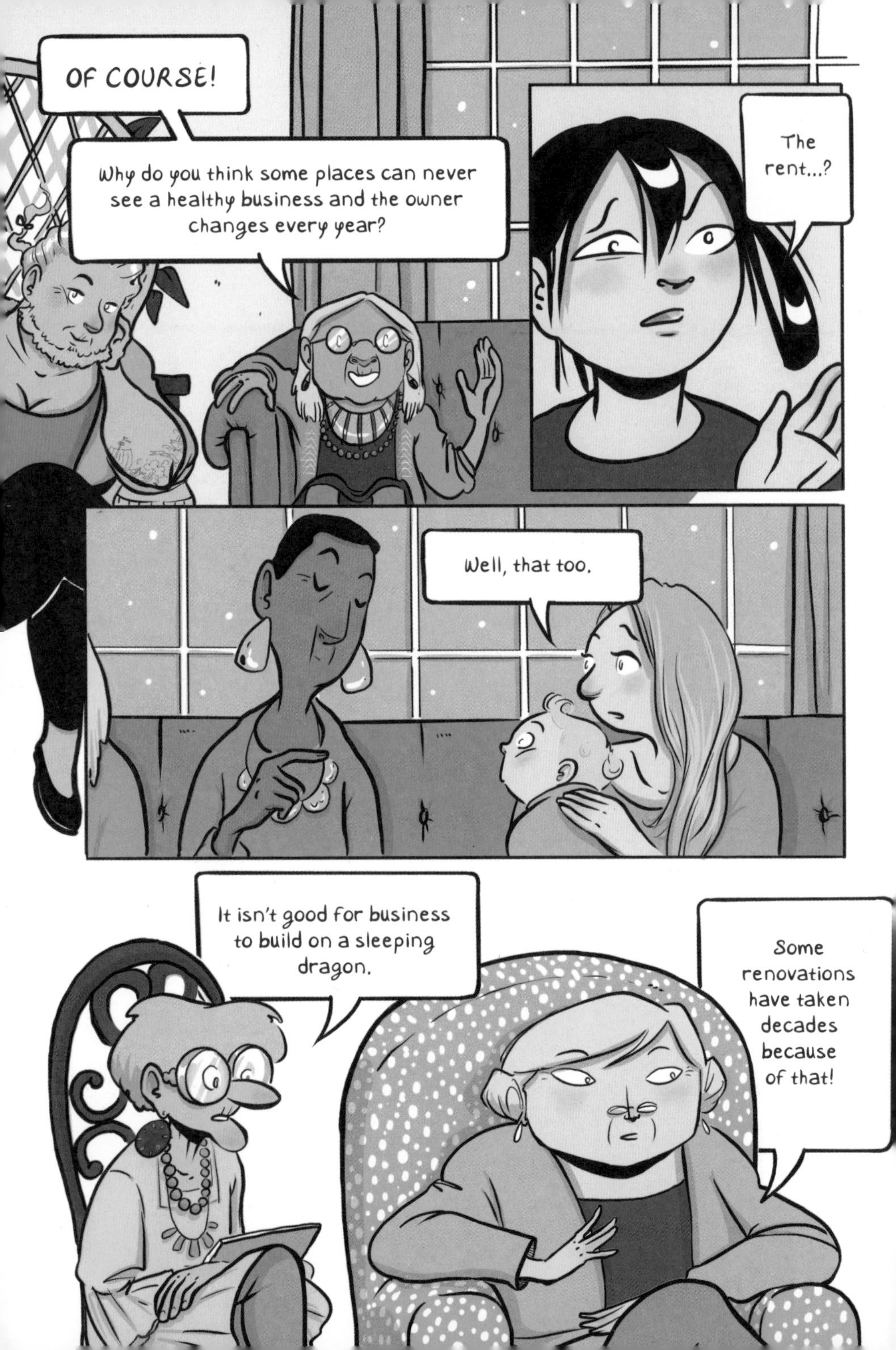
OF COURSE!
Why do you think some places can never see a healthy business and the owner changes every year?
The rent...?
Well, that too.
It isn't good for business to build on a sleeping dragon.
Some renovations have taken decades because of that!

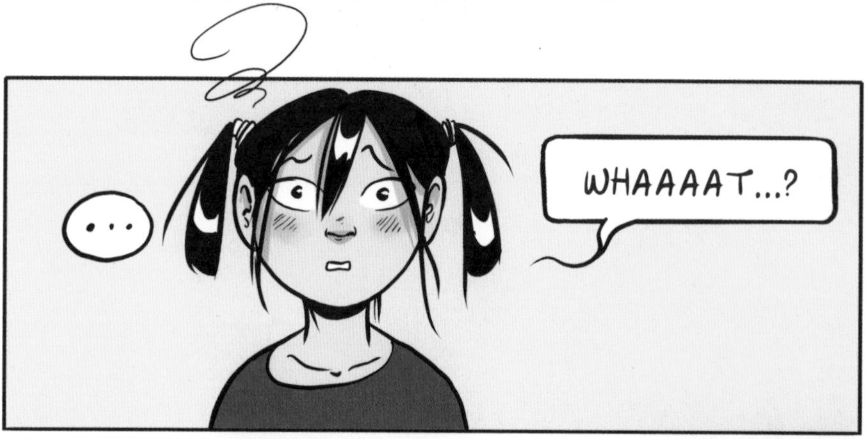
...
WHAAAAT...?

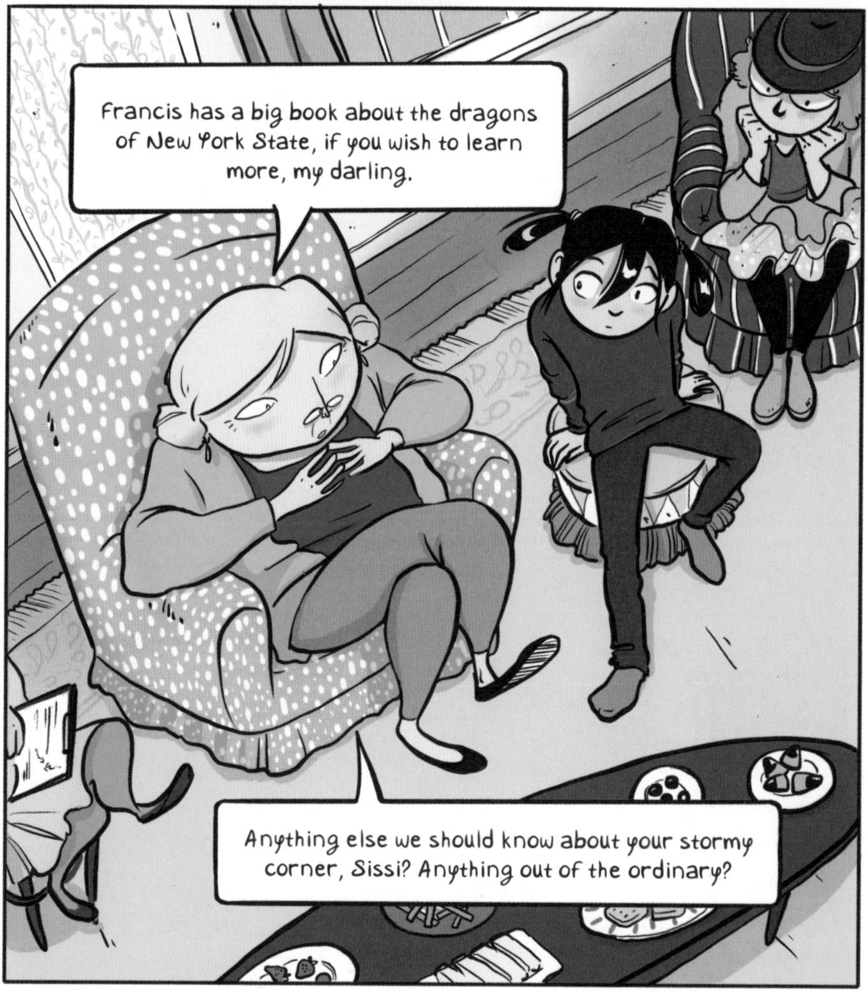
Francis has a big book about the dragons of New York State, if you wish to learn more, my darling.
Anything else we should know about your stormy corner, Sissi? Anything out of the ordinary?

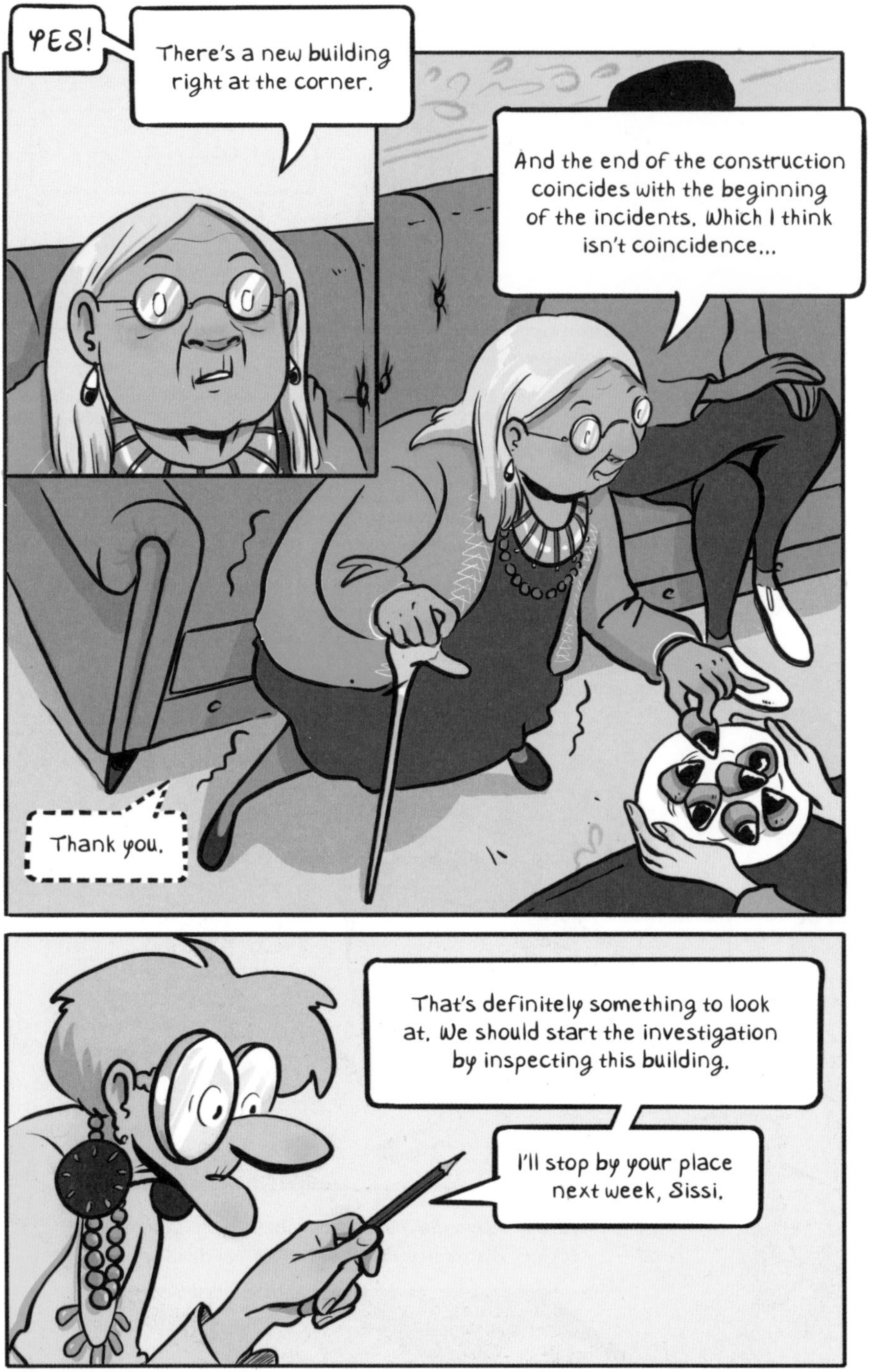
YES!
There's a new building right at the corner.
And the end of the construction coincides with the beginning of the incidents. Which I think isn't coincidence...
Thank you.
That's definitely something to look at. We should start the investigation by inspecting this building.
I'll stop by your place next week, Sissi.

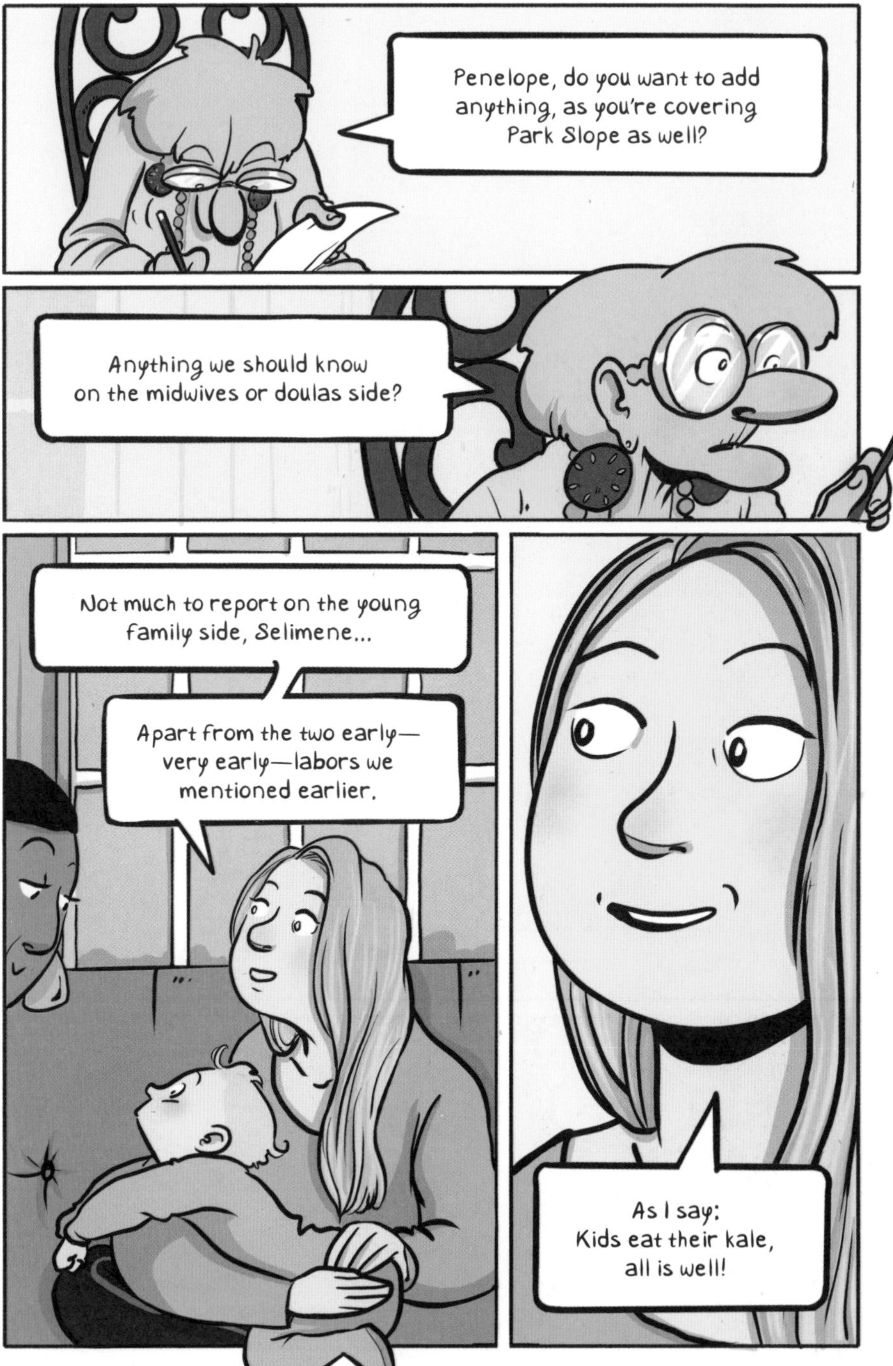
Penelope, do you want to add anything, as you're covering Park Slope as well?
Anything we should know on the midwives or doulas side?
Not much to report on the young family side, Selimene...
Apart from the two early—very early—labors we mentioned earlier.
As I say: Kids eat their kale, all is well!

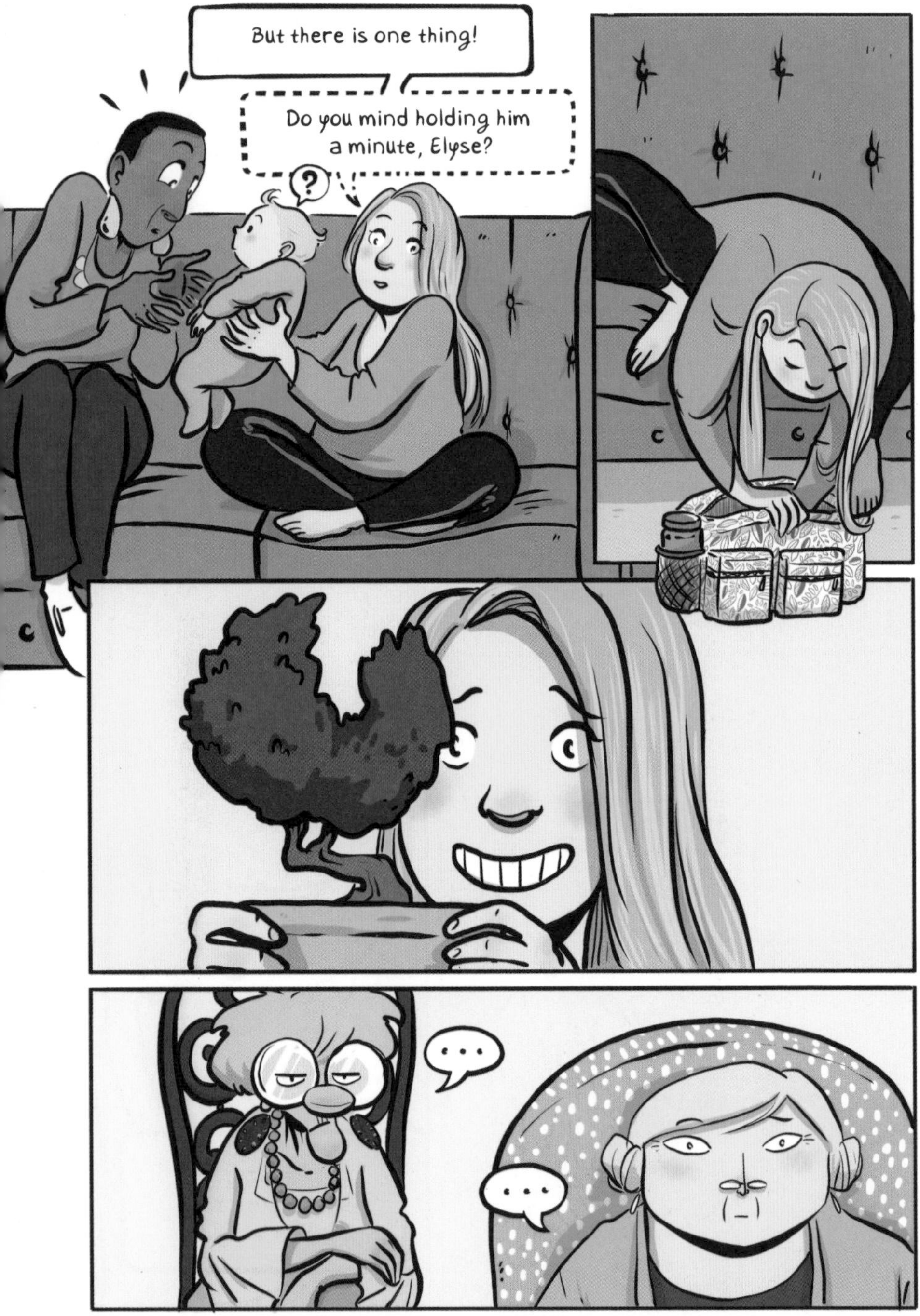
But there is one thing!
Do you mind holding him a minute, Elyse?
?
...
...

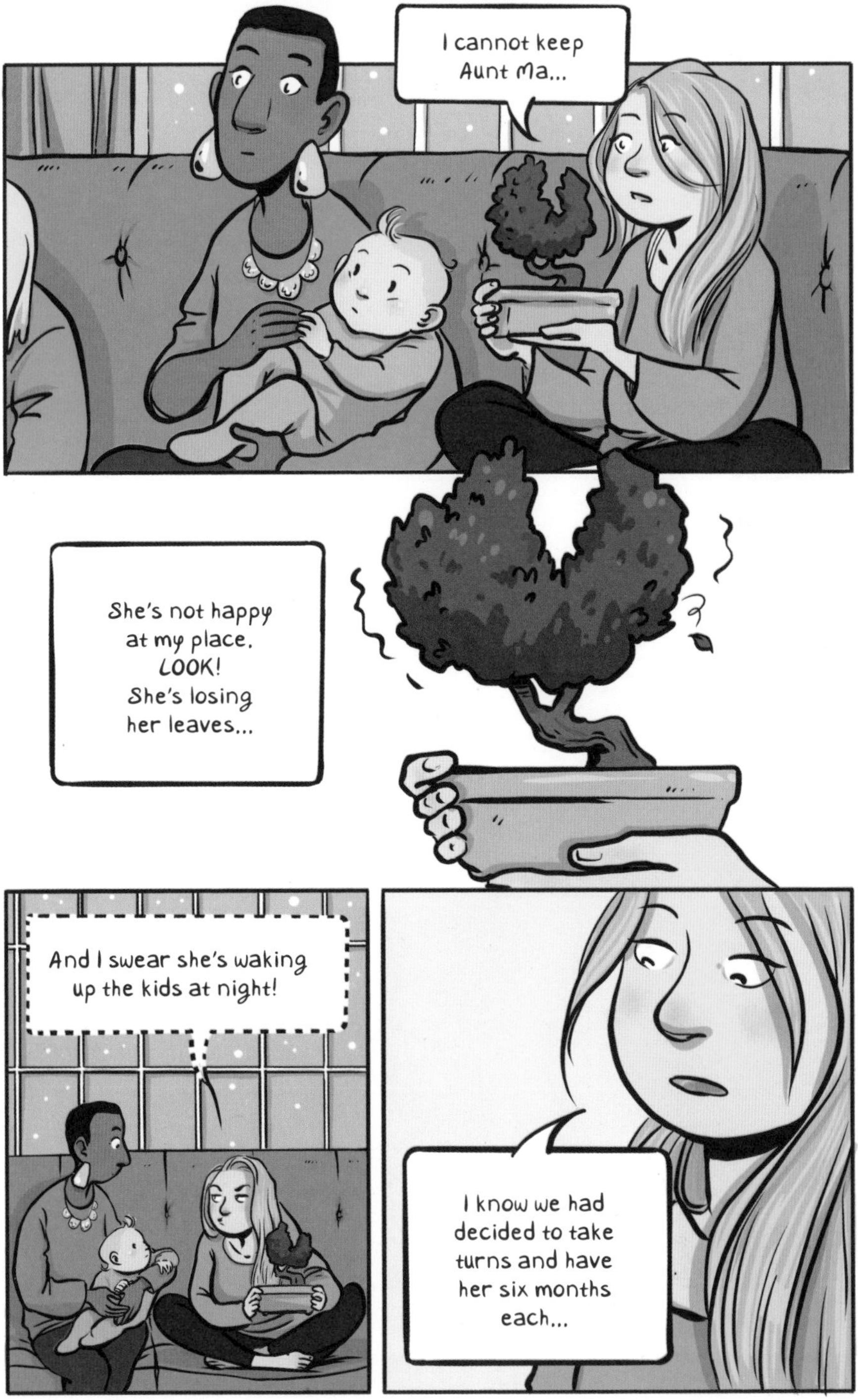
I cannot keep
Aunt Ma...
She's not happy
at my place.
LOOK!
She's losing
her leaves...
And I swear she's waking
up the kids at night!
I know we had
decided to take
turns and have
her six months
each...

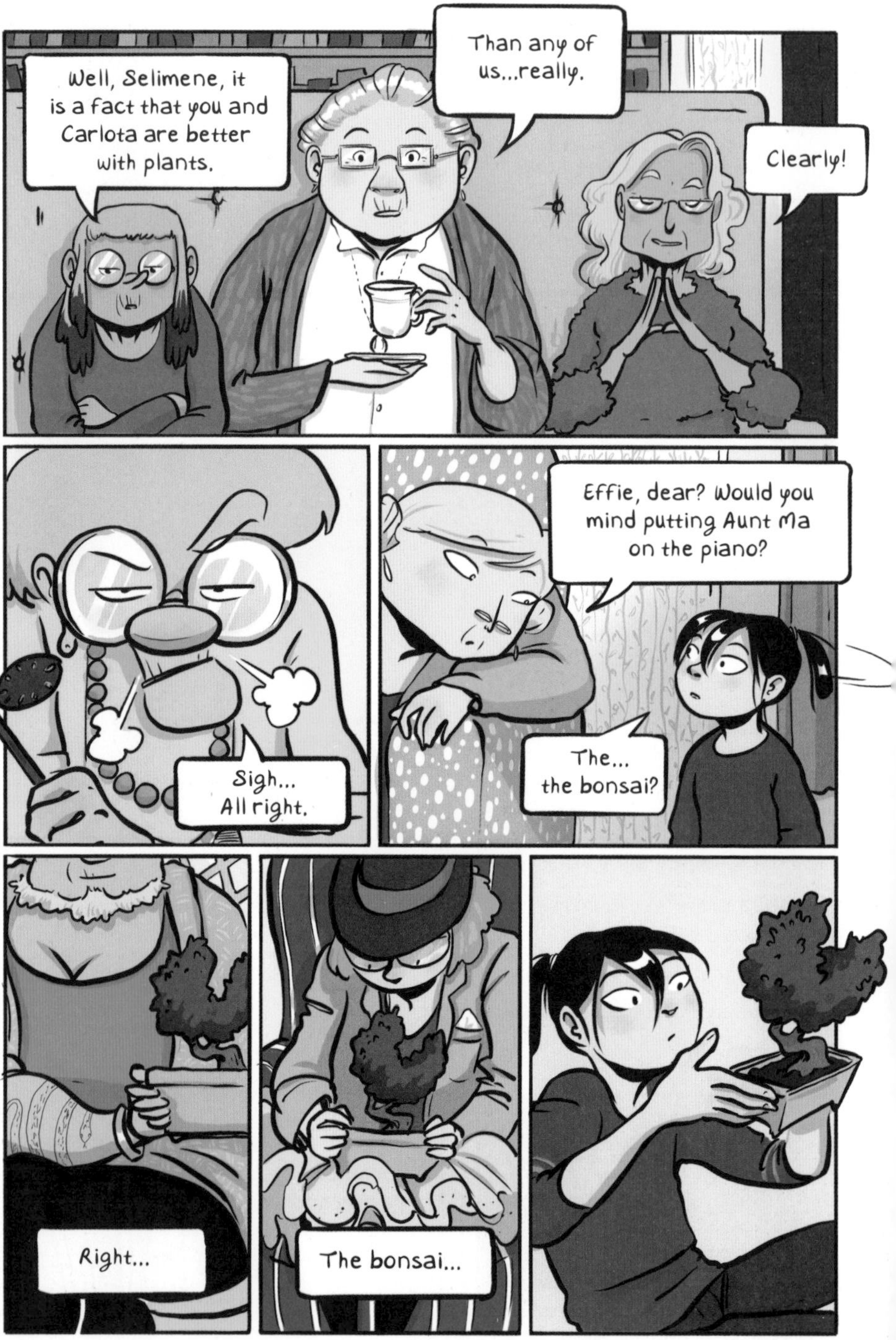
Well, Selimene, it is a fact that you and Carlota are better with plants.
Than any of us...really.
Clearly!
Sigh... All right.
Effie, dear? Would you mind putting Aunt Ma on the piano?
The... the bonsai?
Right...
The bonsai...

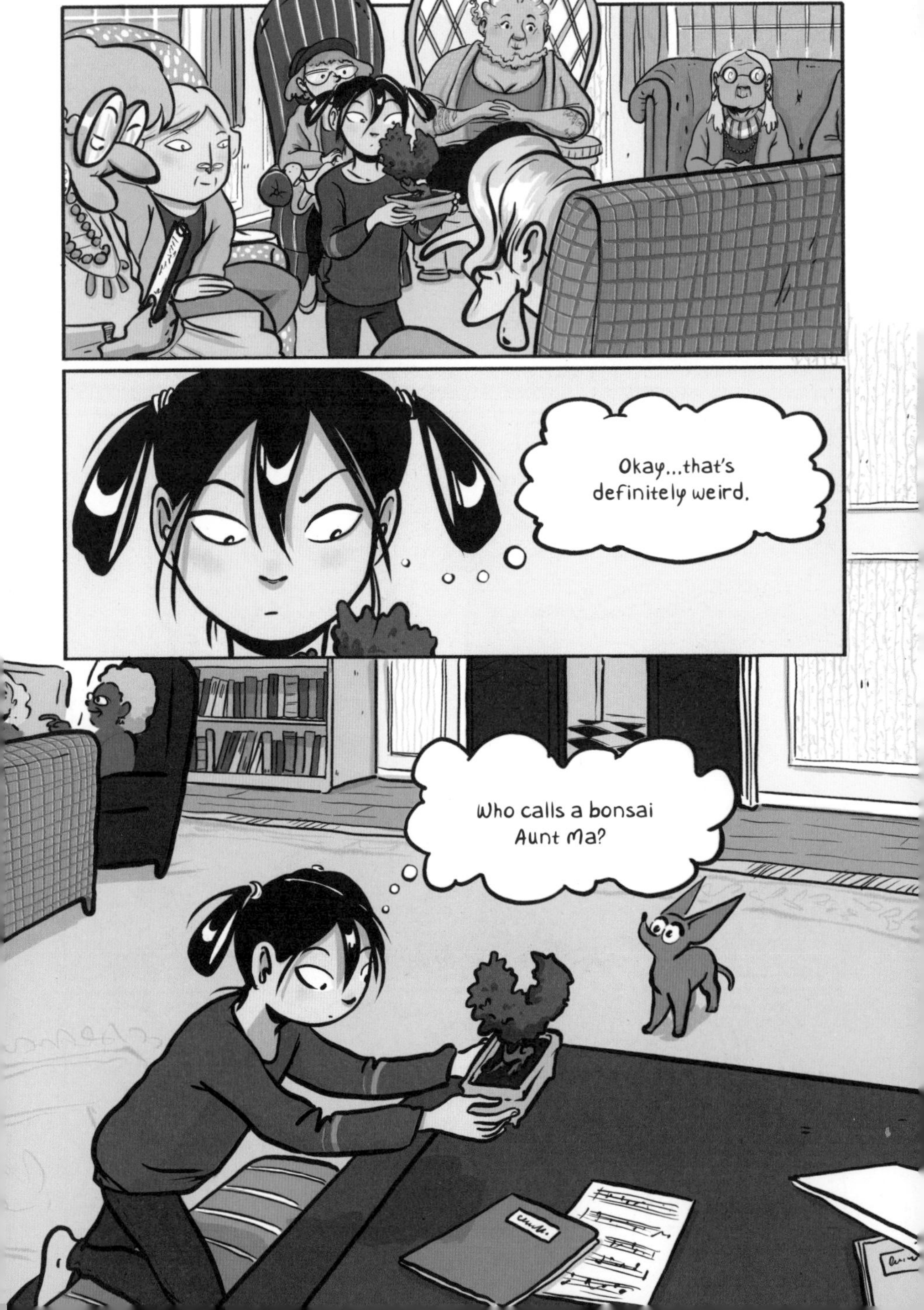

Okay...that's definitely weird.
Who calls a bonsai Aunt Ma?

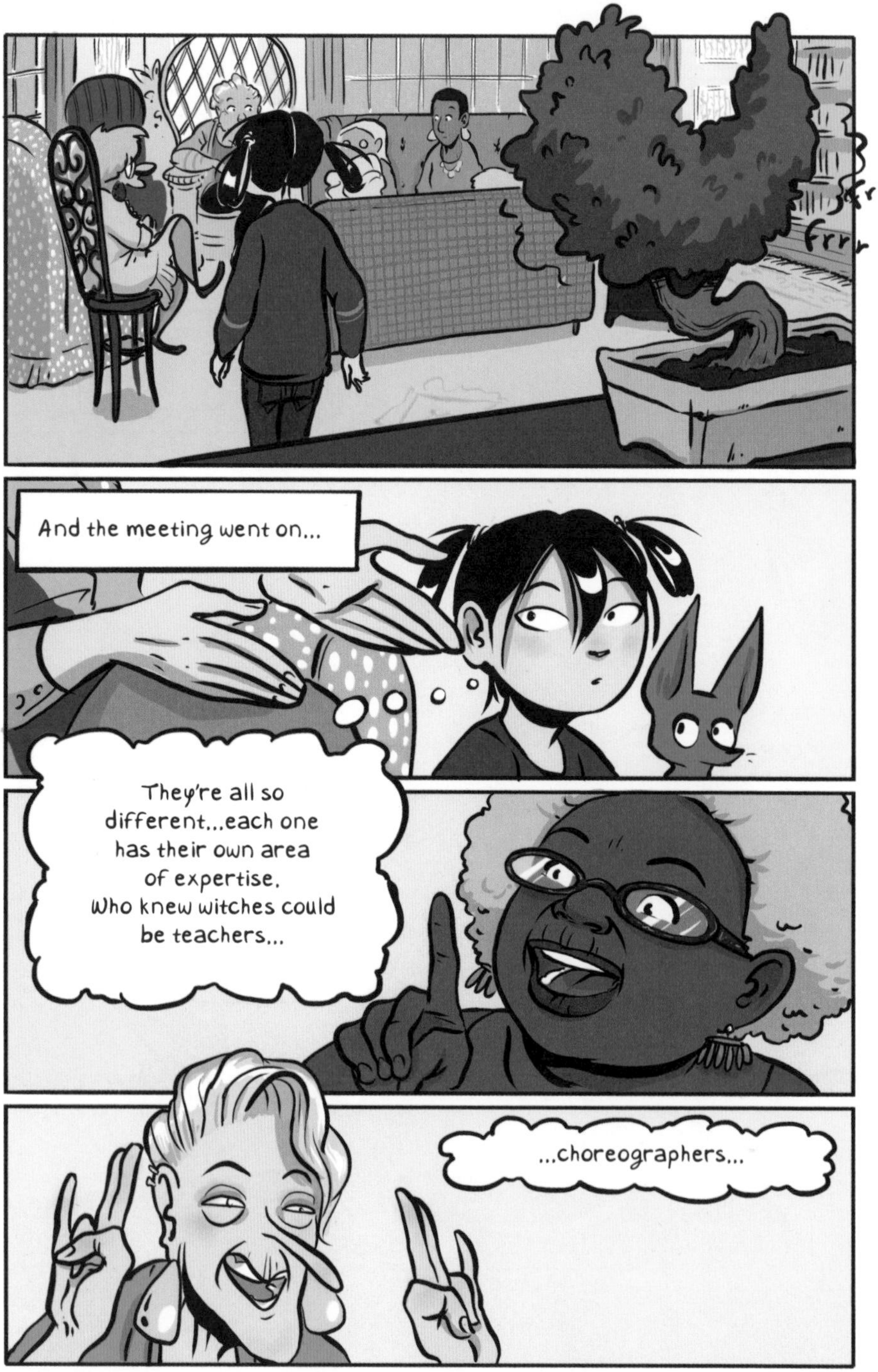
Frrrr
Frrr
And the meeting went on...
They're all so different...each one has their own area of expertise. Who knew witches could be teachers...
...choreographers...

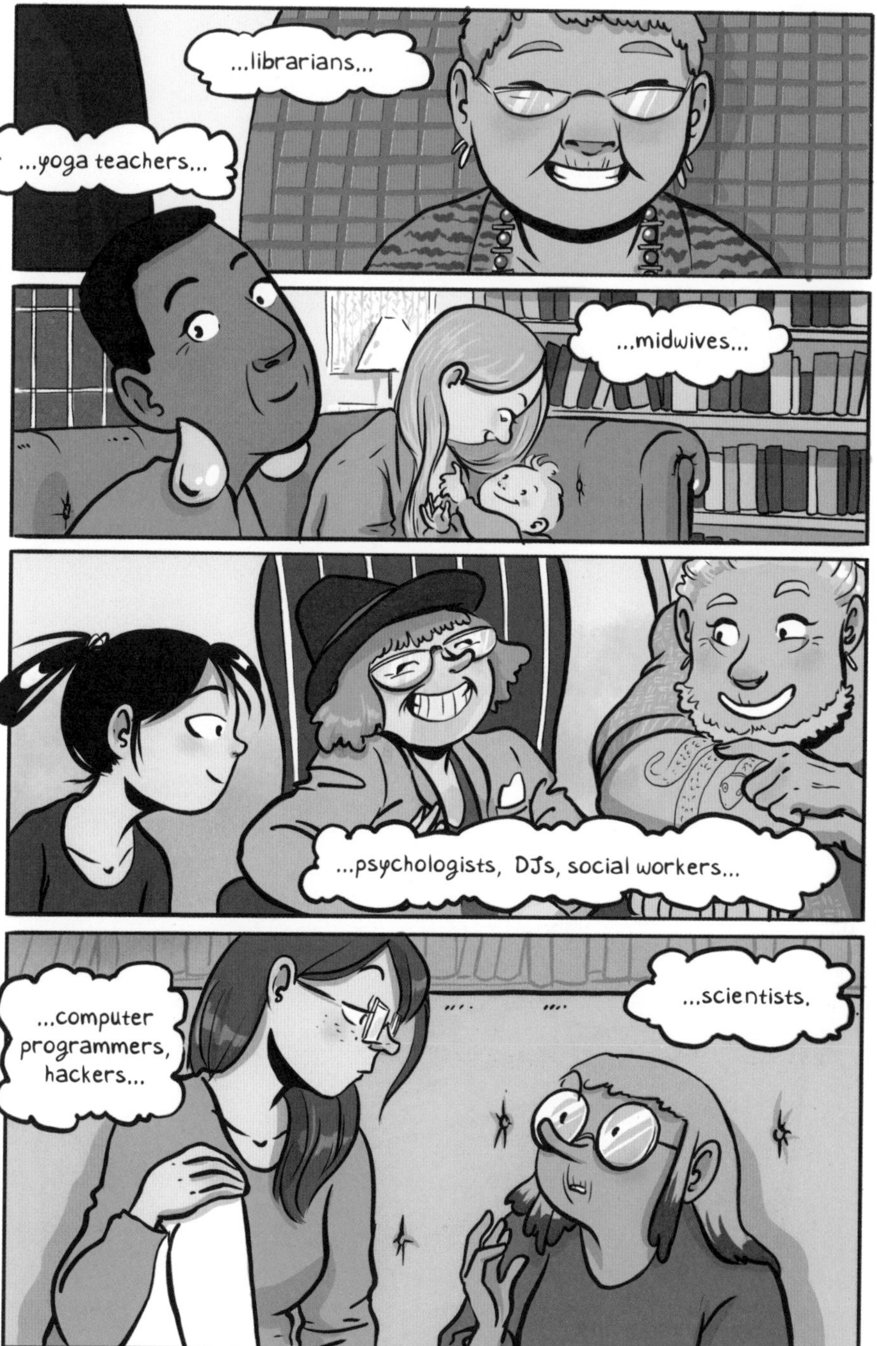
...yoga teachers...
...librarians...
...midwives...
...psychologists, DJs, social workers...
...computer programmers, hackers...
...scientists.

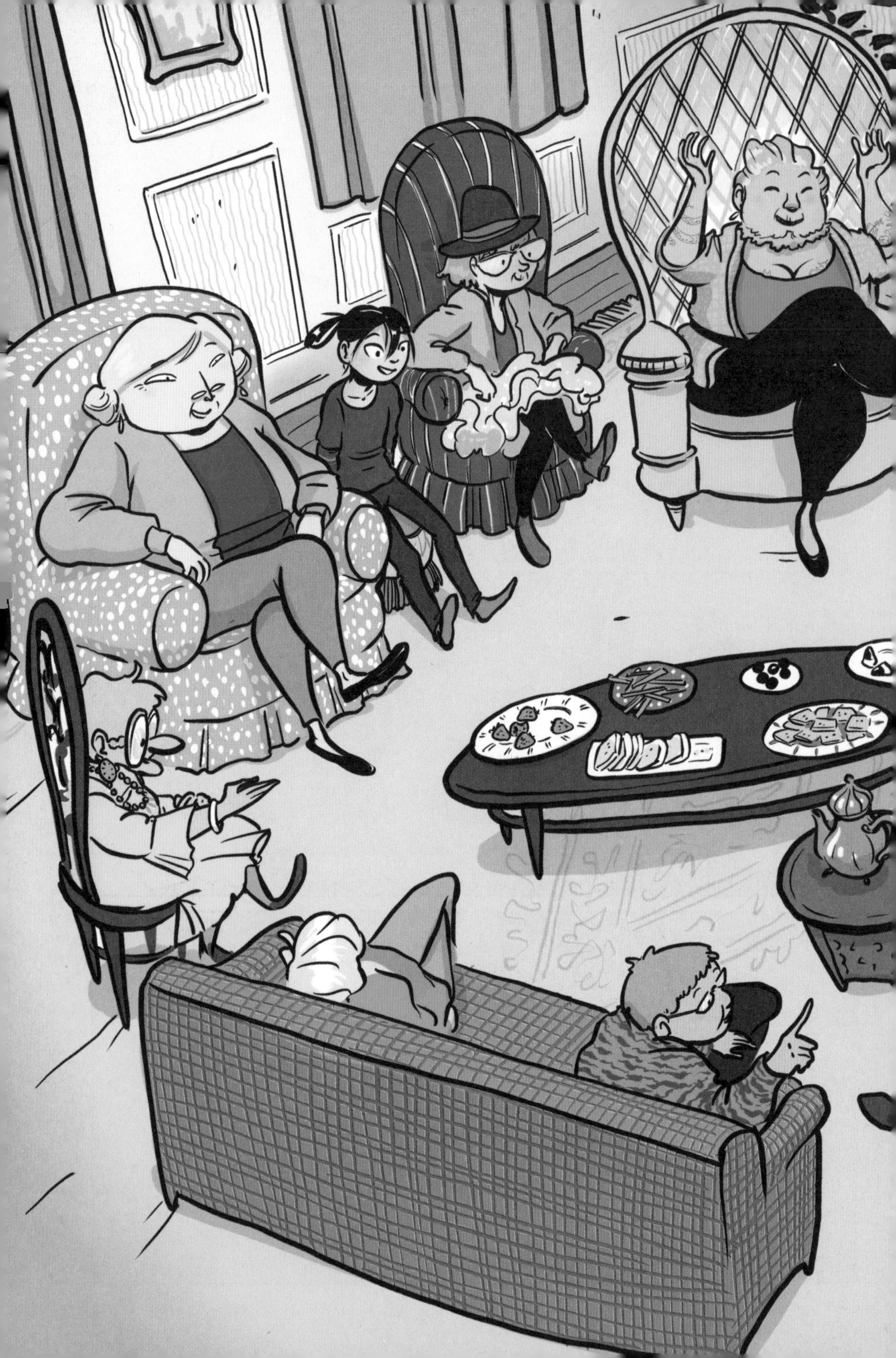

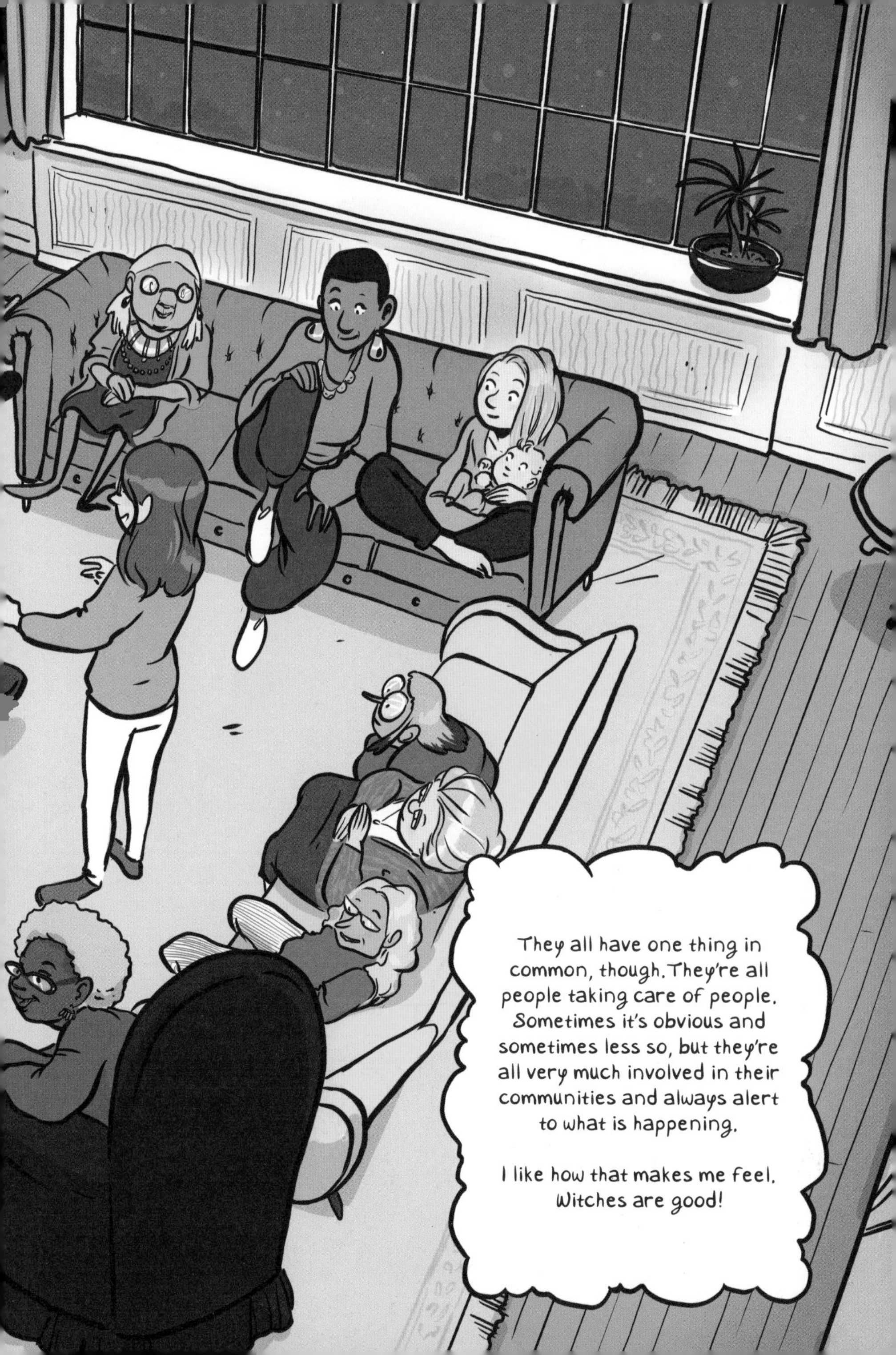
They all have one thing in common, though. They're all people taking care of people. Sometimes it's obvious and sometimes less so, but they're all very much involved in their communities and always alert to what is happening.
I like how that makes me feel. Witches are good!

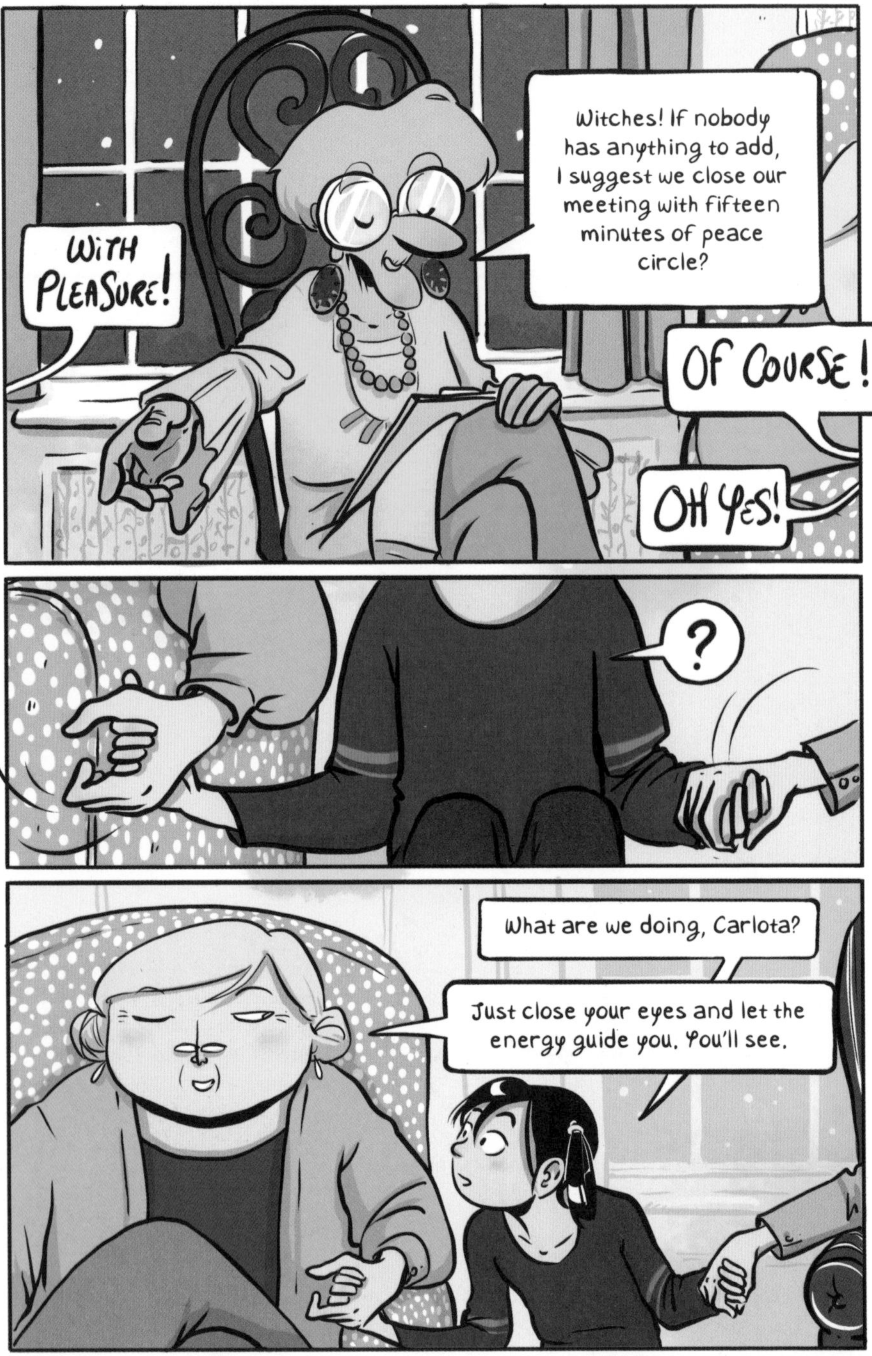
Witches! If nobody has anything to add, I suggest we close our meeting with fifteen minutes of peace circle?
WITH PLEASURE!
OF COURSE!
OH YES!
?
What are we doing, Carlota?
Just close your eyes and let the energy guide you. You'll see.

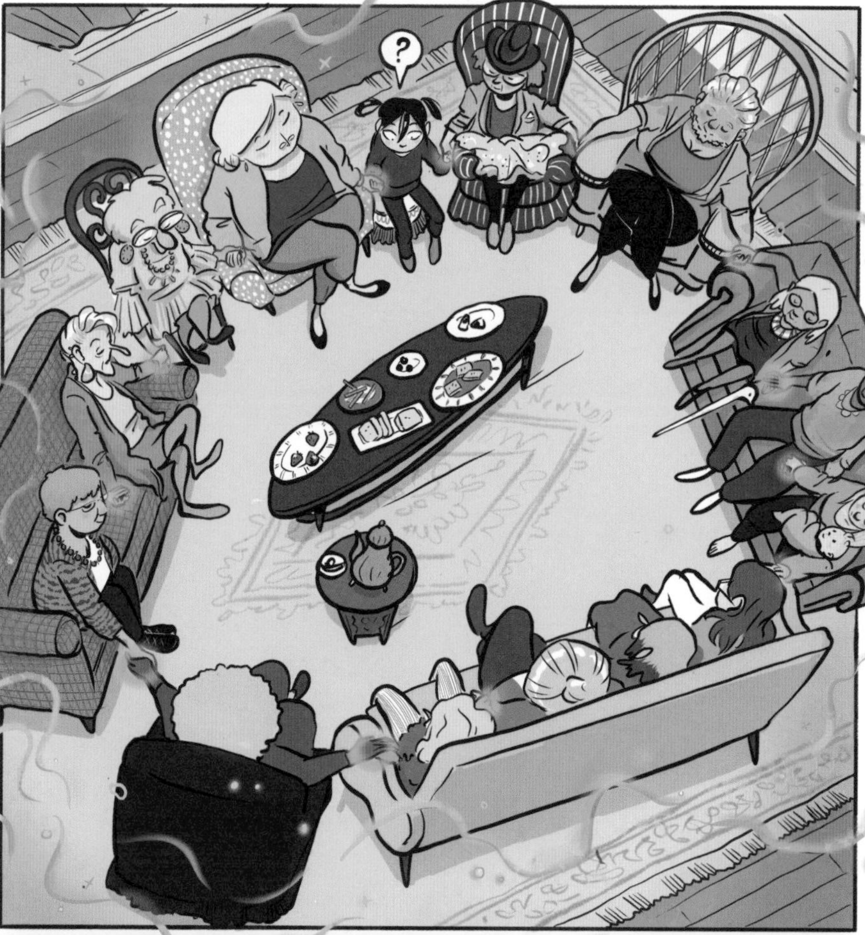
?

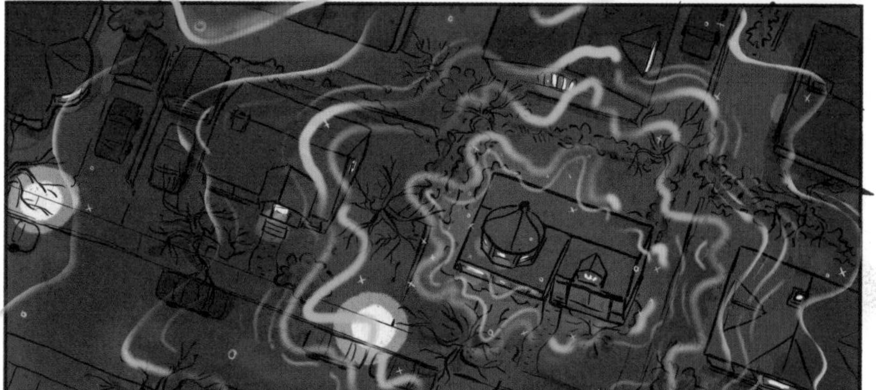

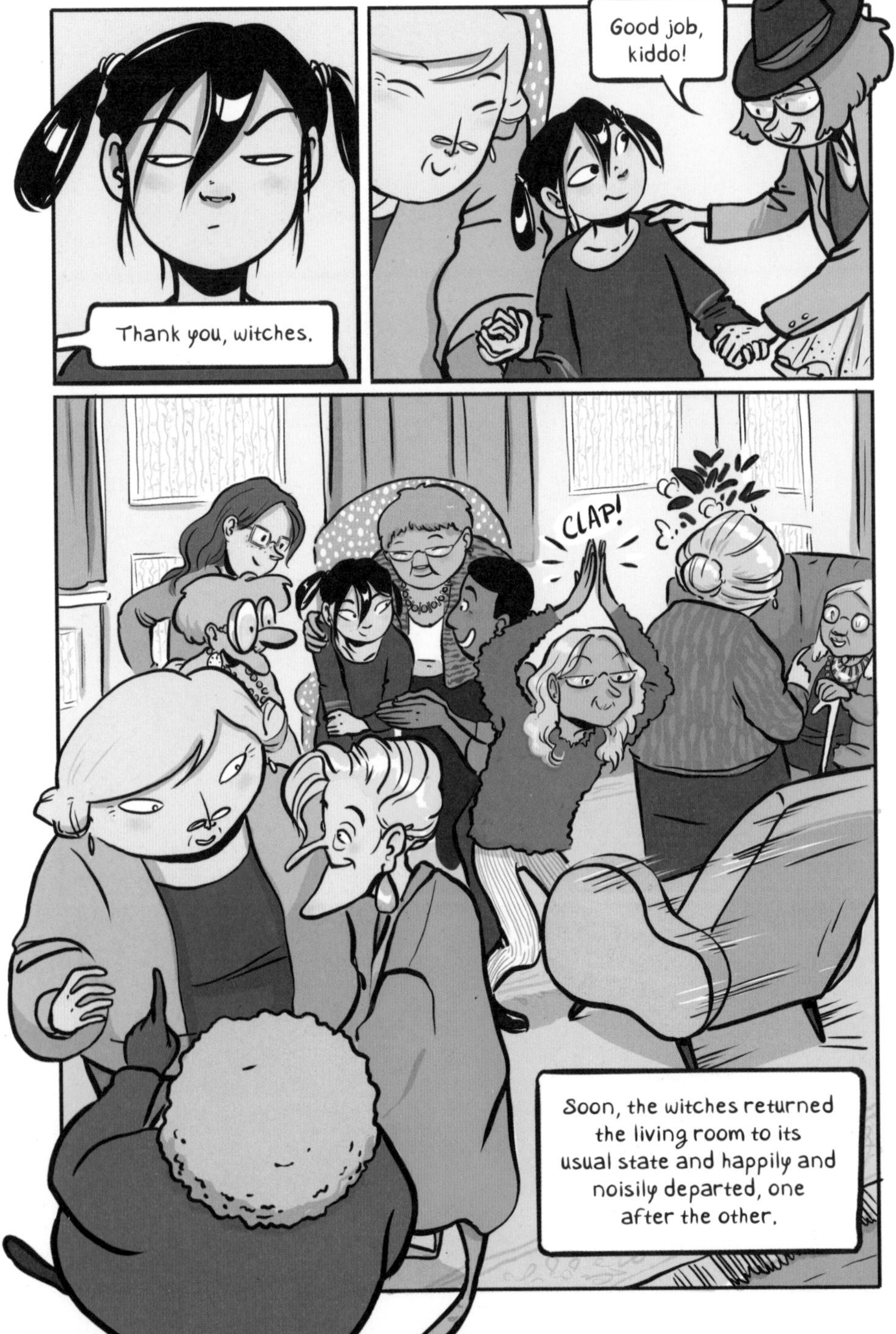
Thank you, witches.
Good job, kiddo!
CLAP!
Soon, the witches returned the living room to its usual state and happily and noisily departed, one after the other.

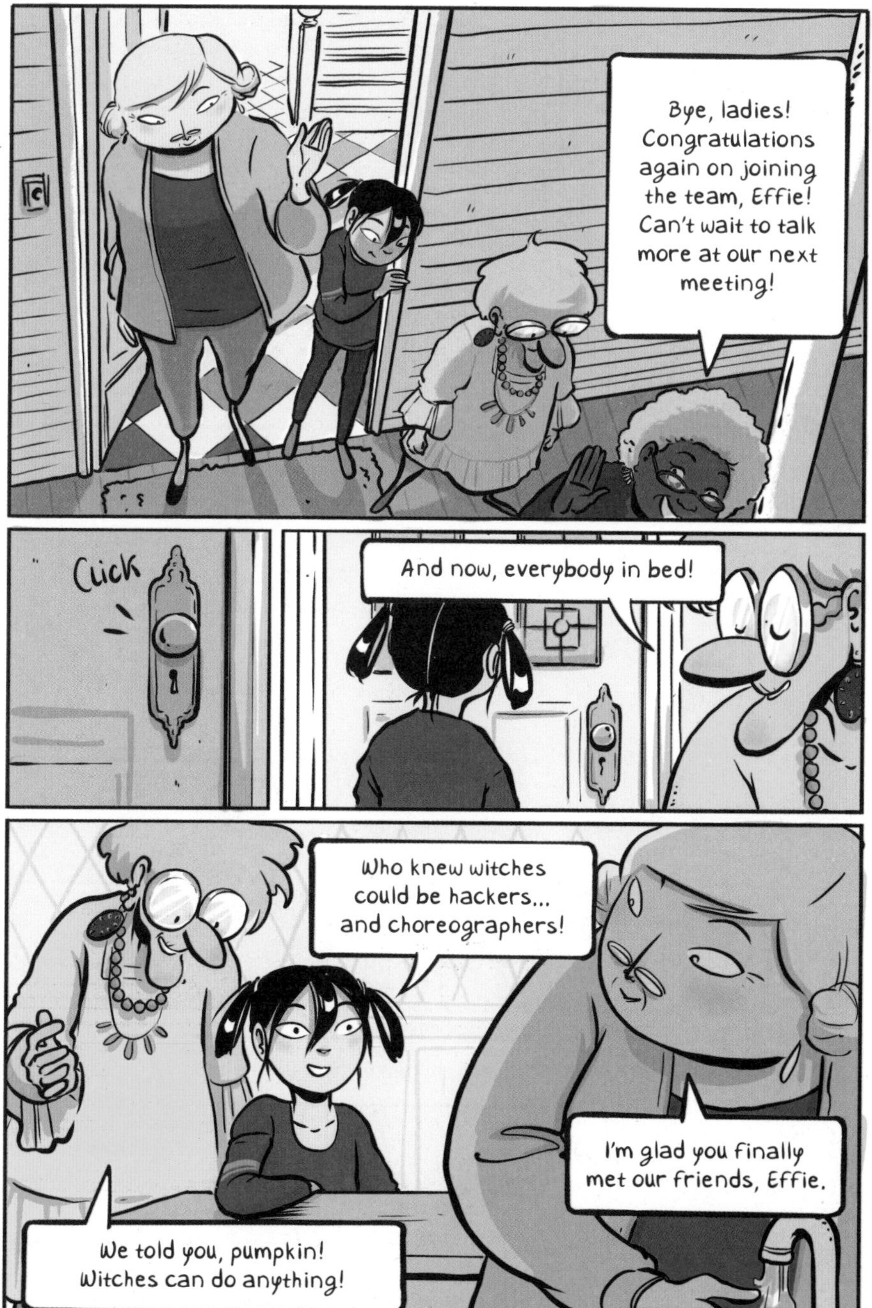
Bye, ladies! Congratulations again on joining the team, Effie! Can't wait to talk more at our next meeting!
Click
And now, everybody in bed!
Who knew witches could be hackers... and choreographers!
I'm glad you finally met our friends, Effie.
We told you, pumpkin! Witches can do anything!

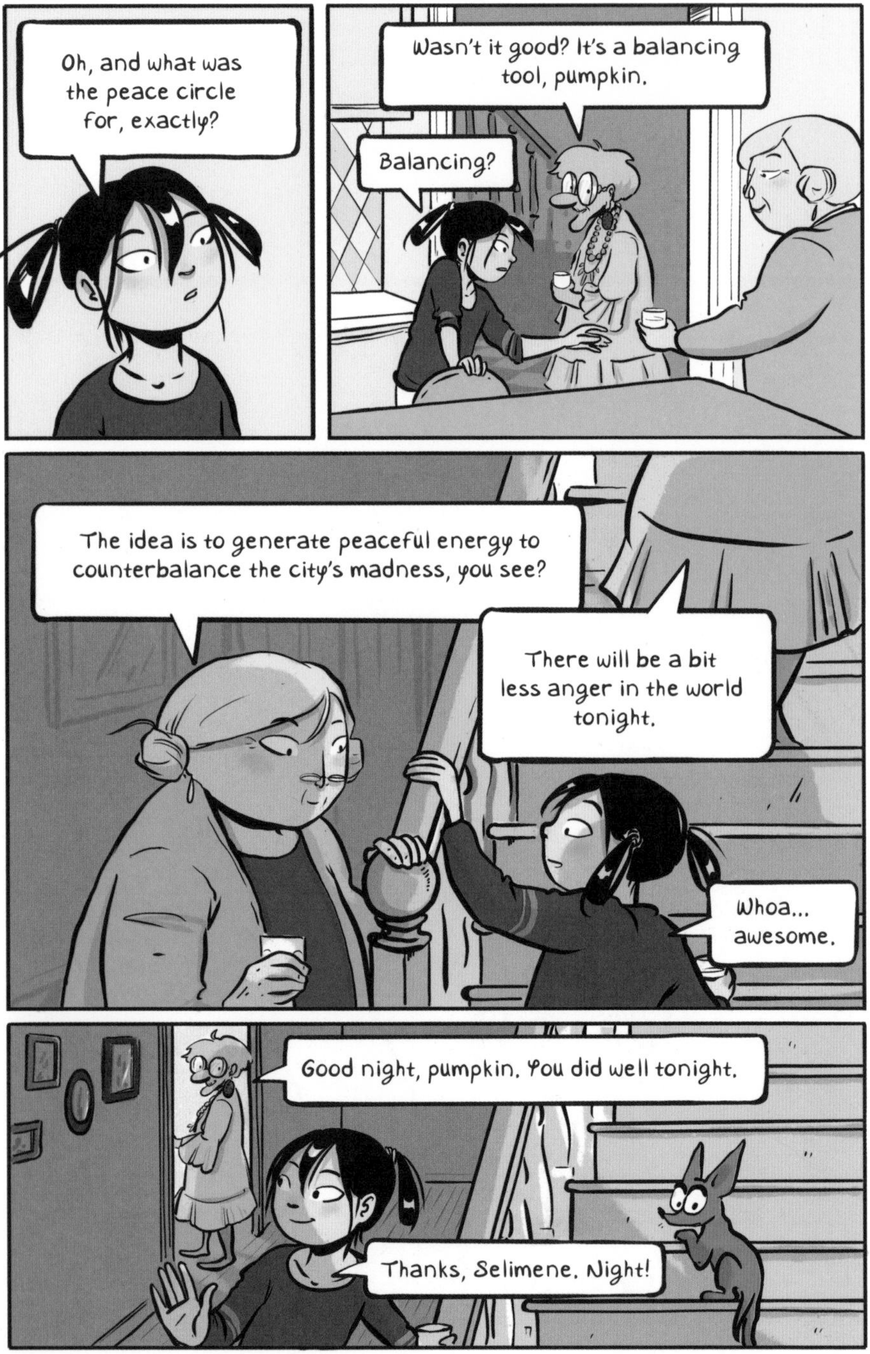
Oh, and what was the peace circle for, exactly?
Wasn't it good? It's a balancing tool, pumpkin.
Balancing?
The idea is to generate peaceful energy to counterbalance the city's madness, you see?
There will be a bit less anger in the world tonight.
Whoa... awesome.
Good night, pumpkin. You did well tonight.
Thanks, Selimene. Night!

Chapter 2

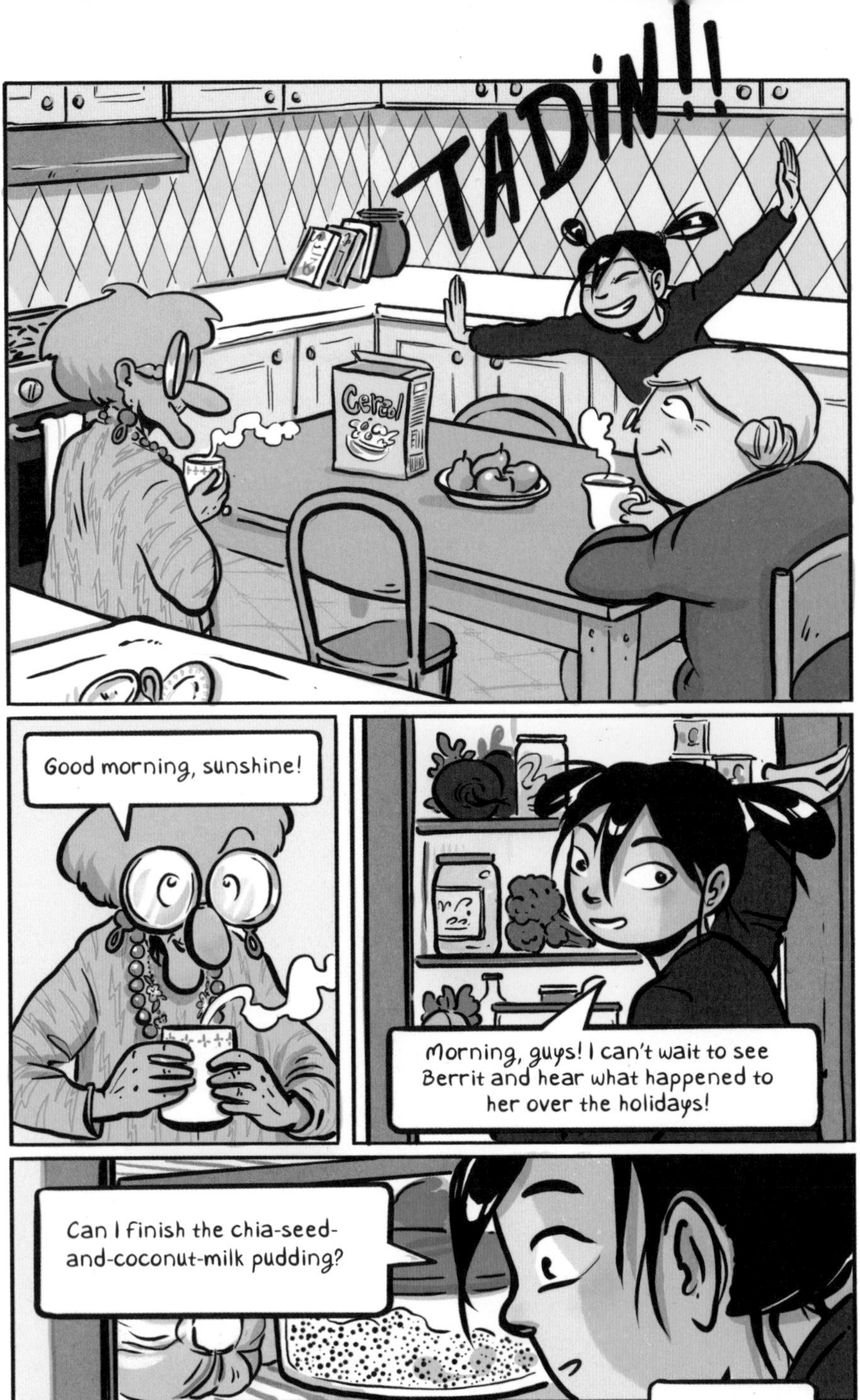
TADIN!!
Cereal
Good morning, sunshine!
Morning, guys! I can't wait to see Berrit and hear what happened to her over the holidays!
Can I finish the chia-seed-and-coconut-milk pudding?
Of course!

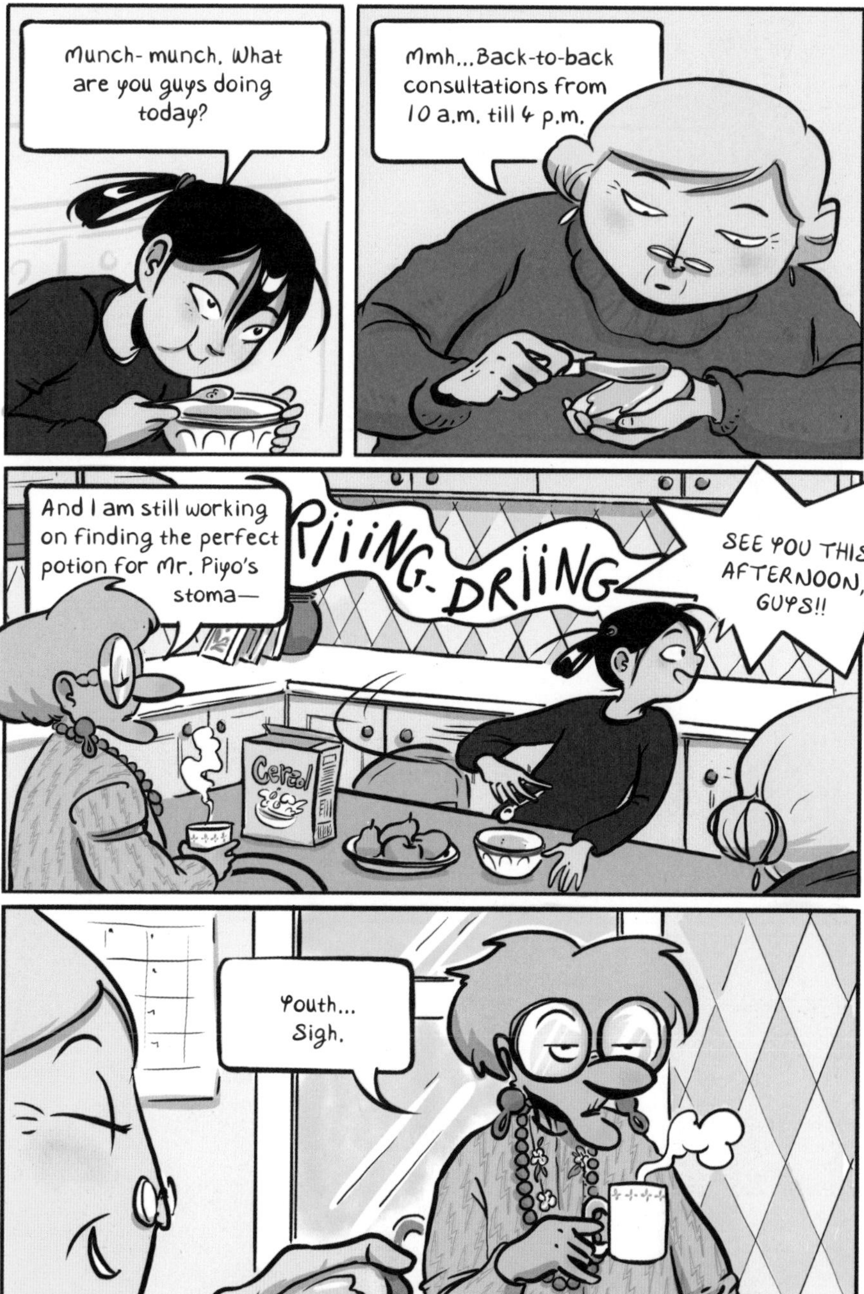
Munch- munch. What are you guys doing today?
Mmh...Back-to-back consultations from 10 a.m. till 4 p.m.
And I am still working on finding the perfect potion for Mr. Piyo's stoma—
DRIING-DRIING
SEE YOU THIS AFTERNOON, GUYS!!
Cereal
Youth... Sigh.

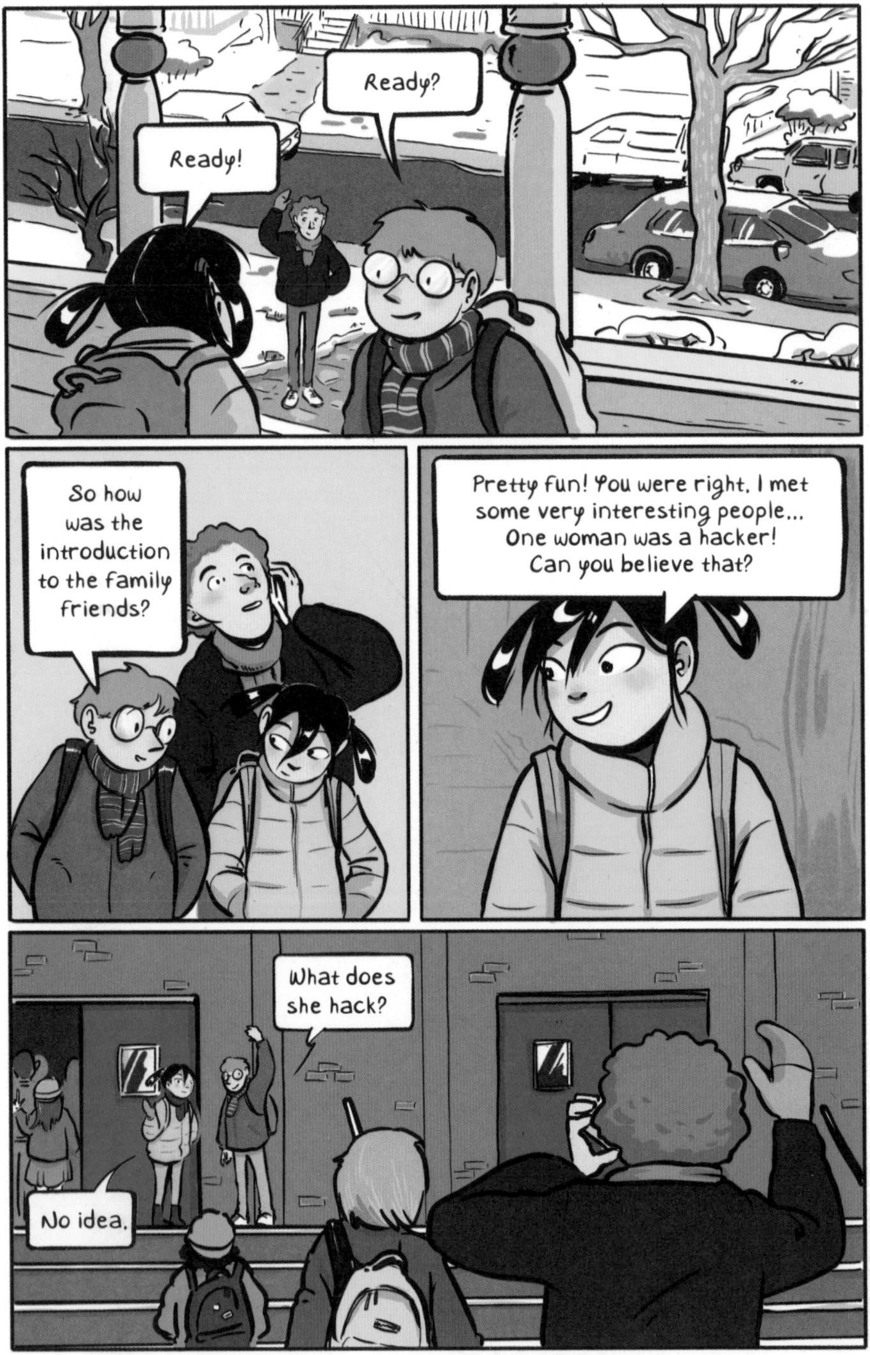
Ready?
Ready!
So how was the introduction to the family friends?
Pretty fun! You were right. I met some very interesting people... One woman was a hacker! Can you believe that?
What does she hack?
No idea.

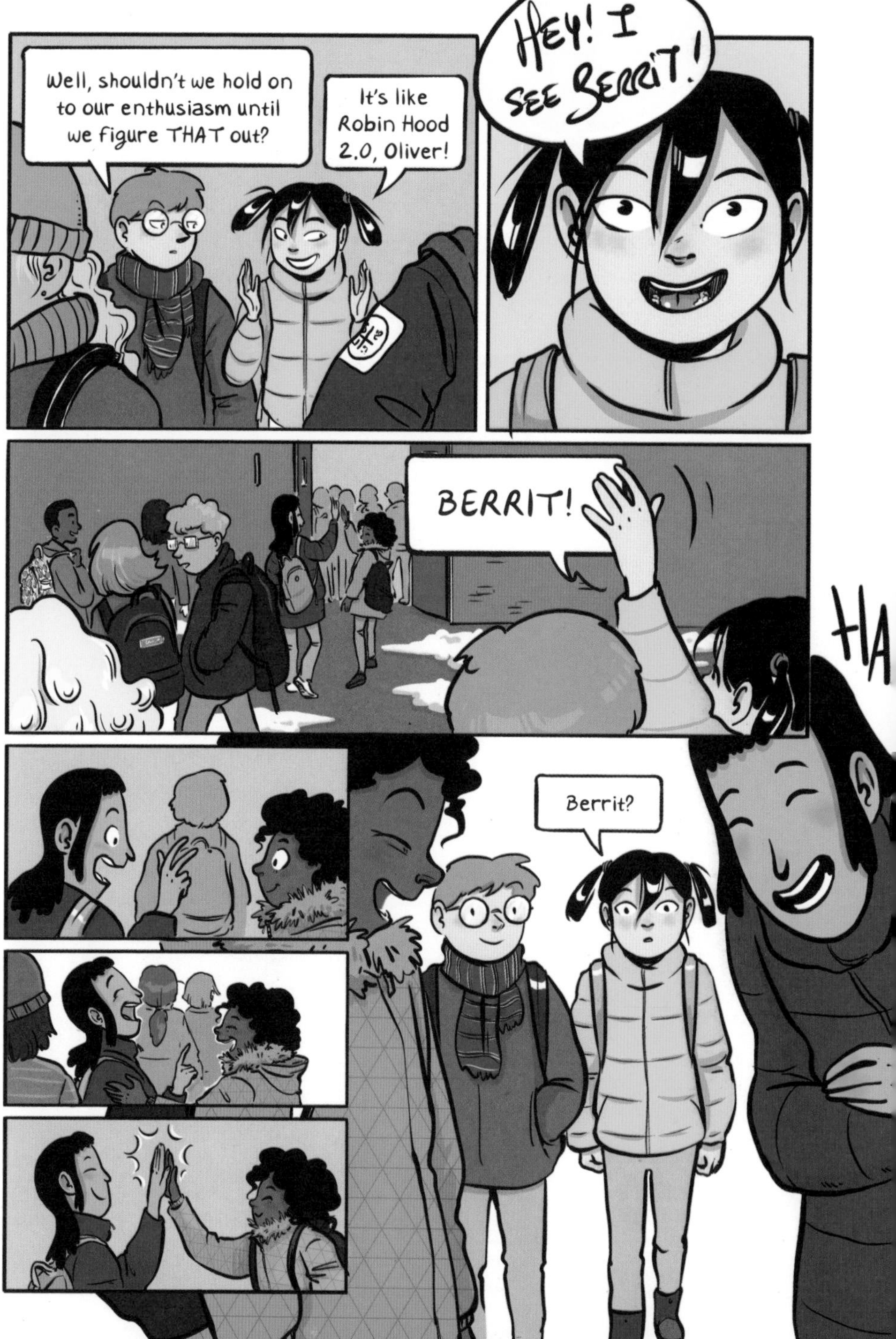
Well, shouldn't we hold on to our enthusiasm until we figure THAT out?
It's like Robin Hood 2.0, Oliver!
HEY! I SEE BERRIT!
BERRIT!
HA
Berrit?

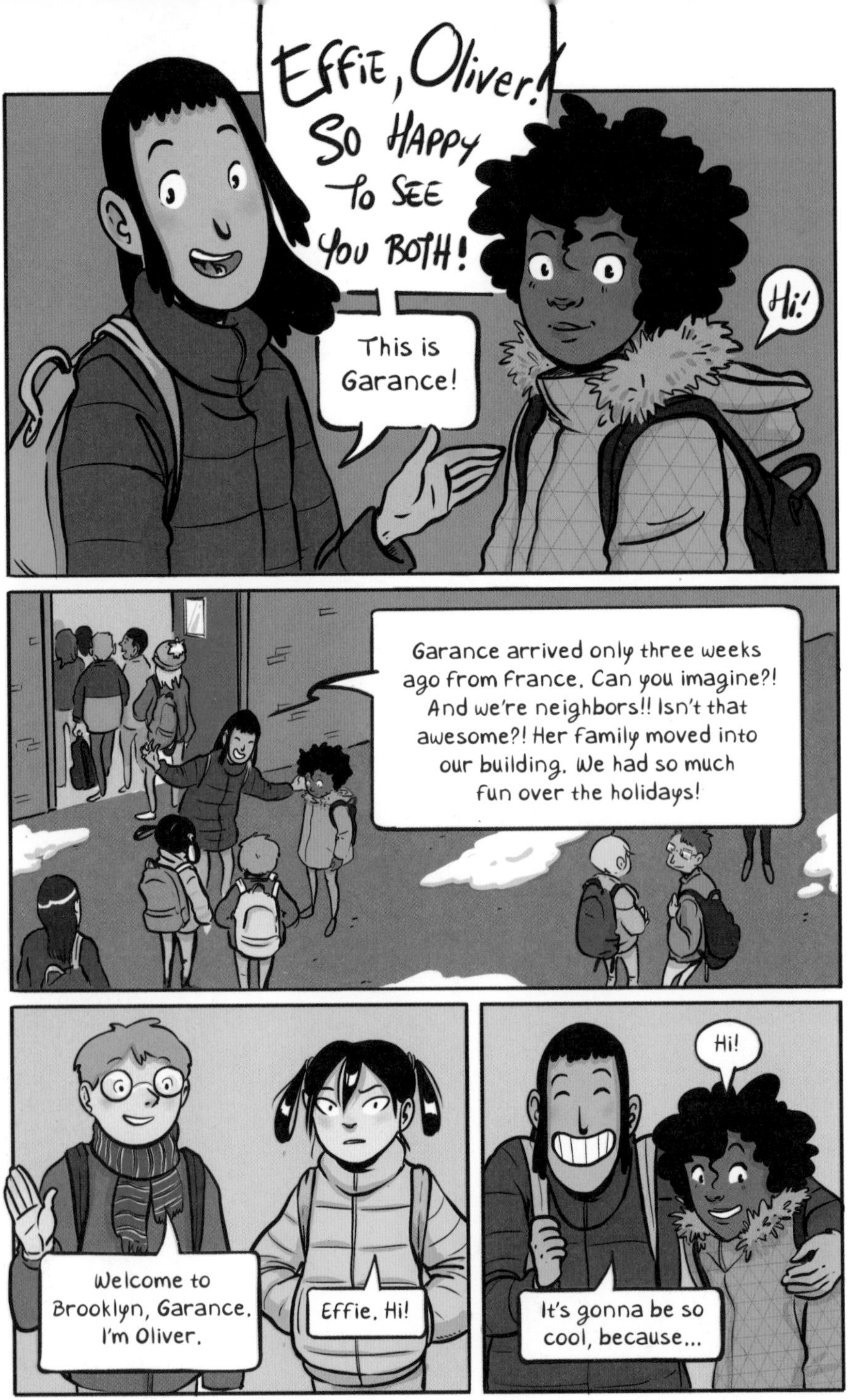
Effie, Oliver! So HAPPY to SEE you BOTH!
This is Garance!
Hi!
Garance arrived only three weeks ago from France. Can you imagine?! And we're neighbors!! Isn't that awesome?! Her family moved into our building. We had so much fun over the holidays!
Welcome to Brooklyn, Garance. I'm Oliver.
Effie. Hi!
Hi!
It's gonna be so cool, because...

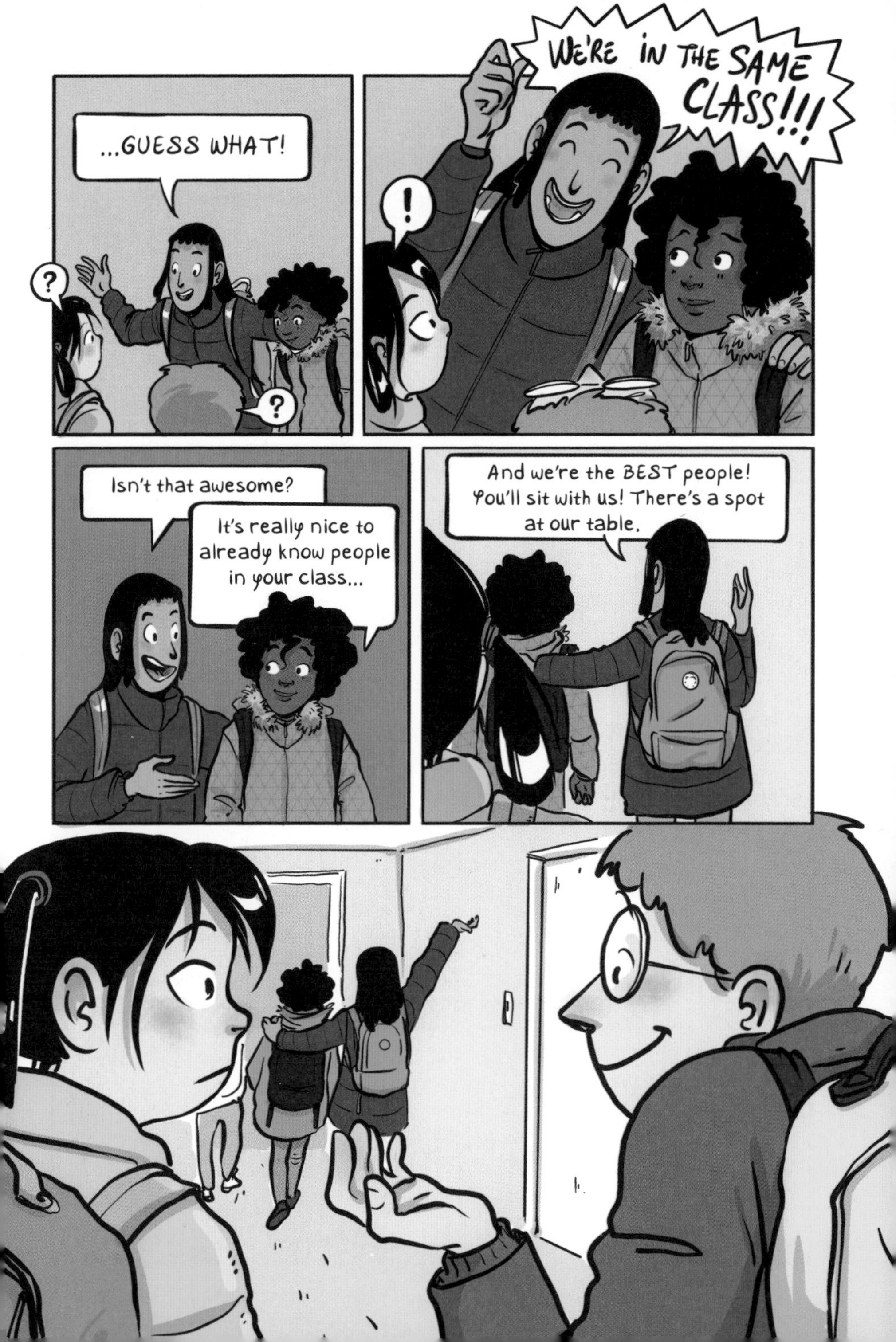
...GUESS WHAT!
?
?
WE'RE IN THE SAME CLASS!!!
!
Isn't that awesome?
It's really nice to already know people in your class...
And we're the BEST people! You'll sit with us! There's a spot at our table.

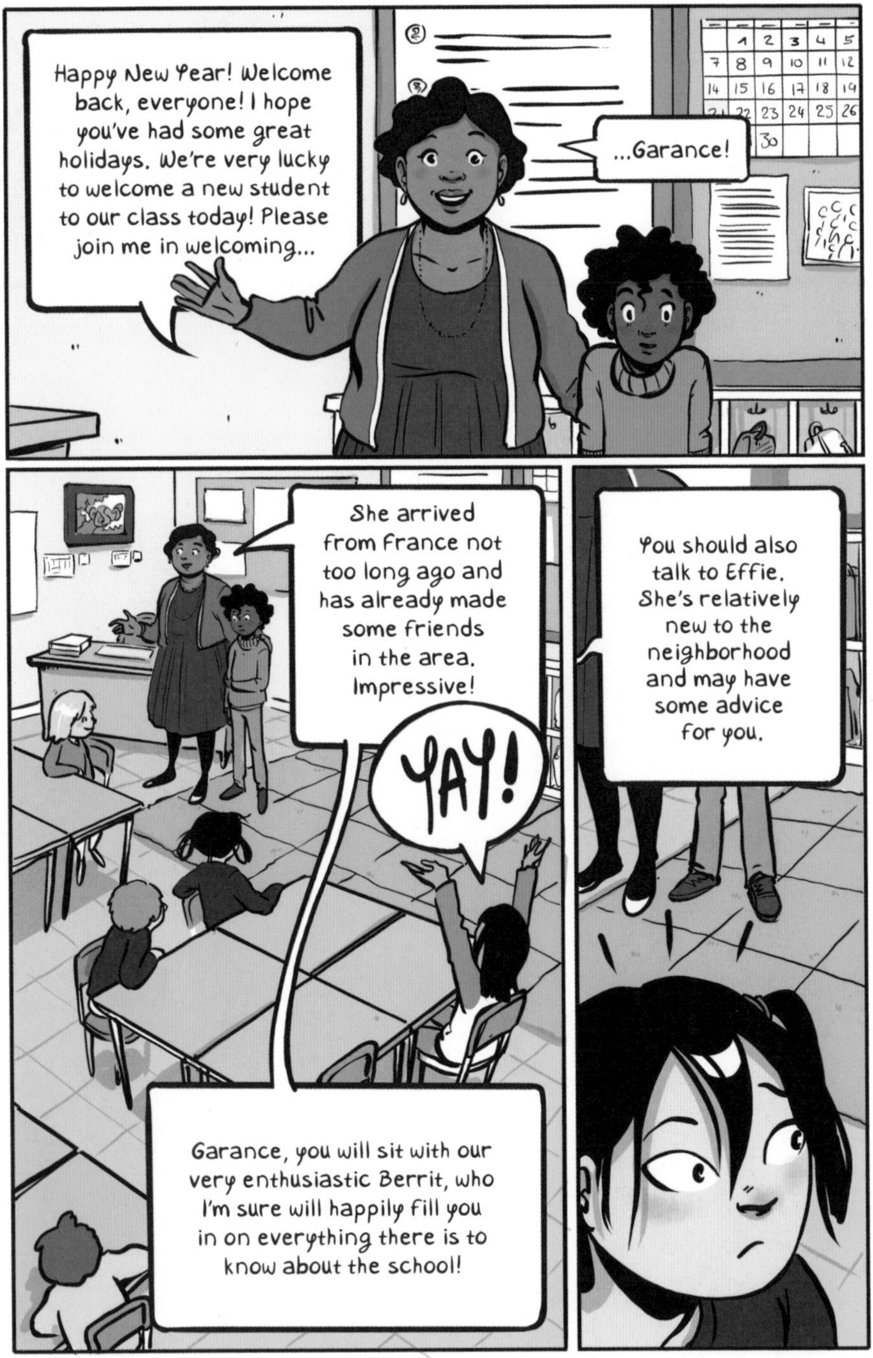
Happy New Year! Welcome back, everyone! I hope you've had some great holidays. We're very lucky to welcome a new student to our class today! Please join me in welcoming...
...Garance!
She arrived from France not too long ago and has already made some friends in the area. Impressive!
YAY!
Garance, you will sit with our very enthusiastic Berrit, who I'm sure will happily fill you in on everything there is to know about the school!
You should also talk to Effie. She's relatively new to the neighborhood and may have some advice for you.

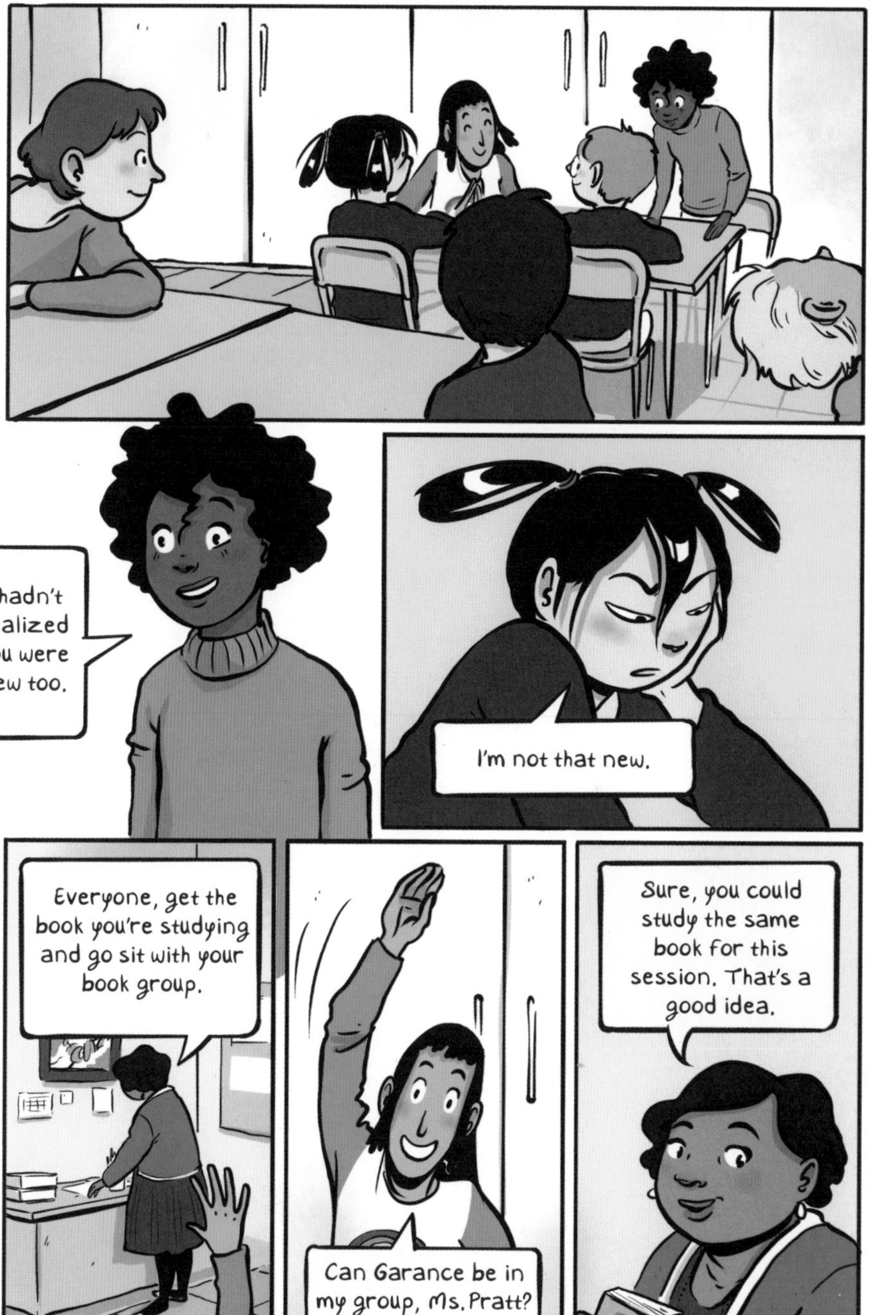

I hadn't realized you were new too.
I'm not that new.
Everyone, get the book you're studying and go sit with your book group.
Can Garance be in my group, Ms. Pratt?
Sure, you could study the same book for this session. That's a good idea.

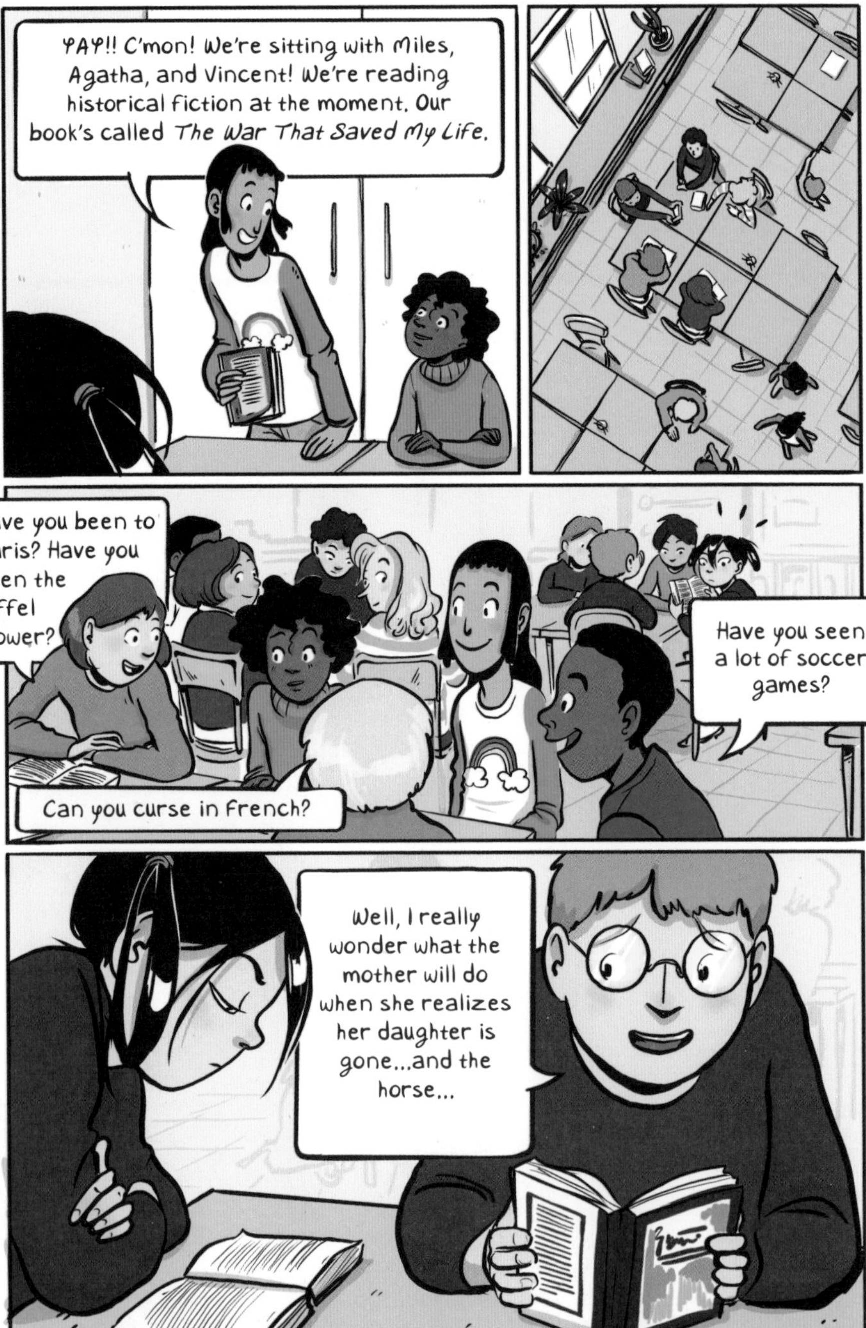
YAY!! C'mon! We're sitting with Miles, Agatha, and Vincent! We're reading historical fiction at the moment. Our book's called *The War That Saved My Life*.
Have you been to Paris? Have you seen the Eiffel Tower?
Have you seen a lot of soccer games?
Can you curse in French?
Well, I really wonder what the mother will do when she realizes her daughter is gone...and the horse...

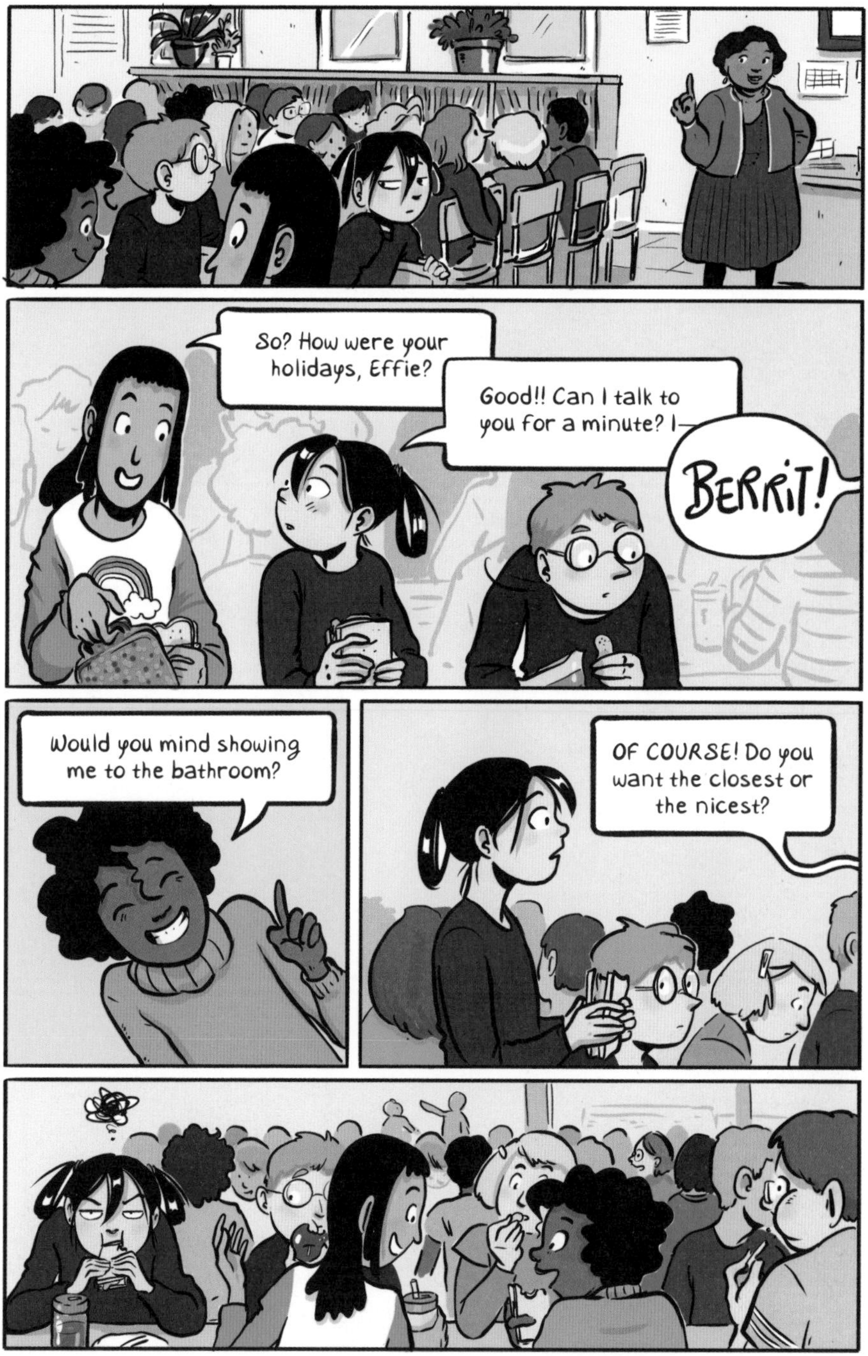
So? How were your holidays, Effie?
Good!! Can I talk to you for a minute? I—
BERRIT!
Would you mind showing me to the bathroom?
OF COURSE! Do you want the closest or the nicest?

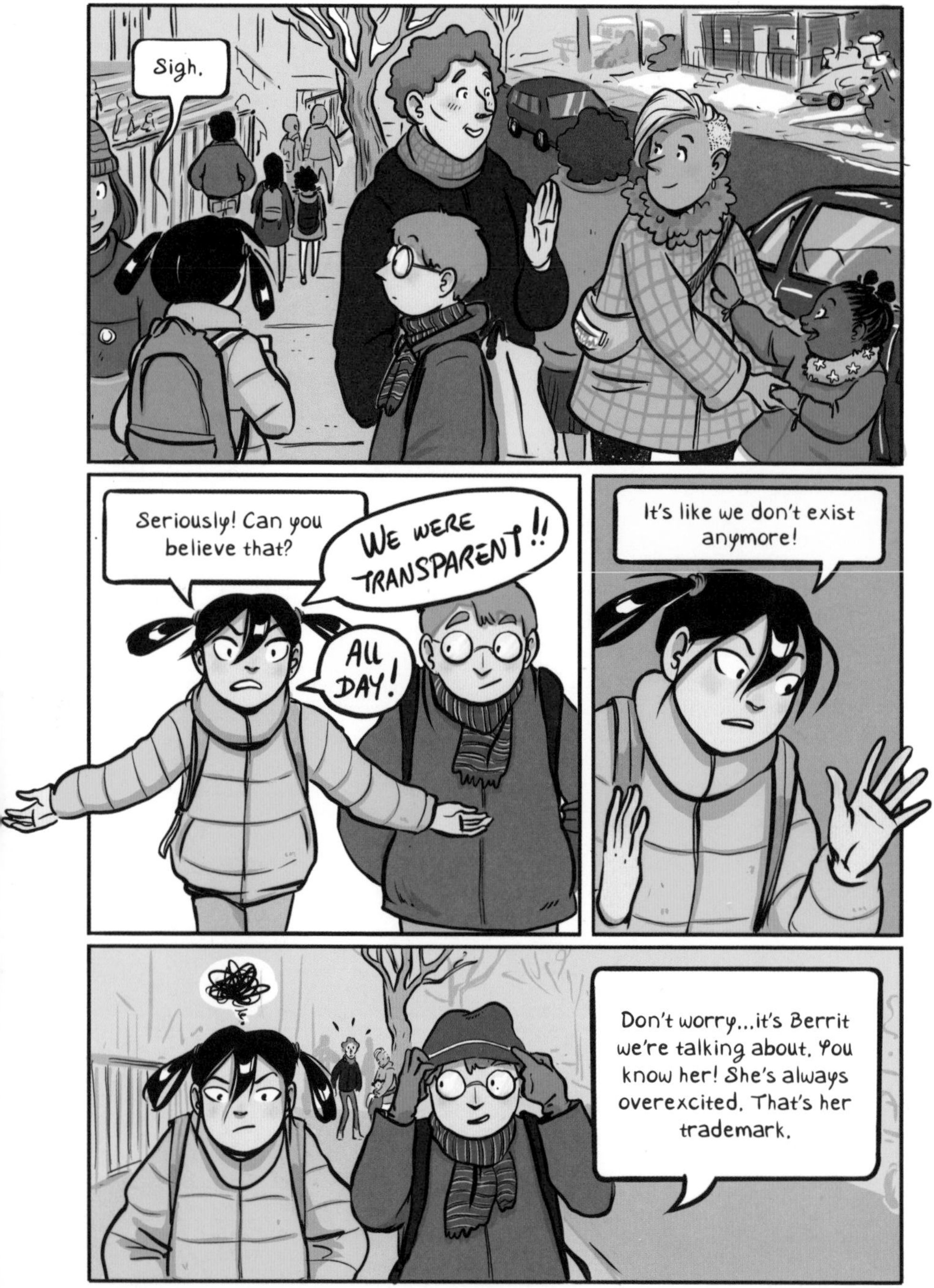
Sigh.
Seriously! Can you believe that?
WE WERE TRANSPARENT!!
ALL DAY!
It's like we don't exist anymore!
Don't worry...it's Berrit we're talking about. You know her! She's always overexcited. That's her trademark.

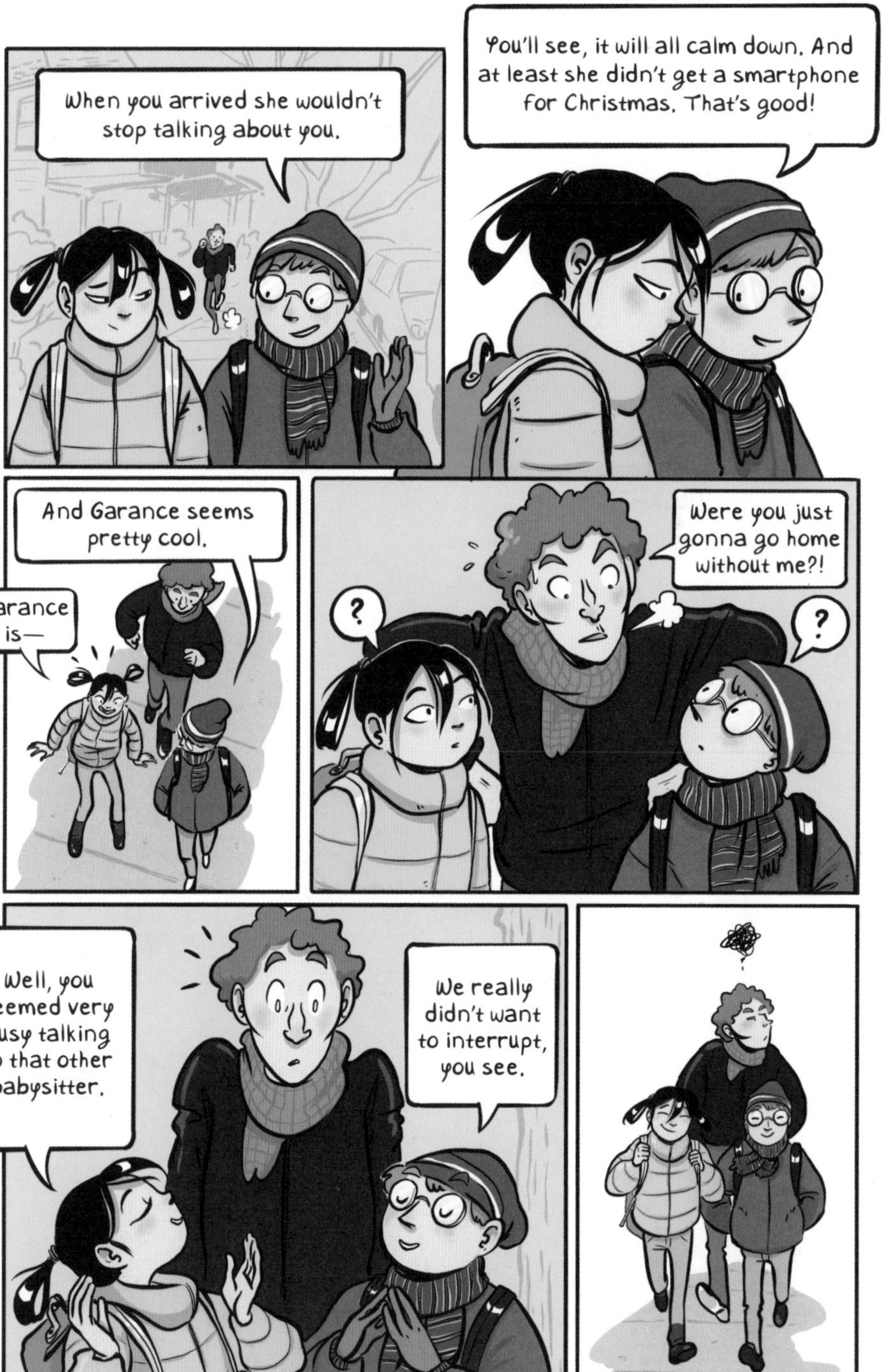
When you arrived she wouldn't stop talking about you.
You'll see, it will all calm down. And at least she didn't get a smartphone for Christmas. That's good!
And Garance seems pretty cool.
Garance is—
Were you just gonna go home without me?!
?
?
Well, you seemed very busy talking to that other babysitter.
We really didn't want to interrupt, you see.

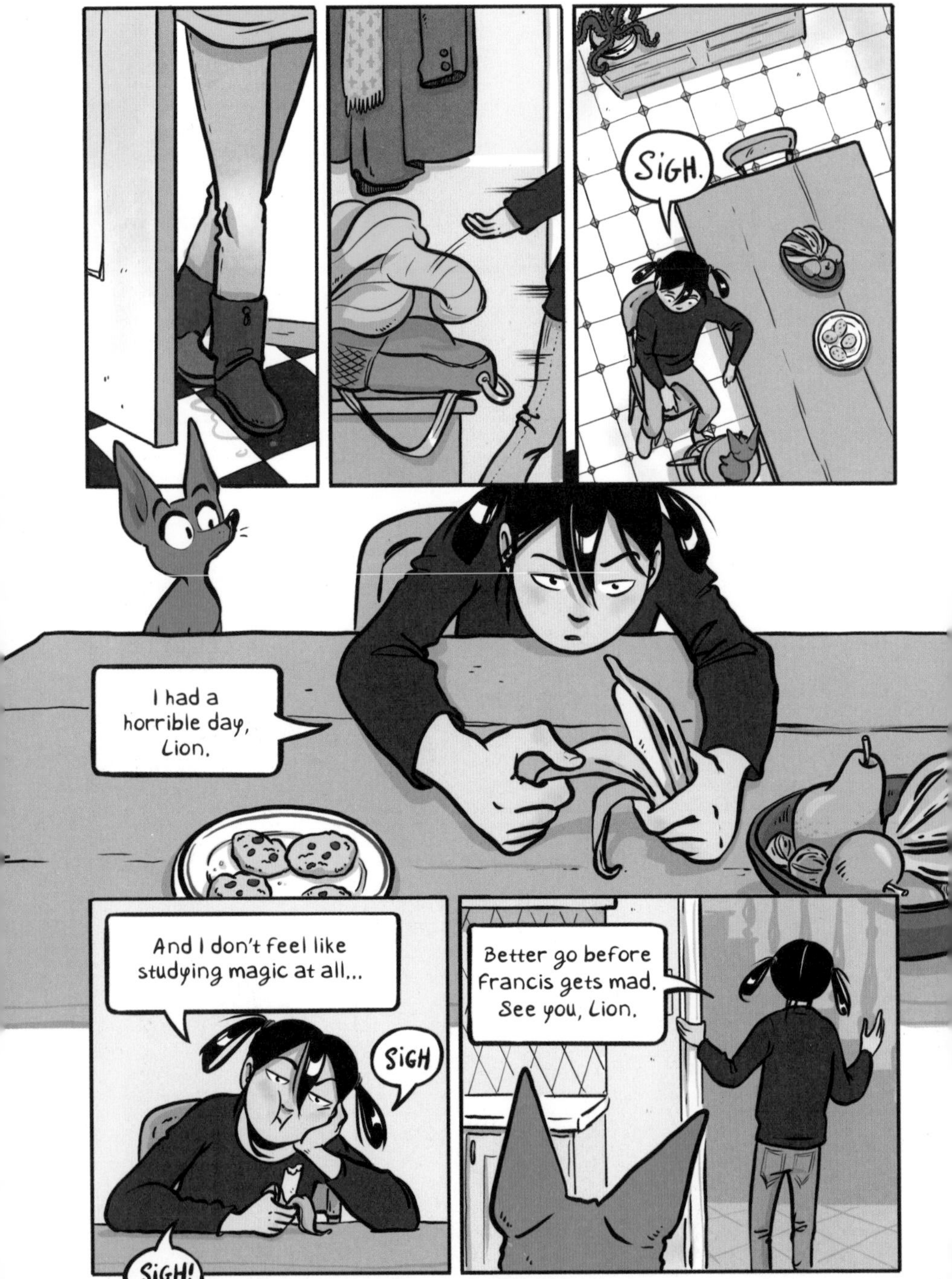
SIGH.
I had a horrible day, Lion.
And I don't feel like studying magic at all...
SIGH
SIGH!
Better go before Francis gets mad. See you, Lion.

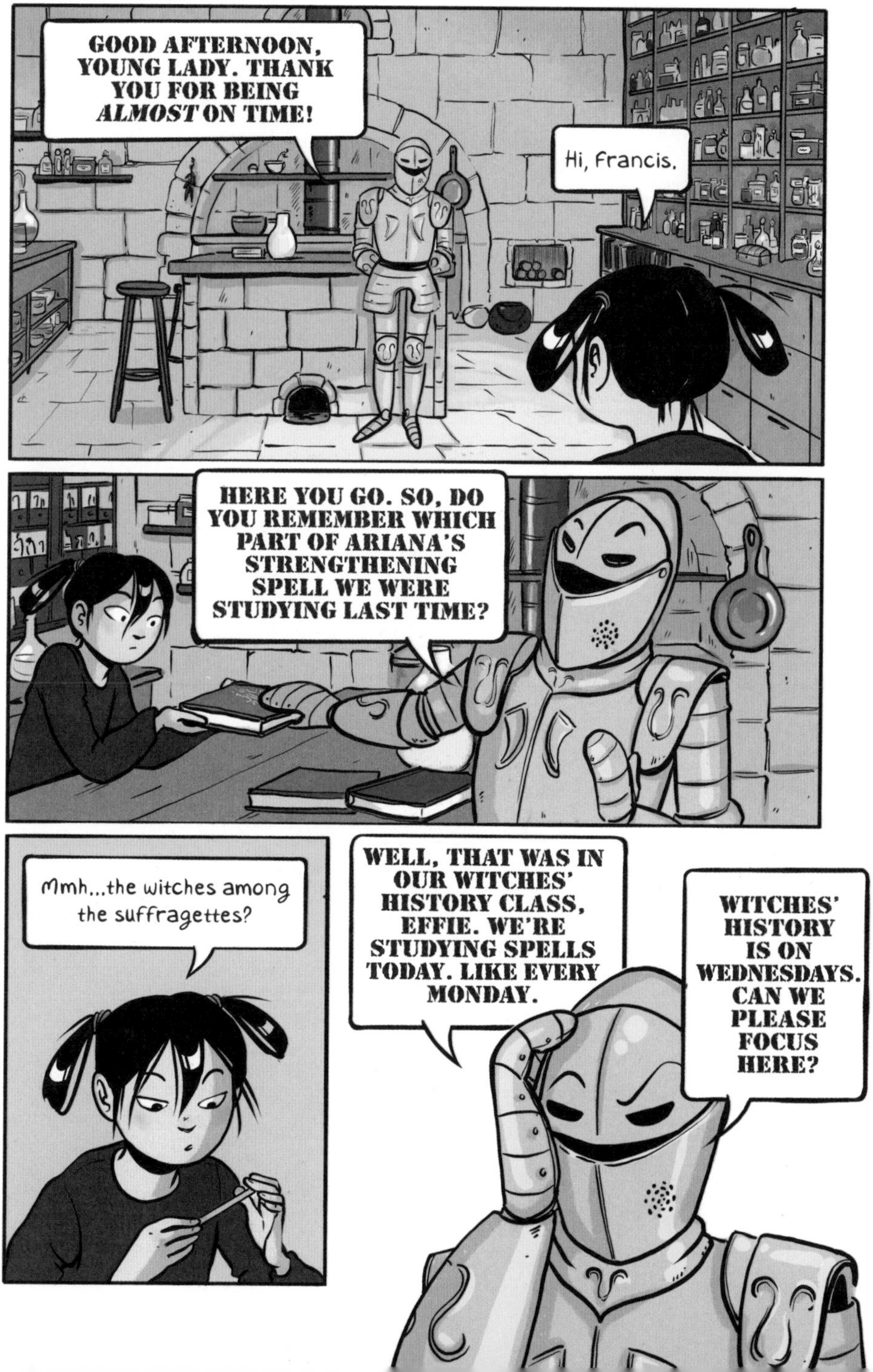
GOOD AFTERNOON, YOUNG LADY. THANK YOU FOR BEING *ALMOST* ON TIME!
Hi, Francis.
HERE YOU GO. SO, DO YOU REMEMBER WHICH PART OF ARIANA'S STRENGTHENING SPELL WE WERE STUDYING LAST TIME?
Mmh...the witches among the suffragettes?
WELL, THAT WAS IN OUR WITCHES' HISTORY CLASS, EFFIE. WE'RE STUDYING SPELLS TODAY. LIKE EVERY MONDAY.
WITCHES' HISTORY IS ON WEDNESDAYS. CAN WE PLEASE FOCUS HERE?

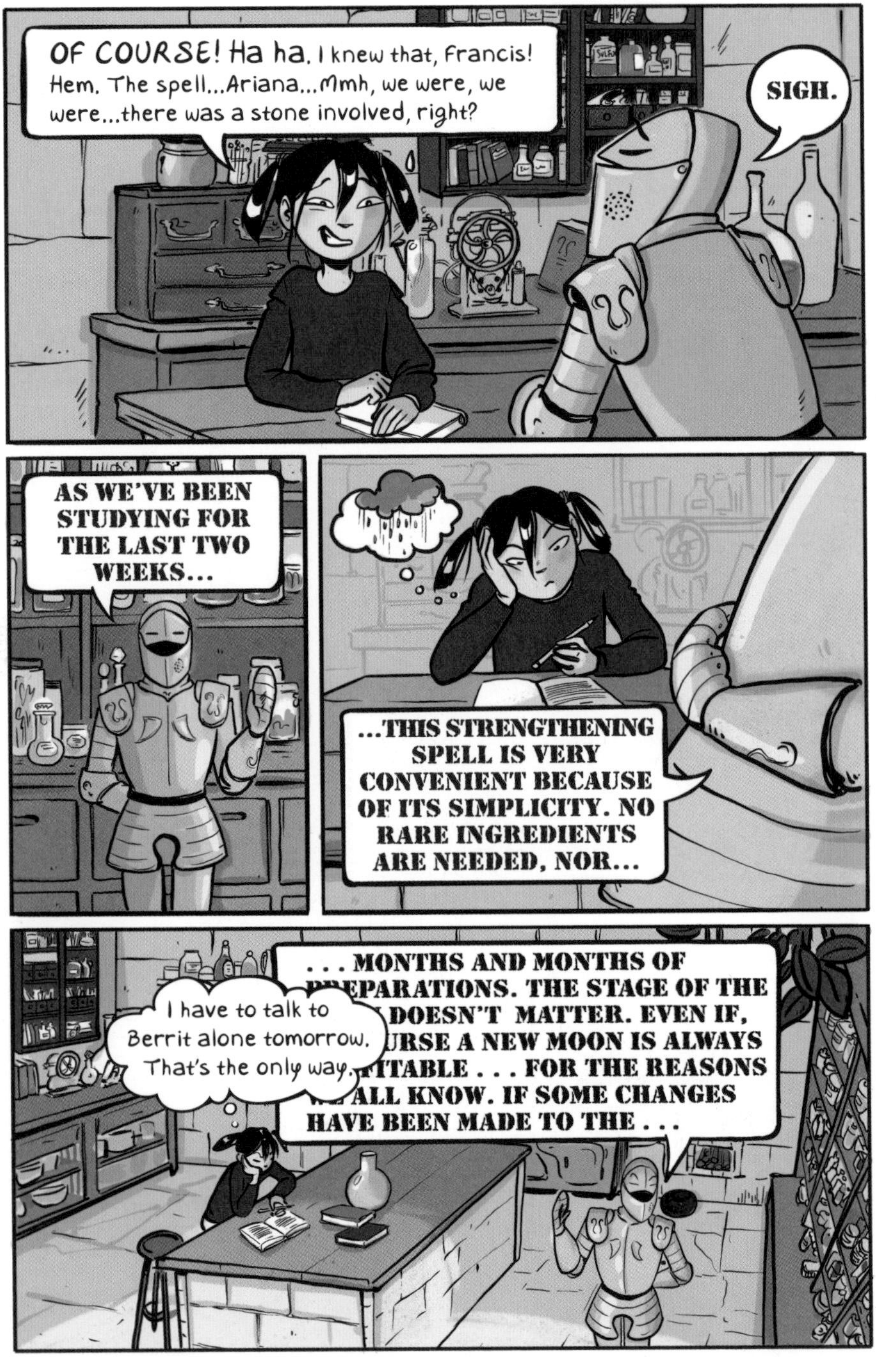
OF COURSE! Ha ha. I knew that, Francis! Hem. The spell...Ariana...Mmh, we were, we were...there was a stone involved, right?
SIGH.
AS WE'VE BEEN STUDYING FOR THE LAST TWO WEEKS...
...THIS STRENGTHENING SPELL IS VERY CONVENIENT BECAUSE OF ITS SIMPLICITY. NO RARE INGREDIENTS ARE NEEDED, NOR...
I have to talk to Berrit alone tomorrow. That's the only way.
. . . MONTHS AND MONTHS OF
EPARATIONS. THE STAGE OF THE
DOESN'T MATTER. EVEN IF,
URSE A NEW MOON IS ALWAYS
FITABLE . . . FOR THE REASONS
ALL KNOW. IF SOME CHANGES
HAVE BEEN MADE TO THE . . .

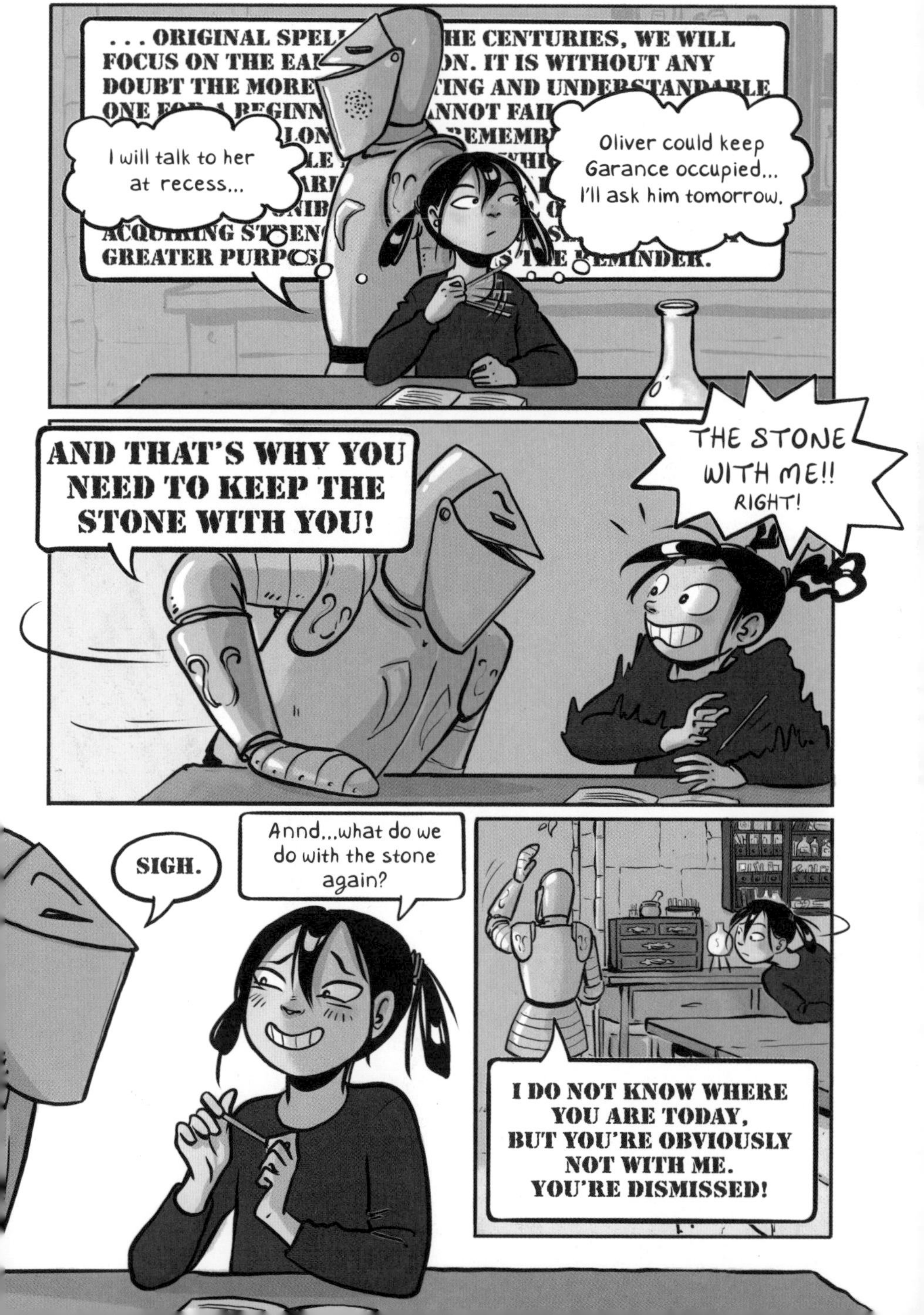

. . . ORIGINAL SPELL ... HE CENTURIES, WE WILL FOCUS ON THE EA ... ON. IT IS WITHOUT ANY DOUBT THE MORE ... TING AND UNDERSTANDABLE ONE FOR A BEGINN ... ACQUIRING ST ... GREATER PURP ... THE REMINDER.
I will talk to her at recess...
Oliver could keep Garance occupied... I'll ask him tomorrow.
AND THAT'S WHY YOU NEED TO KEEP THE STONE WITH YOU!
THE STONE WITH ME!! RIGHT!
SIGH.
Annd...what do we do with the stone again?
I DO NOT KNOW WHERE YOU ARE TODAY, BUT YOU'RE OBVIOUSLY NOT WITH ME. YOU'RE DISMISSED!

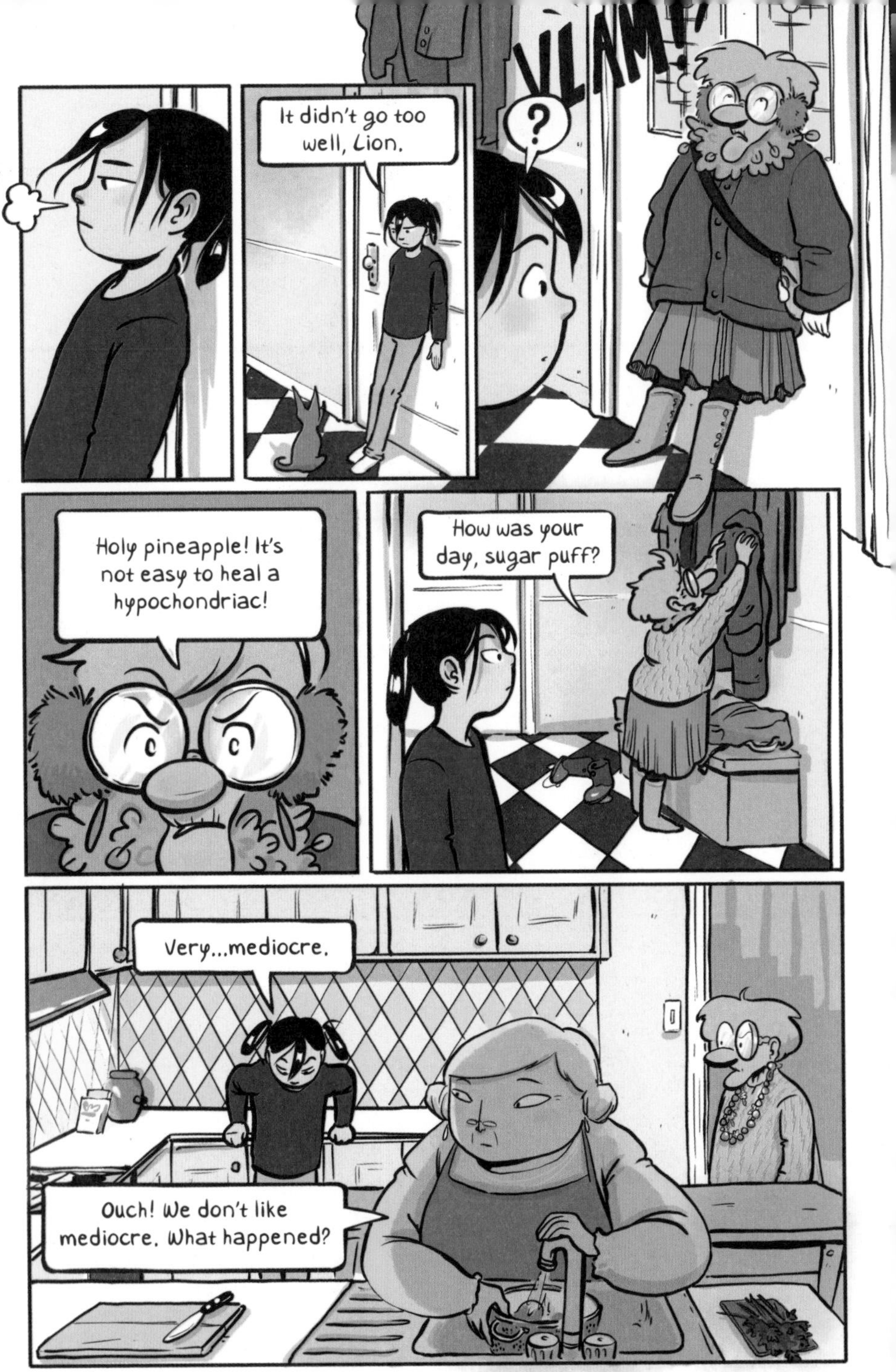

It didn't go too well, Lion.
VLAM!
?
Holy pineapple! It's not easy to heal a hypochondriac!
How was your day, sugar puff?
Very...mediocre.
Ouch! We don't like mediocre. What happened?

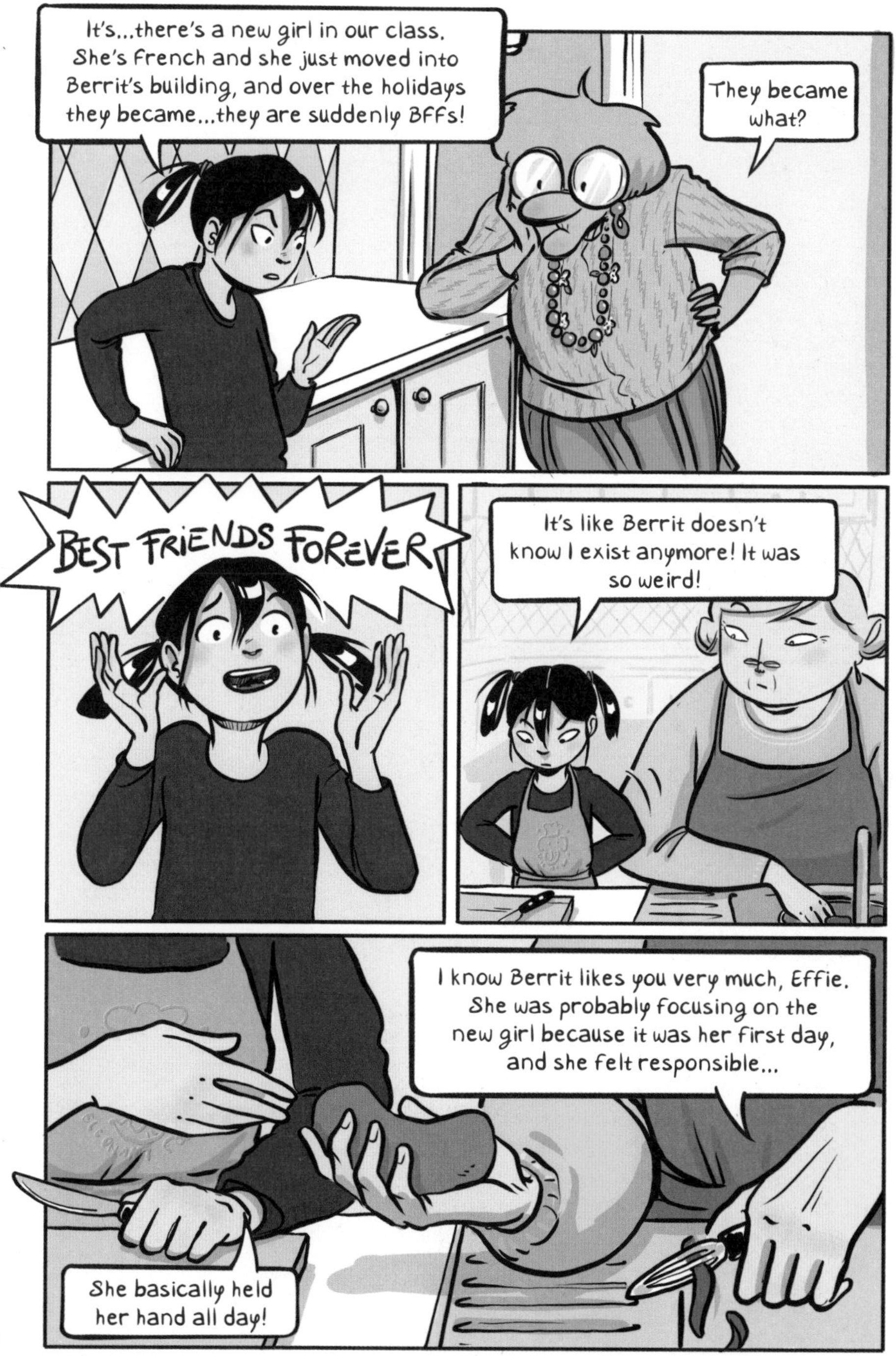
It's...there's a new girl in our class. She's French and she just moved into Berrit's building, and over the holidays they became...they are suddenly BFFs!
They became what?
BEST FRIENDS FOREVER
It's like Berrit doesn't know I exist anymore! It was so weird!
I know Berrit likes you very much, Effie. She was probably focusing on the new girl because it was her first day, and she felt responsible...
She basically held her hand all day!

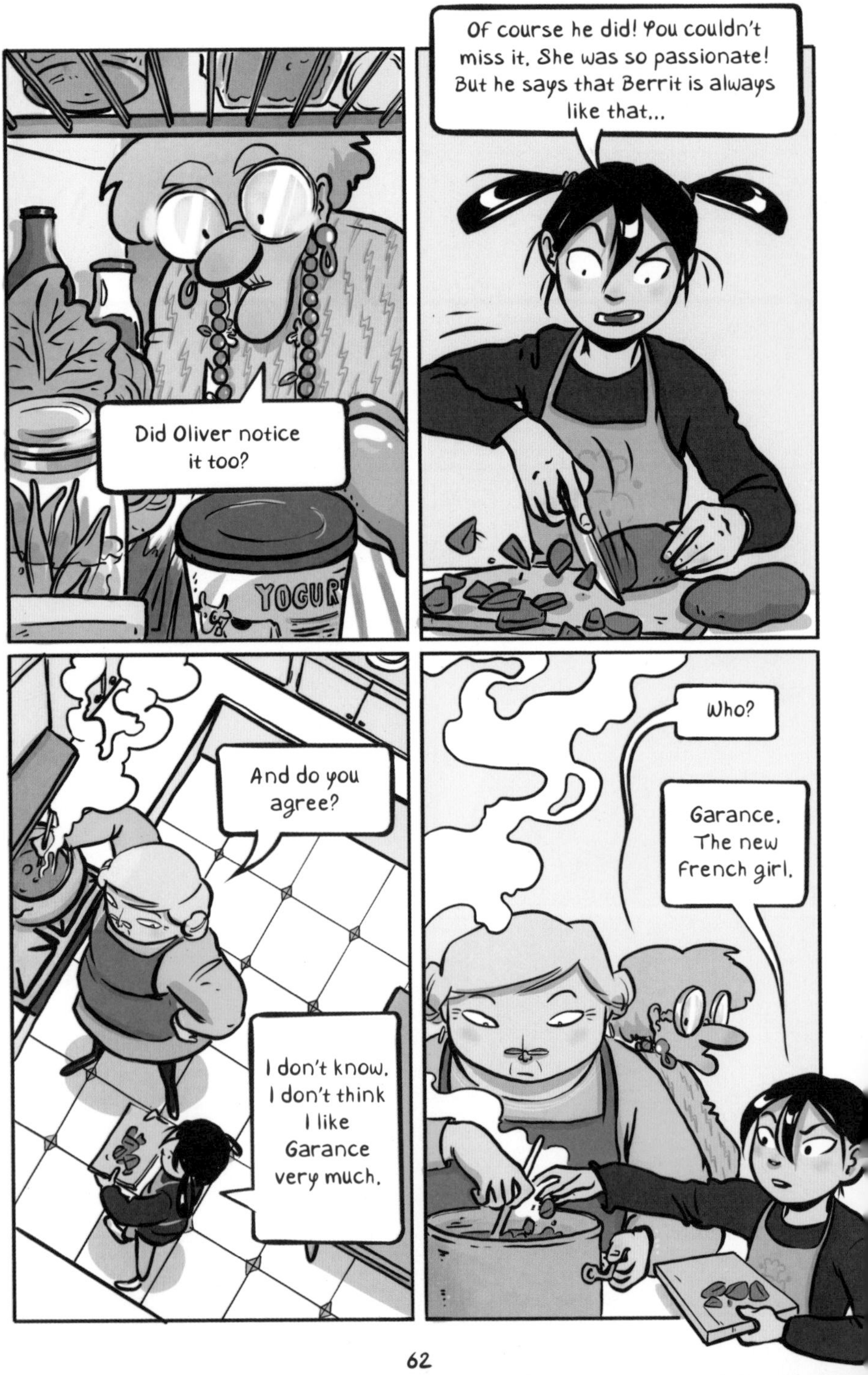
Did Oliver notice it too?
Of course he did! You couldn't miss it. She was so passionate! But he says that Berrit is always like that...
And do you agree?
I don't know. I don't think I like Garance very much.
Who?
Garance. The new French girl.

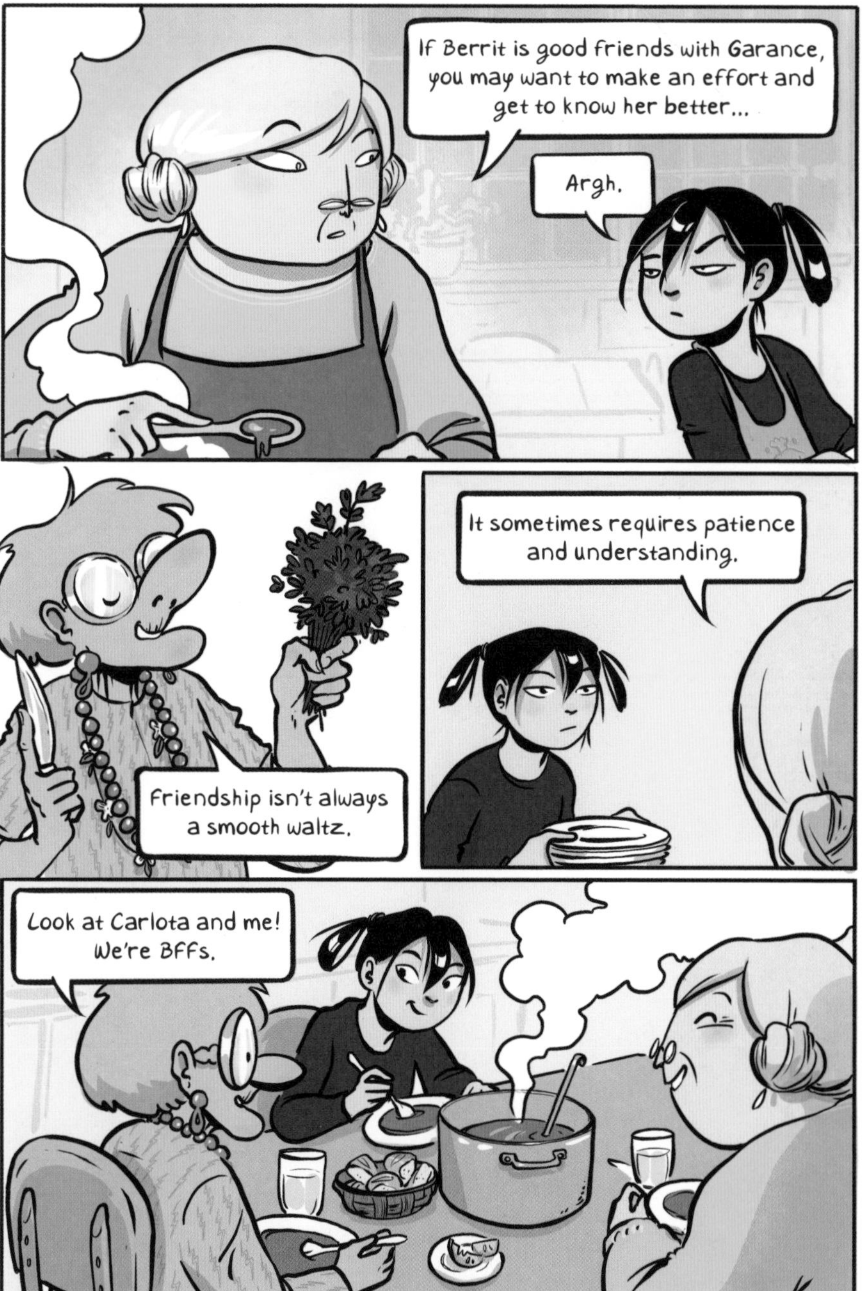
If Berrit is good friends with Garance, you may want to make an effort and get to know her better...
Argh.
Friendship isn't always a smooth waltz.
It sometimes requires patience and understanding.
Look at Carlota and me! We're BFFs.

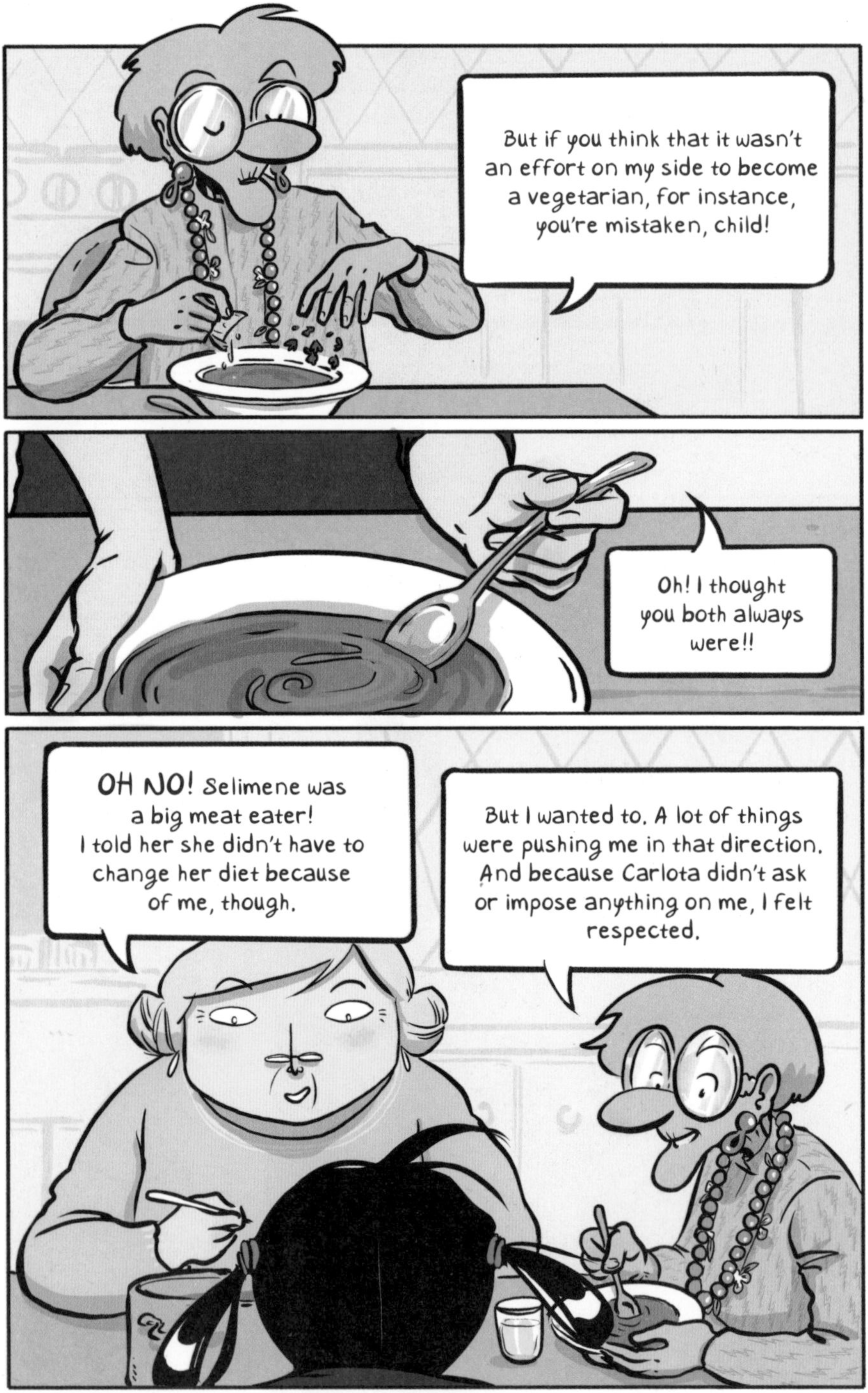
But if you think that it wasn't an effort on my side to become a vegetarian, for instance, you're mistaken, child!
Oh! I thought you both always were!!
OH NO! Selimene was a big meat eater! I told her she didn't have to change her diet because of me, though.
But I wanted to. A lot of things were pushing me in that direction. And because Carlota didn't ask or impose anything on me, I felt respected.

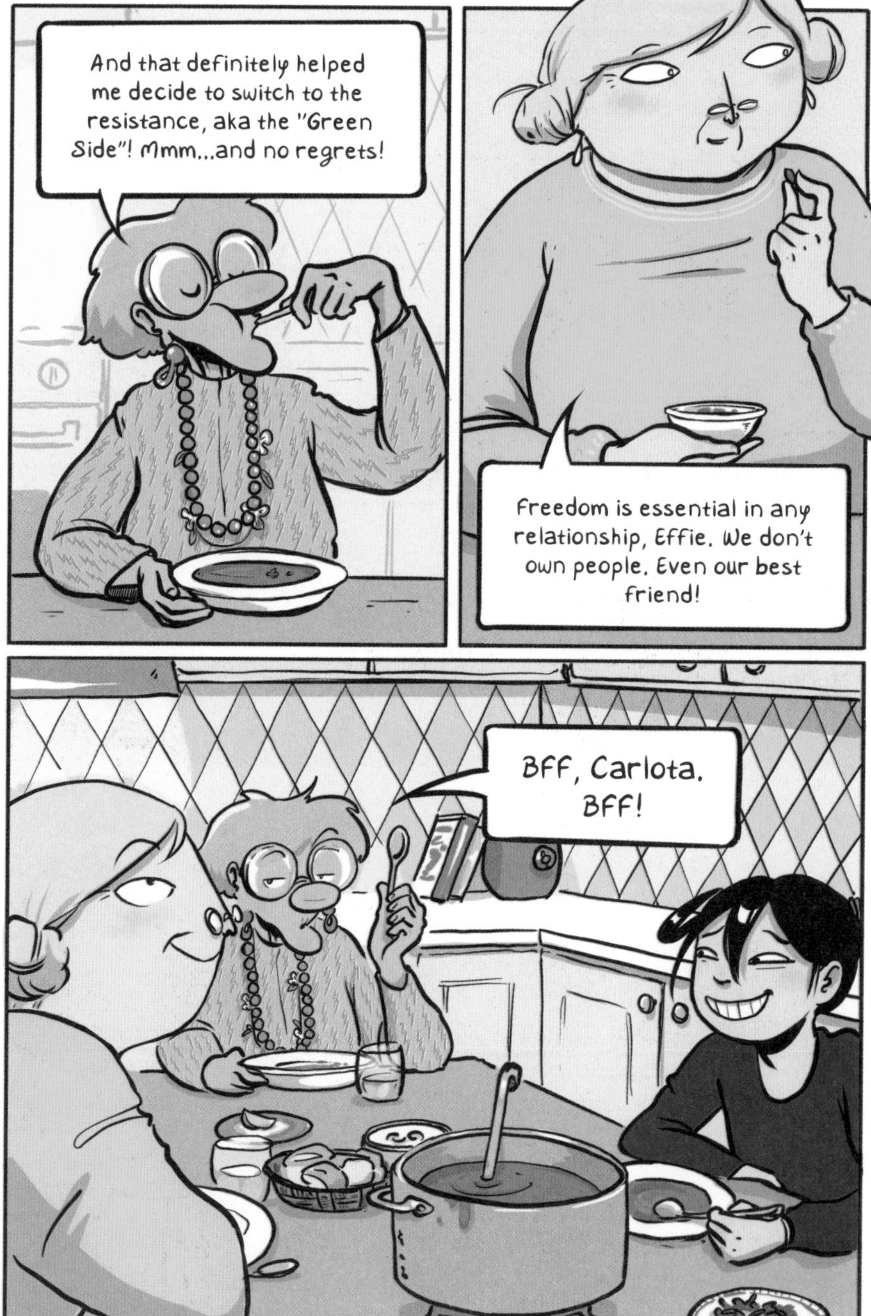

And that definitely helped me decide to switch to the resistance, aka the "Green Side"! Mmm...and no regrets!
Freedom is essential in any relationship, Effie. We don't own people. Even our best friend!
BFF, Carlota. BFF!

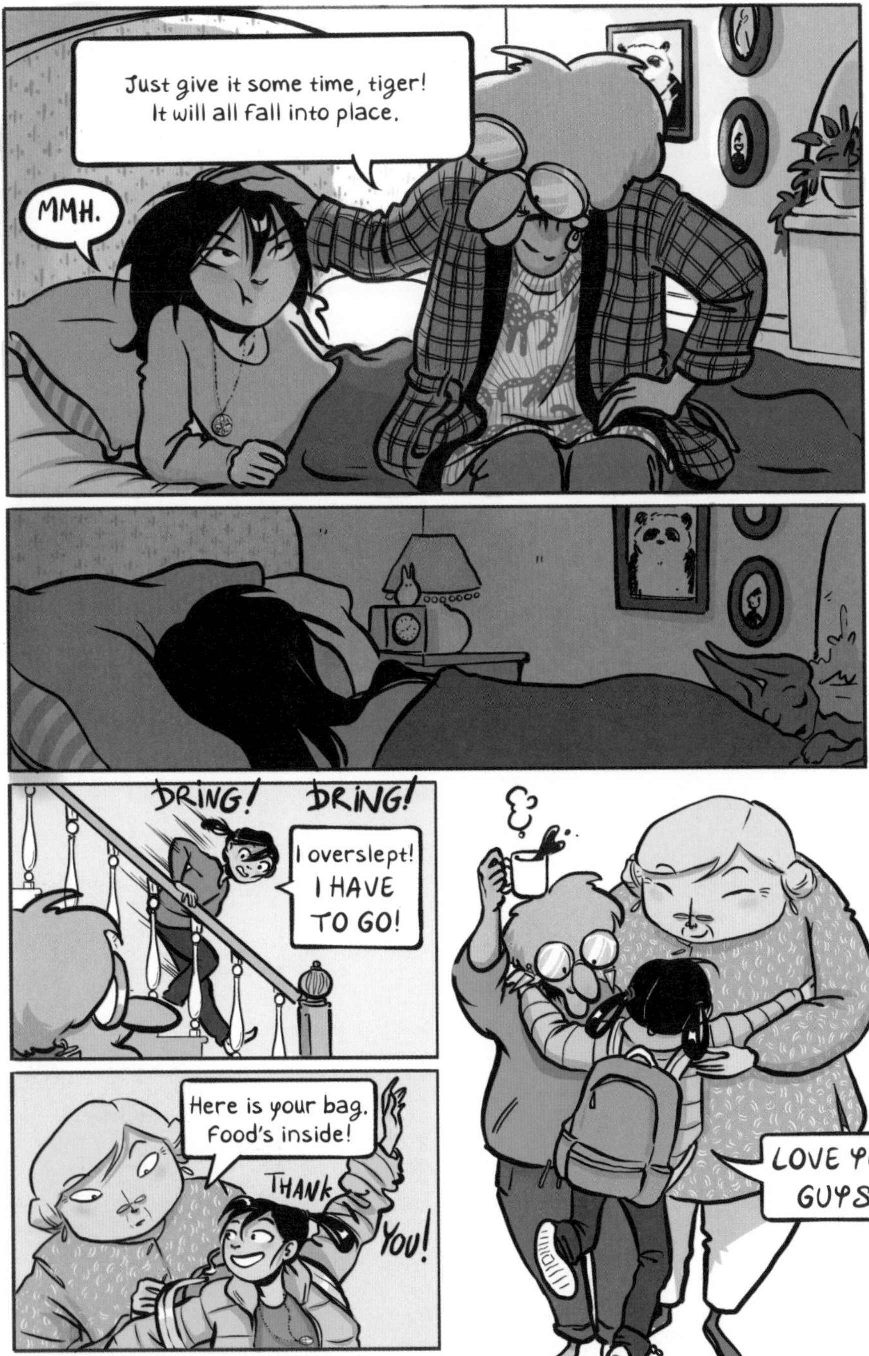

Just give it some time, tiger! It will all fall into place.
MMH.
DRING! DRING!
I overslept! I HAVE TO GO!
Here is your bag. Food's inside!
THANK YOU!
LOVE YOU GUYS!

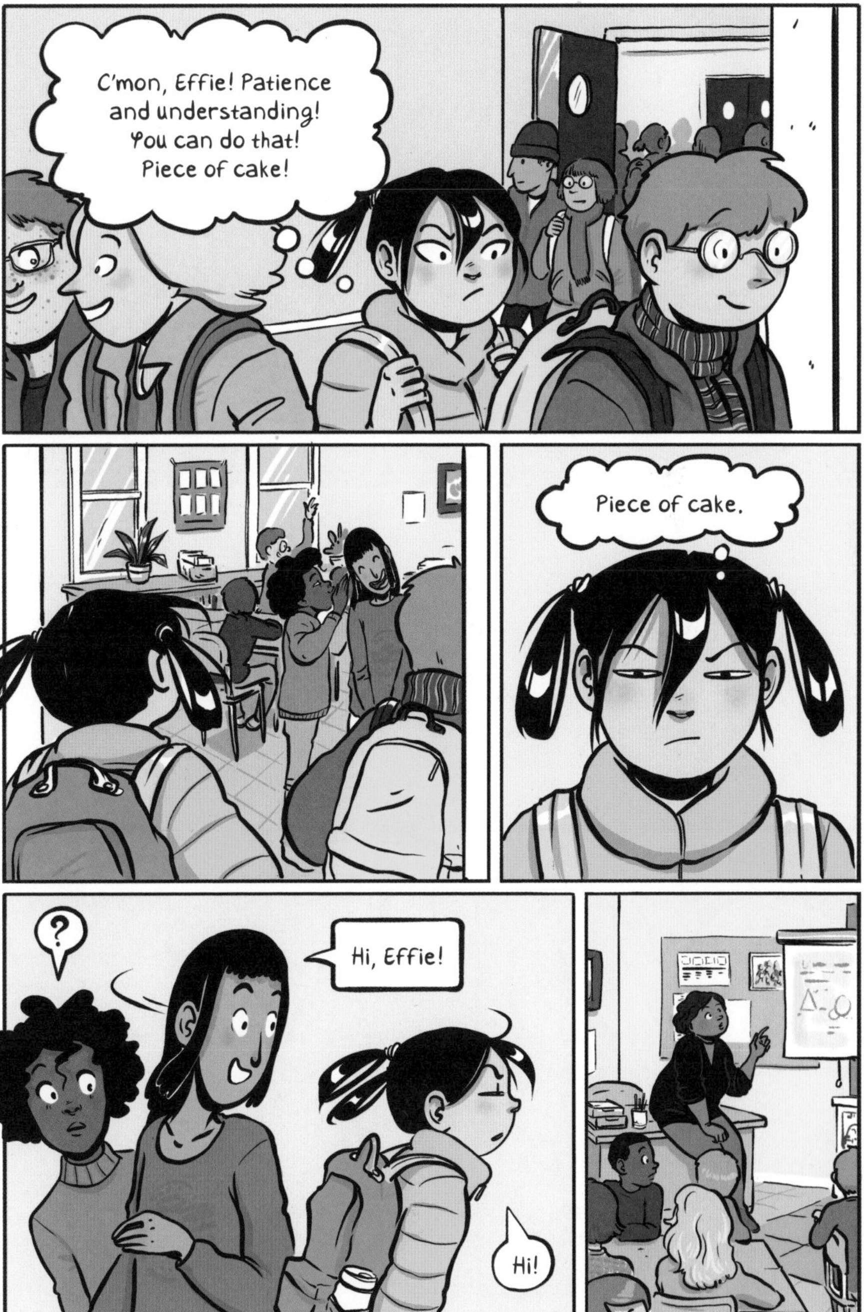
C'mon, Effie! Patience and understanding! You can do that! Piece of cake!
Piece of cake.
?
Hi, Effie!
Hi!

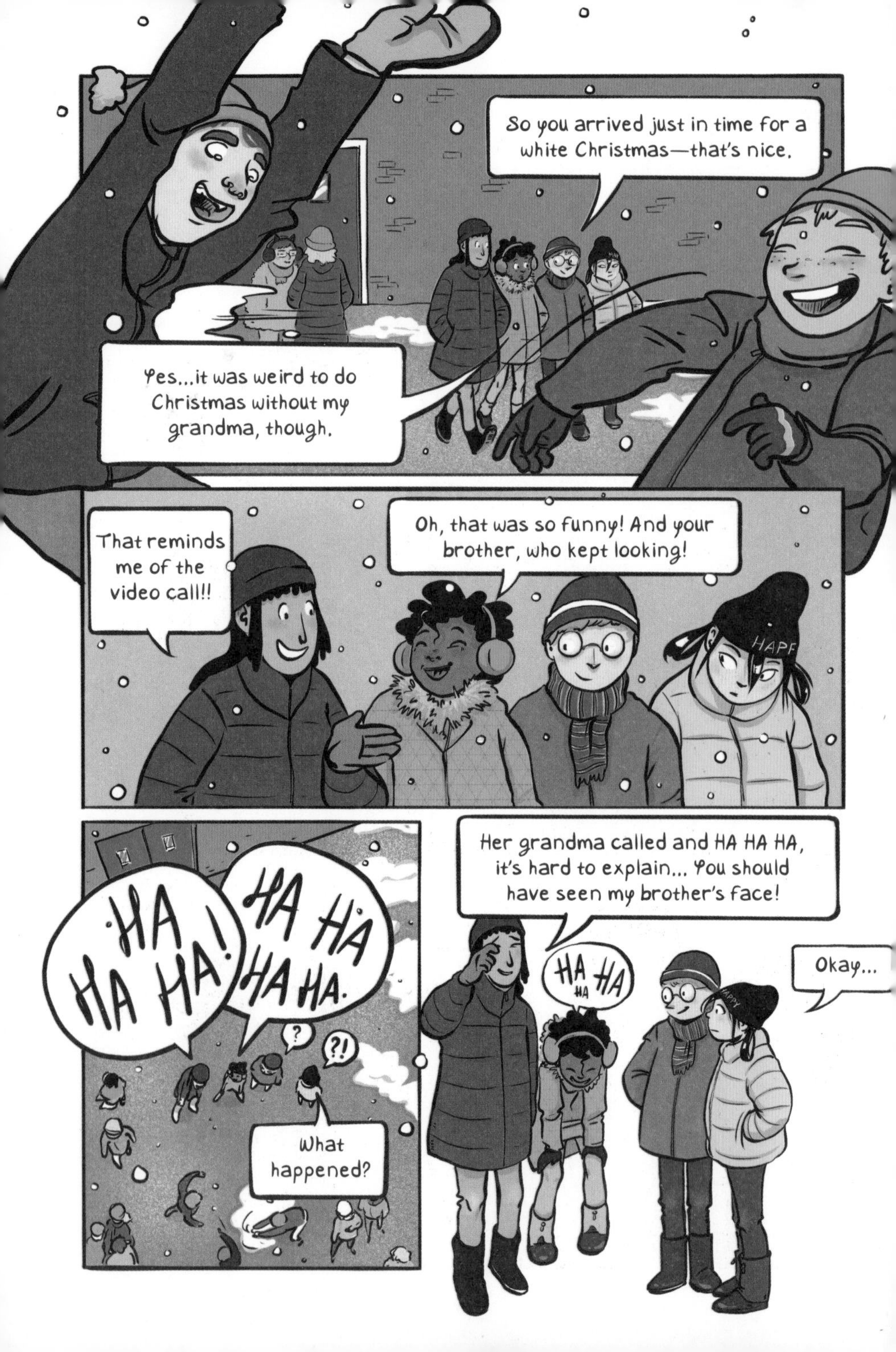
So you arrived just in time for a white Christmas—that's nice.
Yes...it was weird to do Christmas without my grandma, though.
That reminds me of the video call!!
Oh, that was so funny! And your brother, who kept looking!
HAPP
HA HA HA HA!
HA HA HA HA HA.
?
?!
What happened?
Her grandma called and HA HA HA, it's hard to explain... You should have seen my brother's face!
HA HA HA
HAPPY
Okay...

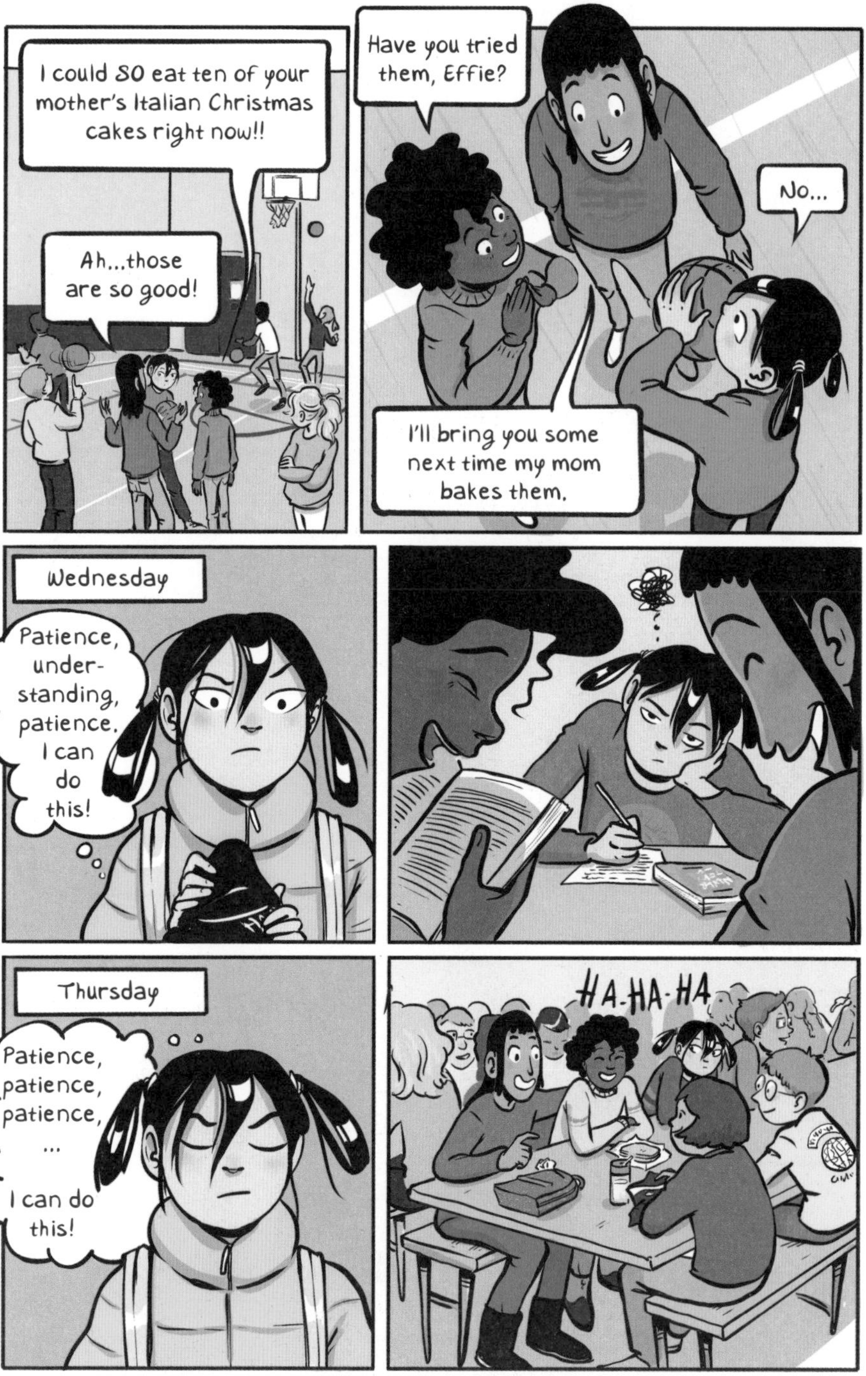
I could SO eat ten of your mother's Italian Christmas cakes right now!!
Ah...those are so good!
Have you tried them, Effie?
No...
I'll bring you some next time my mom bakes them.
Wednesday
Patience, under-standing, patience, I can do this!
Thursday
Patience, patience, patience, ... I can do this!
HA-HA-HA

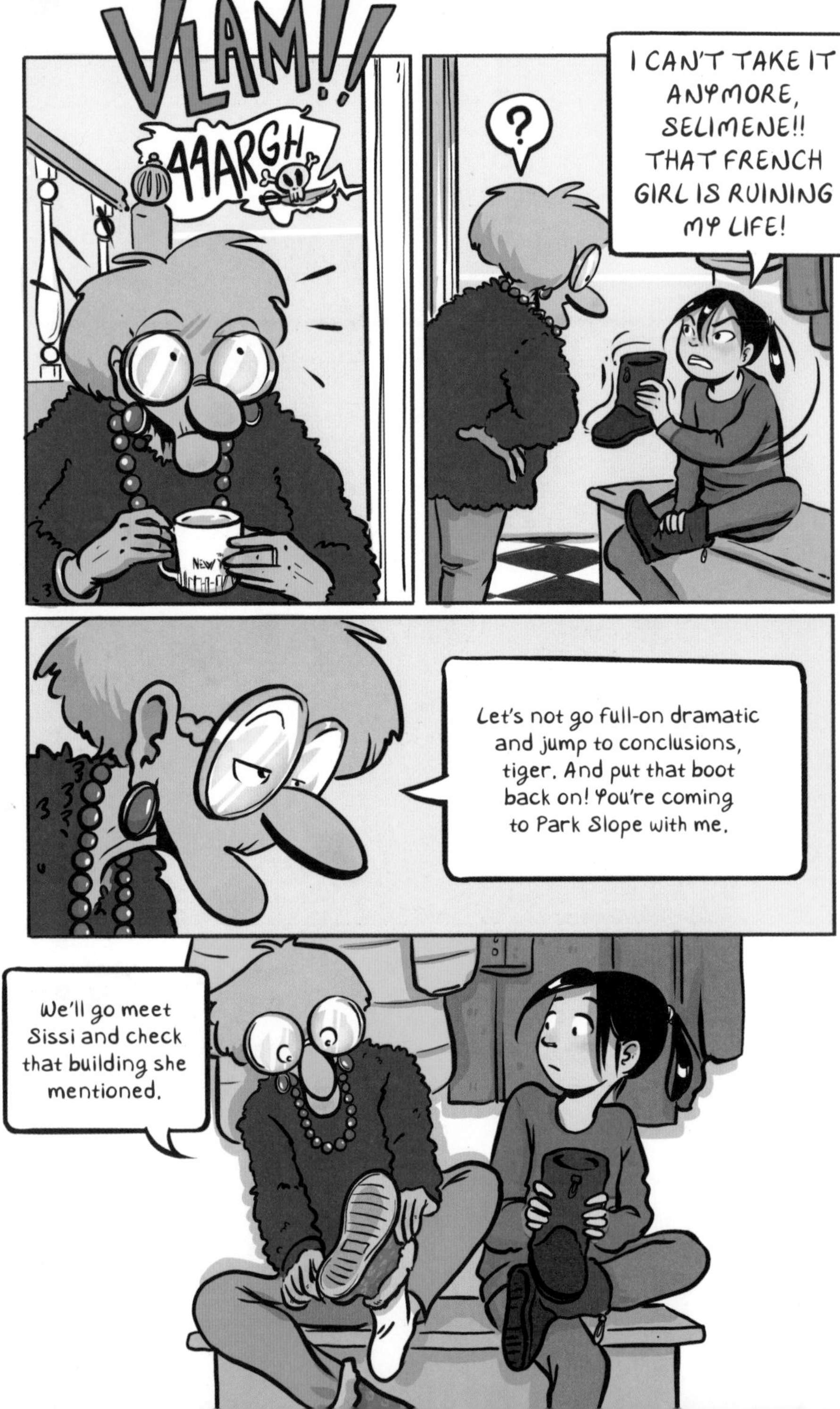
VLAM!!
AAARGH
?
I CAN'T TAKE IT ANYMORE, SELIMENE!! THAT FRENCH GIRL IS RUINING MY LIFE!
Let's not go full-on dramatic and jump to conclusions, tiger. And put that boot back on! You're coming to Park Slope with me.
We'll go meet Sissi and check that building she mentioned.

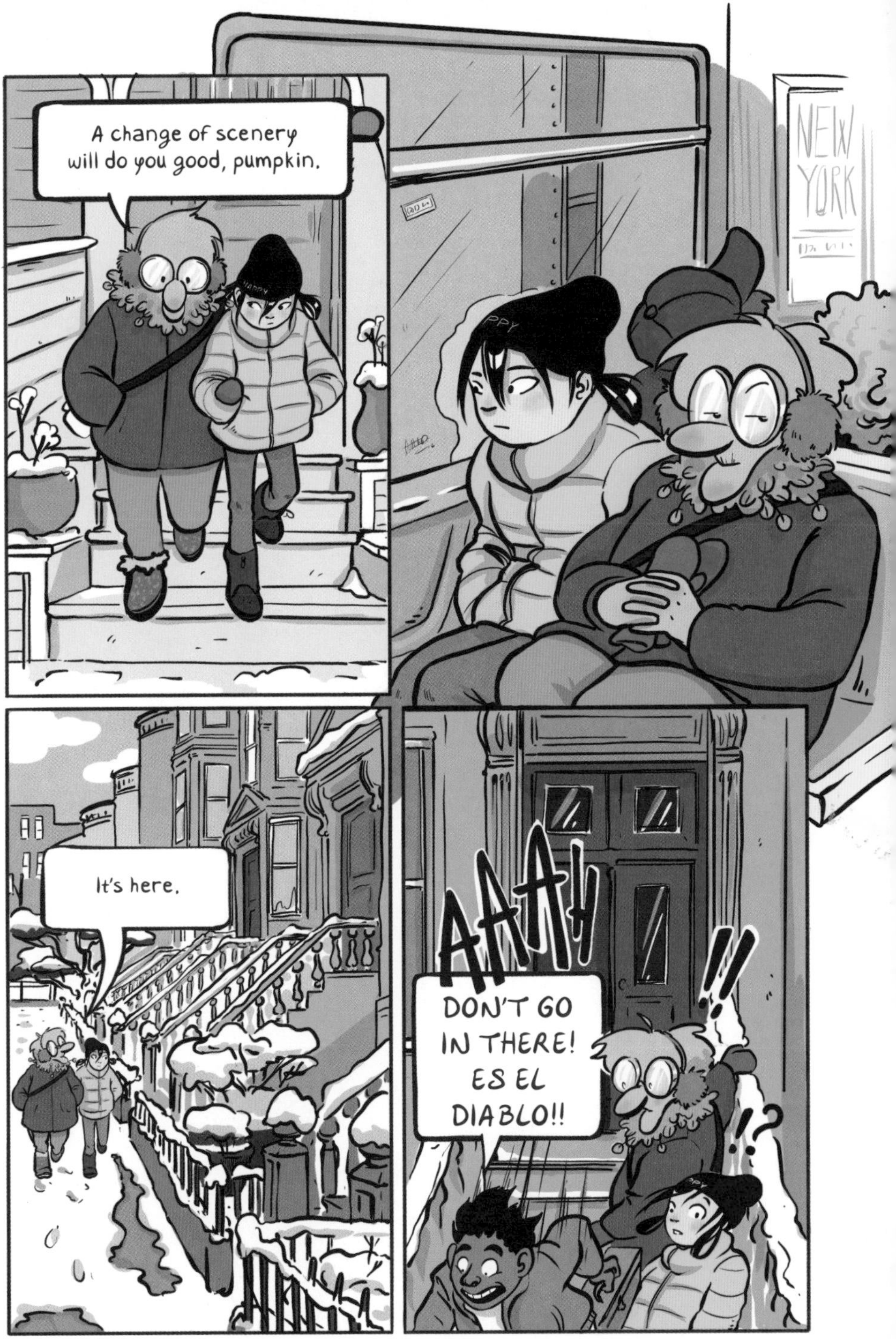

A change of scenery will do you good, pumpkin.
NEW YORK
It's here.
AAAH!!
DON'T GO IN THERE! ES EL DIABLO!!
!?

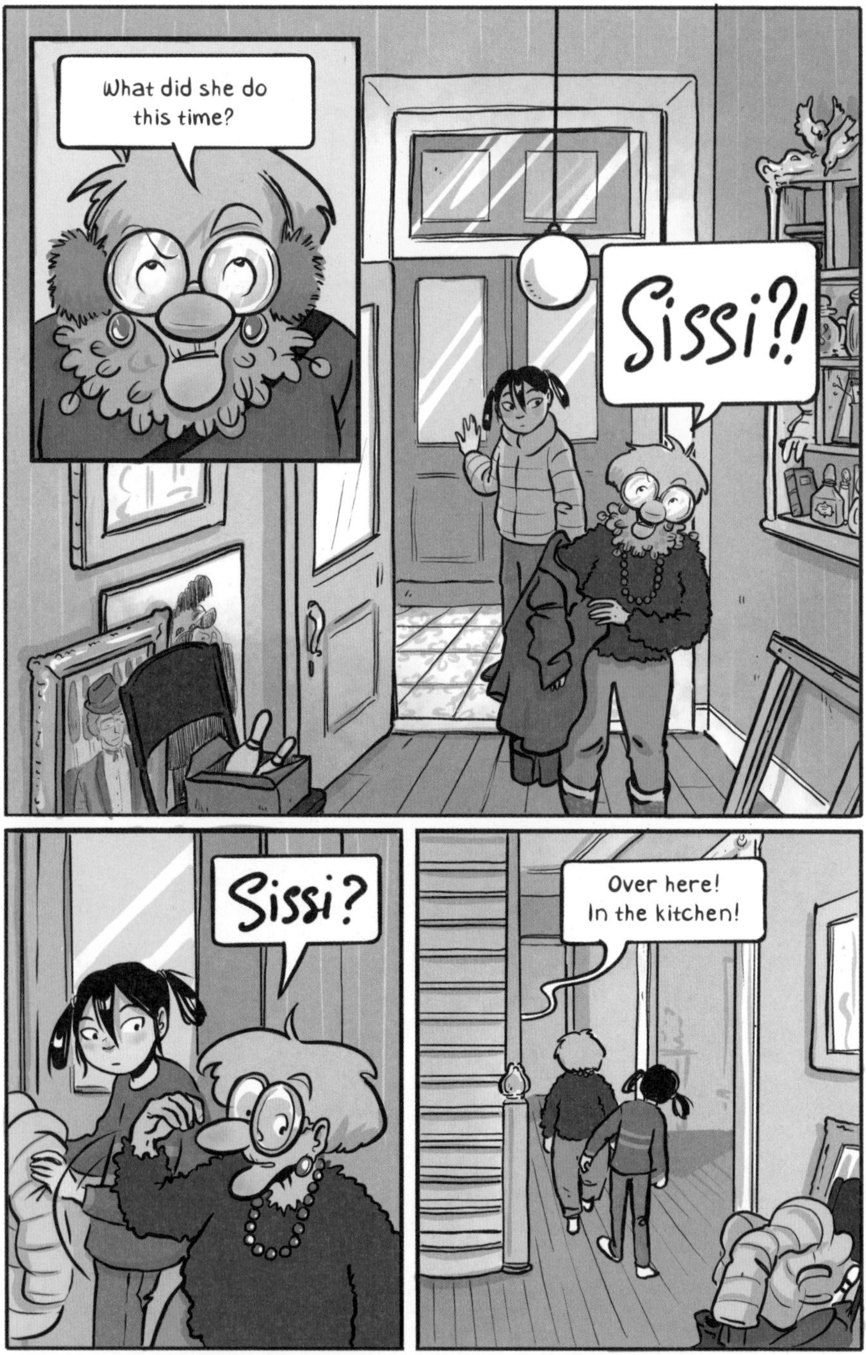
What did she do this time?
Sissi?!
Sissi?
Over here! In the kitchen!

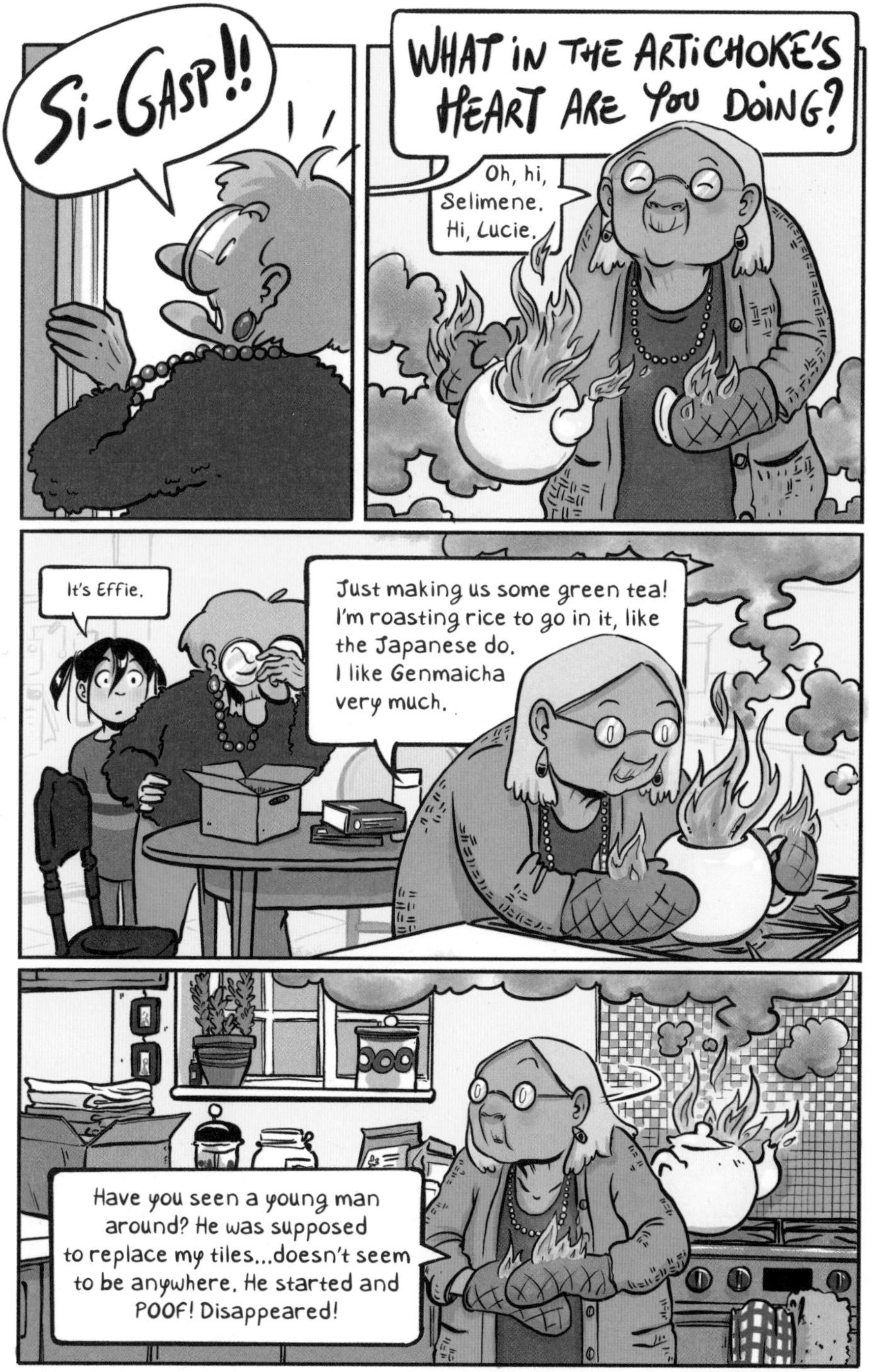
SI-GASP!!
WHAT IN THE ARTICHOKE'S HEART ARE YOU DOING?
Oh, hi, Selimene. Hi, Lucie.
It's Effie.
Just making us some green tea! I'm roasting rice to go in it, like the Japanese do. I like Genmaicha very much.
Have you seen a young man around? He was supposed to replace my tiles...doesn't seem to be anywhere. He started and POOF! Disappeared!

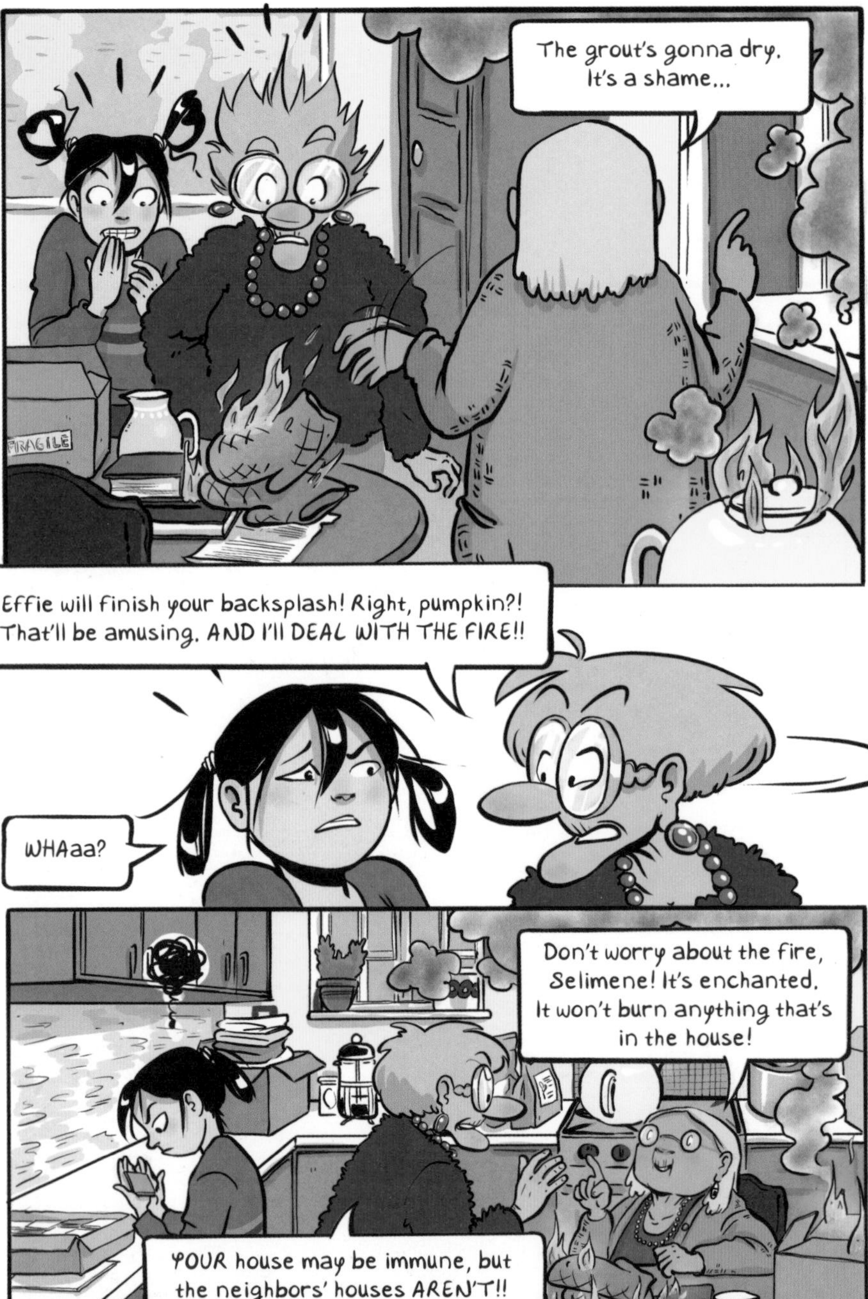
The grout's gonna dry. It's a shame...
FRAGILE
Effie will finish your backsplash! Right, pumpkin?! That'll be amusing. AND I'll DEAL WITH THE FIRE!!
WHAaa?
Don't worry about the fire, Selimene! It's enchanted. It won't burn anything that's in the house!
YOUR house may be immune, but the neighbors' houses AREN'T!!

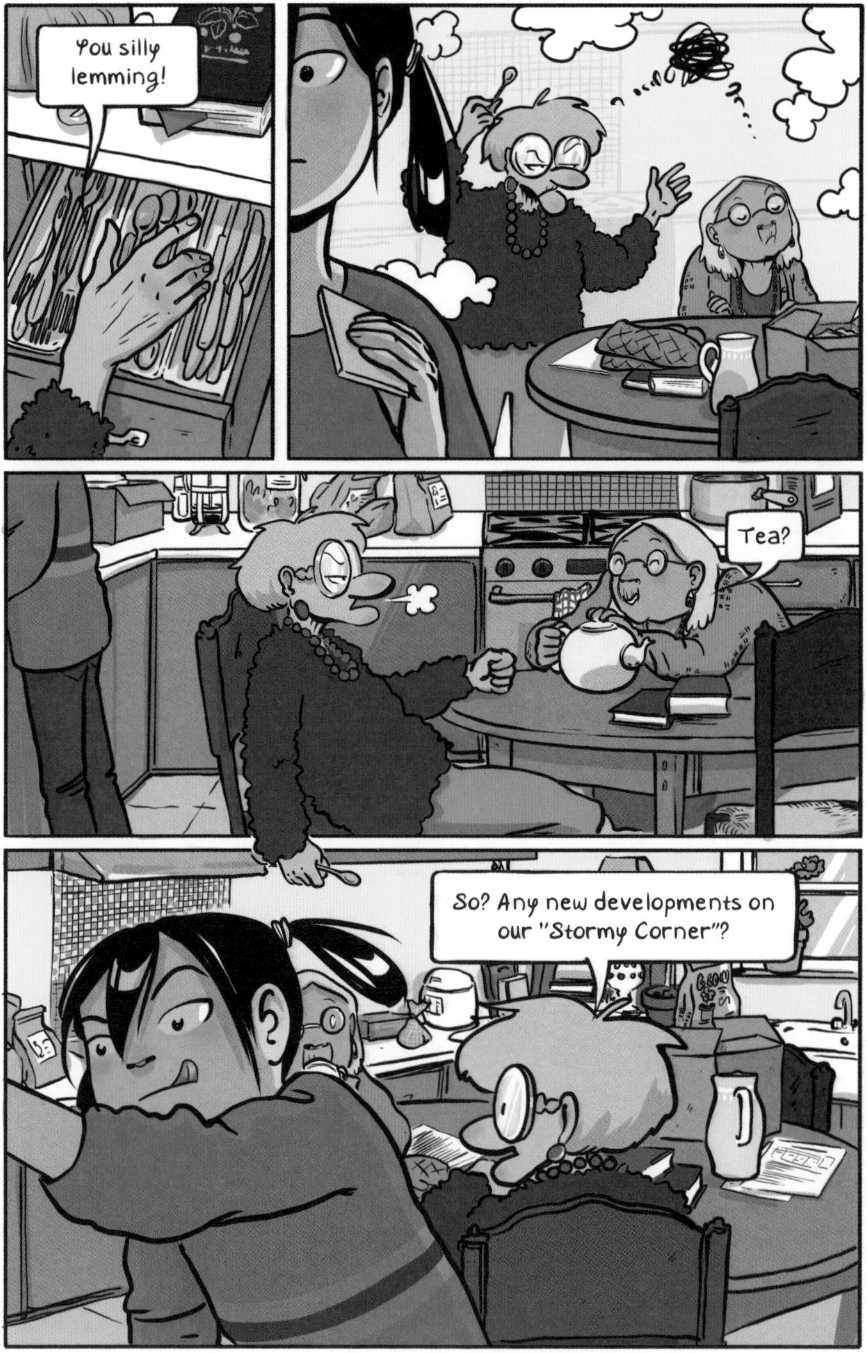
You silly lemming!
Tea?
So? Any new developments on our "Stormy Corner"?

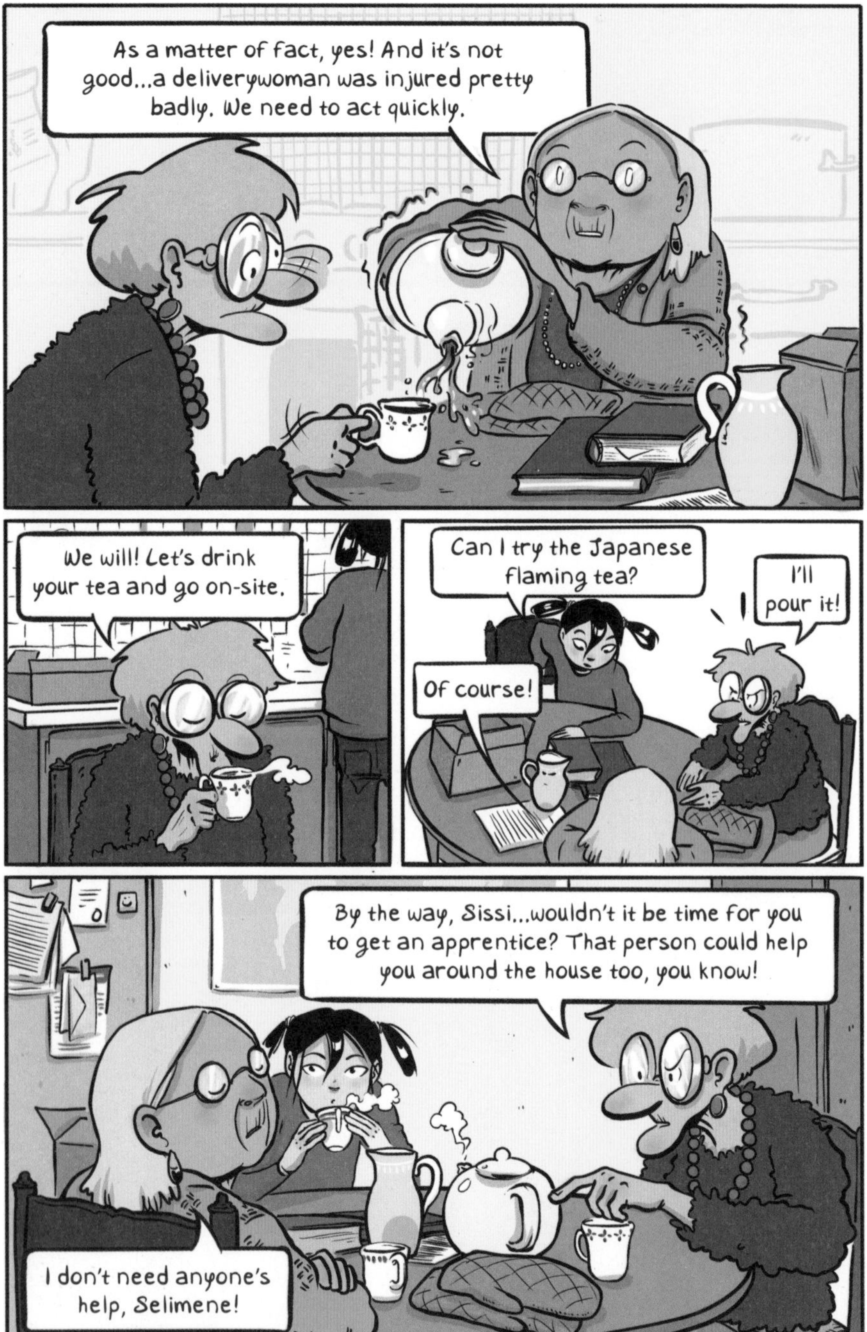

As a matter of fact, yes! And it's not good...a deliverywoman was injured pretty badly. We need to act quickly.
We will! Let's drink your tea and go on-site.
Can I try the Japanese flaming tea?
Of course!
I'll pour it!
By the way, Sissi...wouldn't it be time for you to get an apprentice? That person could help you around the house too, you know!
I don't need anyone's help, Selimene!

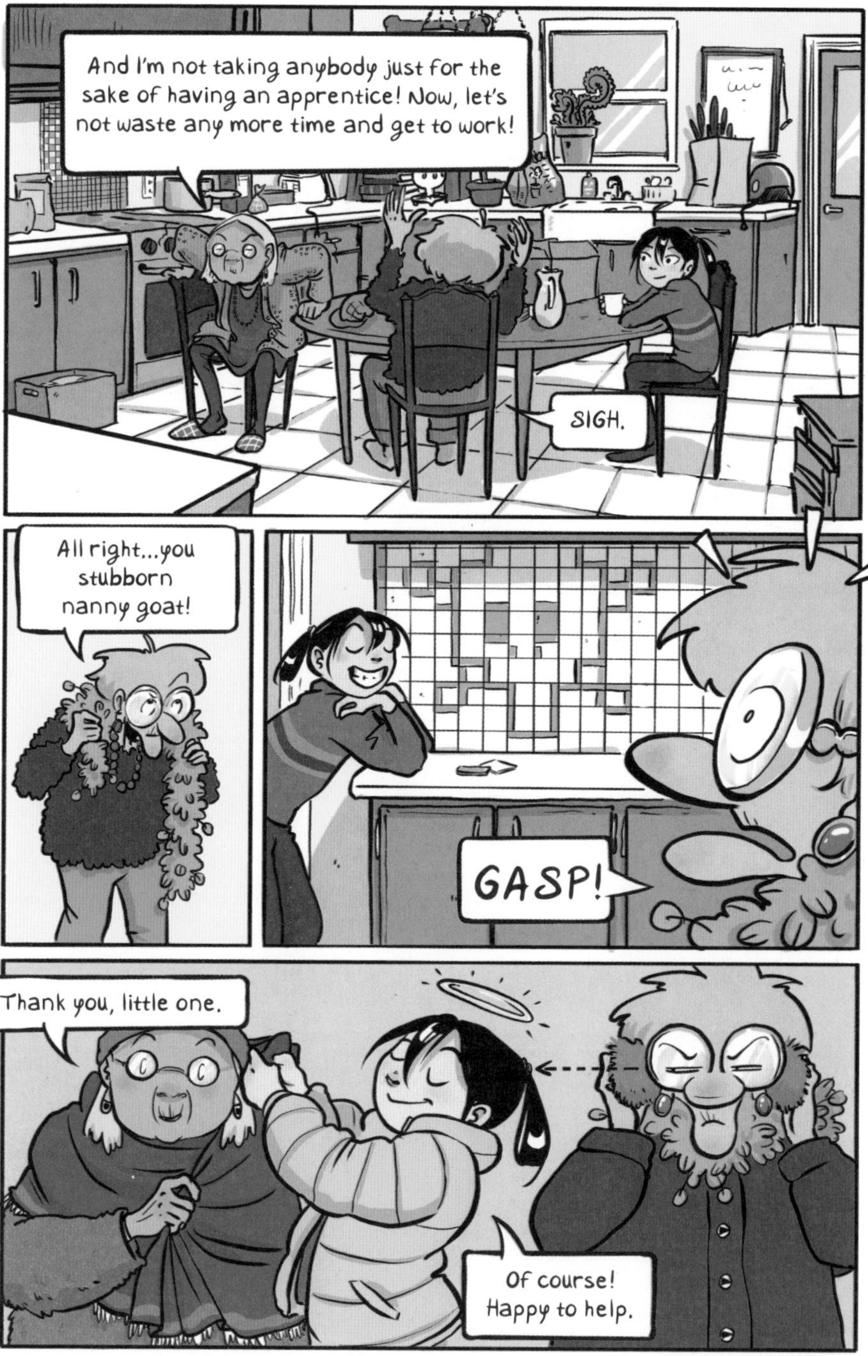
And I'm not taking anybody just for the sake of having an apprentice! Now, let's not waste any more time and get to work!
SIGH.
All right...you stubborn nanny goat!
GASP!
Thank you, little one.
Of course! Happy to help.

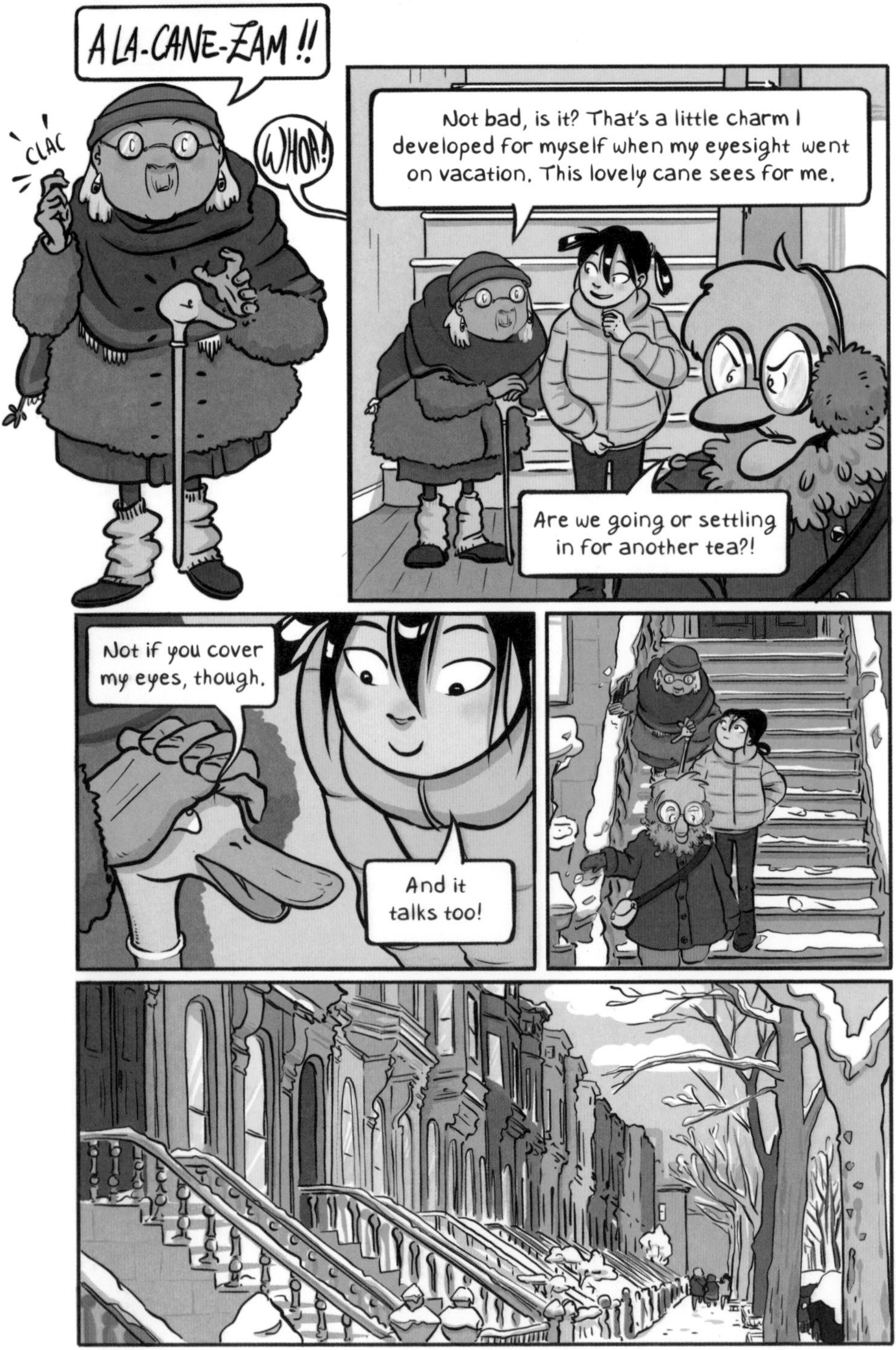
A LA-CANE-ZAM !!
CLAC
WHOA!
Not bad, is it? That's a little charm I developed for myself when my eyesight went on vacation. This lovely cane sees for me.
Are we going or settling in for another tea?!
Not if you cover my eyes, though.
And it talks too!

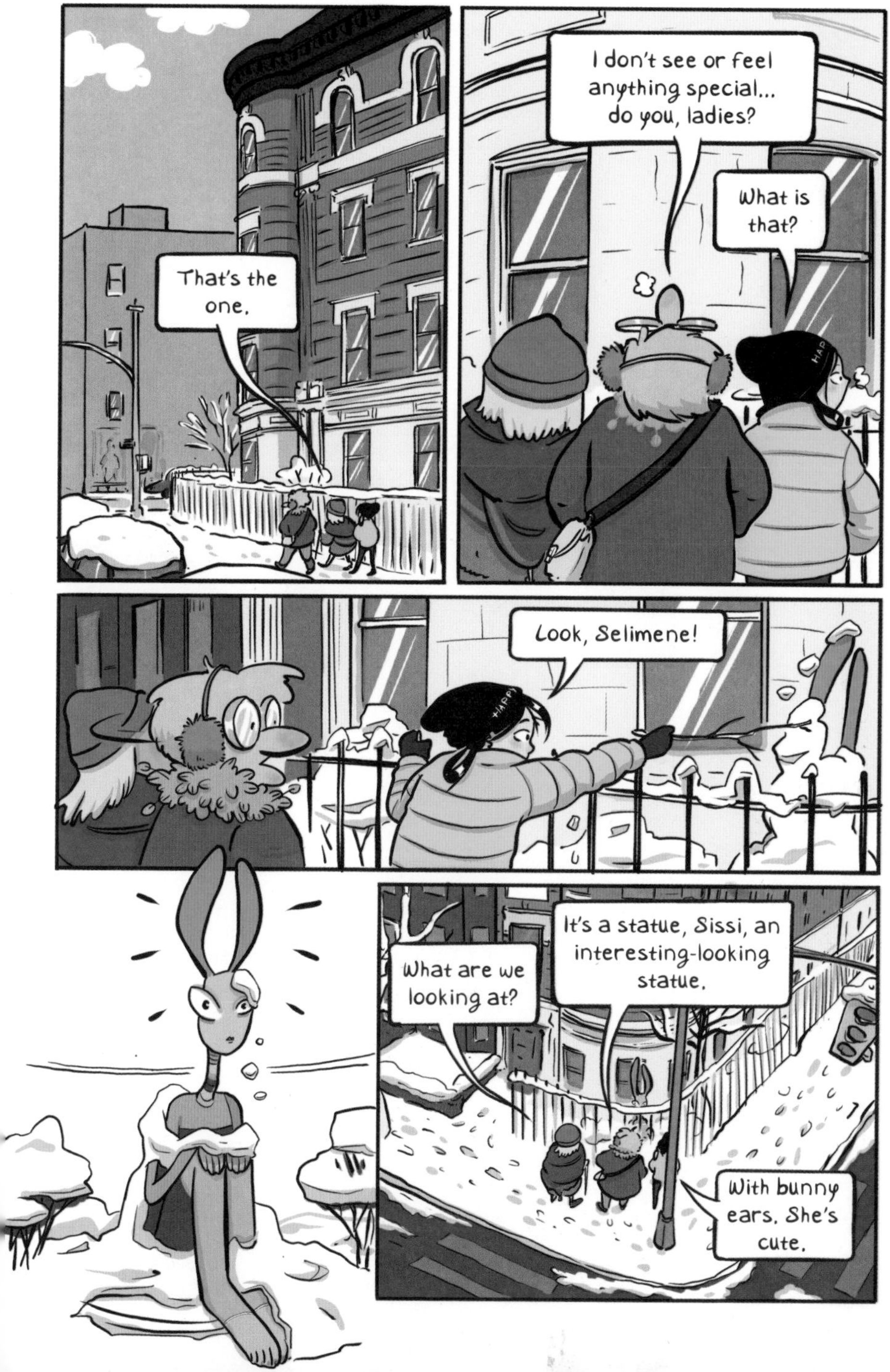
That's the one.
I don't see or feel anything special... do you, ladies?
What is that?
Look, Selimene!
What are we looking at?
It's a statue, Sissi, an interesting-looking statue.
With bunny ears. She's cute.

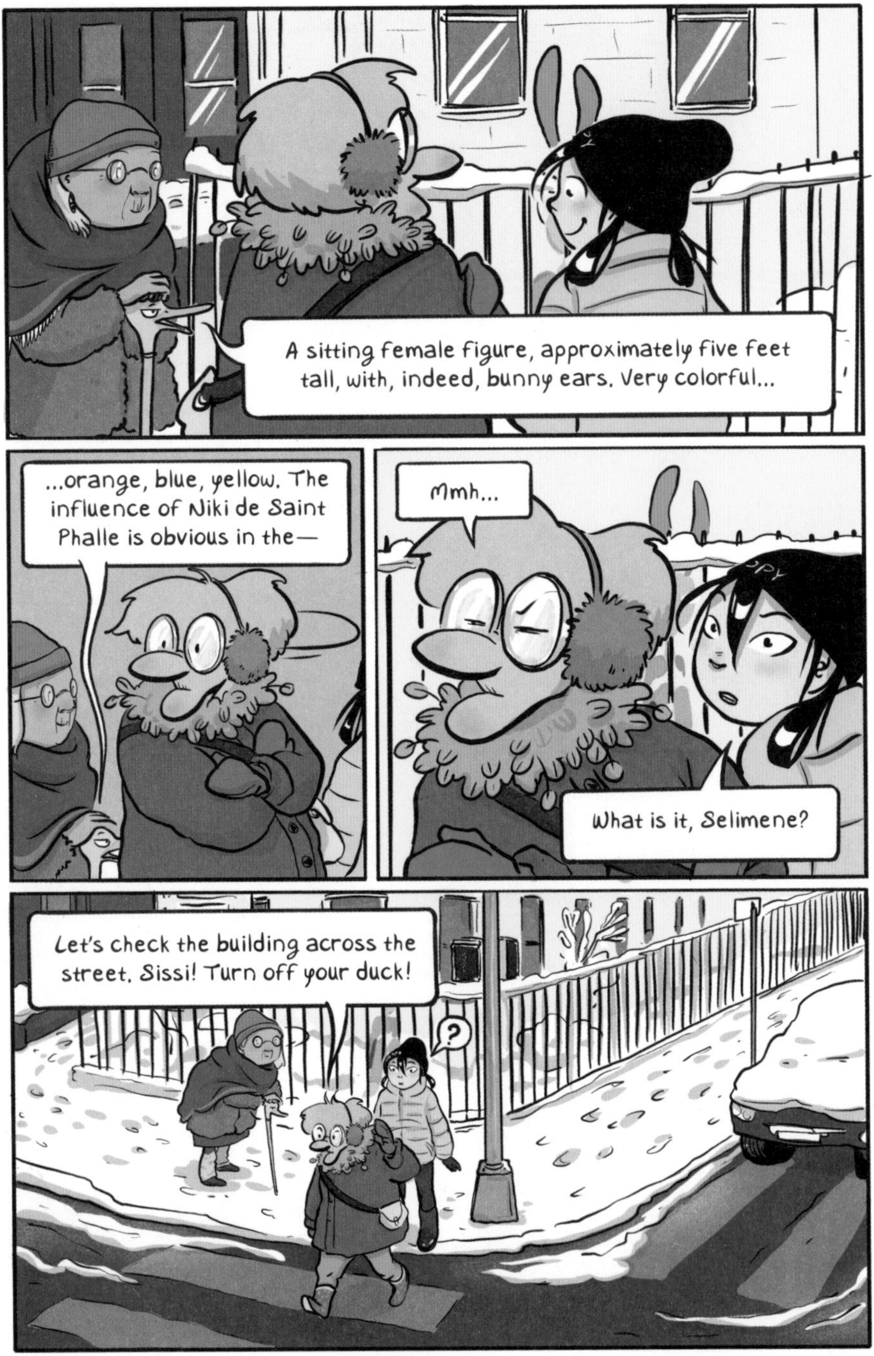
A sitting female figure, approximately five feet tall, with, indeed, bunny ears. Very colorful...
...orange, blue, yellow. The influence of Niki de Saint Phalle is obvious in the—
Mmh...
What is it, Selimene?
Let's check the building across the street, Sissi! Turn off your duck!
?

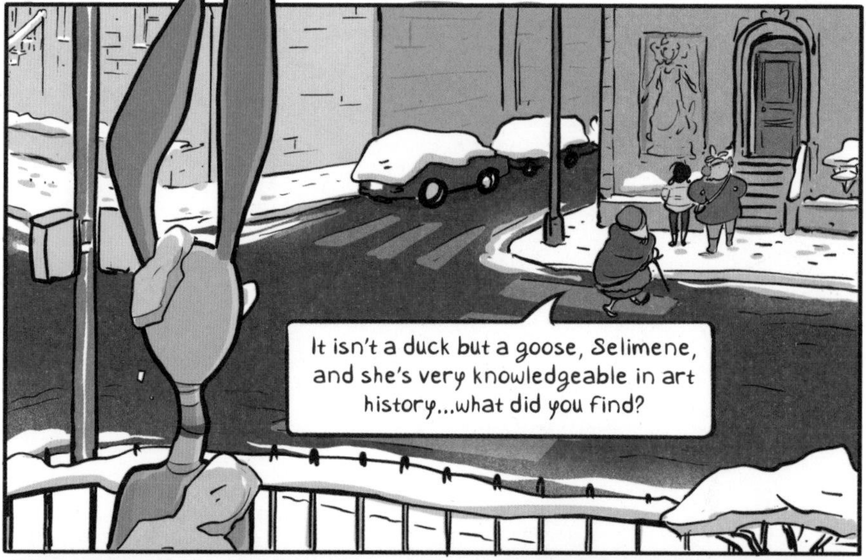
It isn't a duck but a goose, Selimene, and she's very knowledgeable in art history...what did you find?

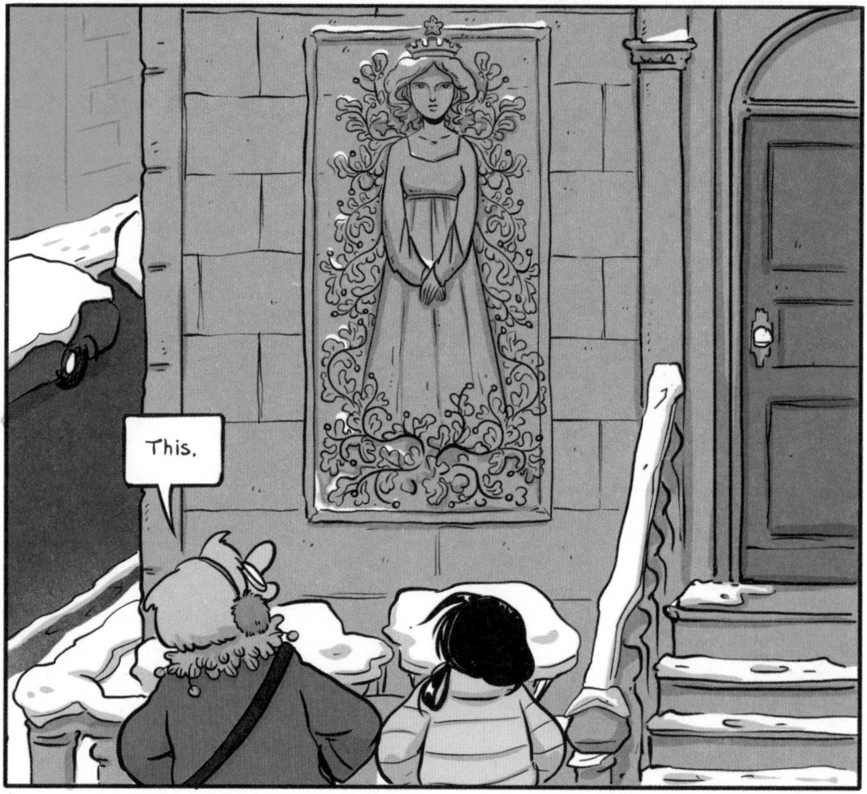
This.

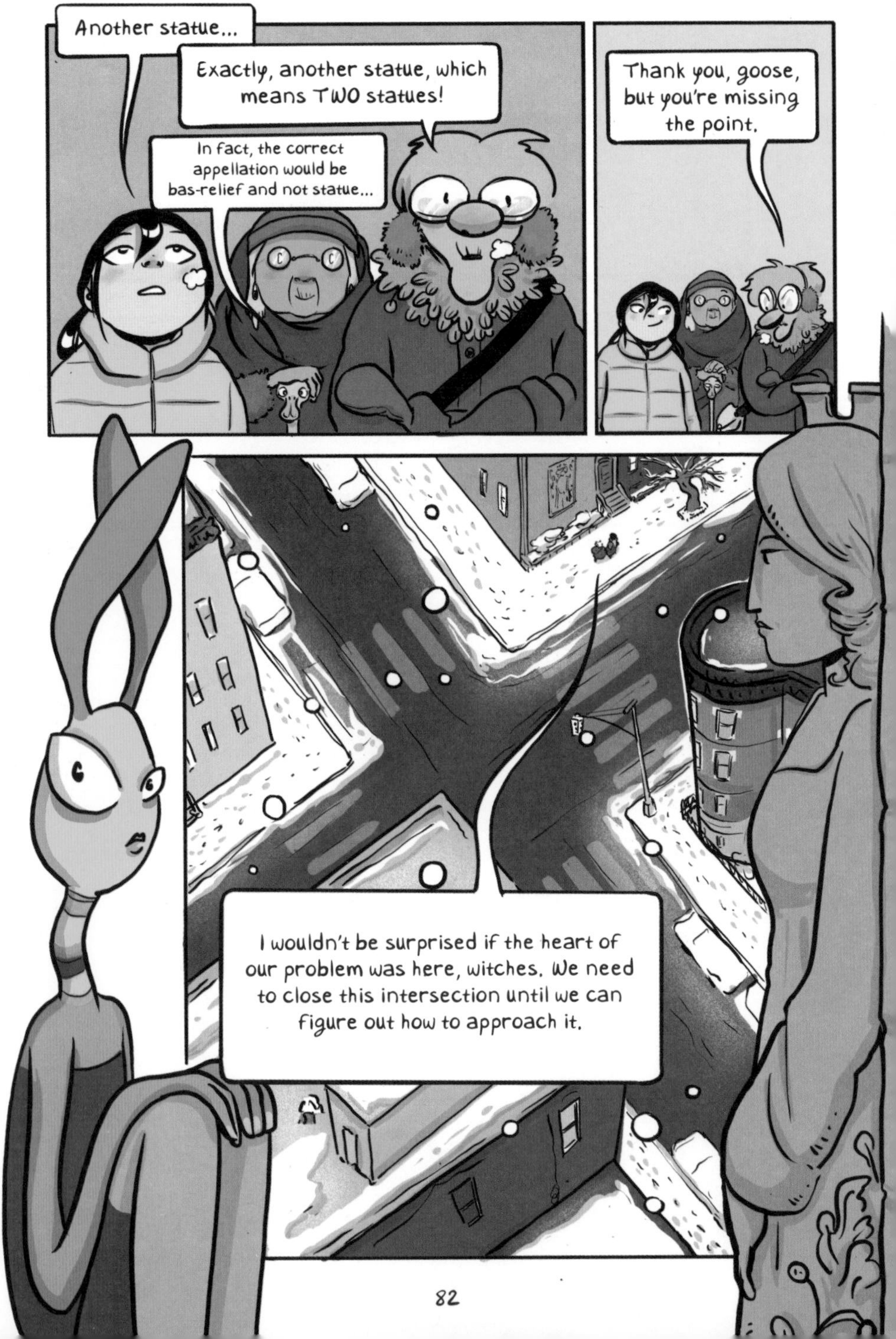
Another statue...
Exactly, another statue, which means TWO statues!
In fact, the correct appellation would be bas-relief and not statue...
Thank you, goose, but you're missing the point.
I wouldn't be surprised if the heart of our problem was here, witches. We need to close this intersection until we can figure out how to approach it.

Are you still in touch with the captain of the nearby police station, Sissi?

Robert? Sure! I'll give him a call.

How was it?

We've got a lead!

Two statues.

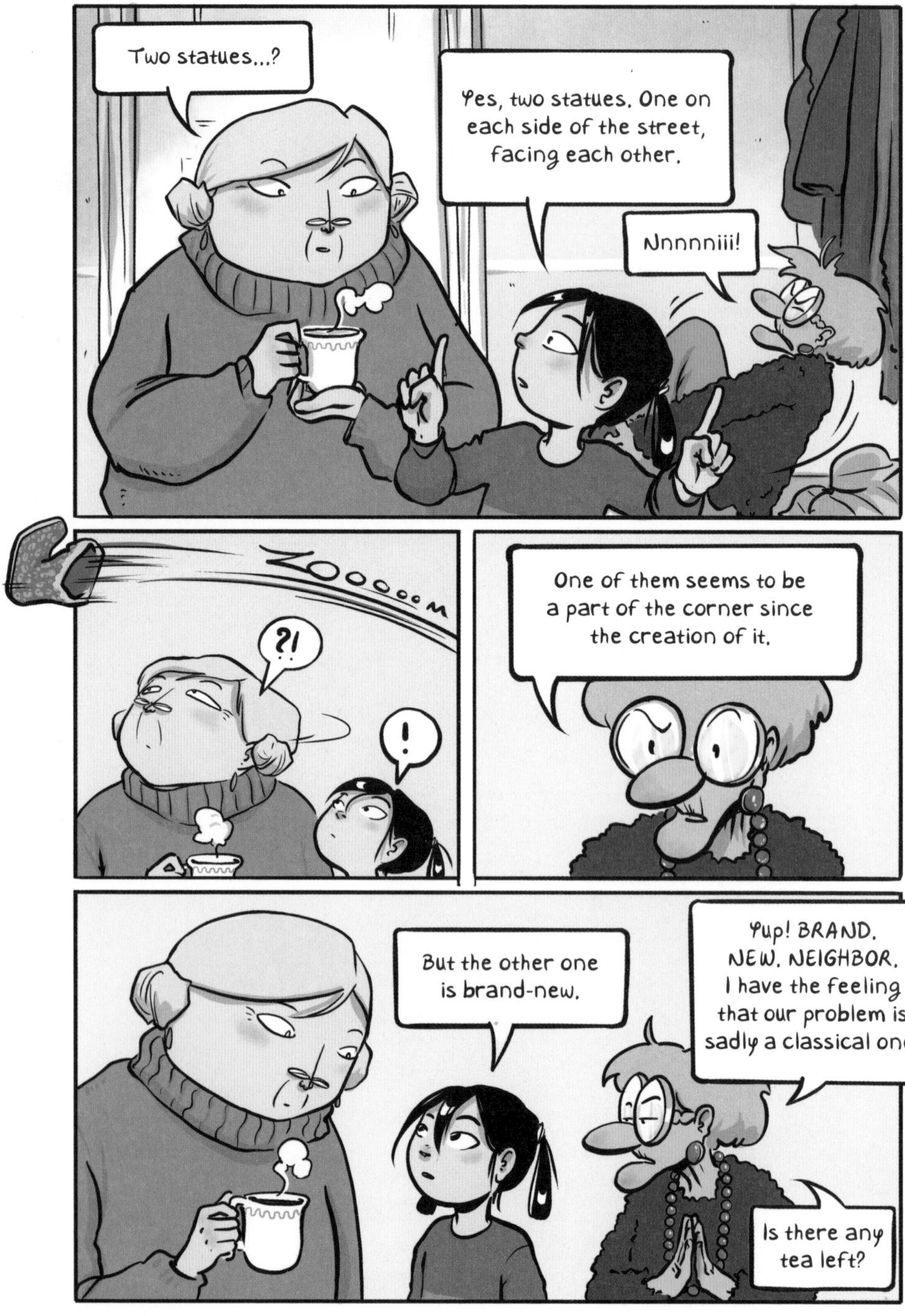
Two statues...?
Yes, two statues. One on each side of the street, facing each other.
Nnnnniii!
ZOOOoooM
?!
!
One of them seems to be a part of the corner since the creation of it.
But the other one is brand-new.
Yup! BRAND. NEW. NEIGHBOR. I have the feeling that our problem is sadly a classical one.
Is there any tea left?

Chapter 3

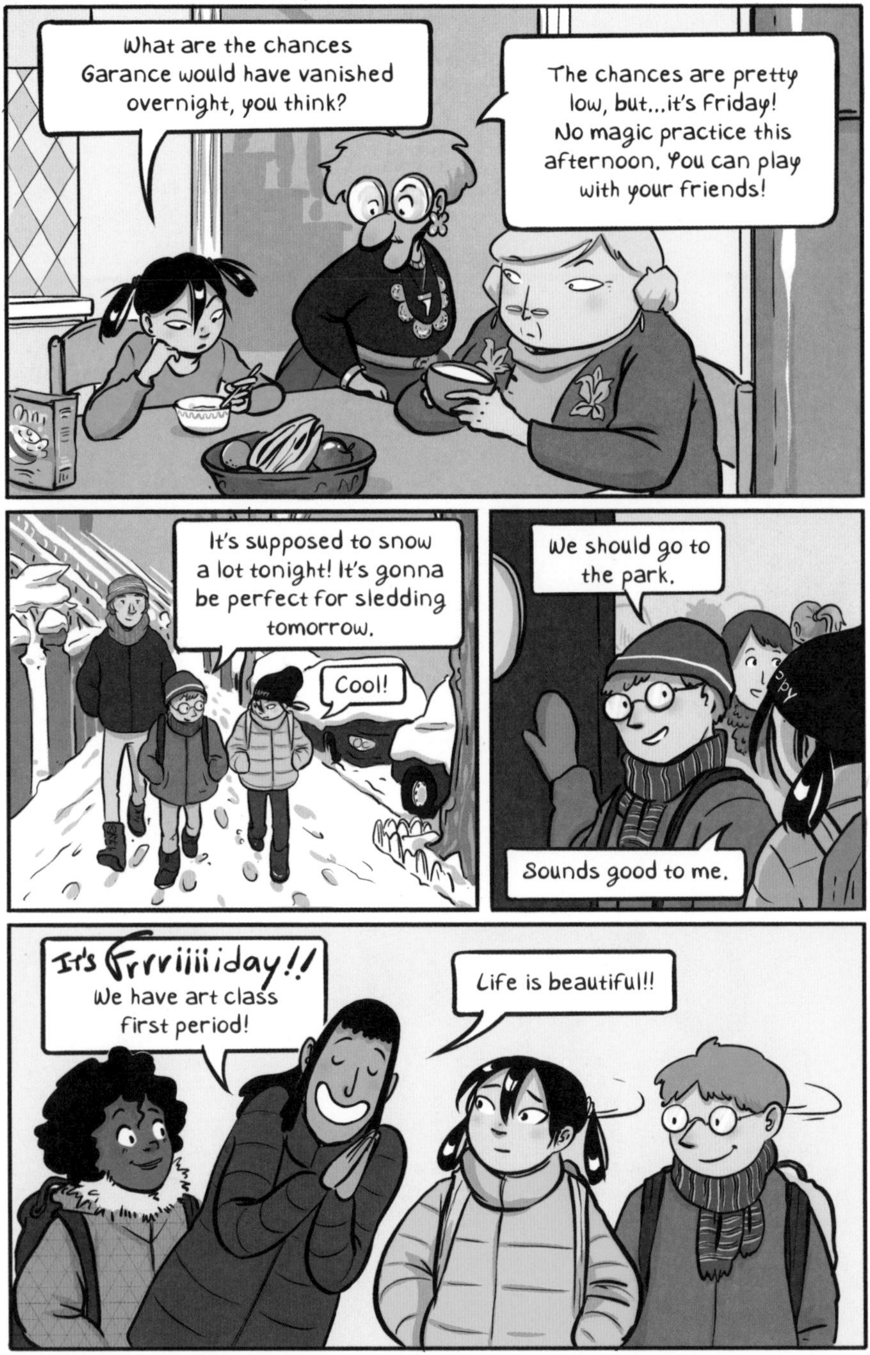
What are the chances Garance would have vanished overnight, you think?
The chances are pretty low, but...it's Friday! No magic practice this afternoon. You can play with your friends!
It's supposed to snow a lot tonight! It's gonna be perfect for sledding tomorrow.
Cool!
We should go to the park.
Sounds good to me.
It's Frrrviiiiiday!! We have art class first period!
Life is beautiful!!

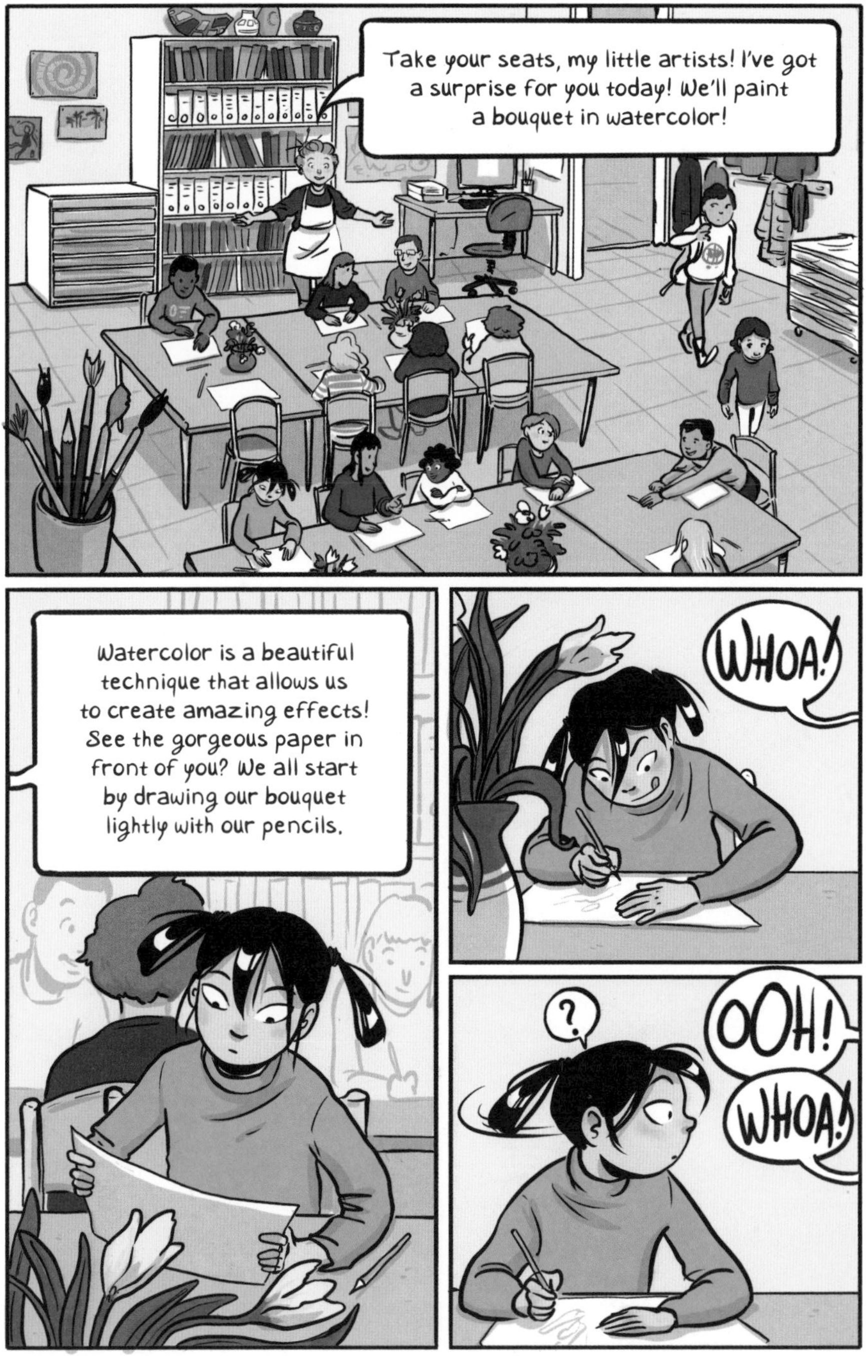
Take your seats, my little artists! I've got a surprise for you today! We'll paint a bouquet in watercolor!
Watercolor is a beautiful technique that allows us to create amazing effects! See the gorgeous paper in front of you? We all start by drawing our bouquet lightly with our pencils.
WHOA!
?
OOH!
WHOA!

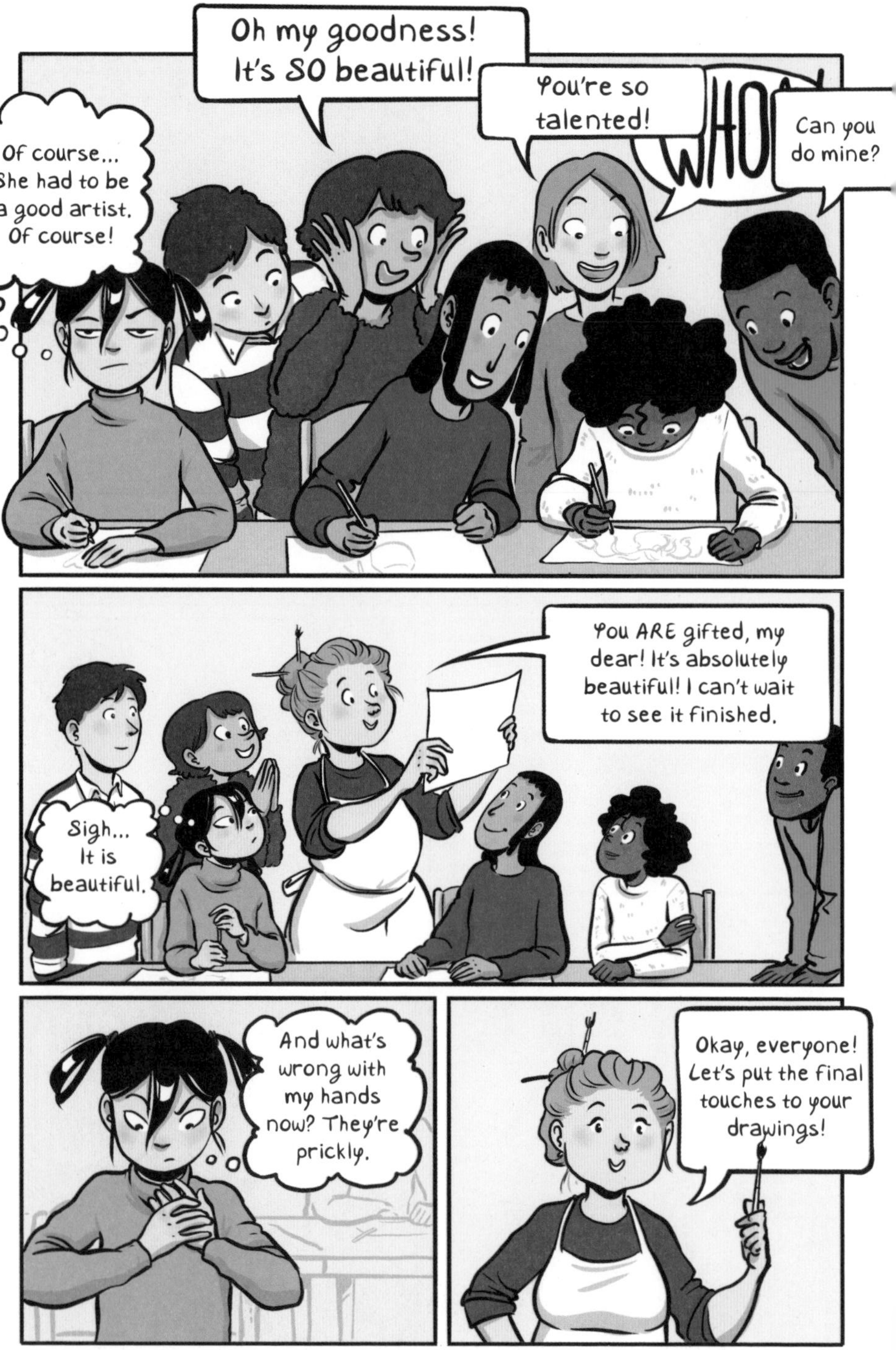
Of course... She had to be a good artist. Of course!
Oh my goodness! It's SO beautiful!
You're so talented!
WHOA
Can you do mine?
You ARE gifted, my dear! It's absolutely beautiful! I can't wait to see it finished.
Sigh... It is beautiful.
And what's wrong with my hands now? They're prickly.
Okay, everyone! Let's put the final touches to your drawings!

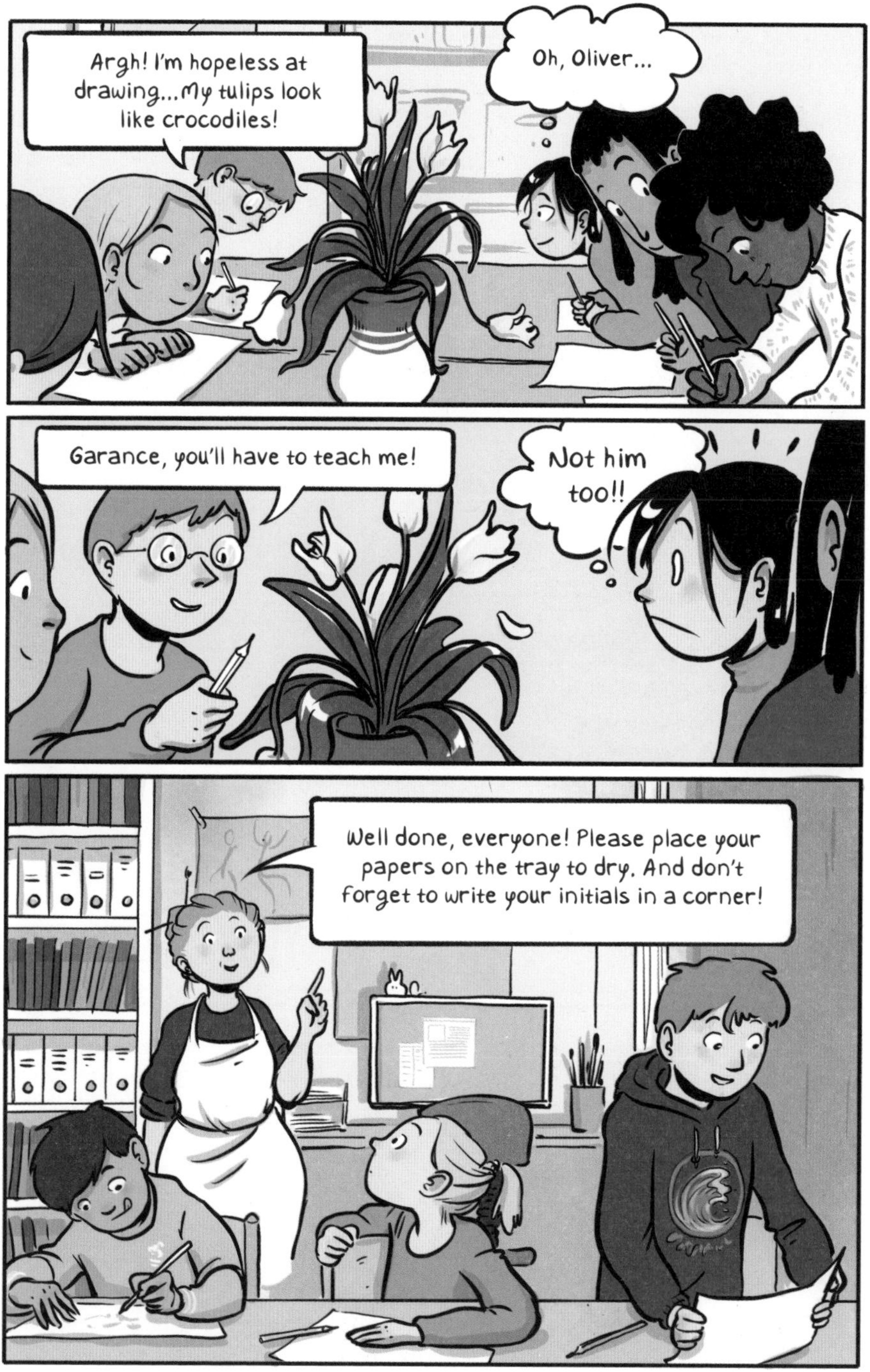
Argh! I'm hopeless at drawing... My tulips look like crocodiles!
Oh, Oliver...
Garance, you'll have to teach me!
Not him too!!
Well done, everyone! Please place your papers on the tray to dry. And don't forget to write your initials in a corner!

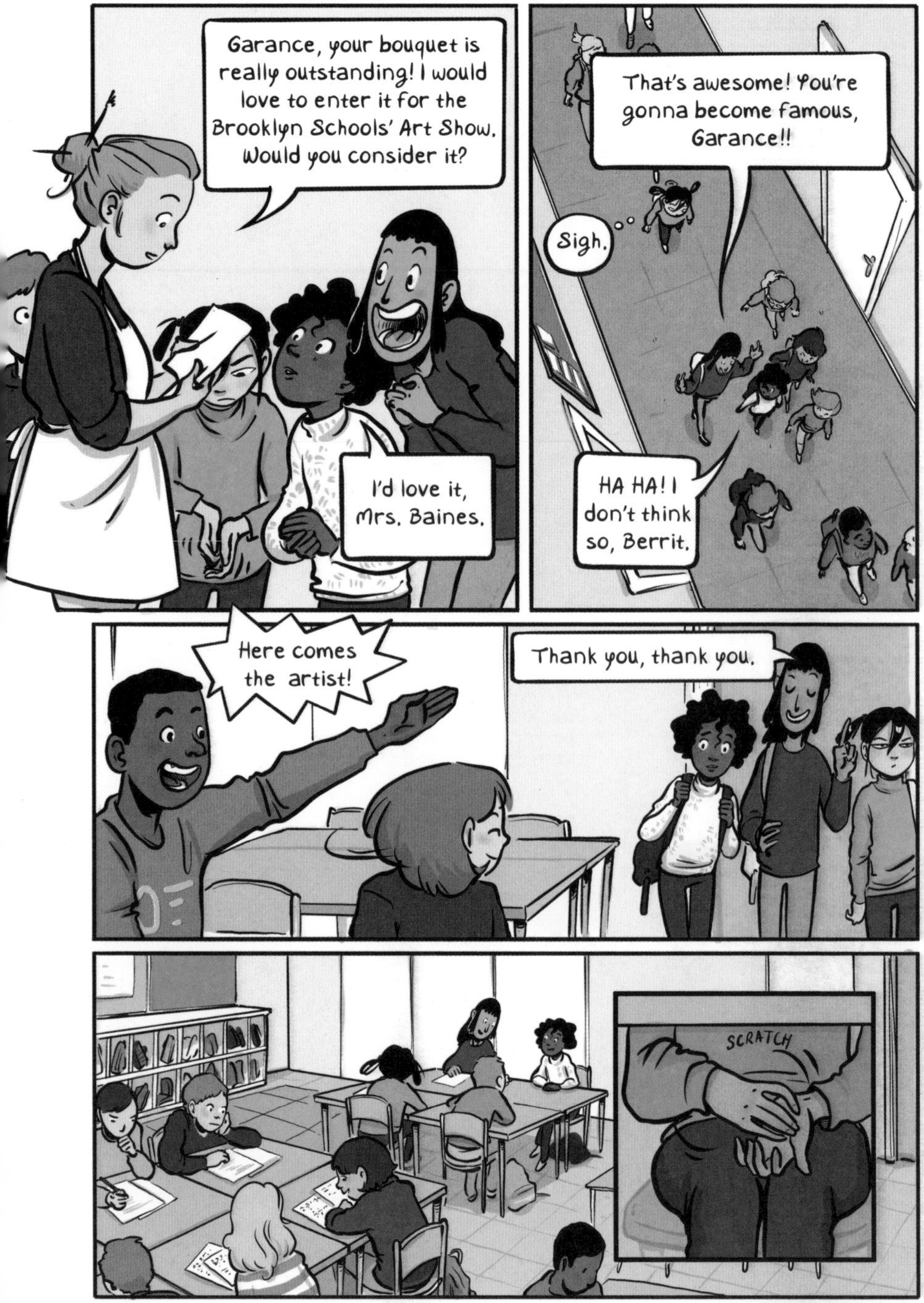
Garance, your bouquet is really outstanding! I would love to enter it for the Brooklyn Schools' Art Show. Would you consider it?
I'd love it, Mrs. Baines.
That's awesome! You're gonna become famous, Garance!!
Sigh.
HA HA! I don't think so, Berrit.
Here comes the artist!
Thank you, thank you.
SCRATCH

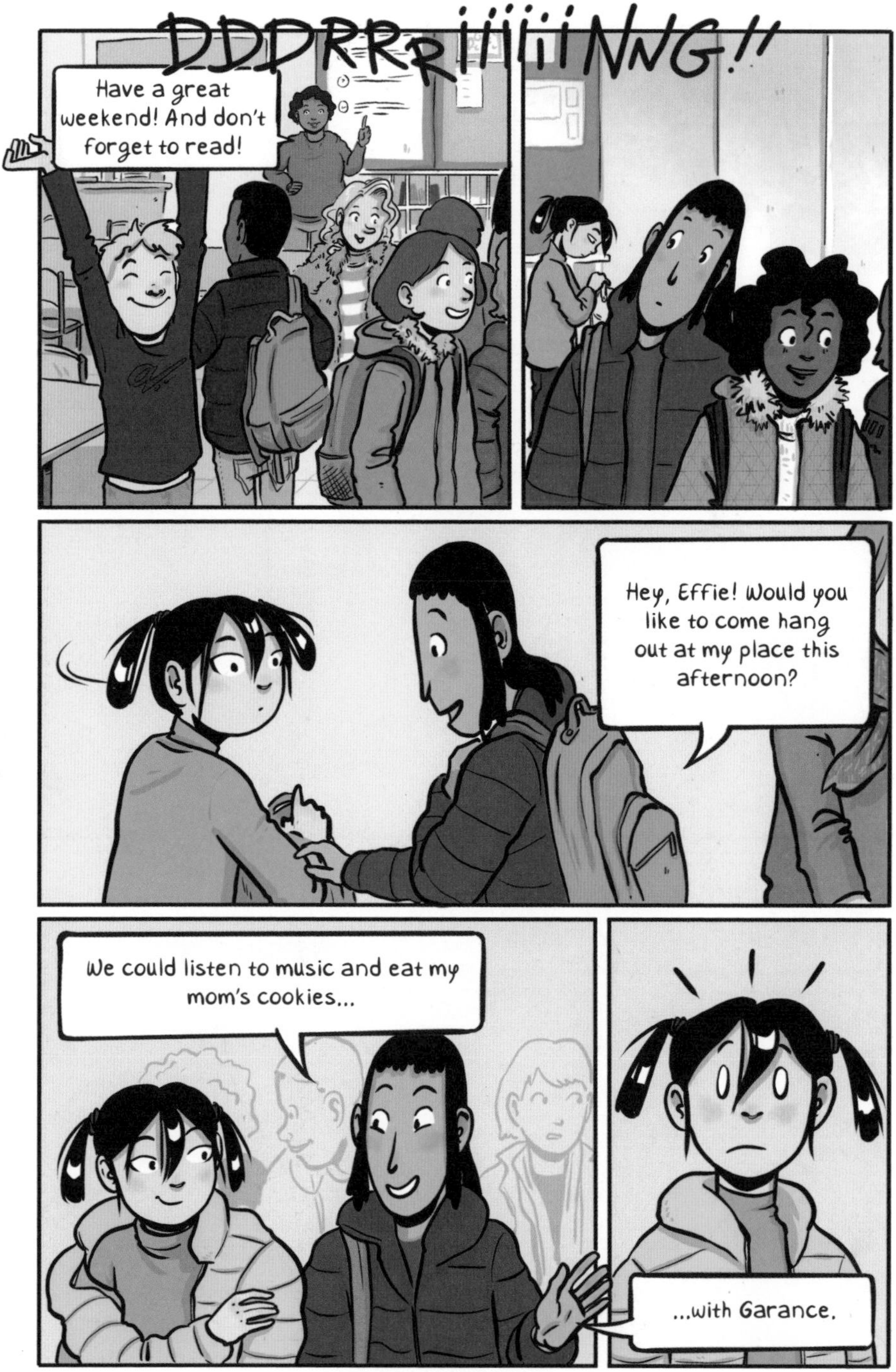
DDDRRRRiiiiiiNNG!!
Have a great weekend! And don't forget to read!
Hey, Effie! Would you like to come hang out at my place this afternoon?
We could listen to music and eat my mom's cookies...
...with Garance.

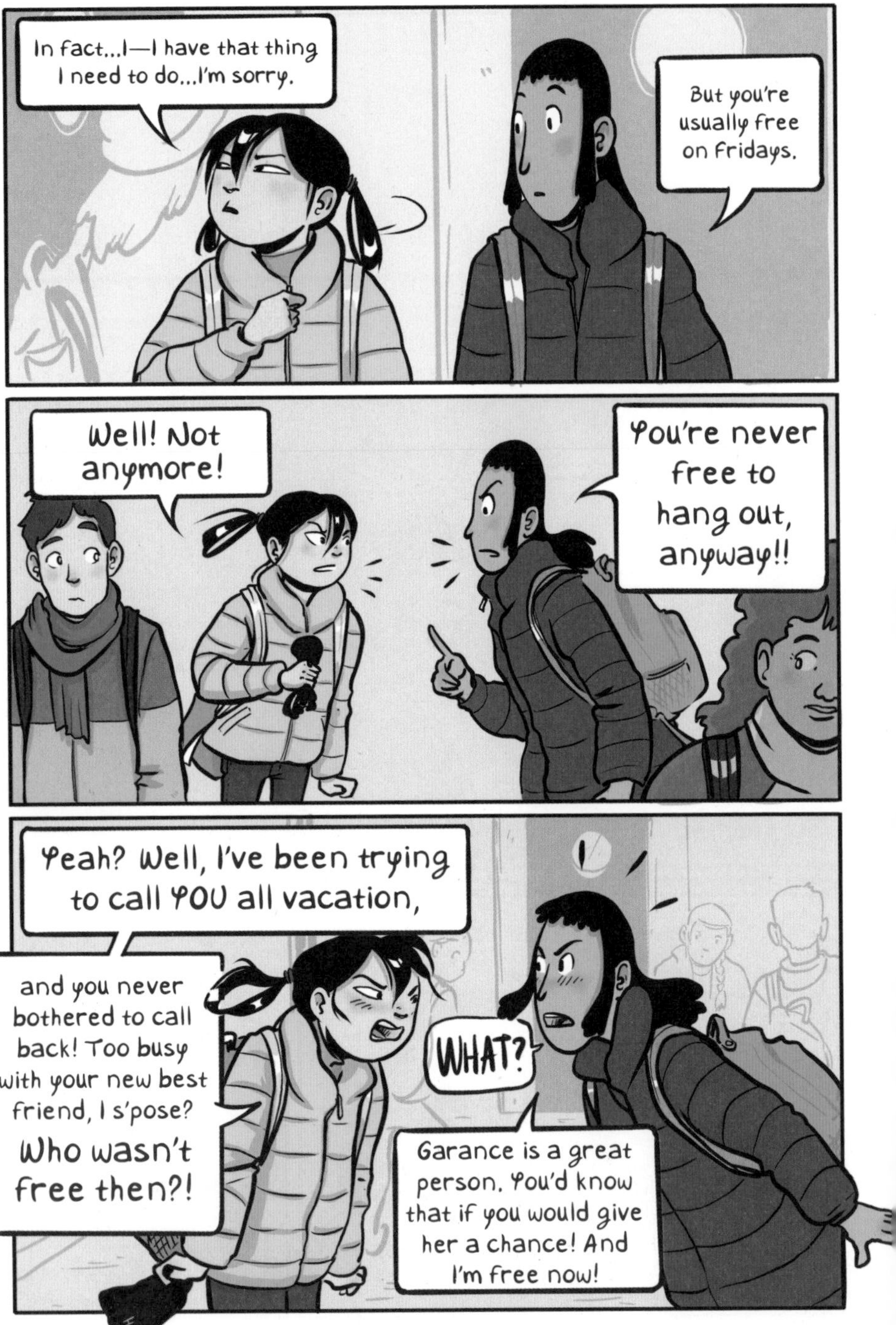
In fact...I—I have that thing I need to do...I'm sorry.
But you're usually free on Fridays.
Well! Not anymore!
You're never free to hang out, anyway!!
Yeah? Well, I've been trying to call YOU all vacation,
and you never bothered to call back! Too busy with your new best friend, I s'pose? Who wasn't free then?!
WHAT?
Garance is a great person. You'd know that if you would give her a chance! And I'm free now!

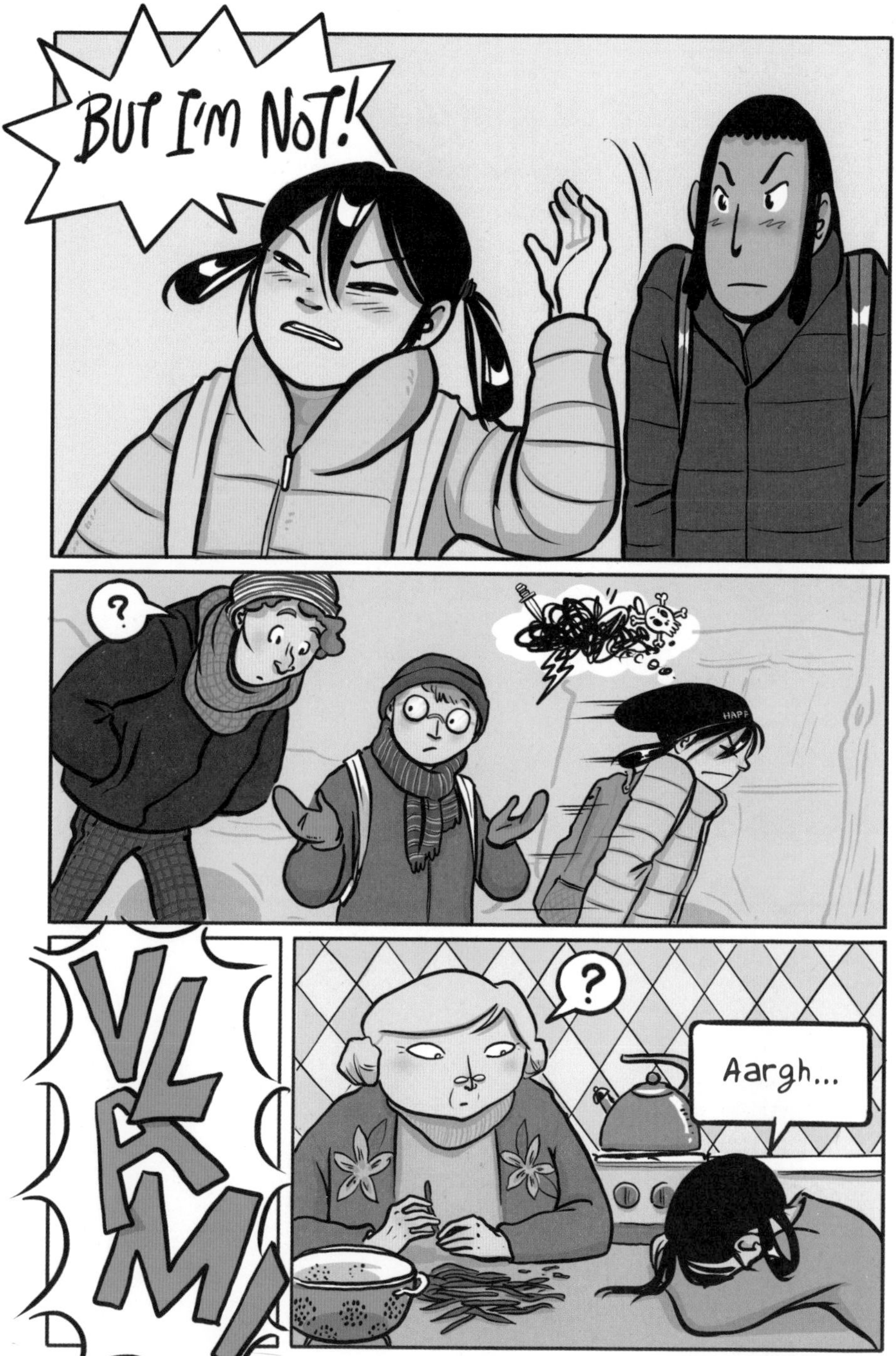
BUT I'M NOT!
?
VLAM!
?
Aargh...

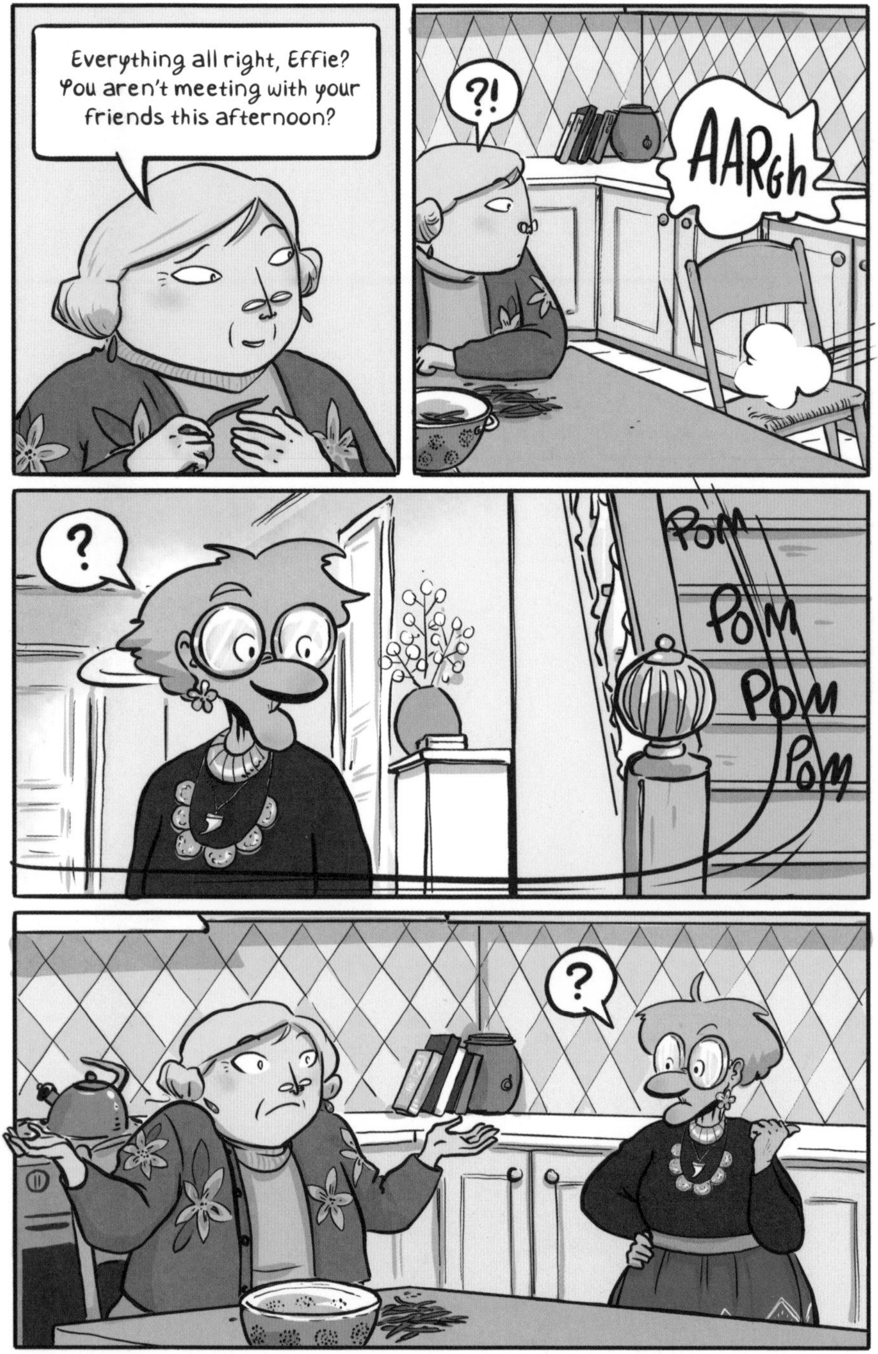
Everything all right, Effie? You aren't meeting with your friends this afternoon?
?!
AARGh
?
POM
POM
POM
POM
?

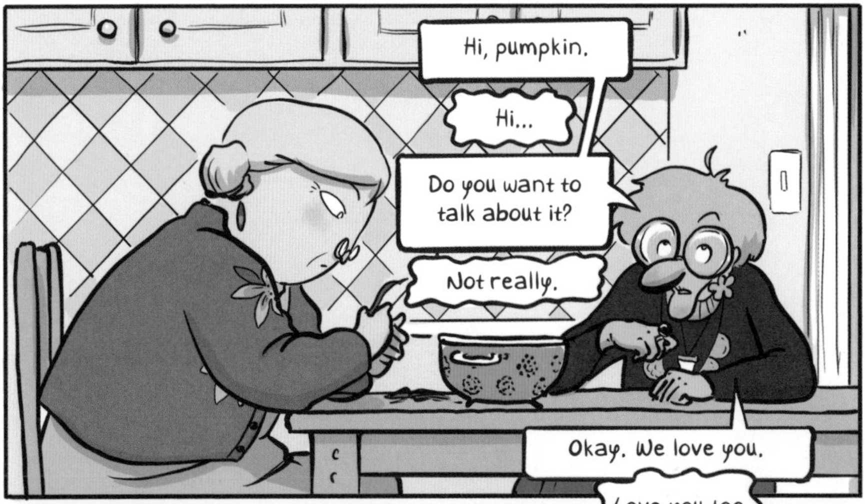

Hi, pumpkin.
Hi...
Do you want to talk about it?
Not really.
Okay. We love you.
Love you too.

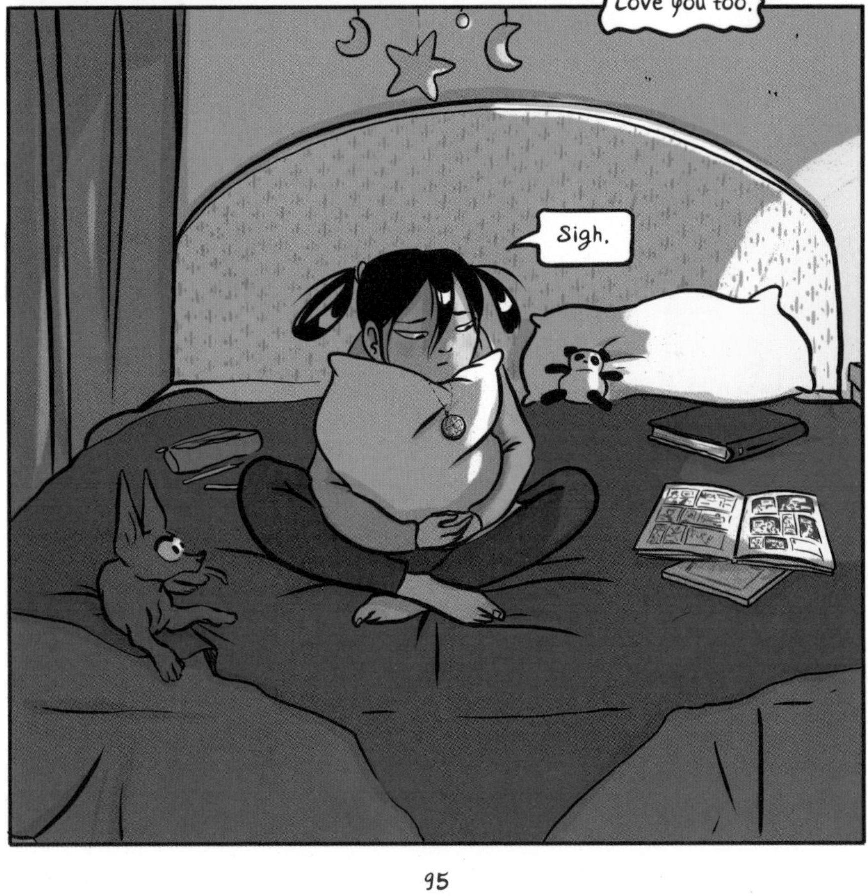

Sigh.

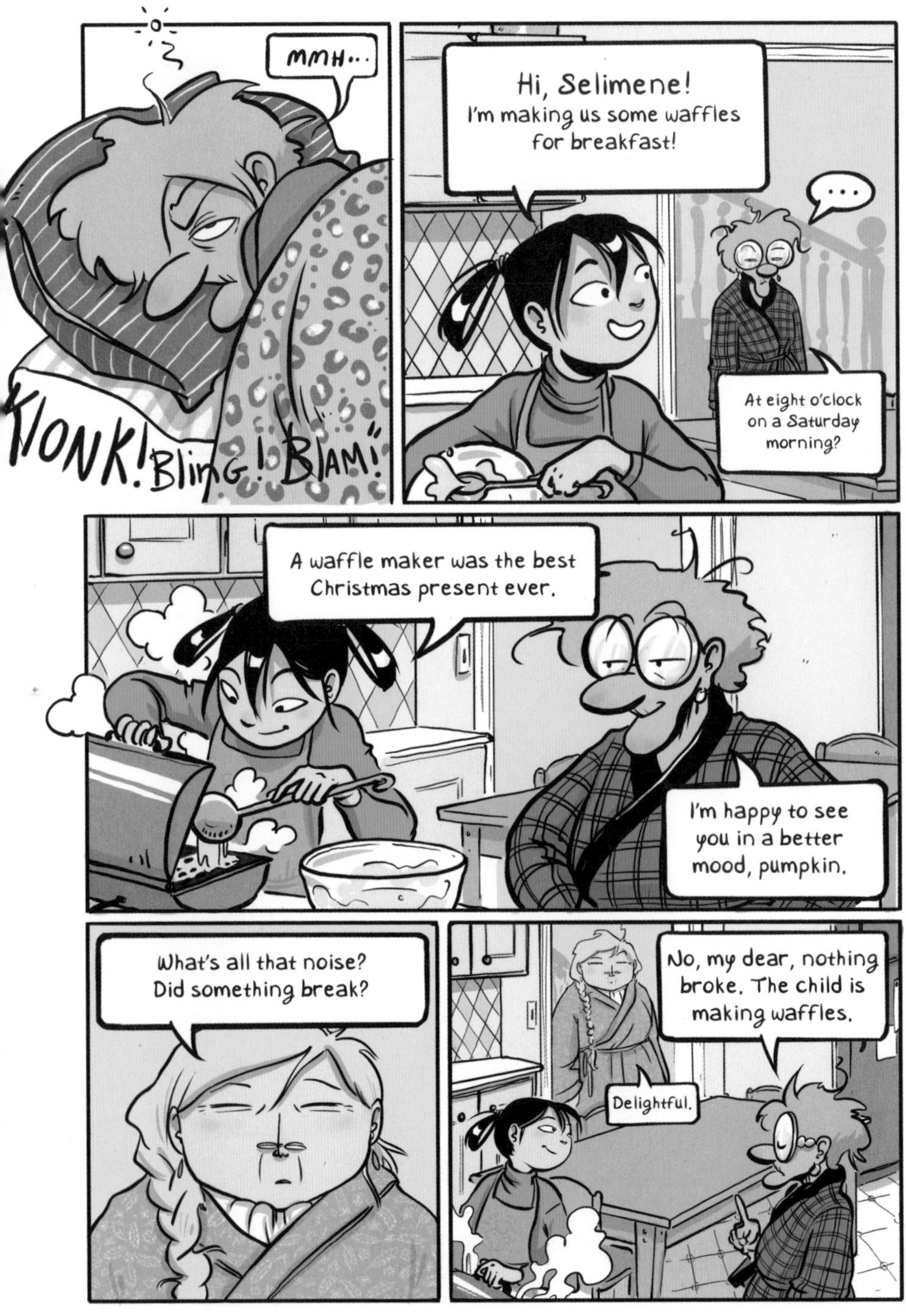
MMH...
KLONK! BLING! BLAM!
Hi, Selimene!
I'm making us some waffles for breakfast!
...
At eight o'clock on a Saturday morning?
A waffle maker was the best Christmas present ever.
I'm happy to see you in a better mood, pumpkin.
What's all that noise? Did something break?
No, my dear, nothing broke. The child is making waffles.
Delightful.

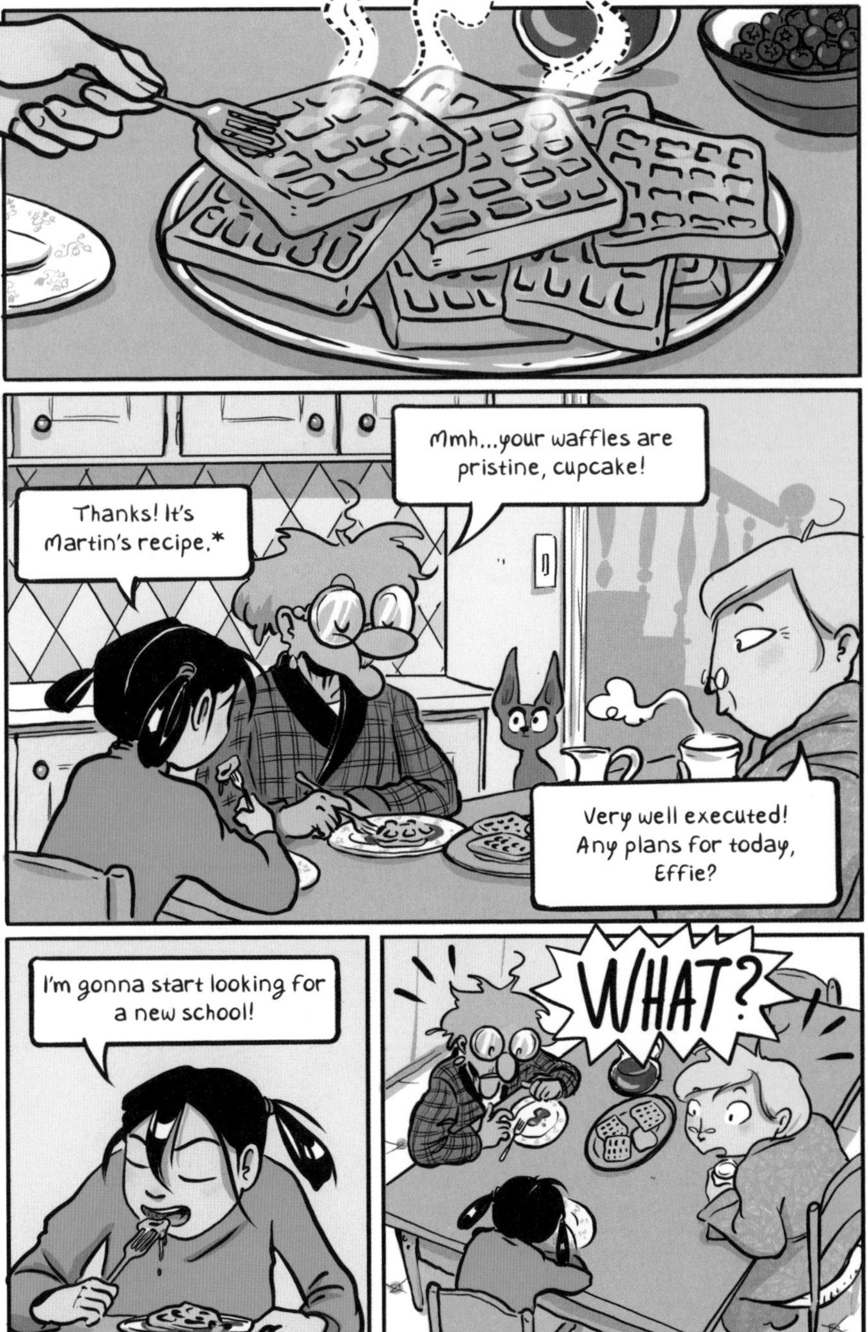
Thanks! It's Martin's recipe.*
Mmh...your waffles are pristine, cupcake!
Very well executed! Any plans for today, Effie?
I'm gonna start looking for a new school!
WHAT?

* See book one.

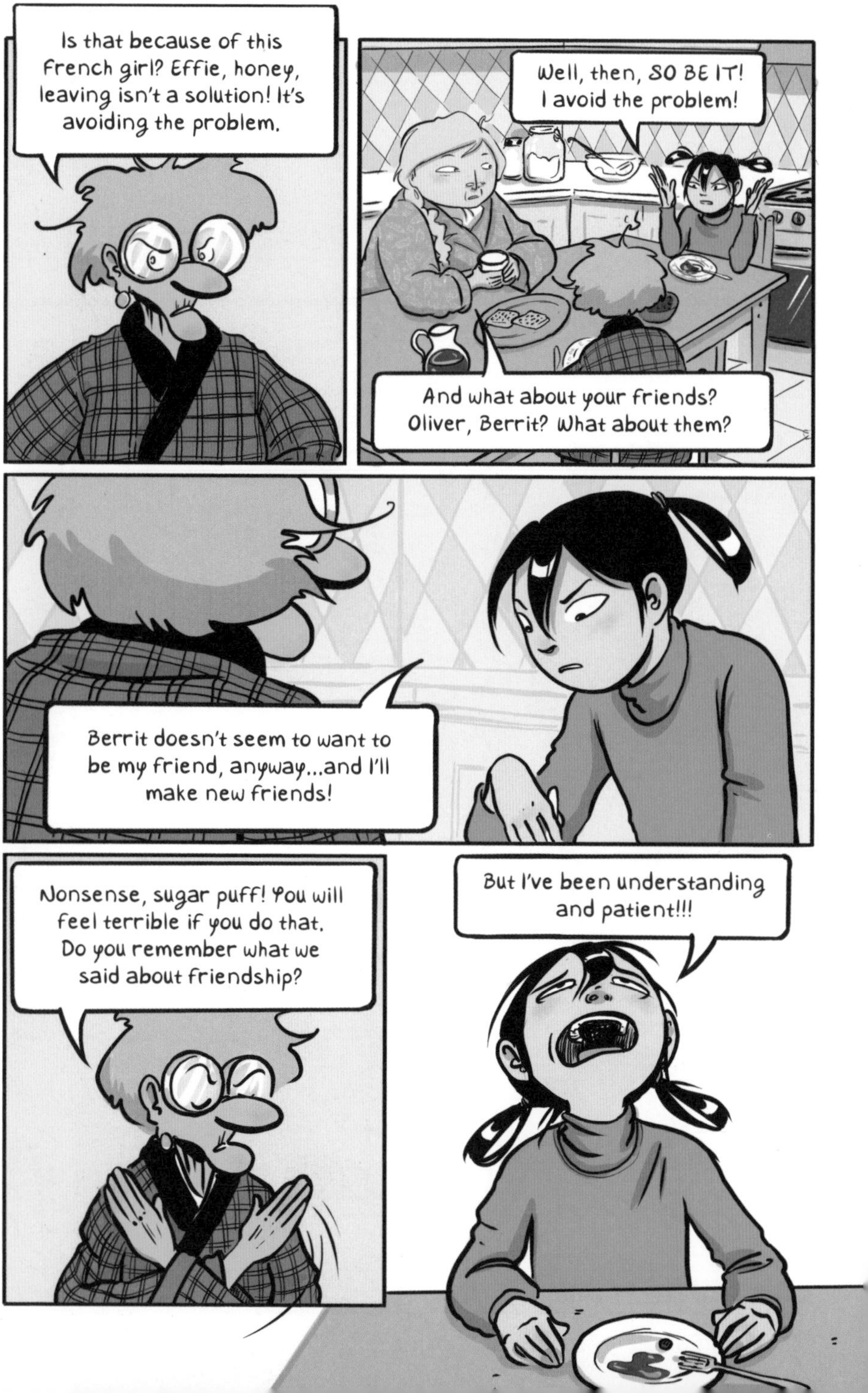
Is that because of this French girl? Effie, honey, leaving isn't a solution! It's avoiding the problem.
Well, then, SO BE IT! I avoid the problem!
And what about your friends? Oliver, Berrit? What about them?
Berrit doesn't seem to want to be my friend, anyway...and I'll make new friends!
Nonsense, sugar puff! You will feel terrible if you do that. Do you remember what we said about friendship?
But I've been understanding and patient!!!

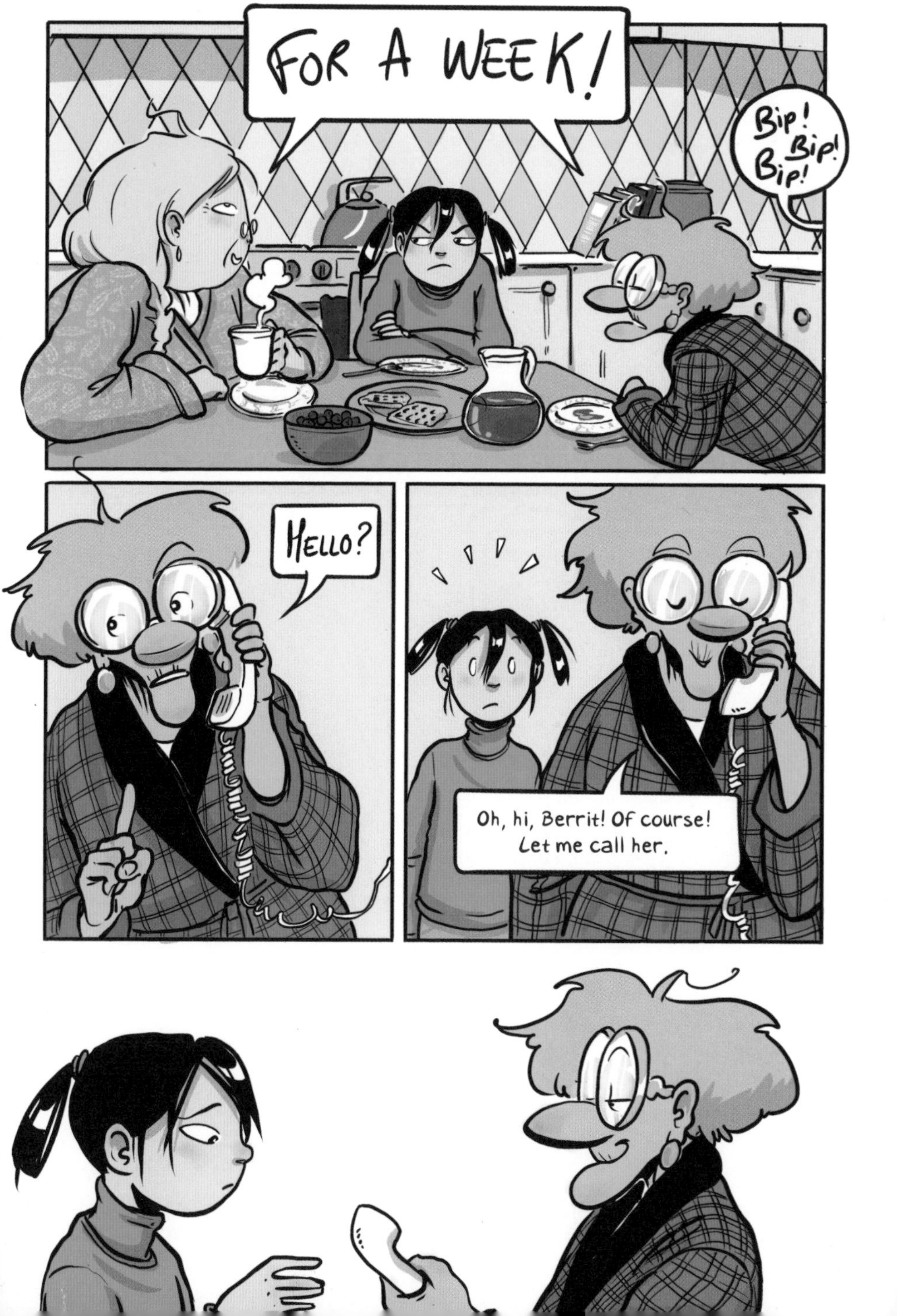
FOR A WEEK!
Bip! Bip! Bip!
HELLO?
Oh, hi, Berrit! Of course! Let me call her.

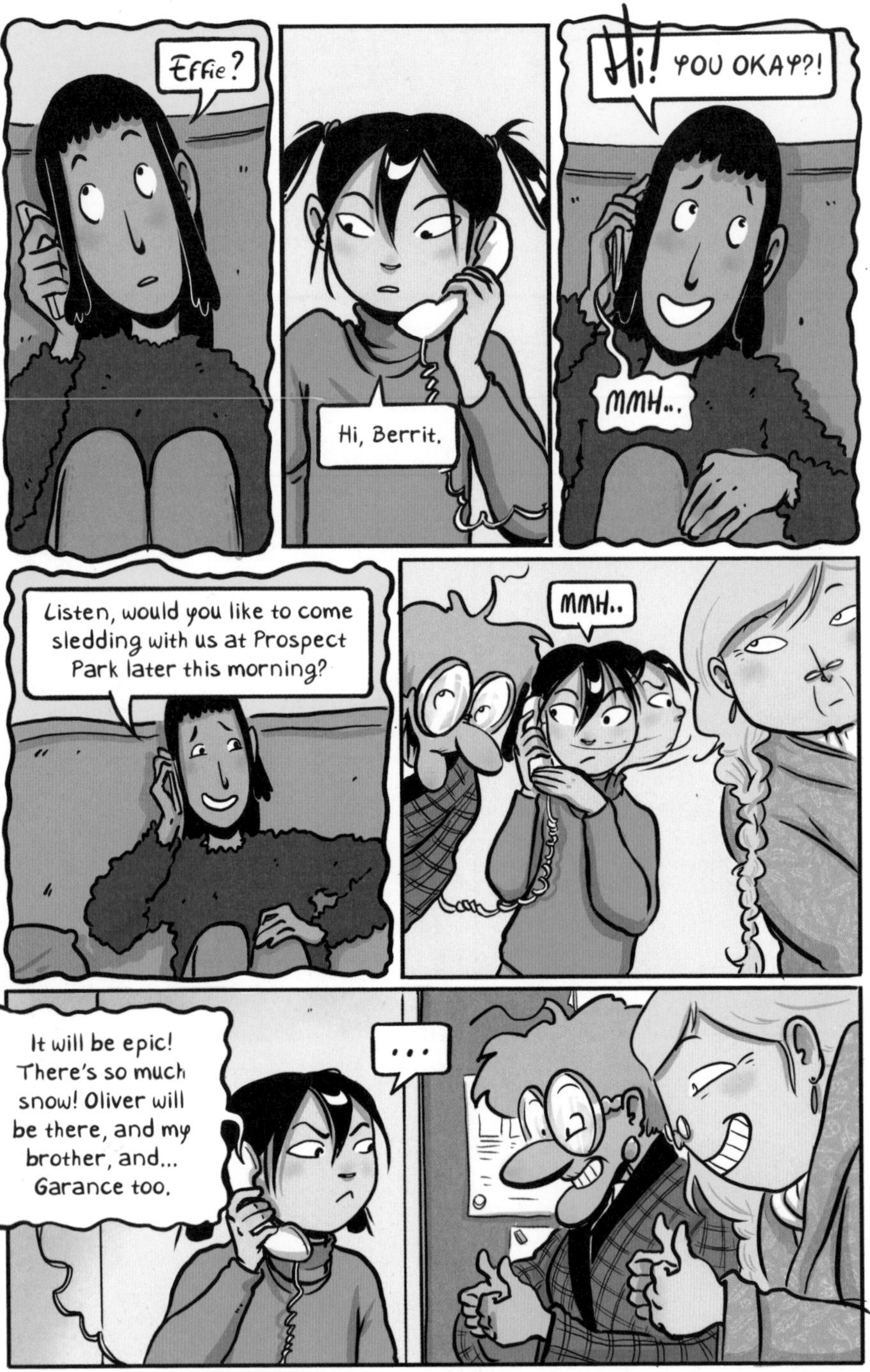

Effie?
Hi, Berrit.
Hi! YOU OKAY?!
MMH...
Listen, would you like to come sledding with us at Prospect Park later this morning?
MMH..
It will be epic! There's so much snow! Oliver will be there, and my brother, and... Garance too.
...

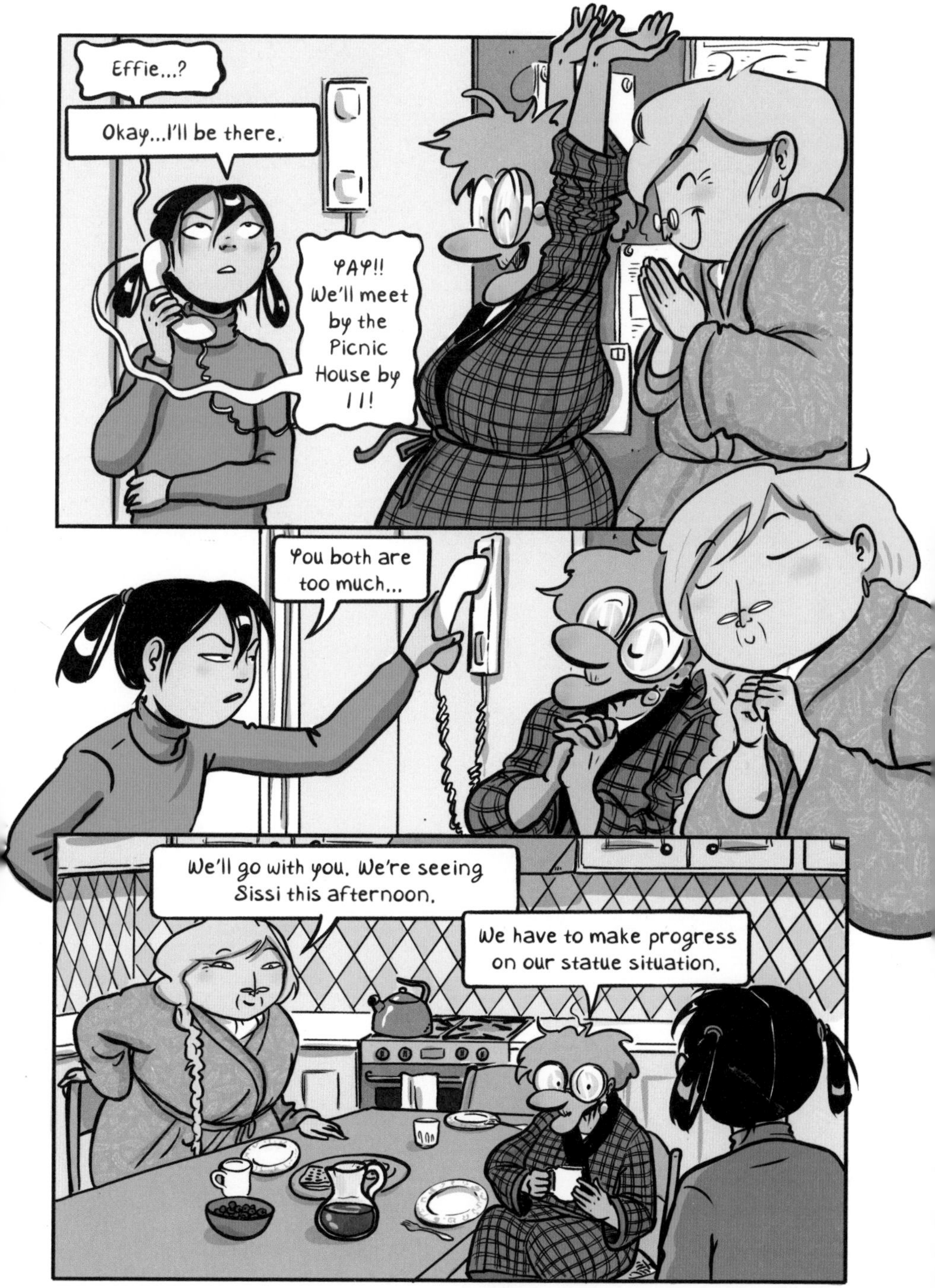
Effie...?
Okay...I'll be there.
YAY!! We'll meet by the Picnic House by 11!
You both are too much...
We'll go with you. We're seeing Sissi this afternoon.
We have to make progress on our statue situation.

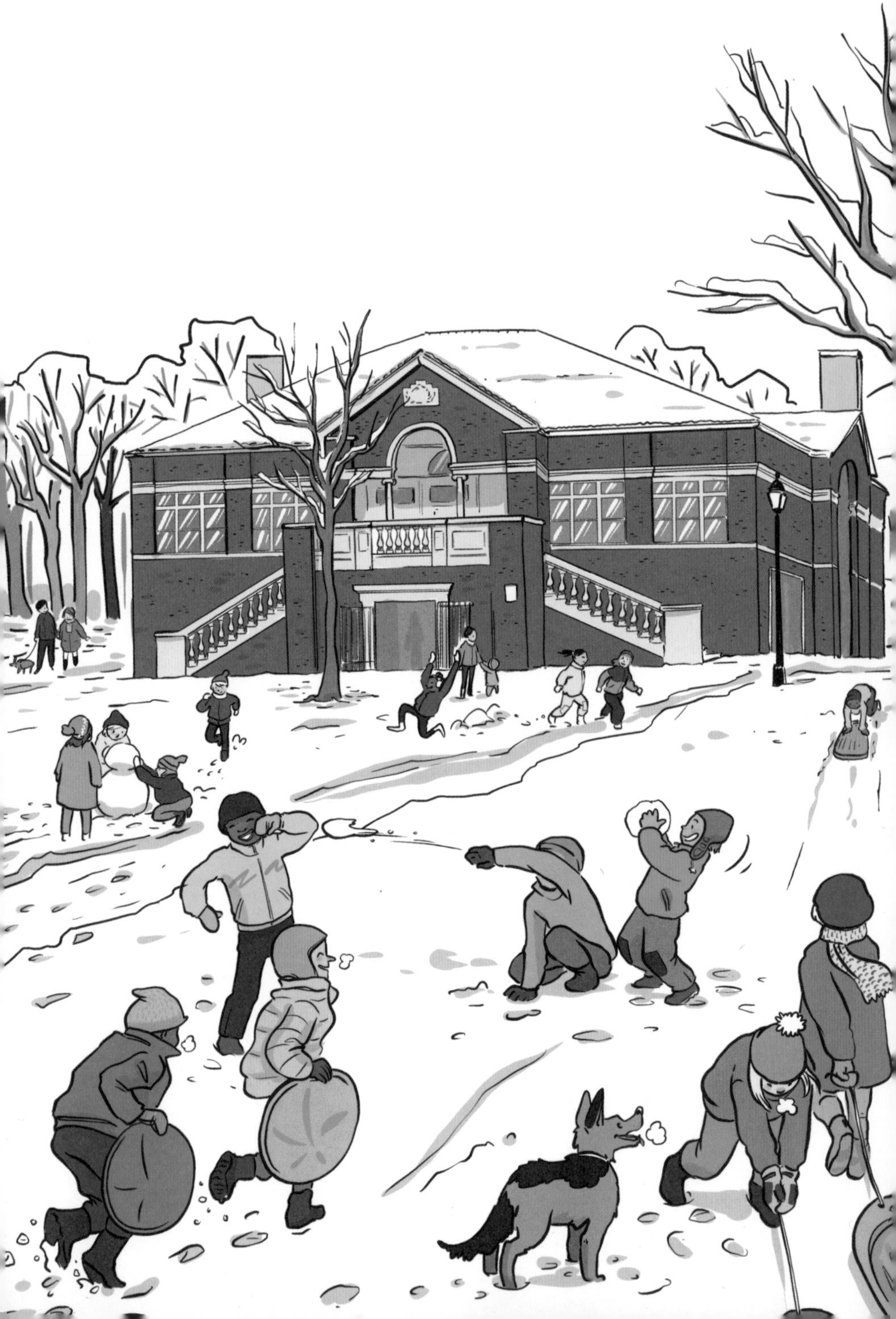

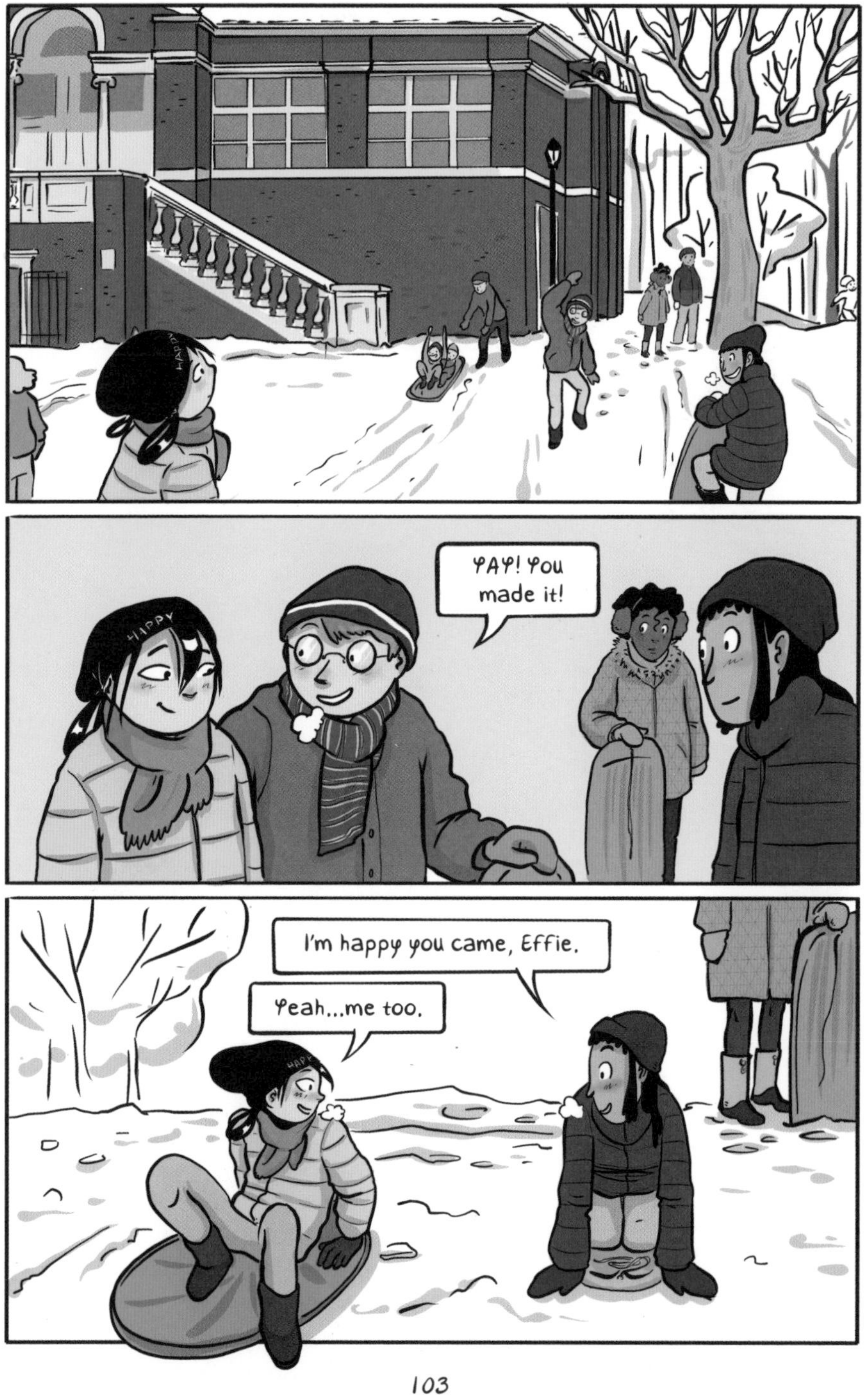
HAPPY
YAY! You made it!
I'm happy you came, Effie.
Yeah...me too.

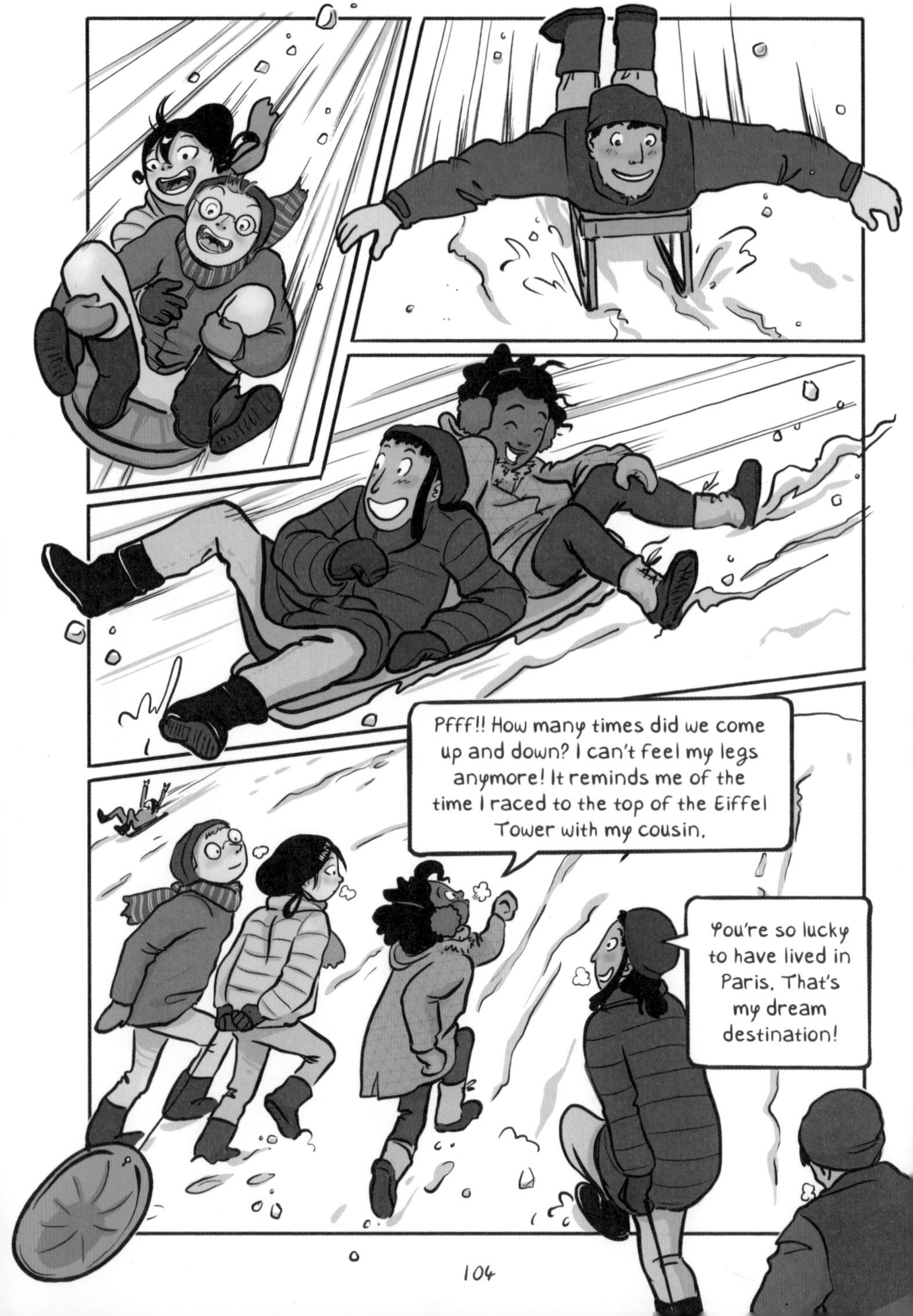
Pfff!! How many times did we come up and down? I can't feel my legs anymore! It reminds me of the time I raced to the top of the Eiffel Tower with my cousin.
You're so lucky to have lived in Paris. That's my dream destination!

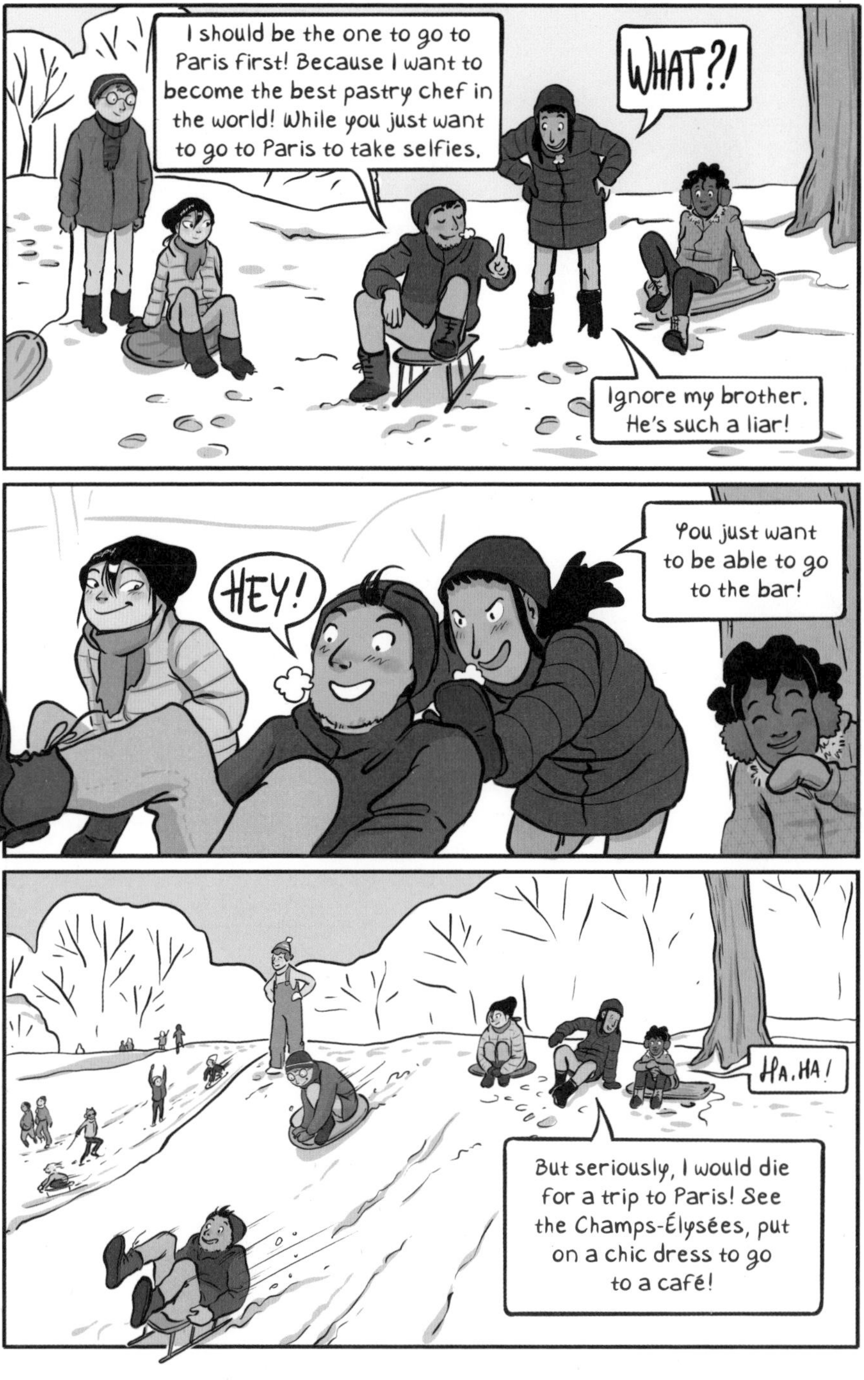
I should be the one to go to Paris first! Because I want to become the best pastry chef in the world! While you just want to go to Paris to take selfies.
WHAT?!
Ignore my brother. He's such a liar!
HEY!
You just want to be able to go to the bar!
HA, HA!
But seriously, I would die for a trip to Paris! See the Champs-Élysées, put on a chic dress to go to a café!

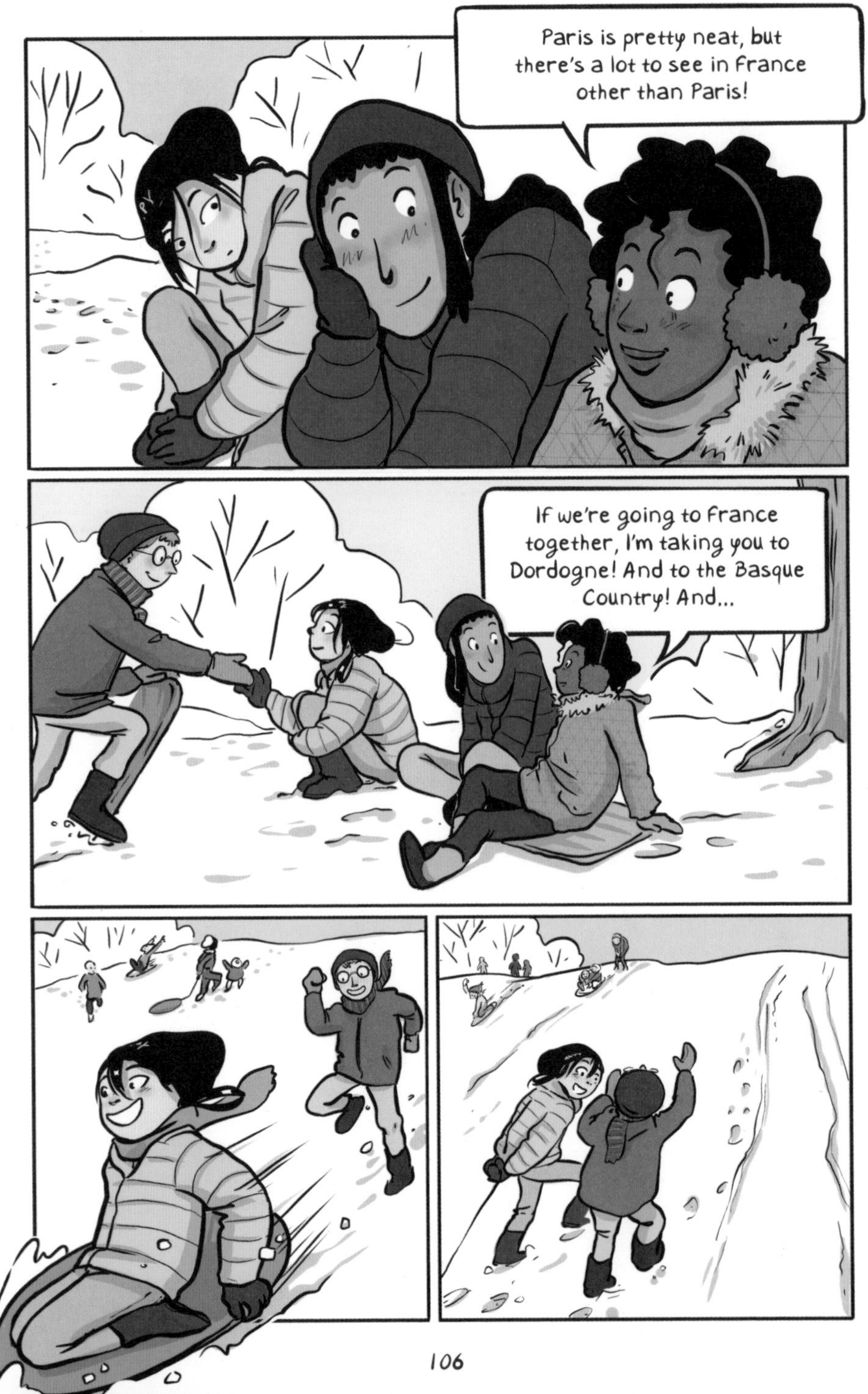
Paris is pretty neat, but there's a lot to see in France other than Paris!
If we're going to France together, I'm taking you to Dordogne! And to the Basque Country! And...

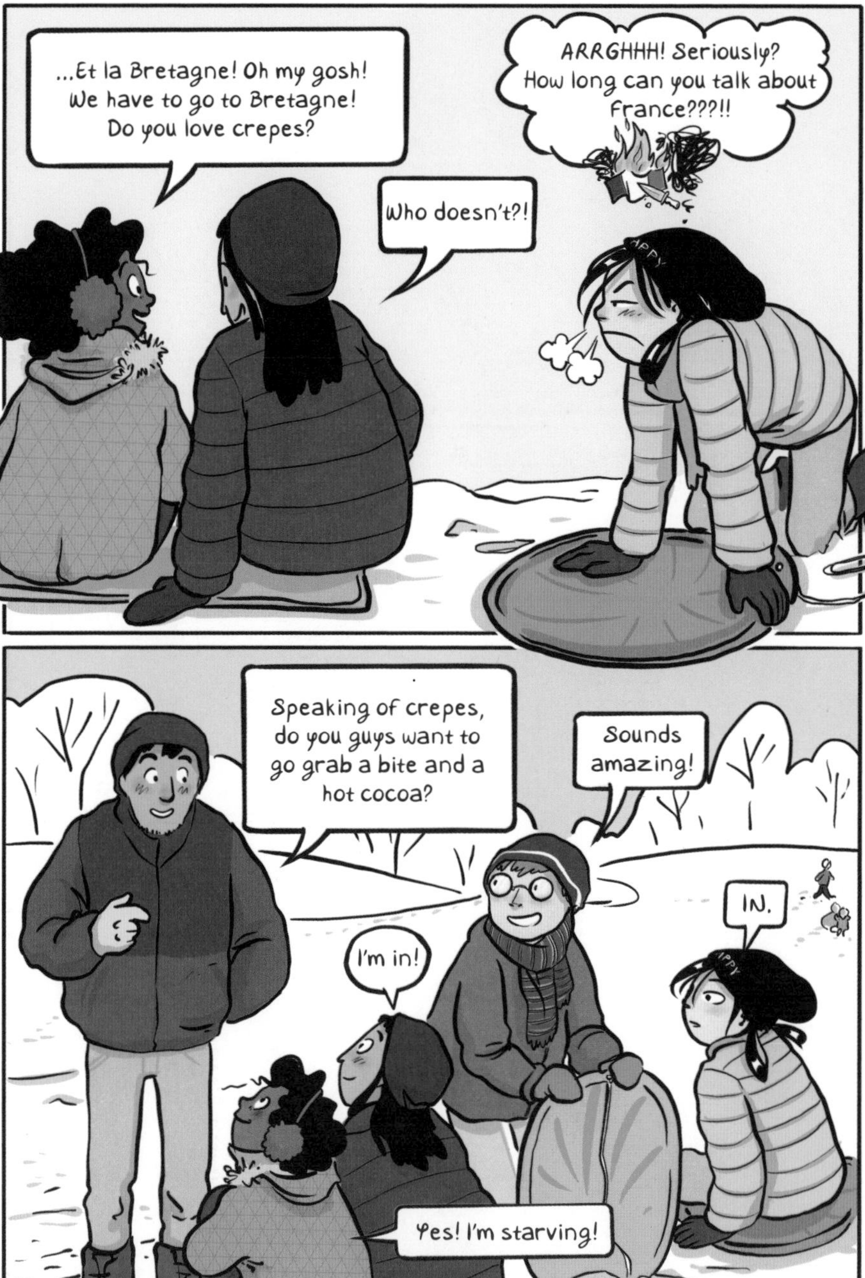
...Et la Bretagne! Oh my gosh! We have to go to Bretagne! Do you love crepes?
Who doesn't?!
ARRGHHH! Seriously? How long can you talk about France???!!
Speaking of crepes, do you guys want to go grab a bite and a hot cocoa?
Sounds amazing!
IN.
I'm in!
Yes! I'm starving!

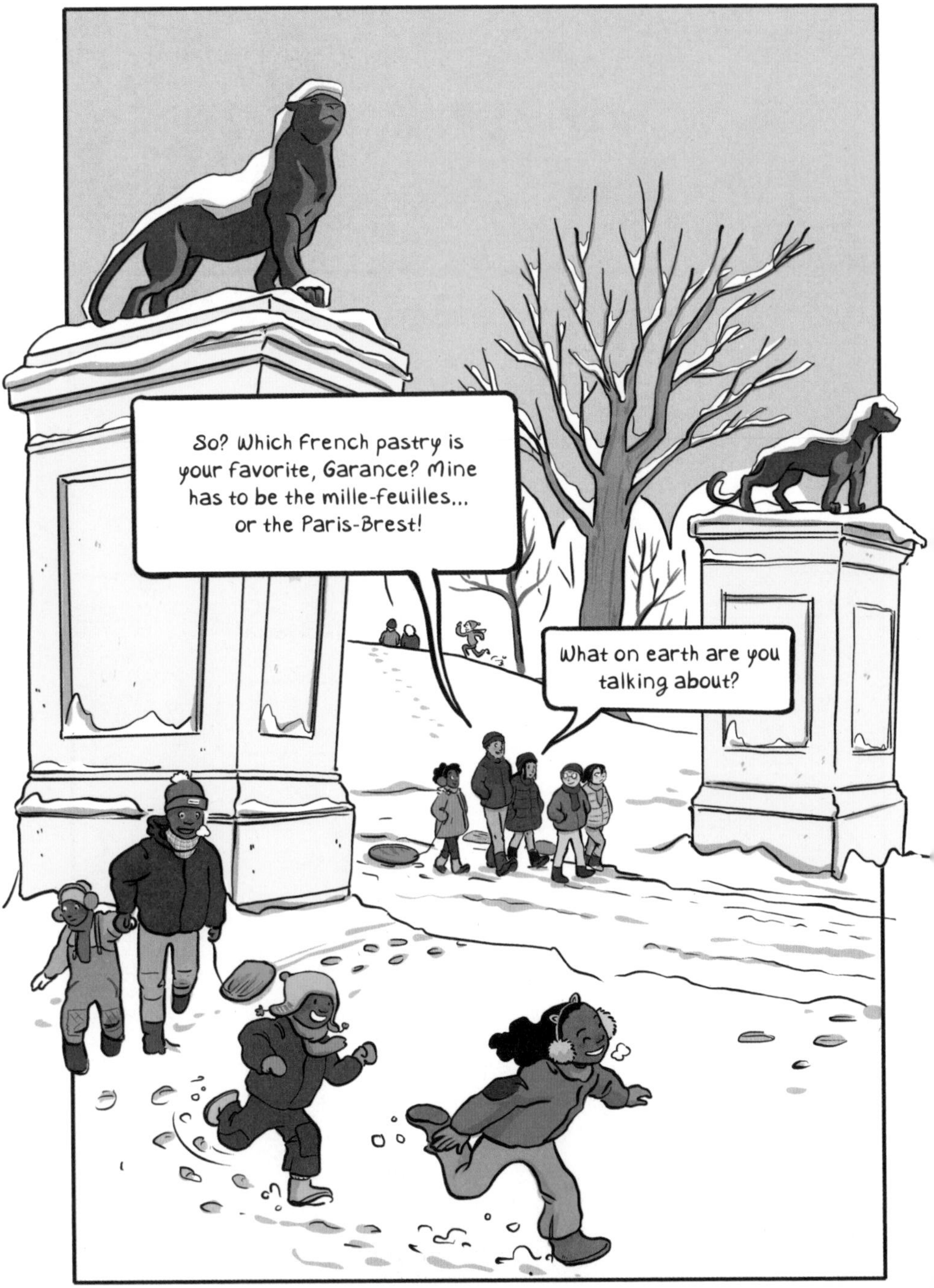
So? Which French pastry is your favorite, Garance? Mine has to be the mille-feuilles... or the Paris-Brest!
What on earth are you talking about?

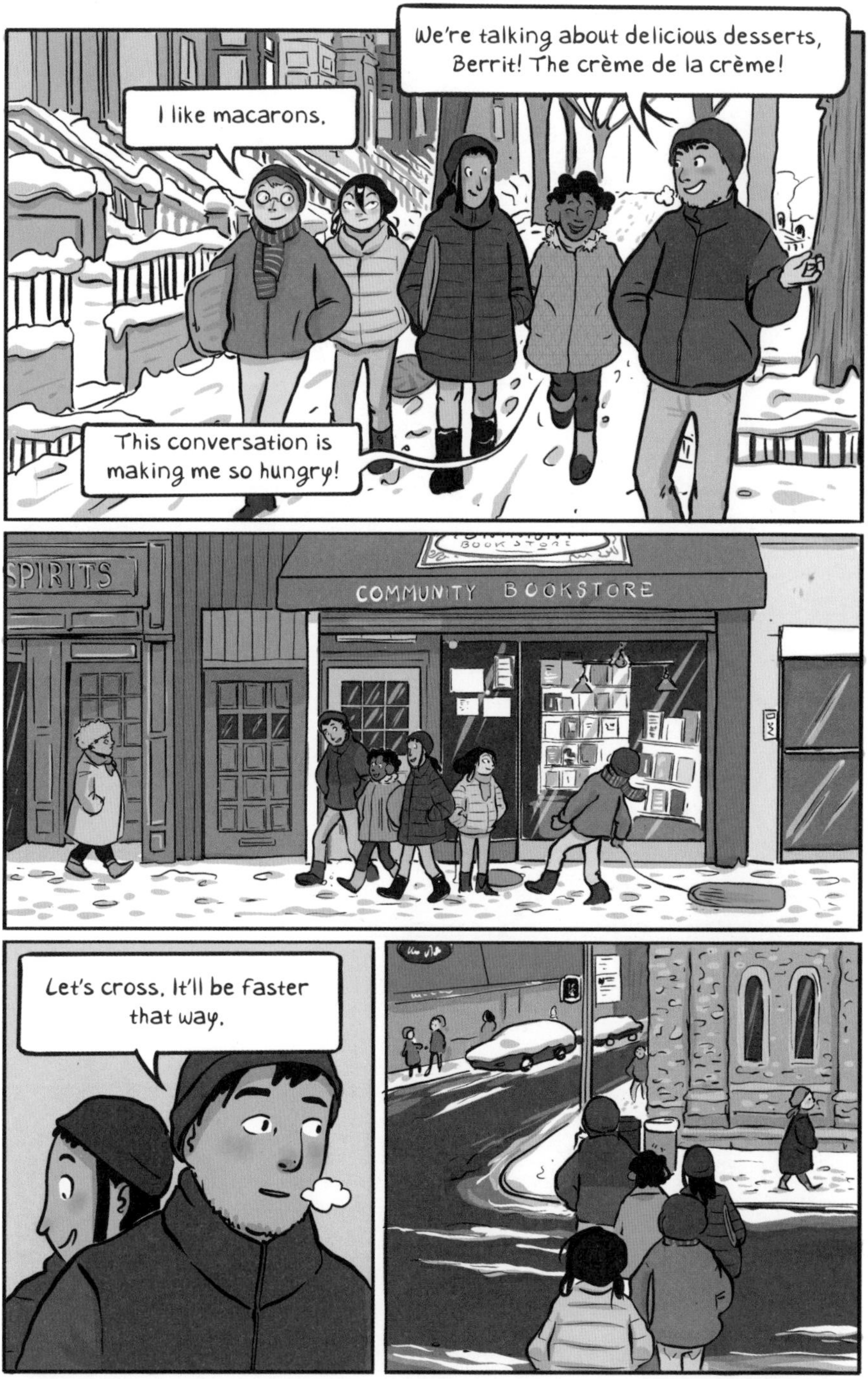
I like macarons.
We're talking about delicious desserts, Berrit! The crème de la crème!
This conversation is making me so hungry!
SPIRITS
COMMUNITY BOOKSTORE
Let's cross. It'll be faster that way.

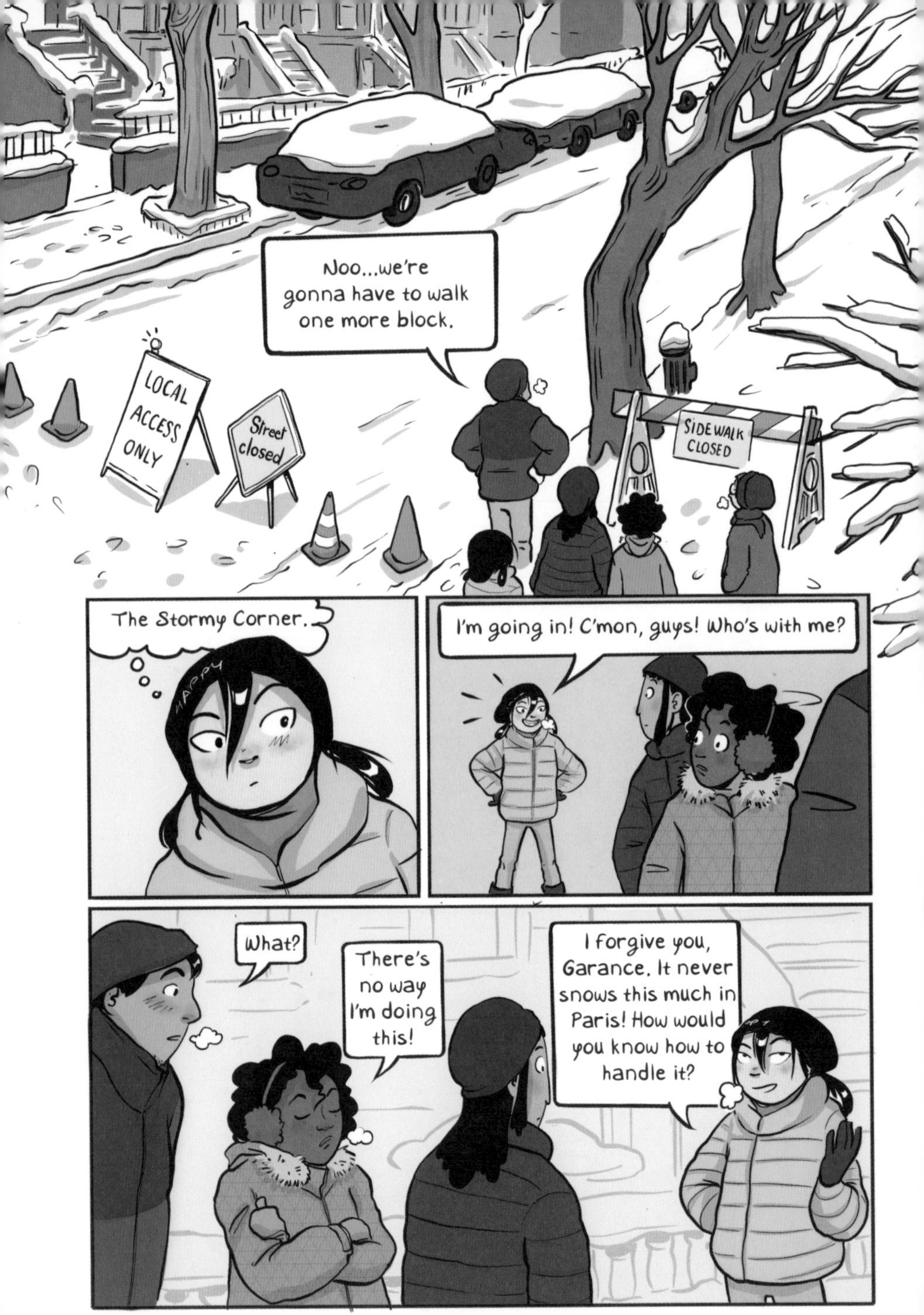

Noo...we're gonna have to walk one more block.
LOCAL ACCESS ONLY
Street closed
SIDEWALK CLOSED
The Stormy Corner.
I'm going in! C'mon, guys! Who's with me?
What?
There's no way I'm doing this!
I forgive you, Garance. It never snows this much in Paris! How would you know how to handle it?

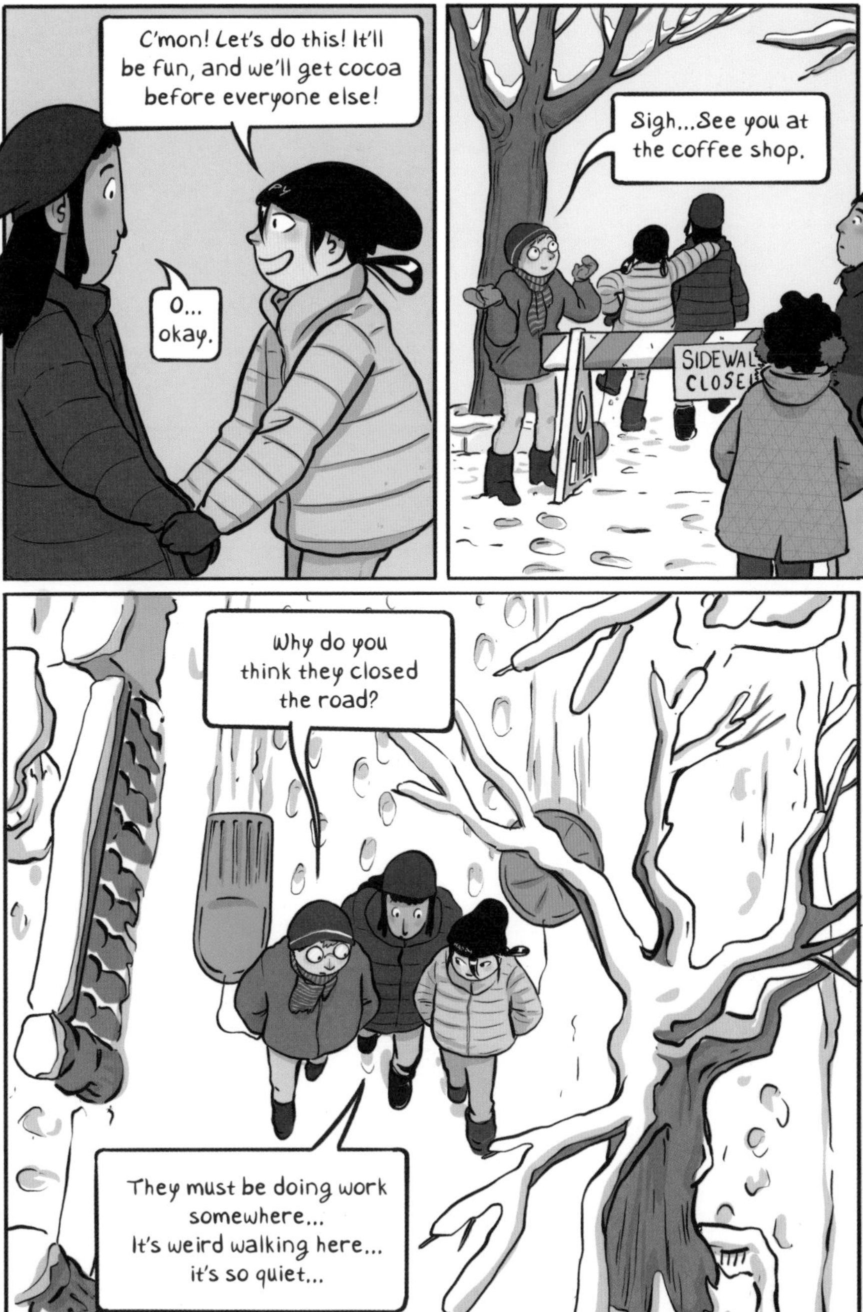
C'mon! Let's do this! It'll be fun, and we'll get cocoa before everyone else!
O... okay.
Sigh...See you at the coffee shop.
SIDEWAL CLOSE
Why do you think they closed the road?
They must be doing work somewhere...
It's weird walking here... it's so quiet...

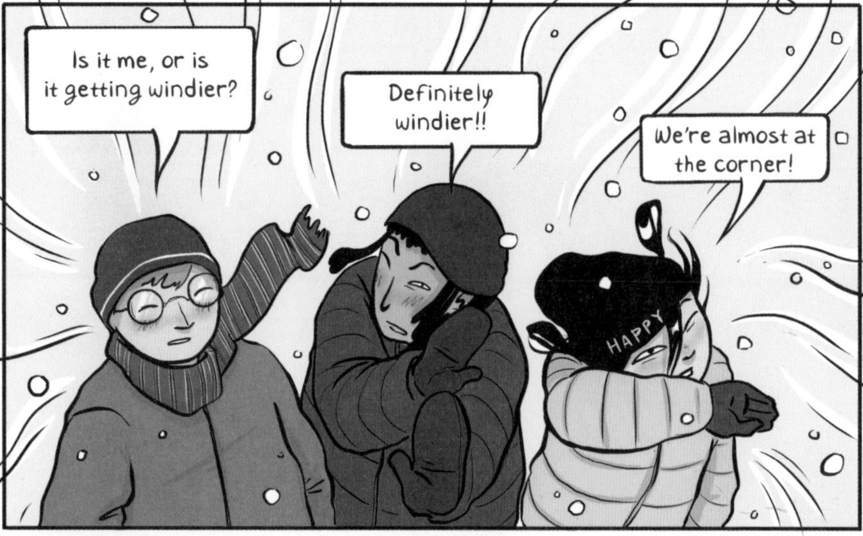
Is it me, or is it getting windier?
Definitely windier!!
We're almost at the corner!
HAPPY

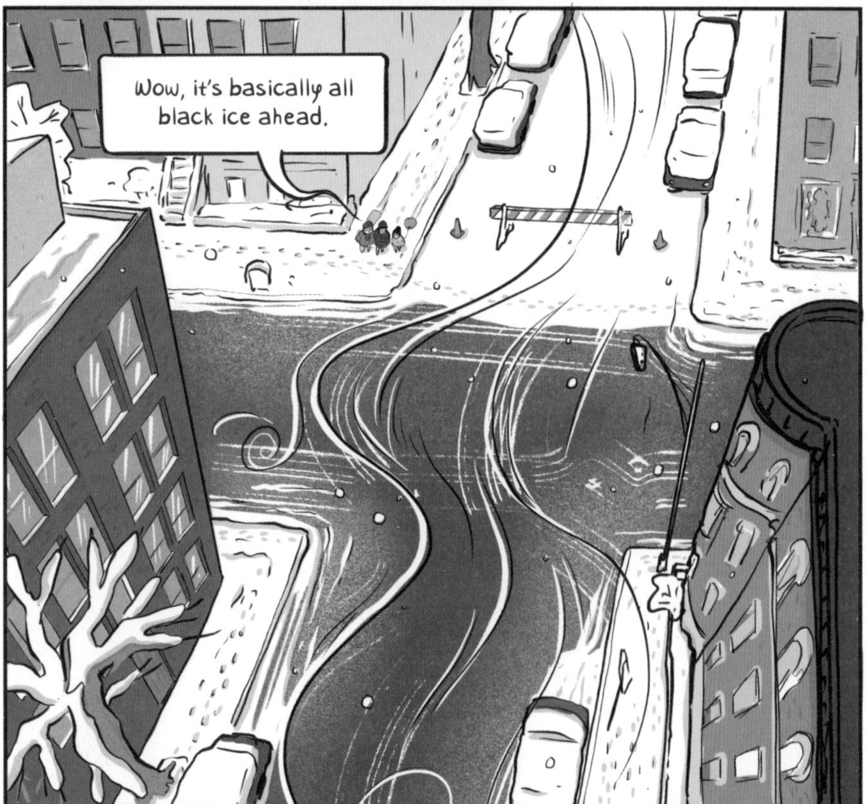
Wow, it's basically all black ice ahead.

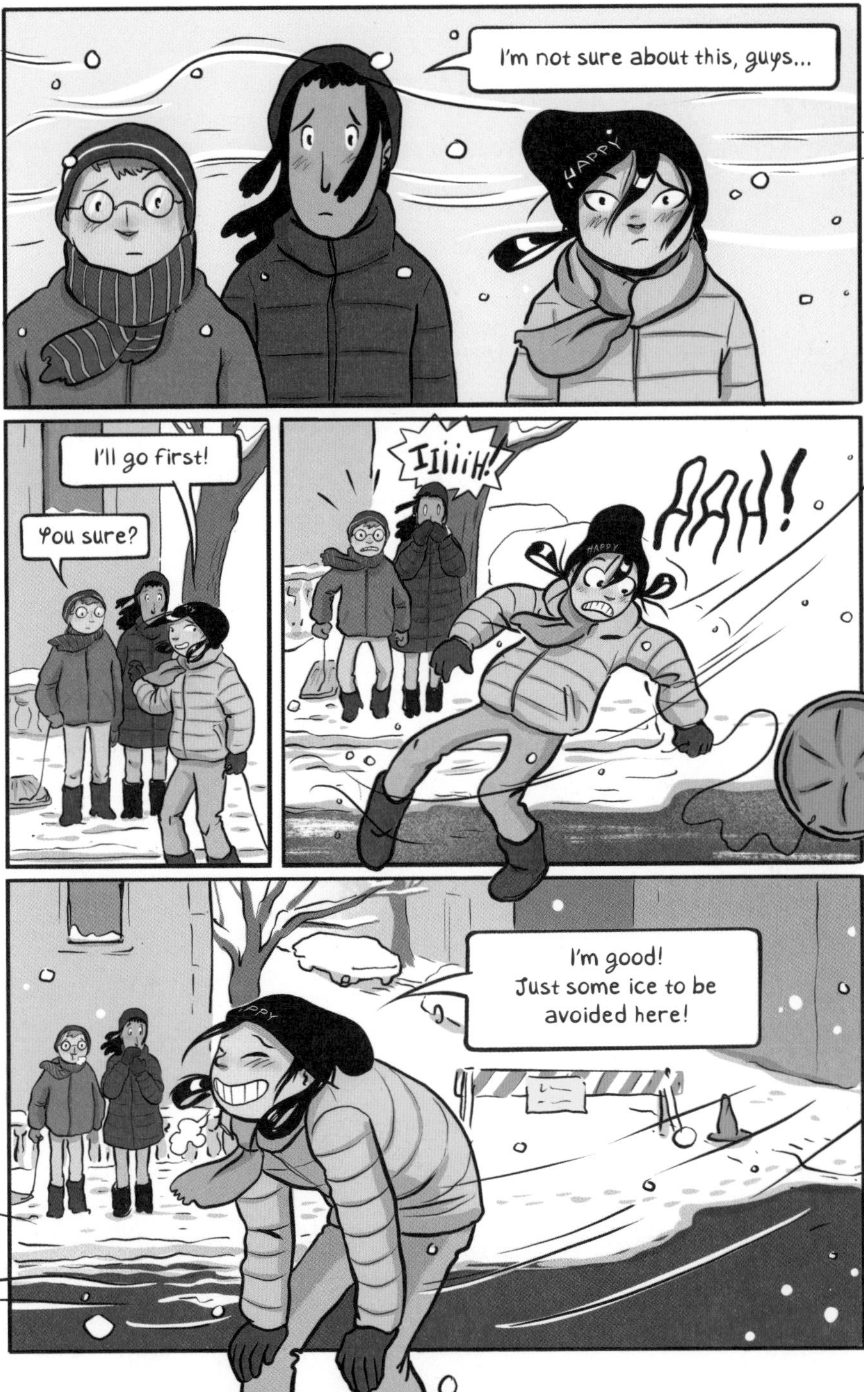
I'm not sure about this, guys...
I'll go first!
You sure?
IIiiiH!
AAH!
I'm good!
Just some ice to be avoided here!

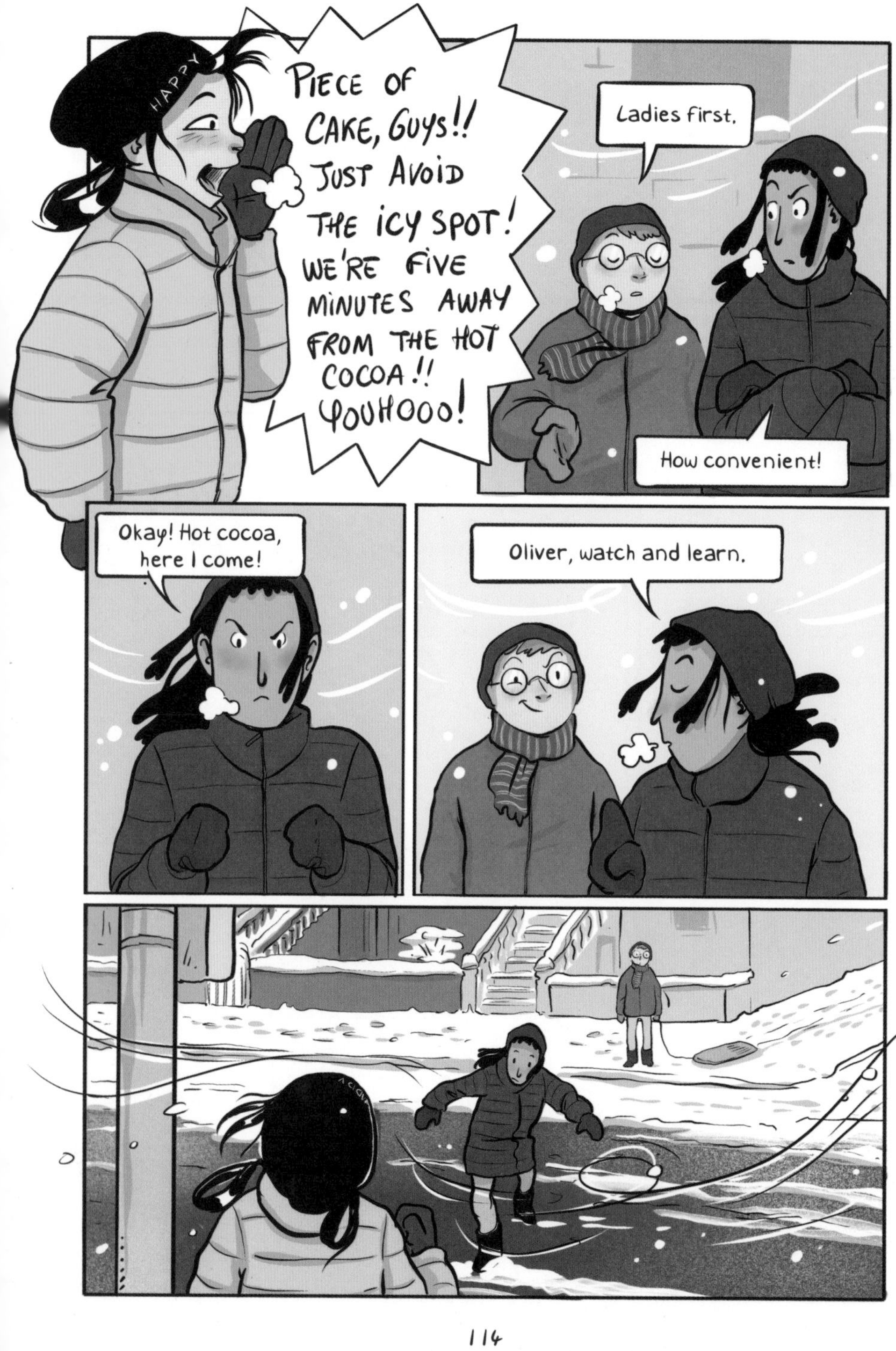
HAPPY
PIECE OF CAKE, GUYS!! JUST AVOID THE ICY SPOT! WE'RE FIVE MINUTES AWAY FROM THE HOT COCOA!! YOUHOOO!
Ladies first.
How convenient!
Okay! Hot cocoa, here I come!
Oliver, watch and learn.

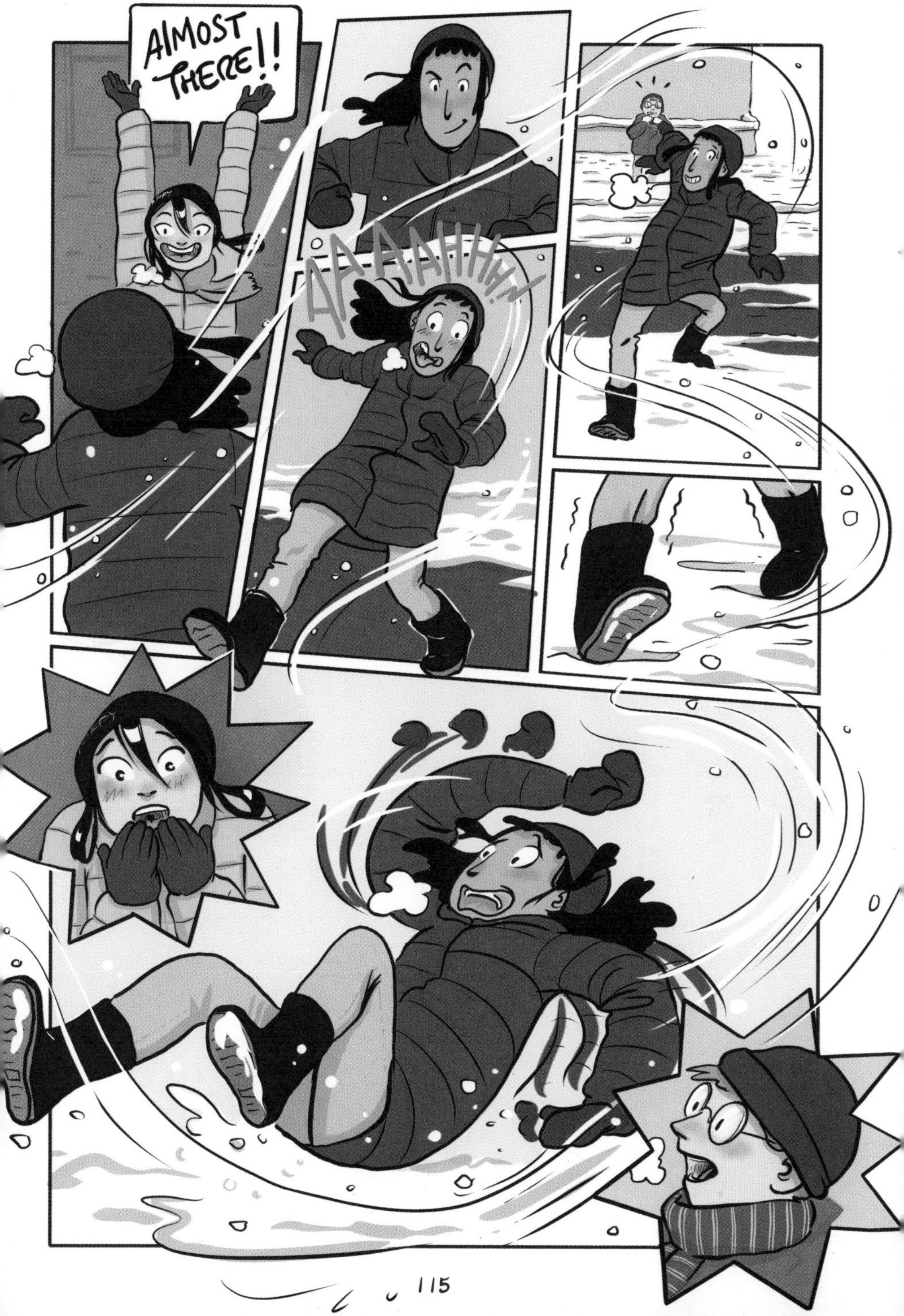
ALMOST THERE!!
AAAAHHHH!

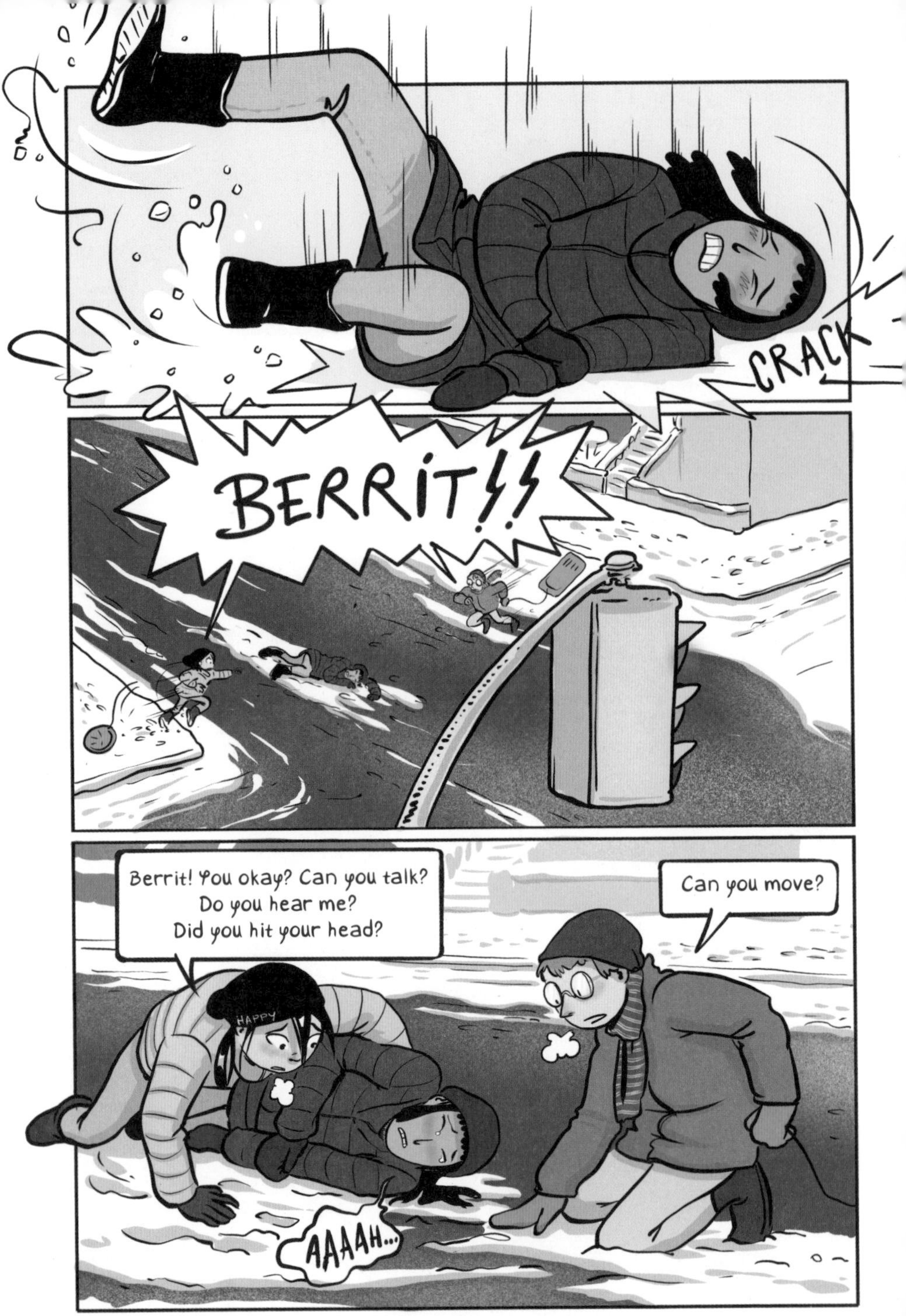
CRACK
BERRIT!!
Berrit! You okay? Can you talk? Do you hear me? Did you hit your head?
Can you move?
AAAAH...

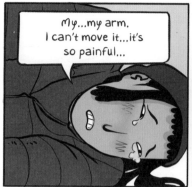

My...my arm. I can't move it...it's so painful...

You're...you're gonna be okay.

Let's get you out of here.

AAAAh Ah! SOB

It hurts SO MUCH... SOB.

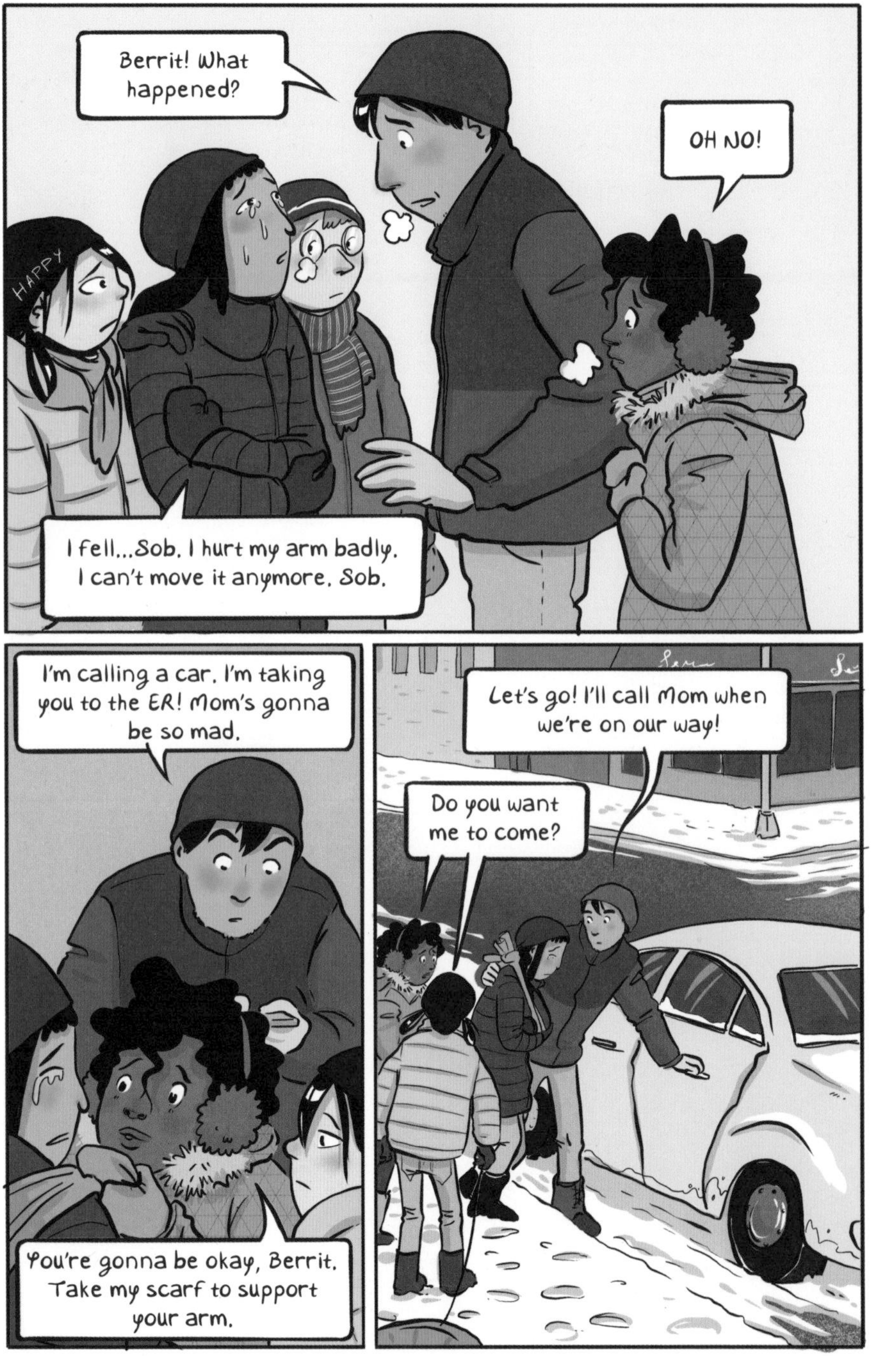
Berrit! What happened?
OH NO!
I fell...Sob. I hurt my arm badly. I can't move it anymore. Sob.
I'm calling a car. I'm taking you to the ER! Mom's gonna be so mad.
You're gonna be okay, Berrit. Take my scarf to support your arm.
Let's go! I'll call Mom when we're on our way!
Do you want me to come?

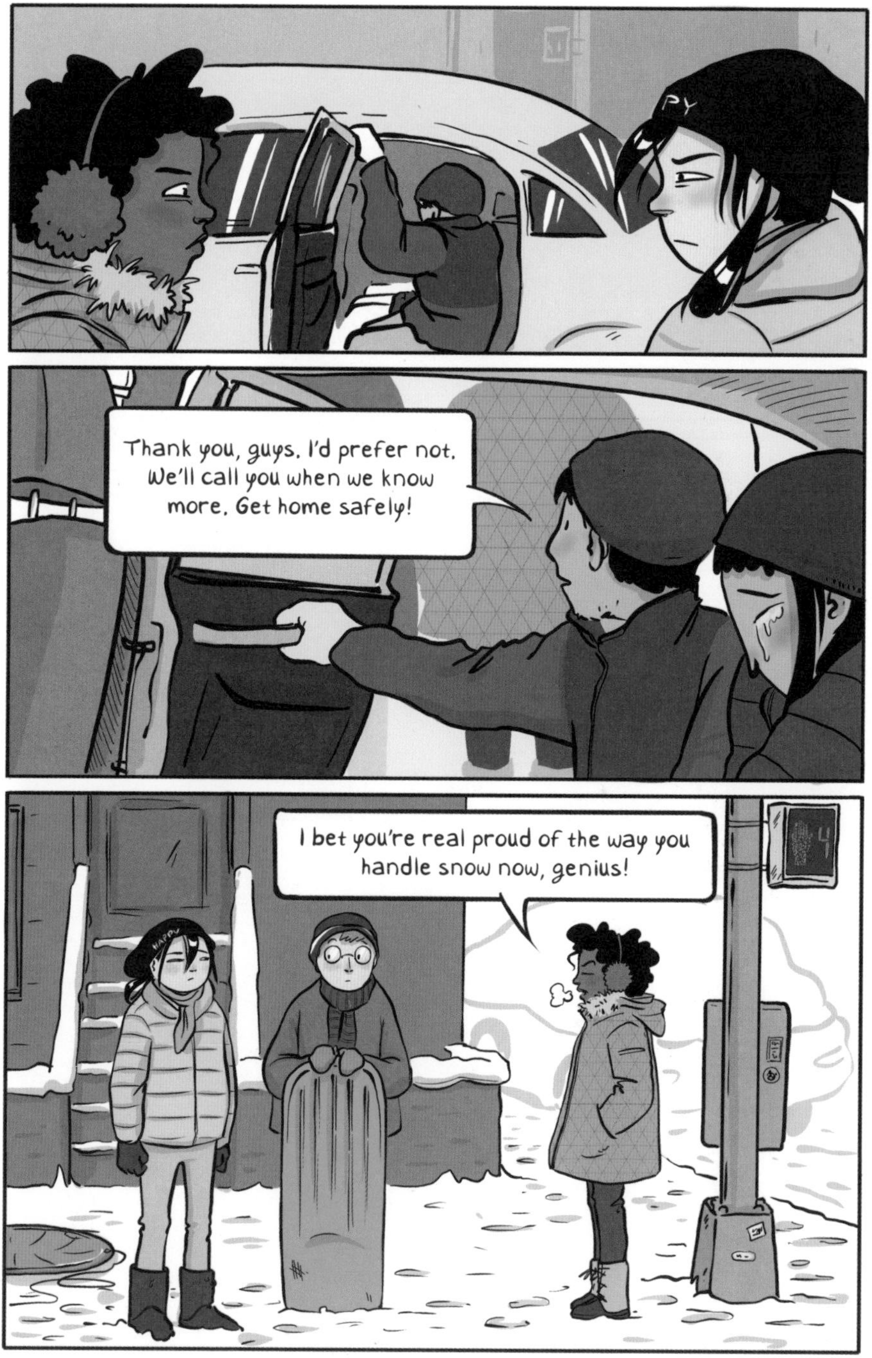

Thank you, guys. I'd prefer not. We'll call you when we know more. Get home safely!
I bet you're real proud of the way you handle snow now, genius!

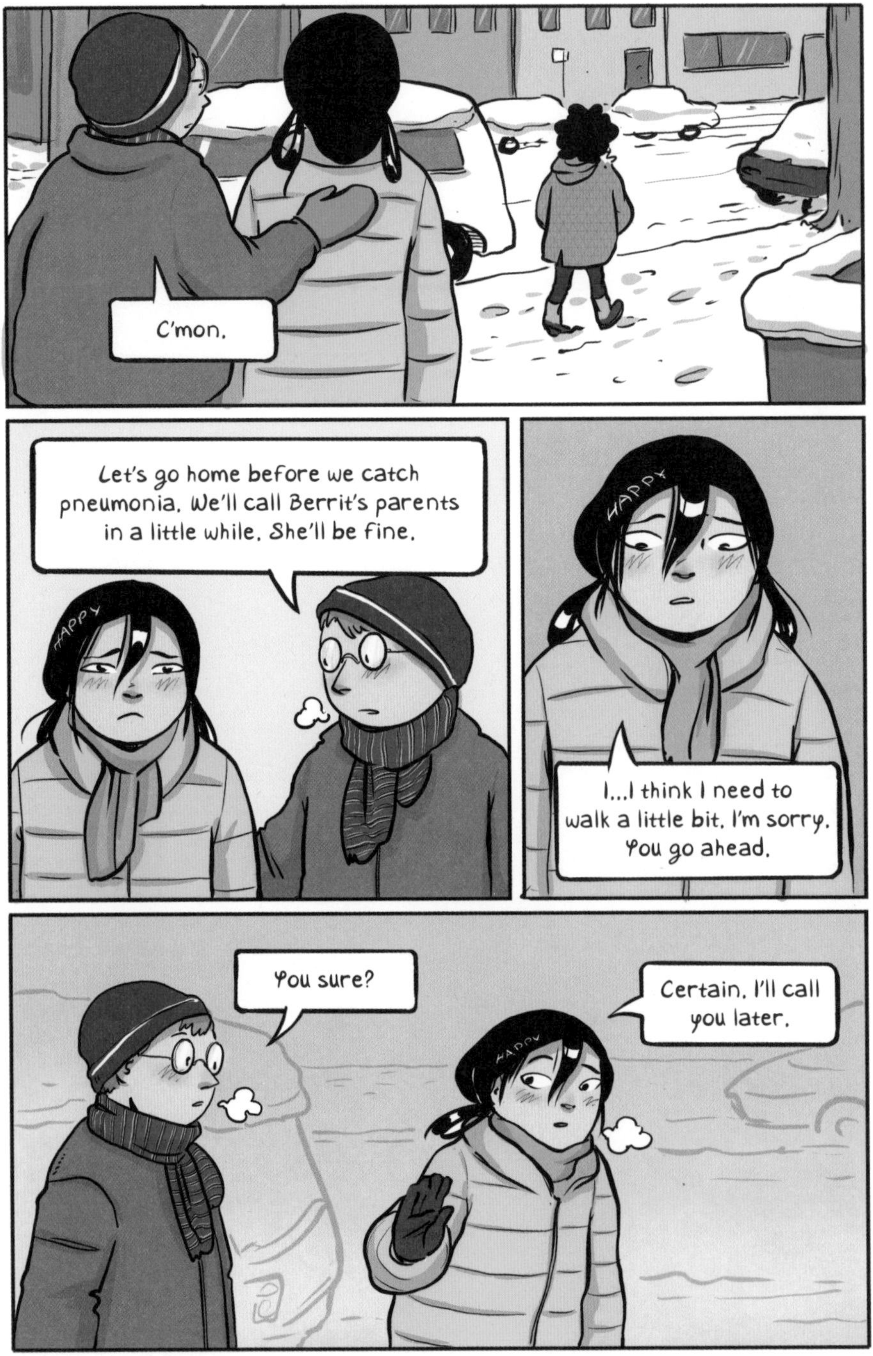
C'mon.
Let's go home before we catch pneumonia. We'll call Berrit's parents in a little while. She'll be fine.
HAPPY
HAPPY
I...I think I need to walk a little bit. I'm sorry. You go ahead.
You sure?
Certain. I'll call you later.
HAPPY

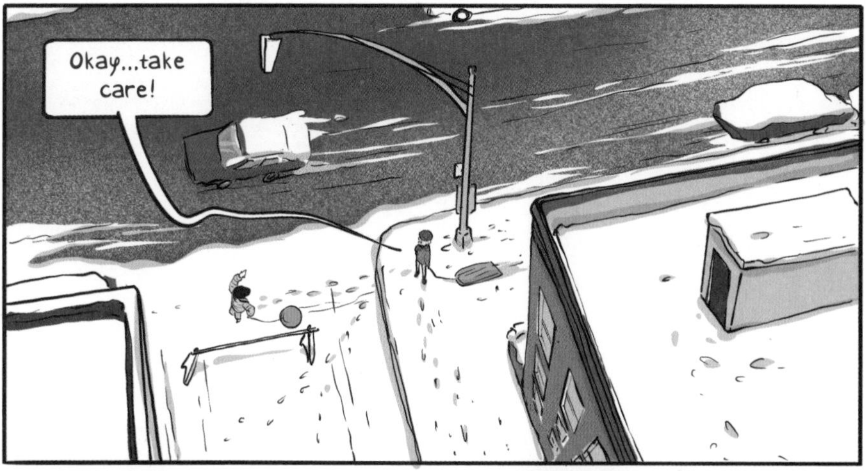
Okay...take care!

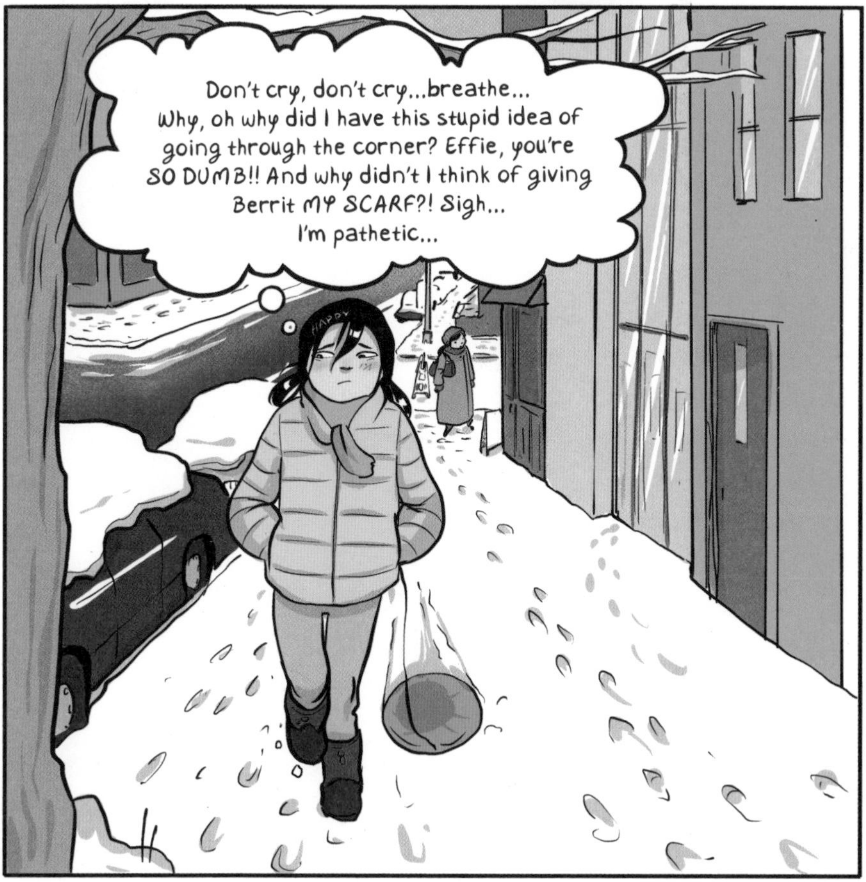
Don't cry, don't cry...breathe... Why, oh why did I have this stupid idea of going through the corner? Effie, you're SO DUMB!! And why didn't I think of giving Berrit MY SCARF?! Sigh... I'm pathetic...

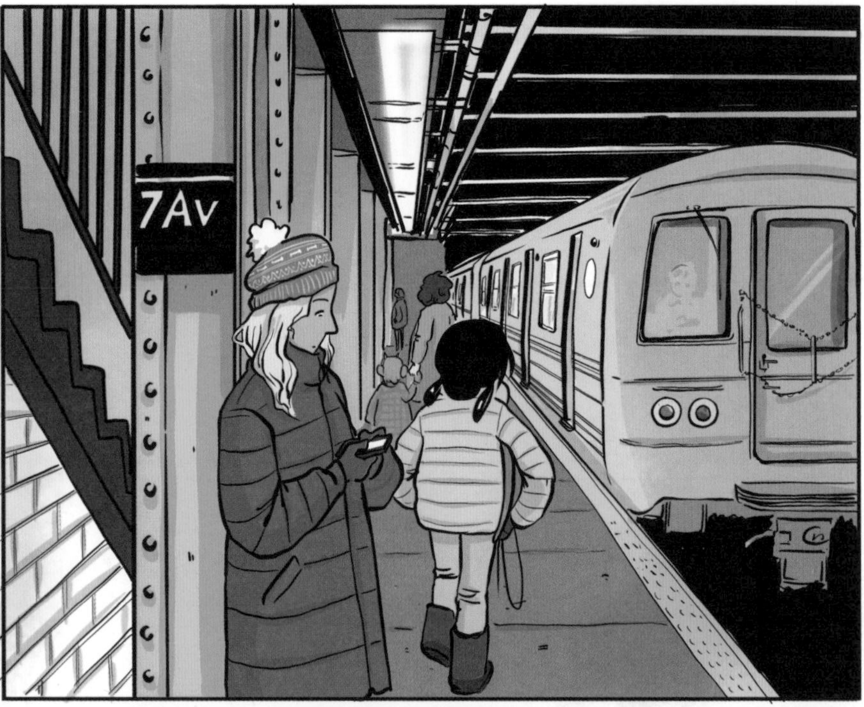
7Av

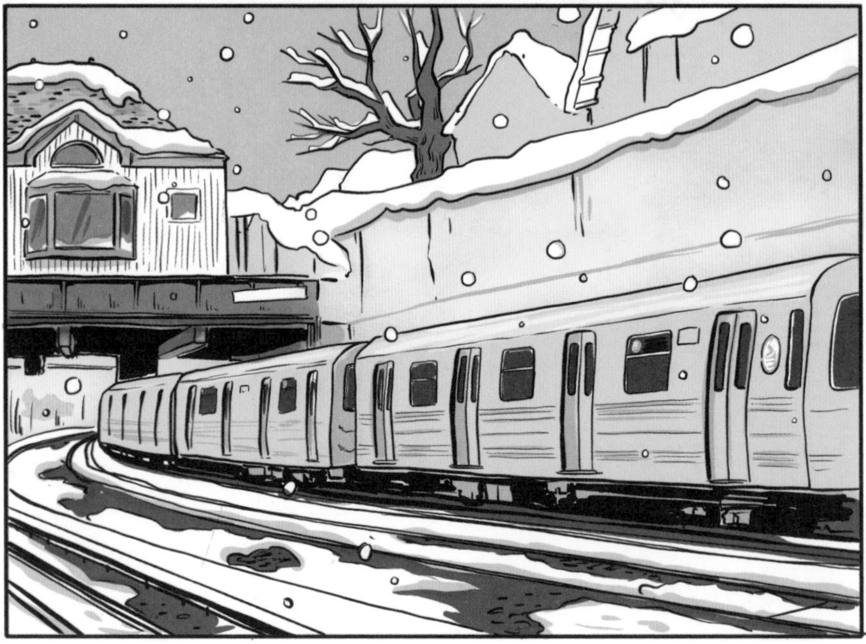

Chapter 4

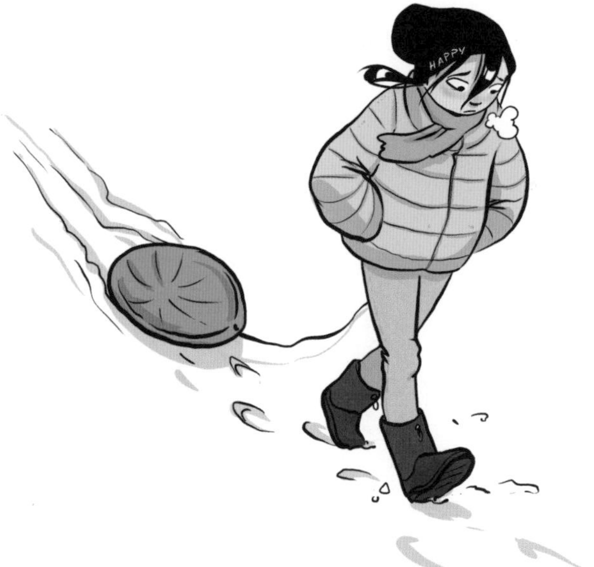
HAPPY

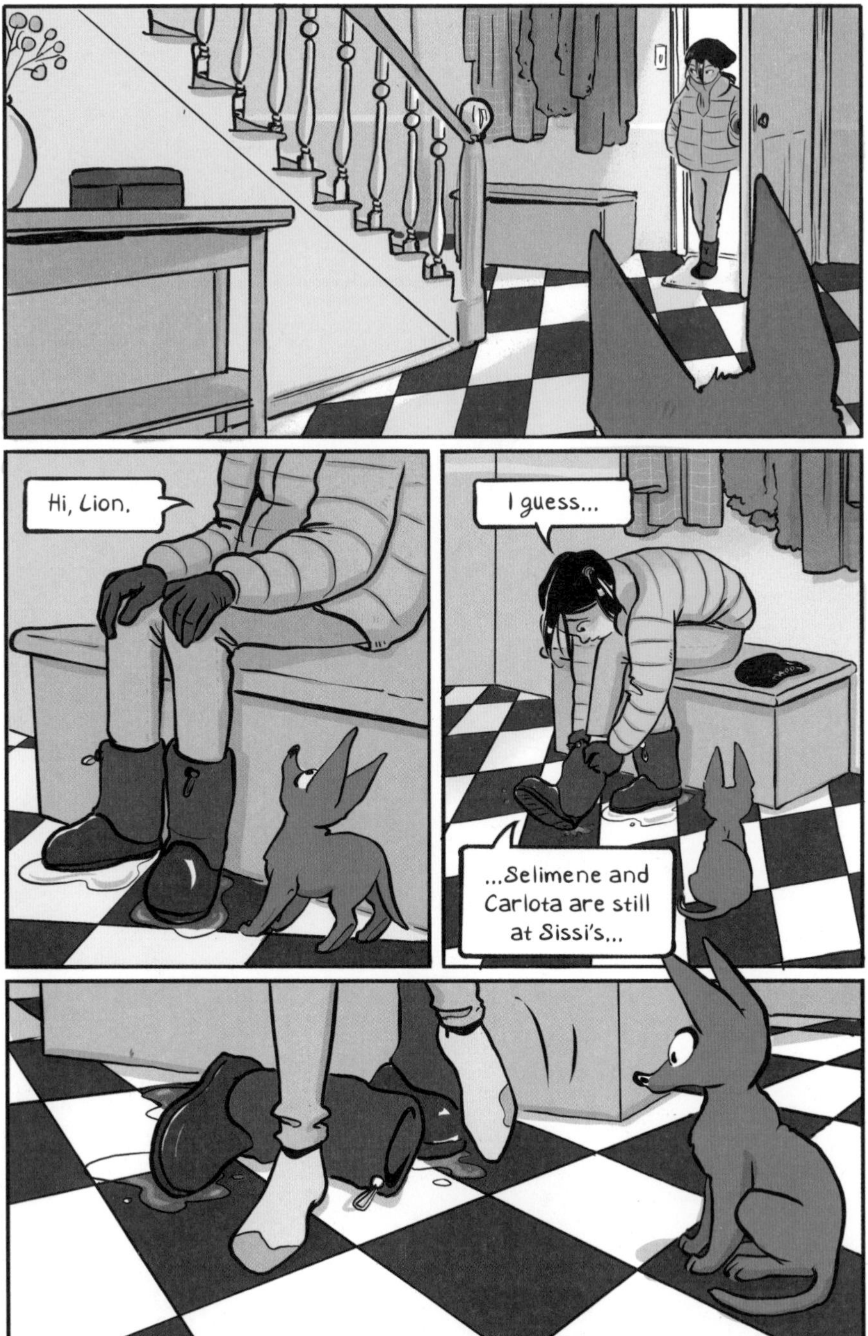
Hi, Lion.
I guess...
...Selimene and Carlota are still at Sissi's...

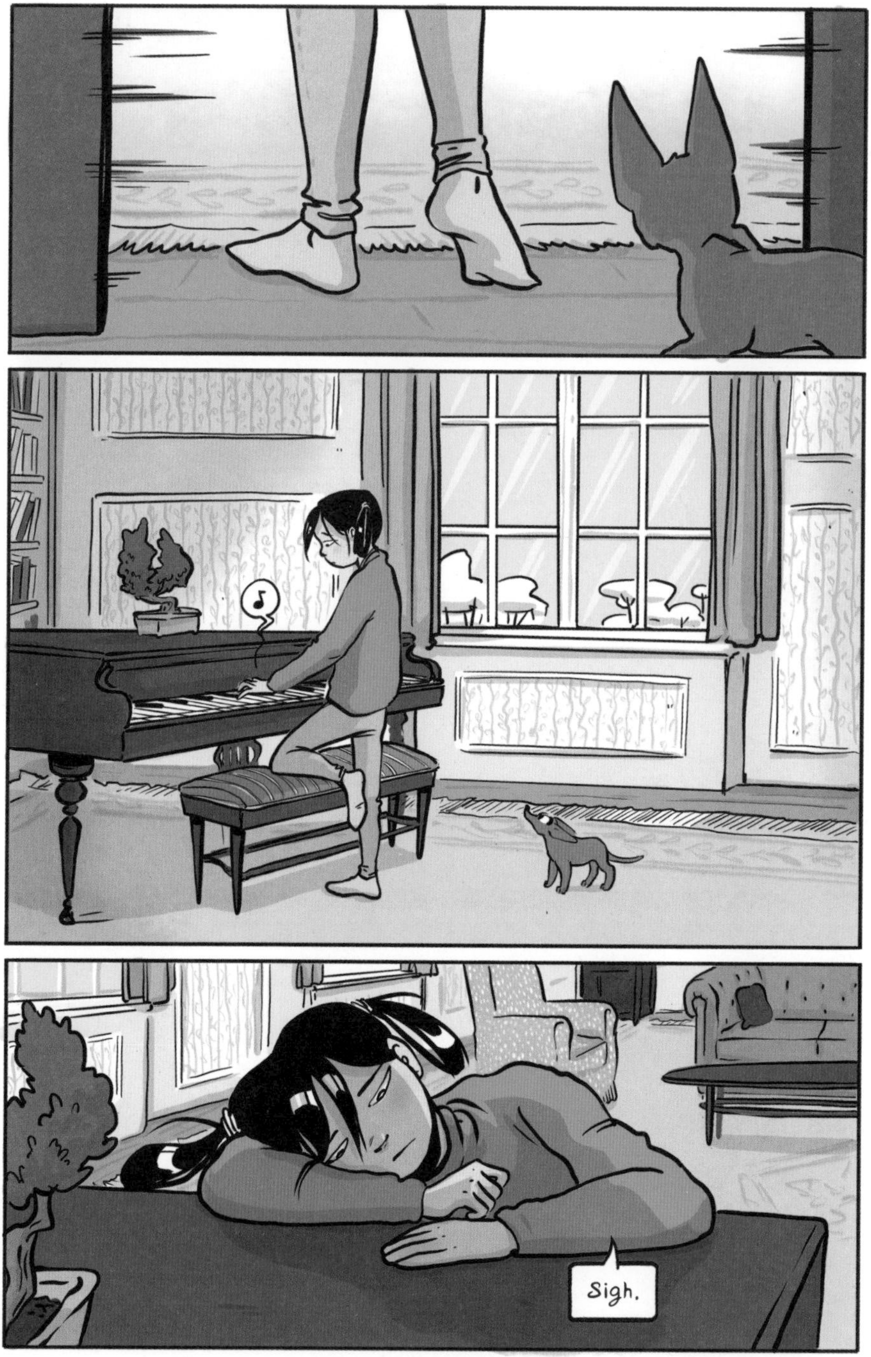
Sigh.

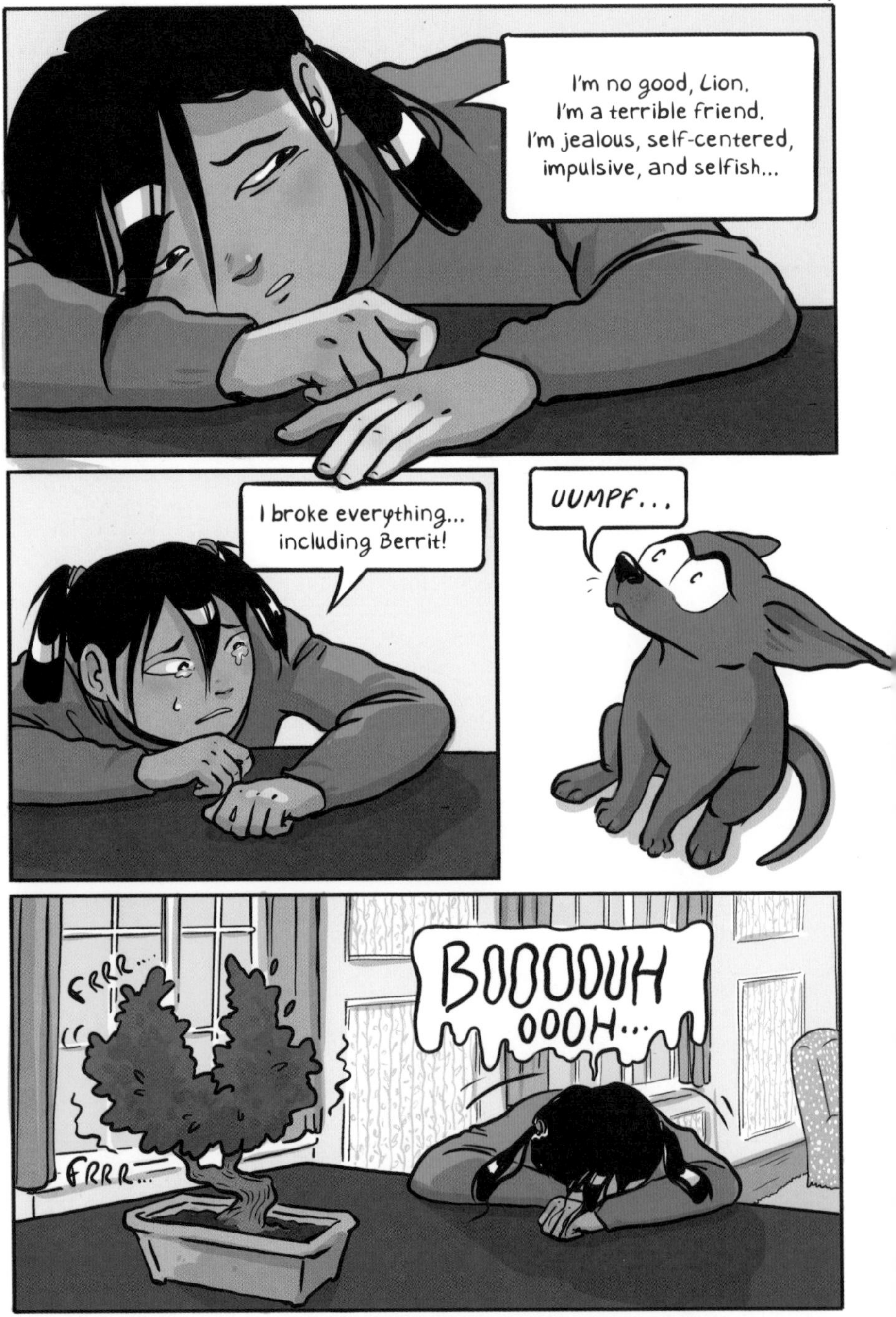

I'm no good, Lion.
I'm a terrible friend.
I'm jealous, self-centered,
impulsive, and selfish...
I broke everything...
including Berrit!
UUMPF...
FRRR...
BOOOOUH
OOOH...
FRRR...

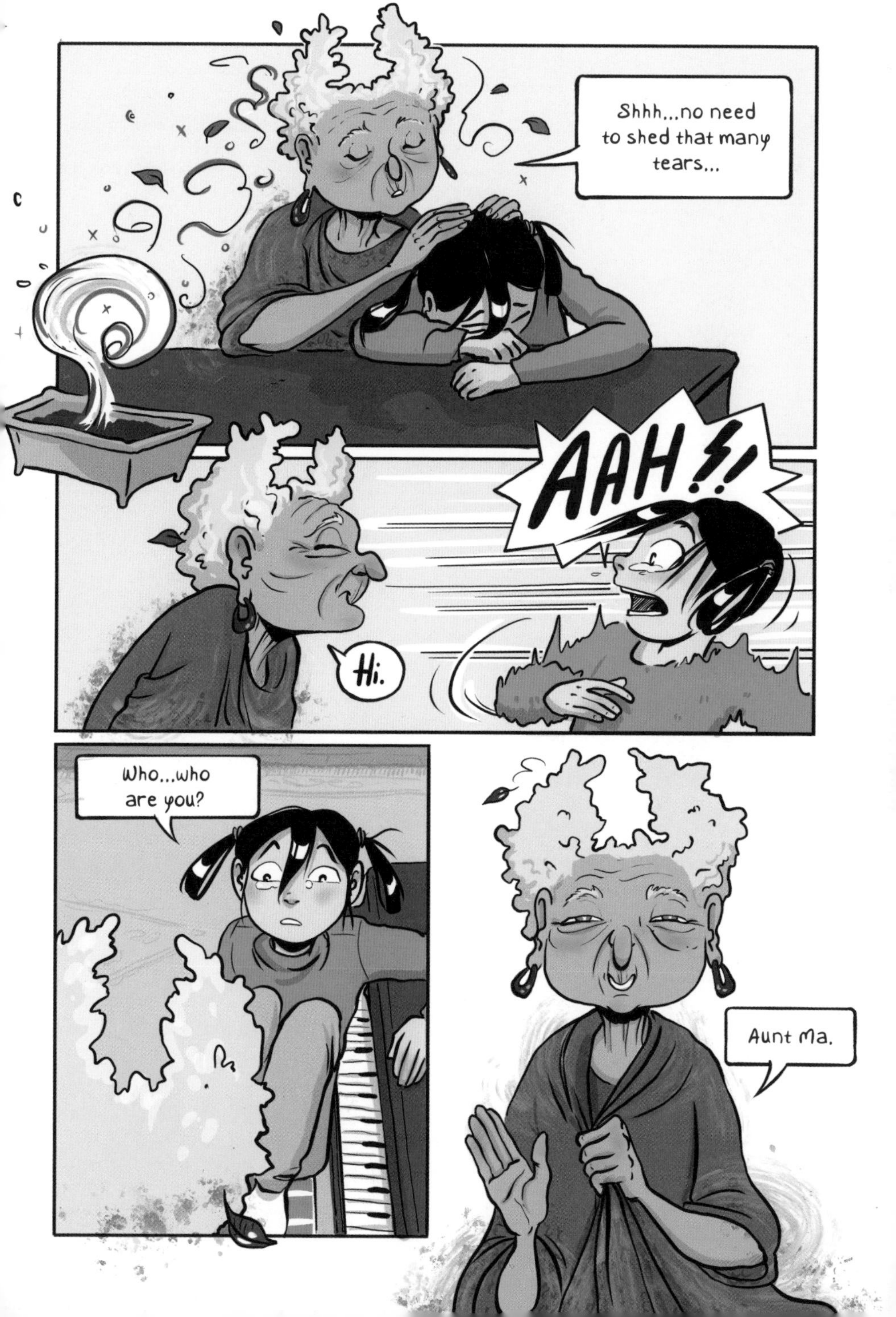
Shhh...no need to shed that many tears...
AAH!!
Hi.
Who...who are you?
Aunt Ma.

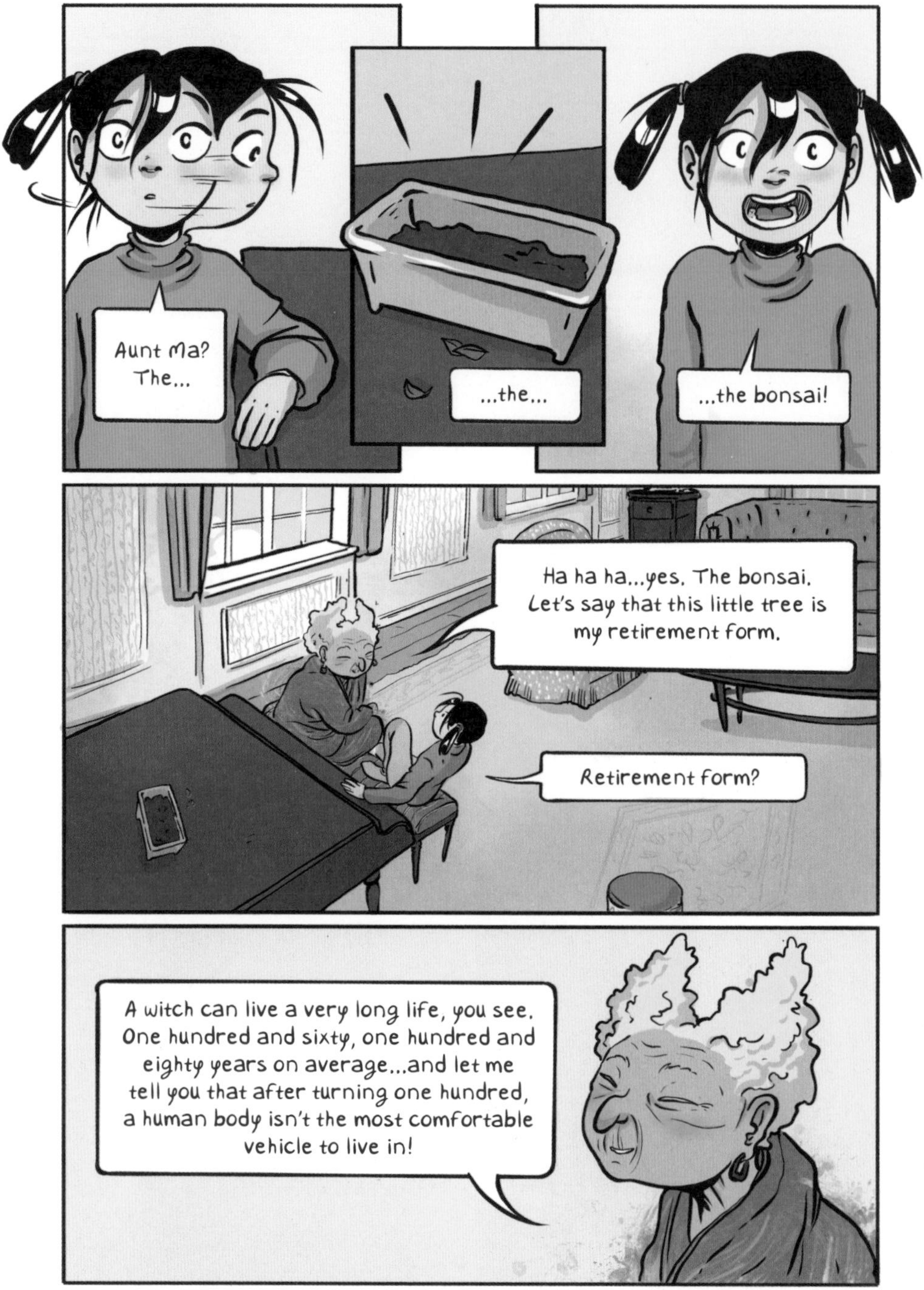
Aunt Ma? The...
...the...
...the bonsai!
Ha ha ha...yes. The bonsai. Let's say that this little tree is my retirement form.
Retirement form?
A witch can live a very long life, you see. One hundred and sixty, one hundred and eighty years on average...and let me tell you that after turning one hundred, a human body isn't the most comfortable vehicle to live in!

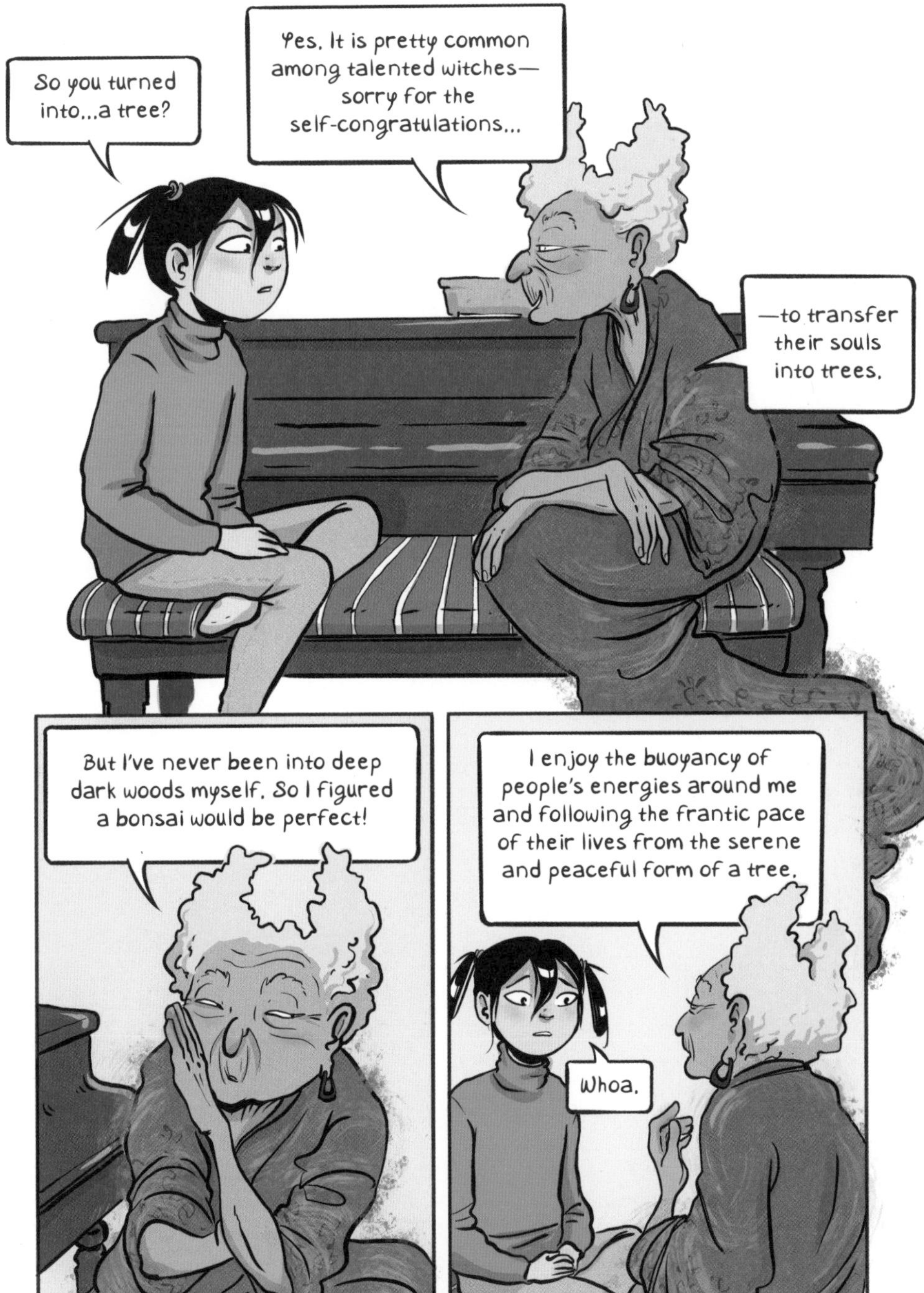
So you turned into...a tree?
Yes. It is pretty common among talented witches—sorry for the self-congratulations...
—to transfer their souls into trees.
But I've never been into deep dark woods myself. So I figured a bonsai would be perfect!
I enjoy the buoyancy of people's energies around me and following the frantic pace of their lives from the serene and peaceful form of a tree.
Whoa.

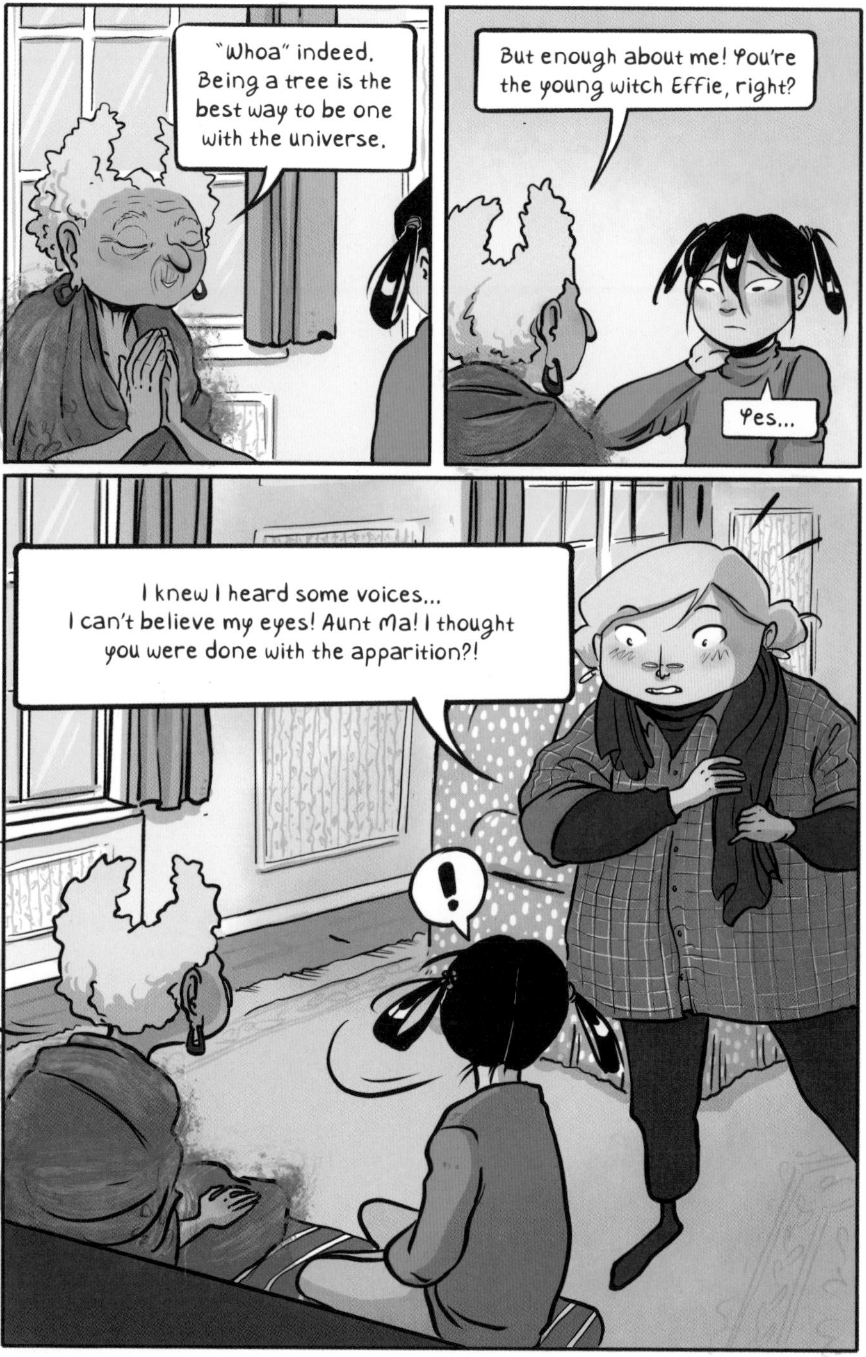
"Whoa" indeed. Being a tree is the best way to be one with the universe.
But enough about me! You're the young witch Effie, right?
Yes...
I knew I heard some voices... I can't believe my eyes! Aunt Ma! I thought you were done with the apparition?!
!

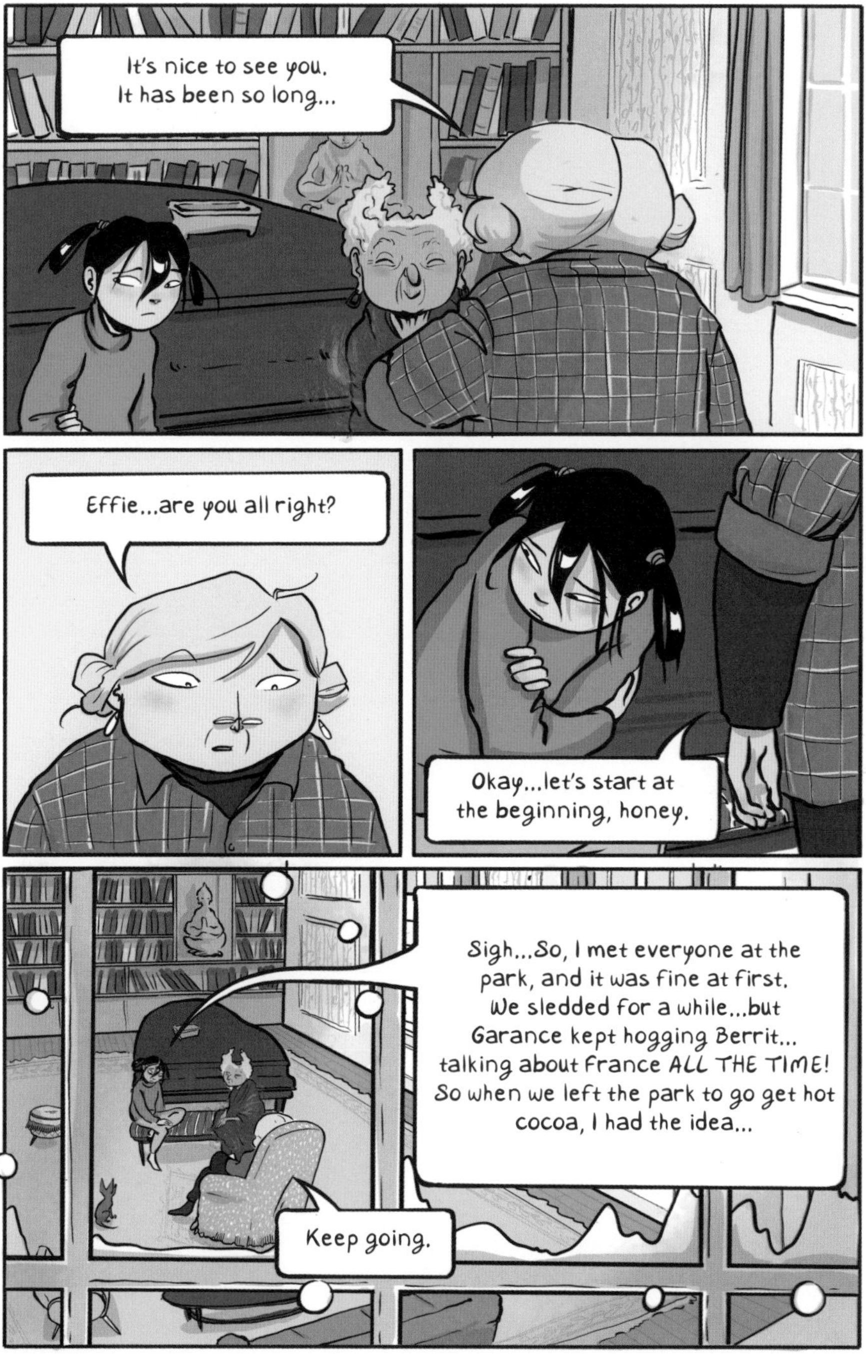
It's nice to see you. It has been so long...
Effie...are you all right?
Okay...let's start at the beginning, honey.
Sigh...So, I met everyone at the park, and it was fine at first. We sledded for a while...but Garance kept hogging Berrit... talking about France ALL THE TIME! So when we left the park to go get hot cocoa, I had the idea...
Keep going.

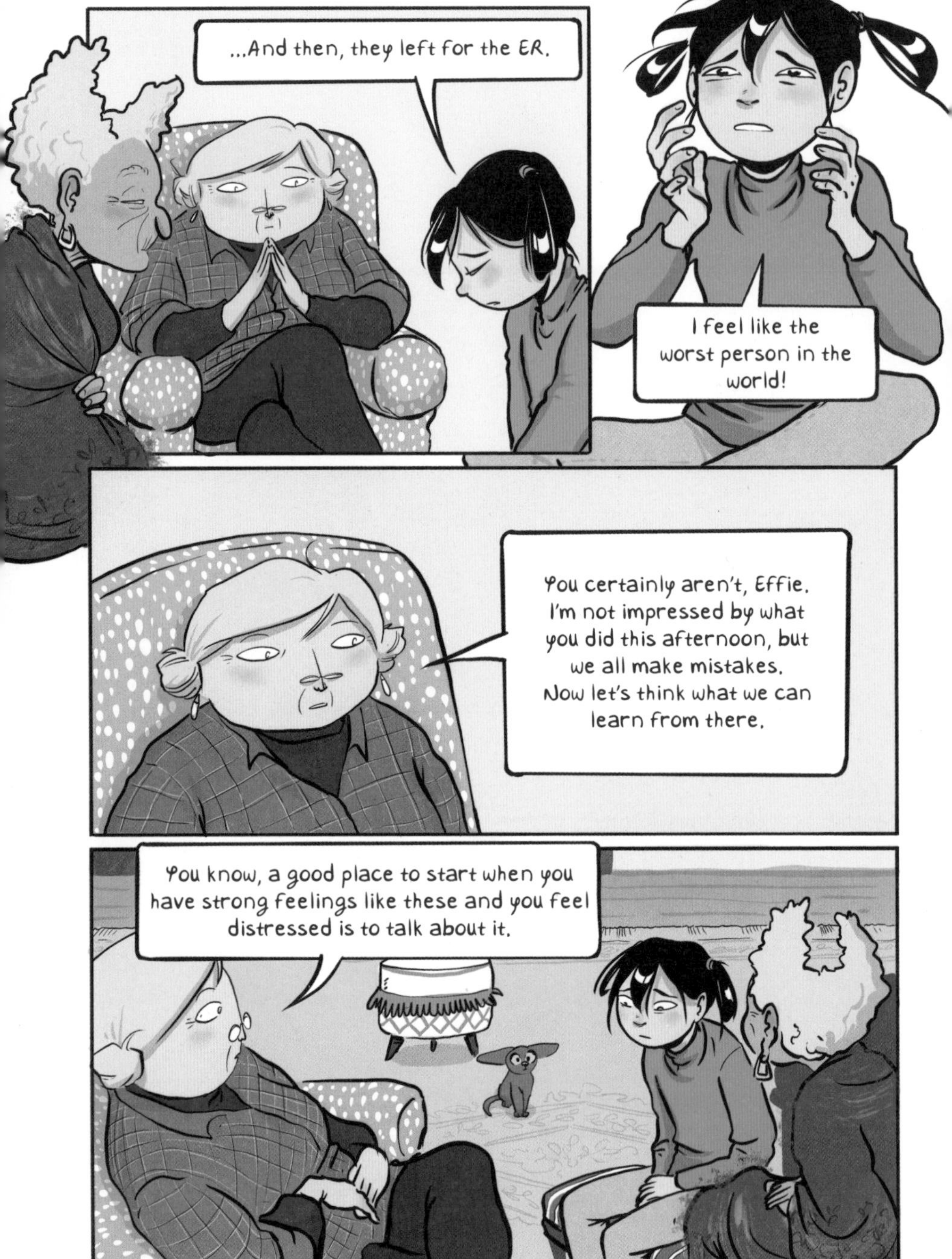
...And then, they left for the ER.
I feel like the worst person in the world!
You certainly aren't, Effie. I'm not impressed by what you did this afternoon, but we all make mistakes. Now let's think what we can learn from there.
You know, a good place to start when you have strong feelings like these and you feel distressed is to talk about it.

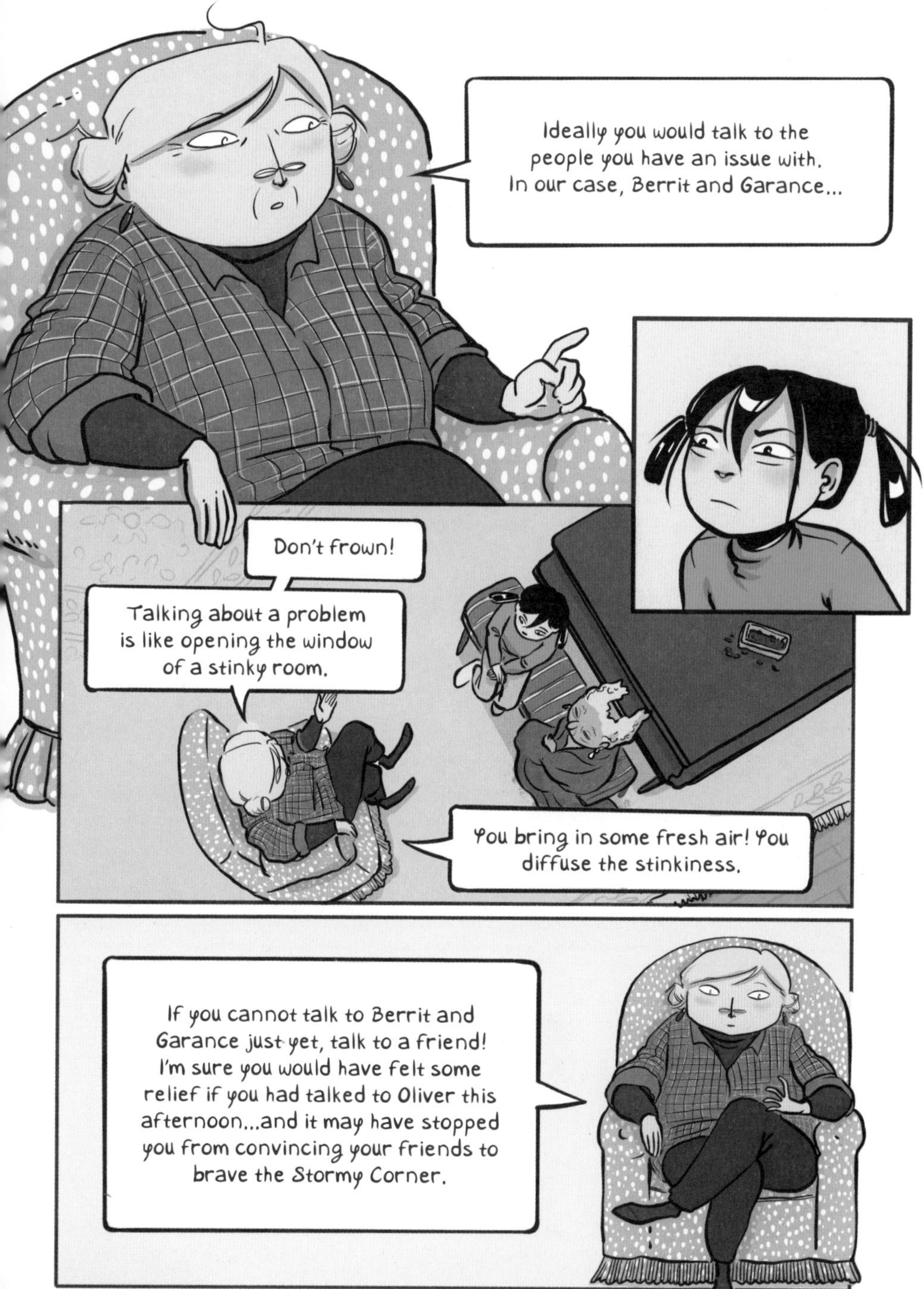
Ideally you would talk to the people you have an issue with. In our case, Berrit and Garance...
Don't frown!
Talking about a problem is like opening the window of a stinky room.
You bring in some fresh air! You diffuse the stinkiness.
If you cannot talk to Berrit and Garance just yet, talk to a friend! I'm sure you would have felt some relief if you had talked to Oliver this afternoon...and it may have stopped you from convincing your friends to brave the Stormy Corner.

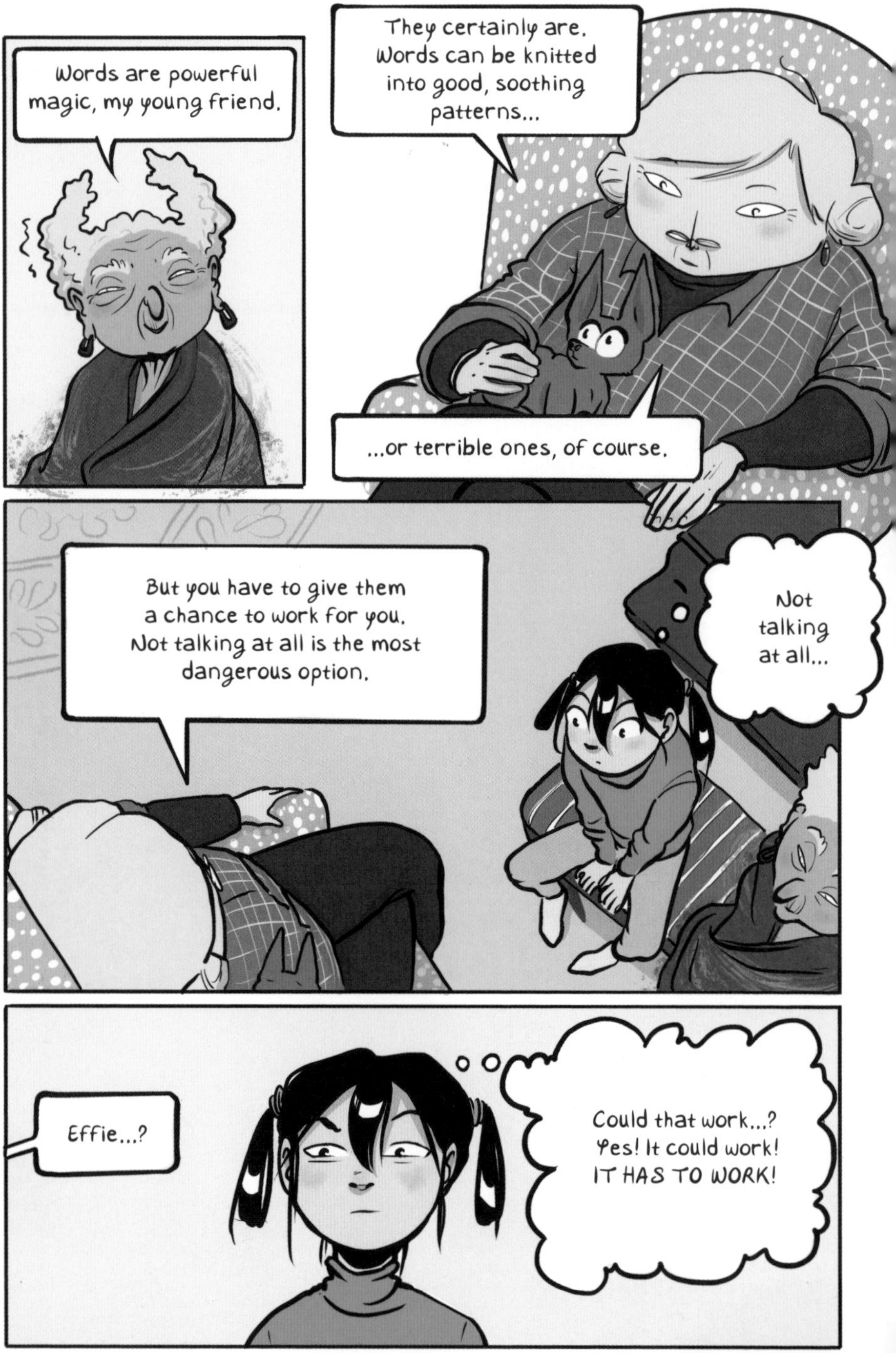
Words are powerful magic, my young friend.
They certainly are. Words can be knitted into good, soothing patterns...
...or terrible ones, of course.
But you have to give them a chance to work for you. Not talking at all is the most dangerous option.
Not talking at all...
Effie...?
Could that work...? Yes! It could work! IT HAS TO WORK!

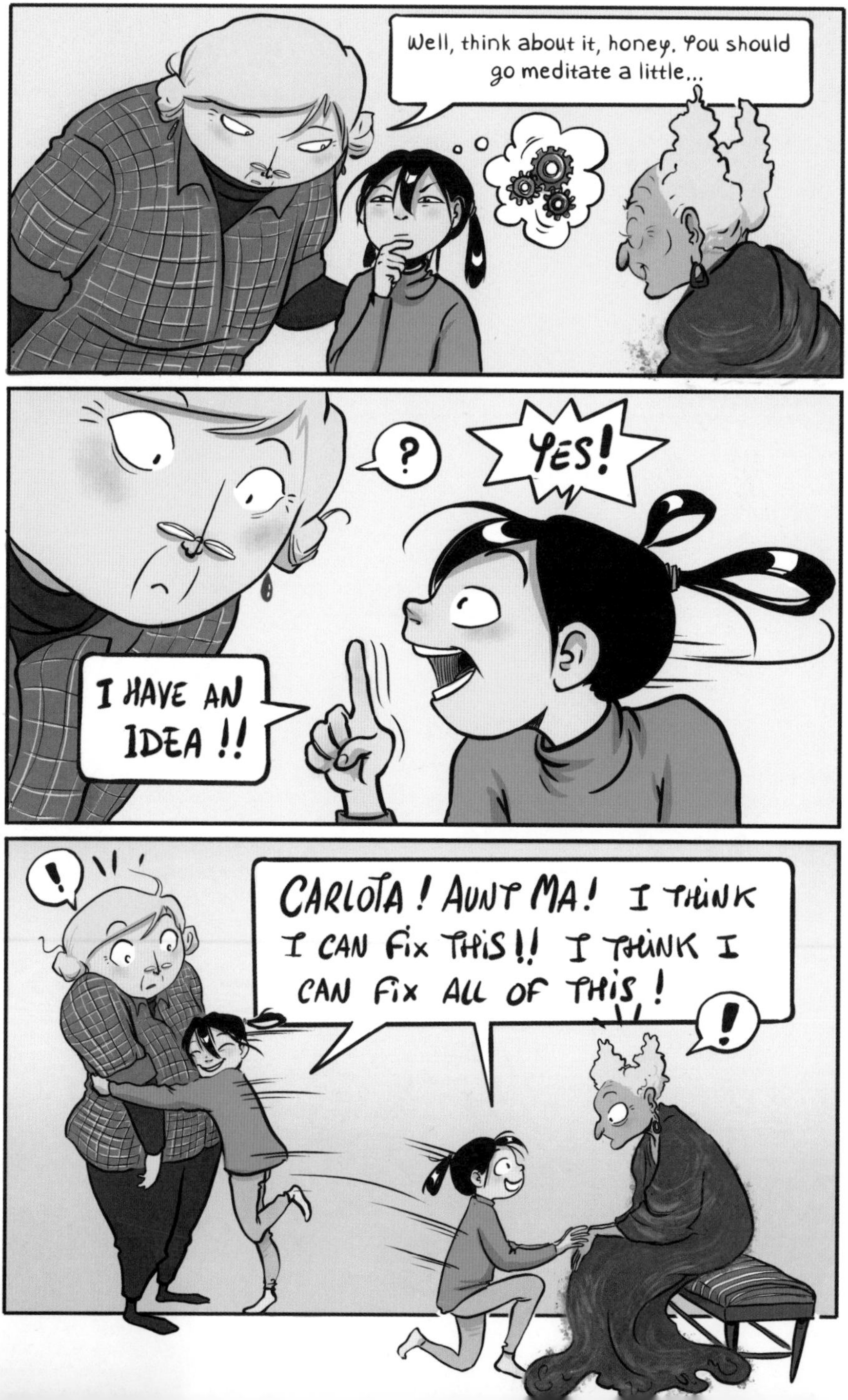

Well, think about it, honey. You should go meditate a little...
?
YES!
I HAVE AN IDEA !!
!
CARLOTA! AUNT MA! I THINK I CAN FIX THIS!! I THINK I CAN FIX ALL OF THIS!
!

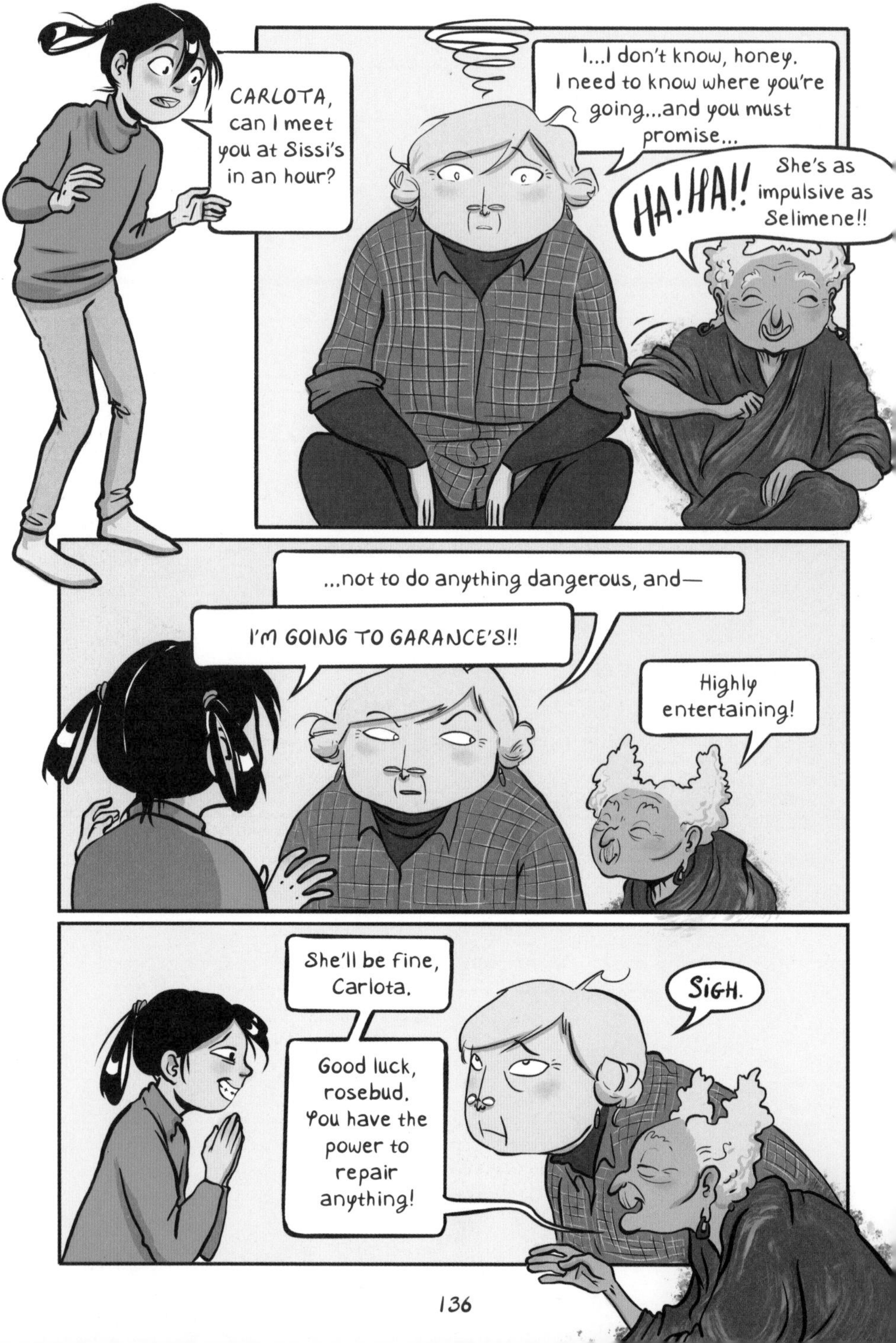
CARLOTA, can I meet you at Sissi's in an hour?
I...I don't know, honey. I need to know where you're going...and you must promise...
HA!HA!! She's as impulsive as Selimene!!
...not to do anything dangerous, and—
I'M GOING TO GARANCE'S!!
Highly entertaining!
She'll be fine, Carlota.
Good luck, rosebud. You have the power to repair anything!
SIGH.

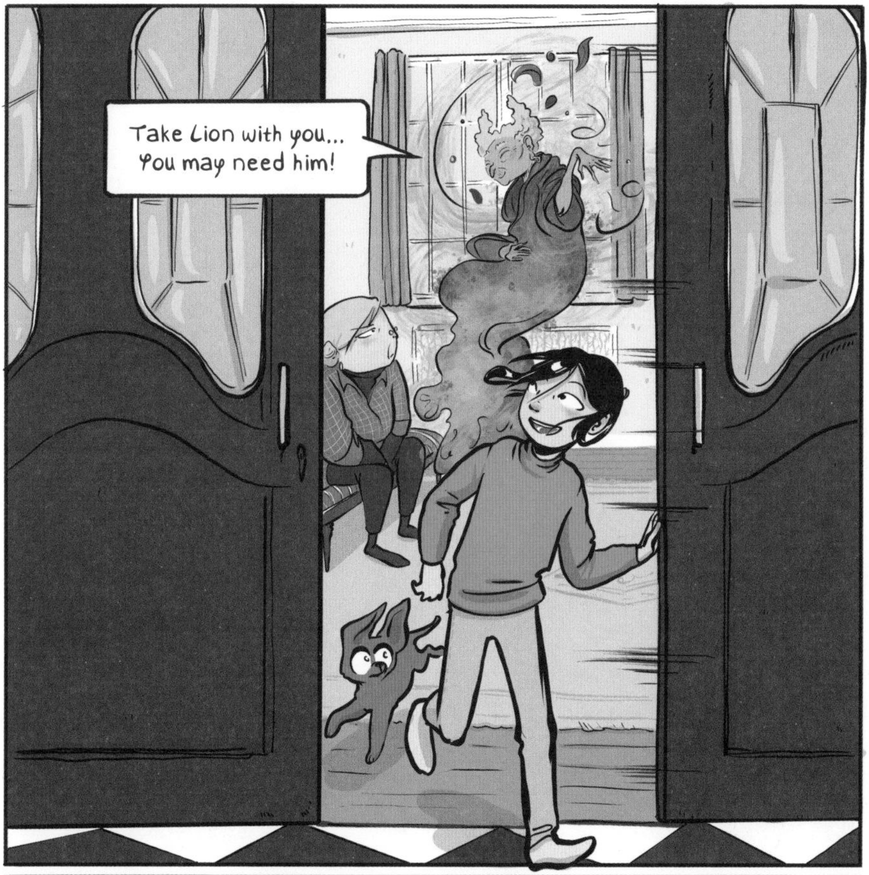
Take Lion with you...
You may need him!

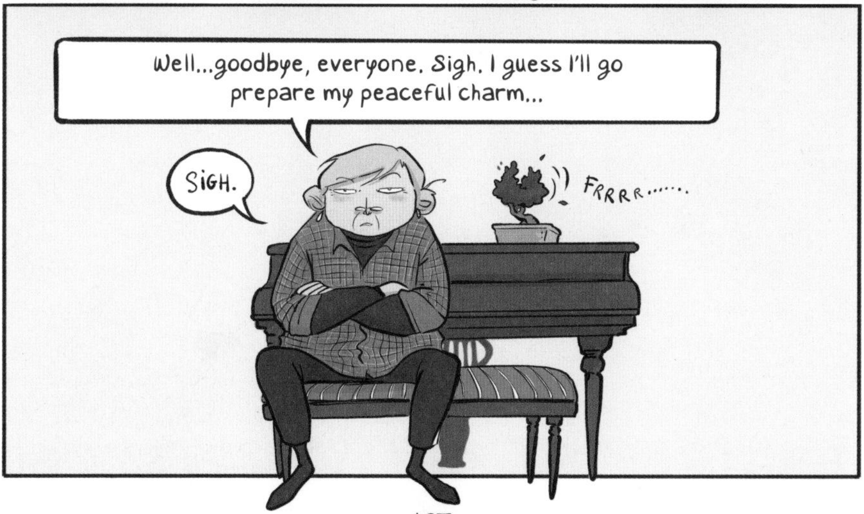
Well...goodbye, everyone. Sigh. I guess I'll go prepare my peaceful charm...
SIGH.
FRRRR......

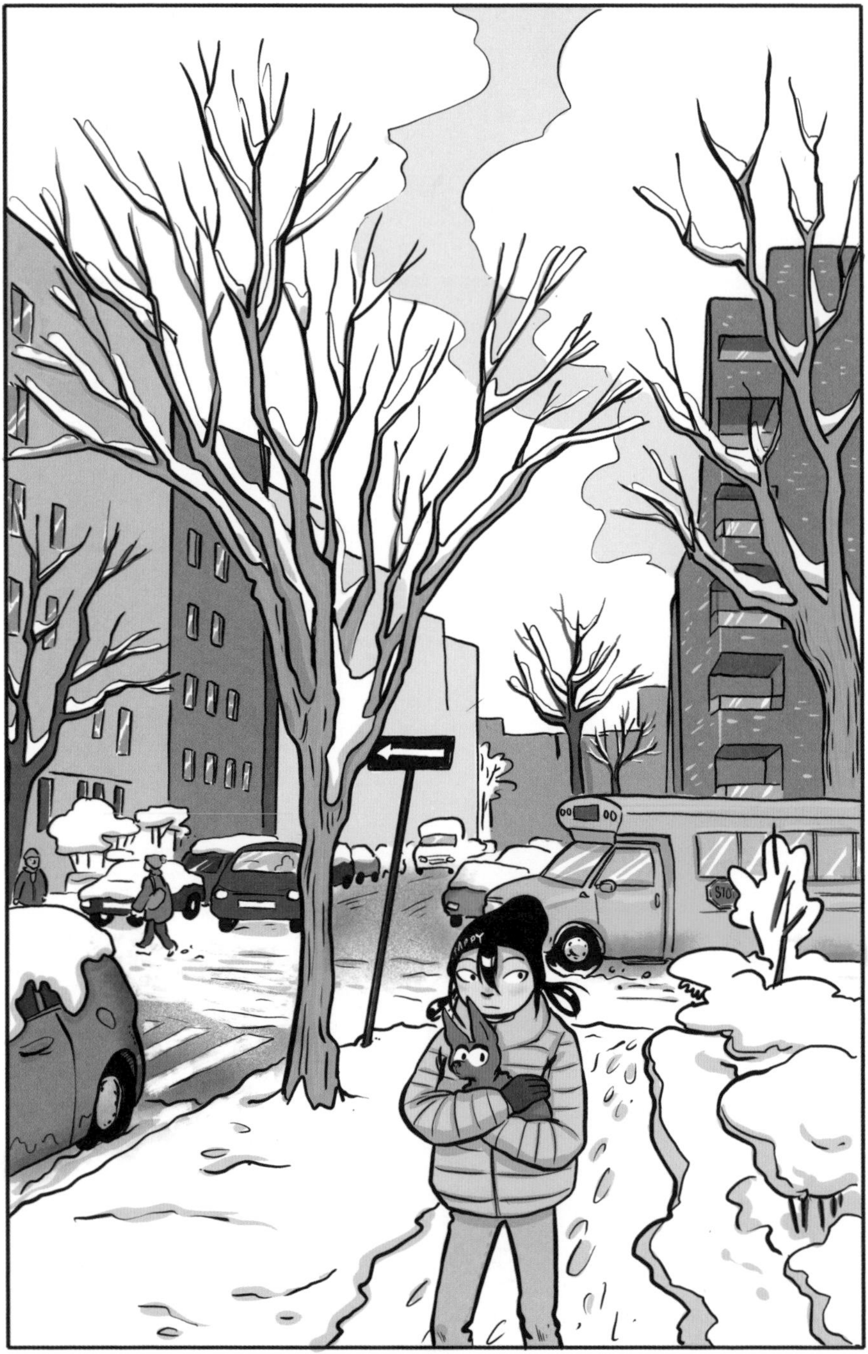

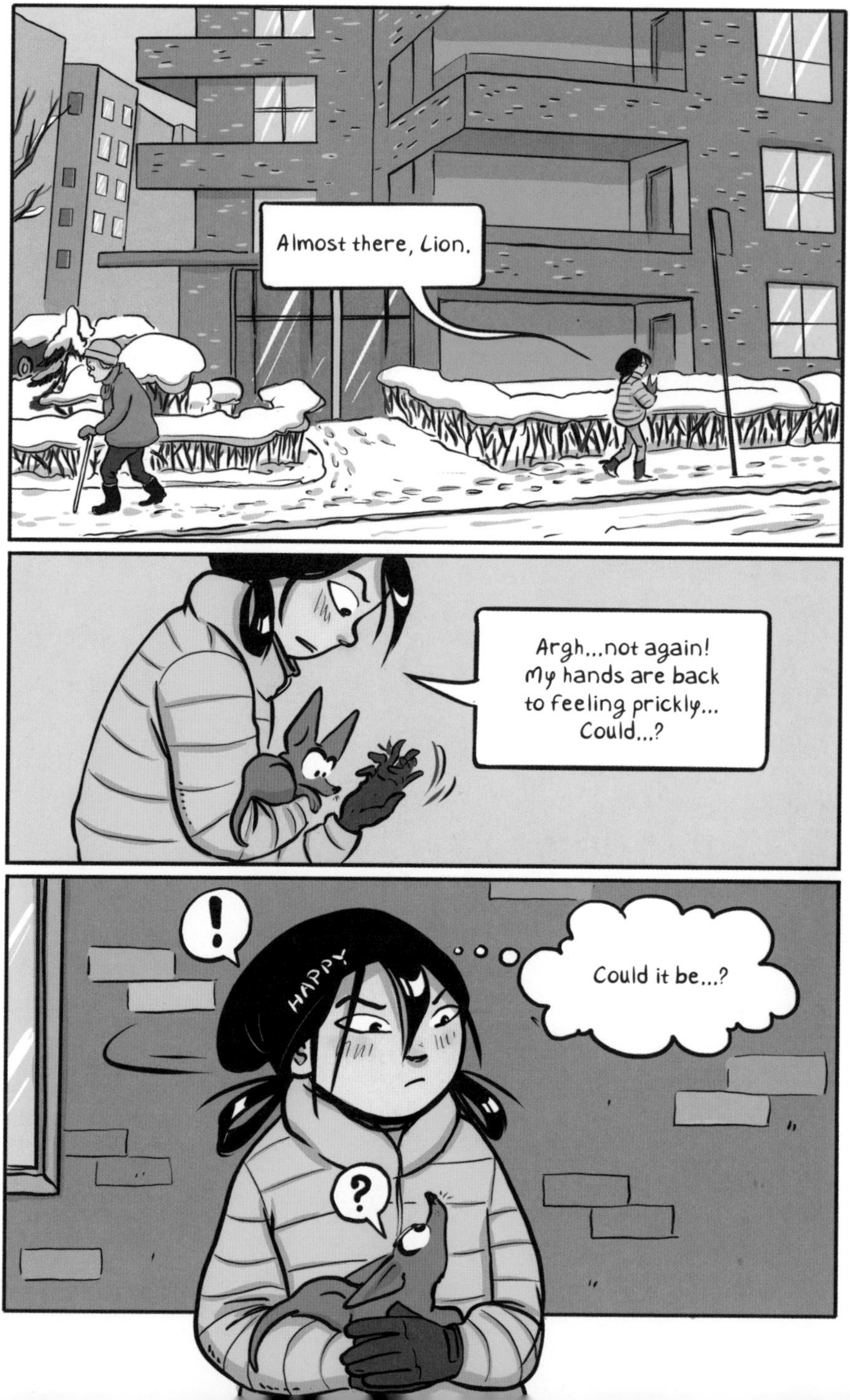
Almost there, Lion.
Argh...not again! My hands are back to feeling prickly... Could...?
!
Could it be...?
HAPPY
?

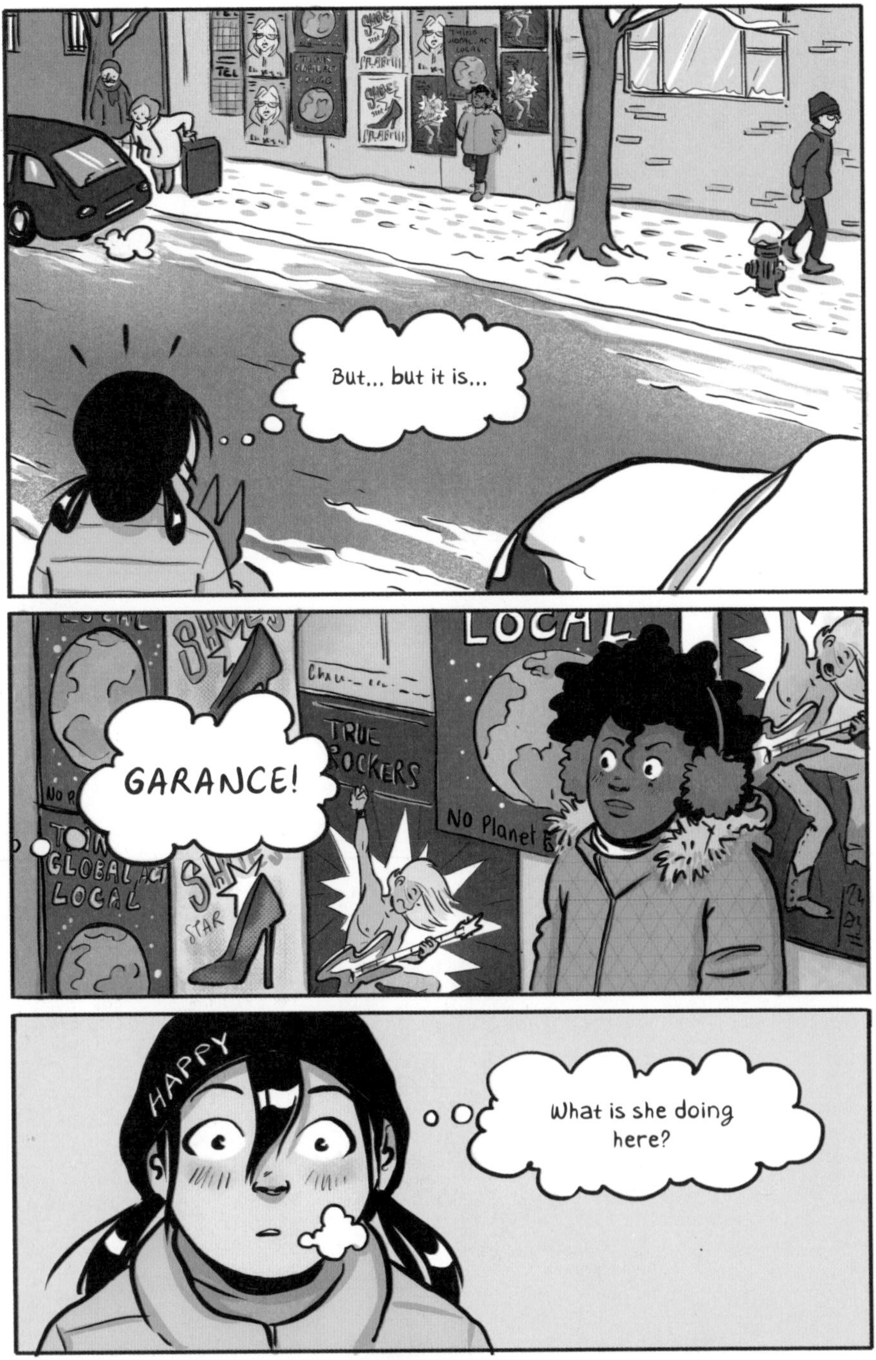
But... but it is...
GARANCE!
TRUE ROCKERS
LOCAL
No Planet
STAR
HAPPY
What is she doing here?

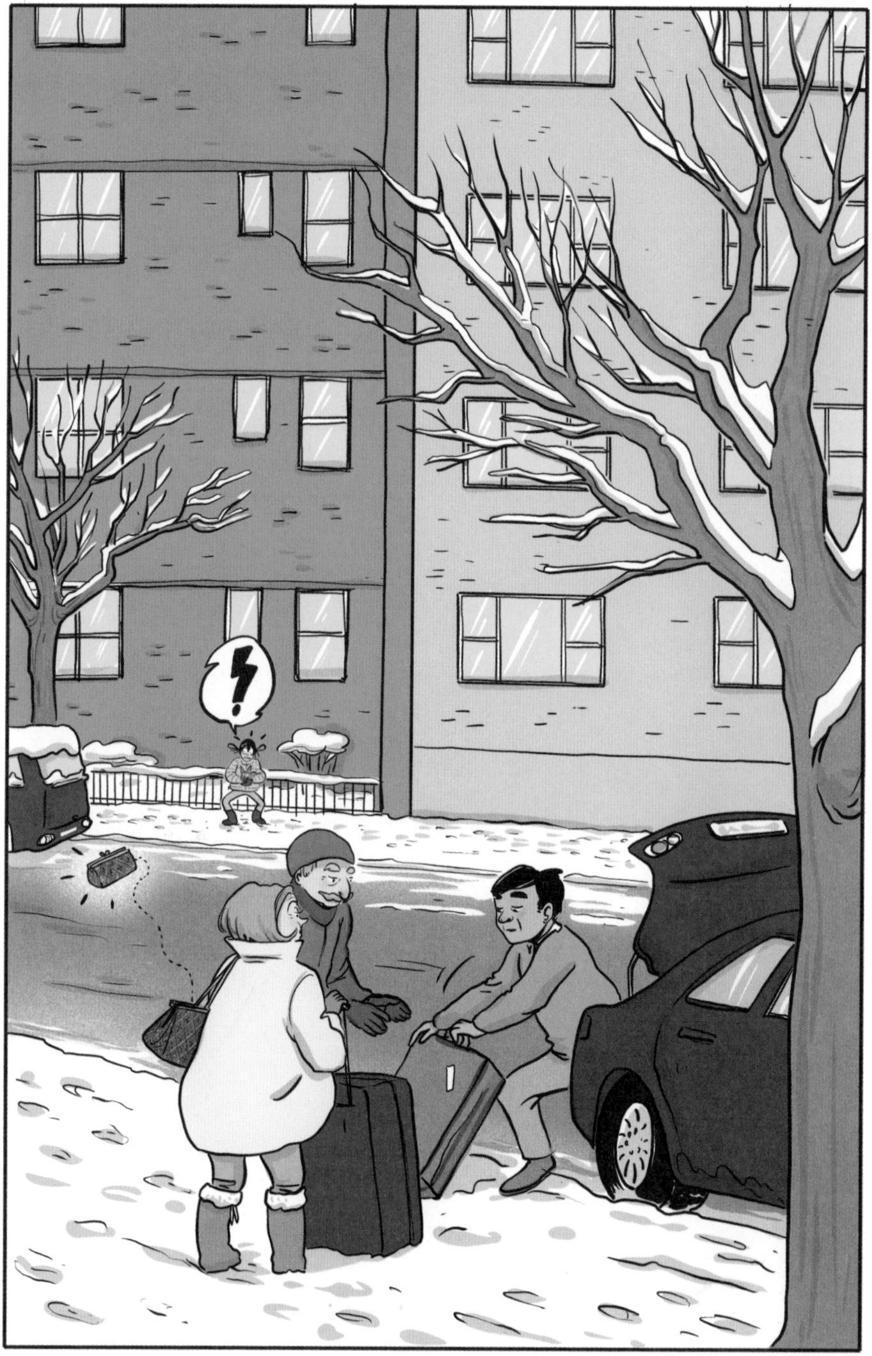

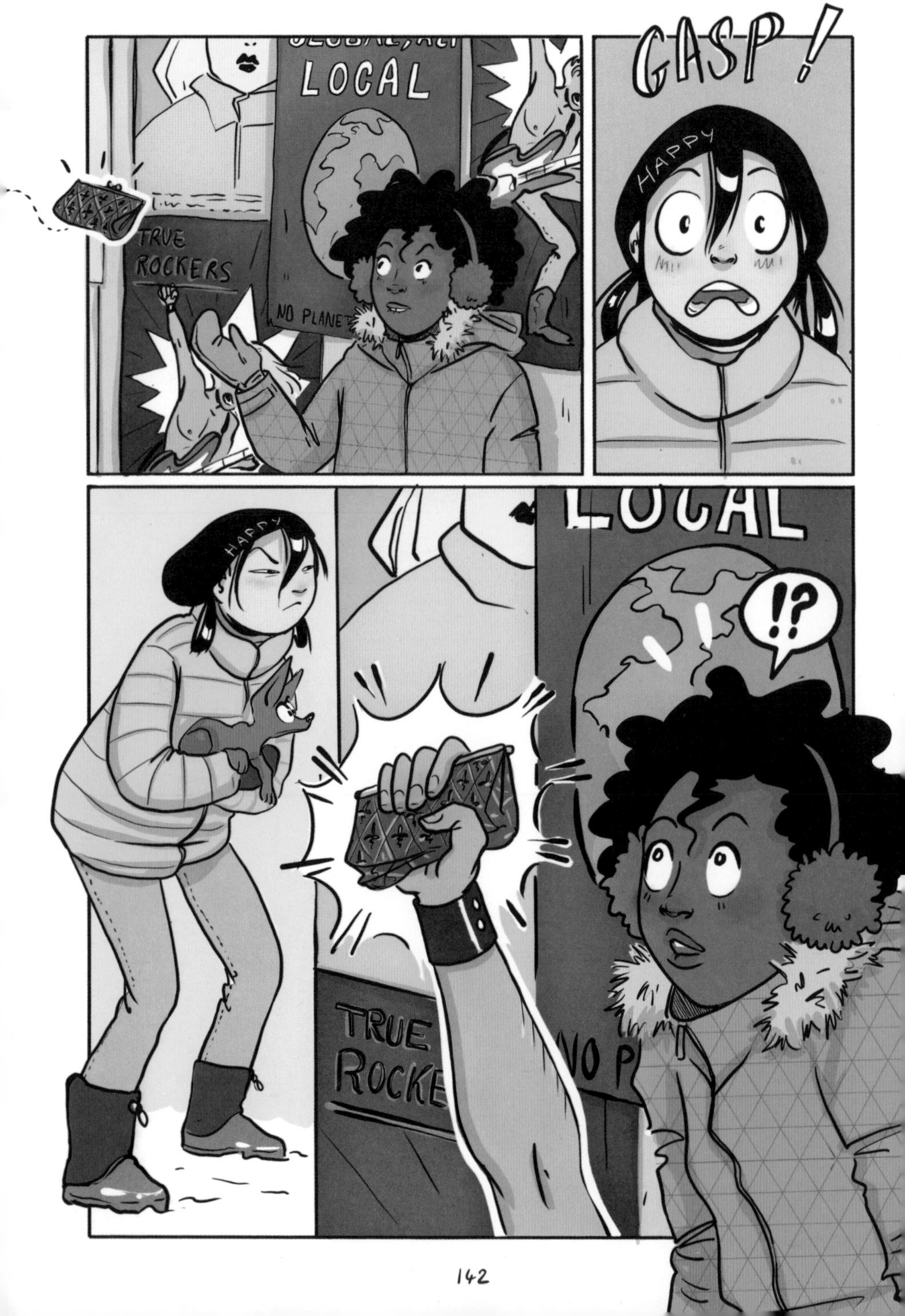
LOCAL
TRUE
ROCKERS
NO PLANET
GASP!
HAPPY
HAPPY
LOCAL
!?
TRUE
ROCKE
NO P

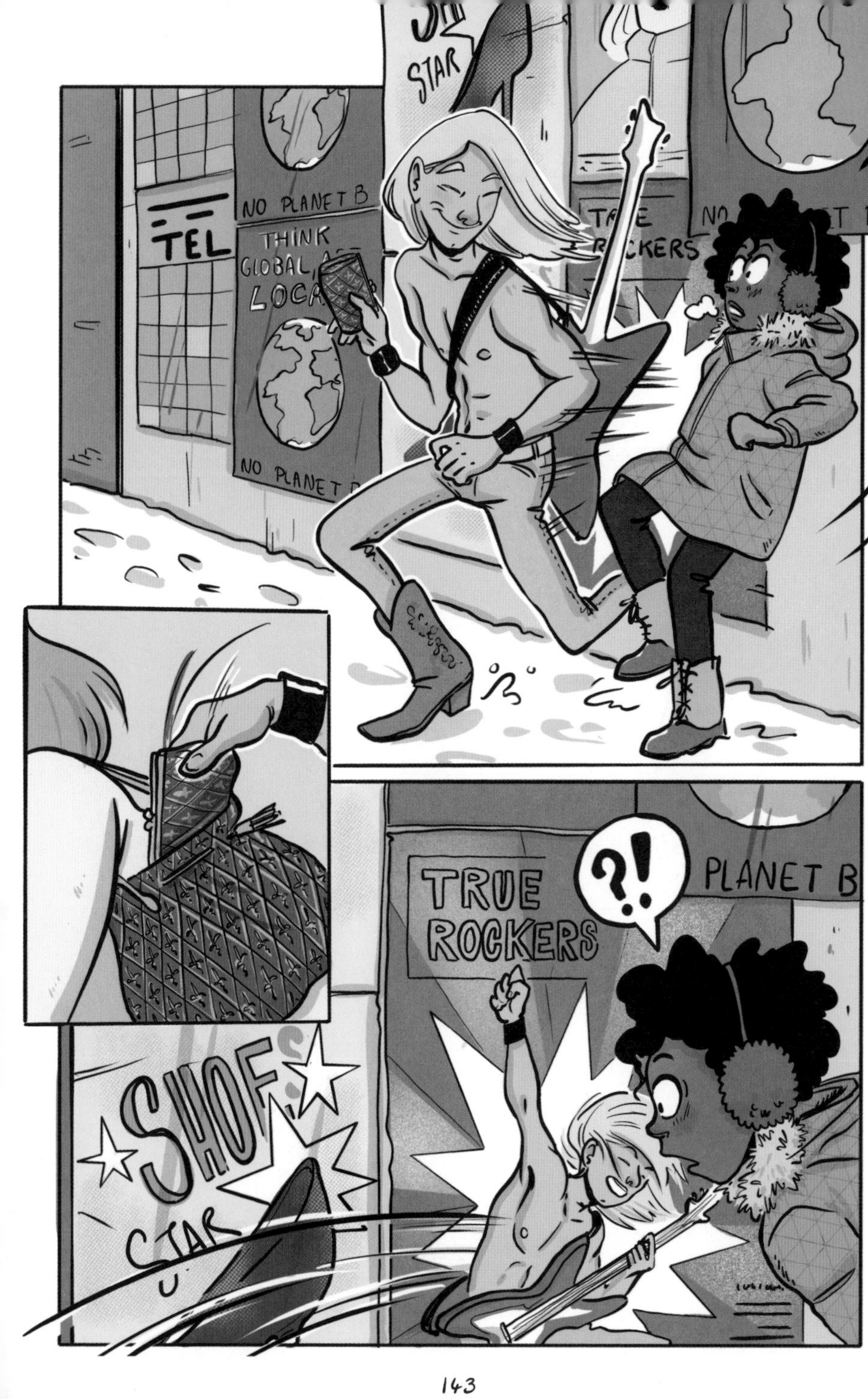
STAR
NO PLANET B
TEL
THINK GLOBAL,
NO PLANET B
TRUE ROCKERS
?!
PLANET B
SHOF

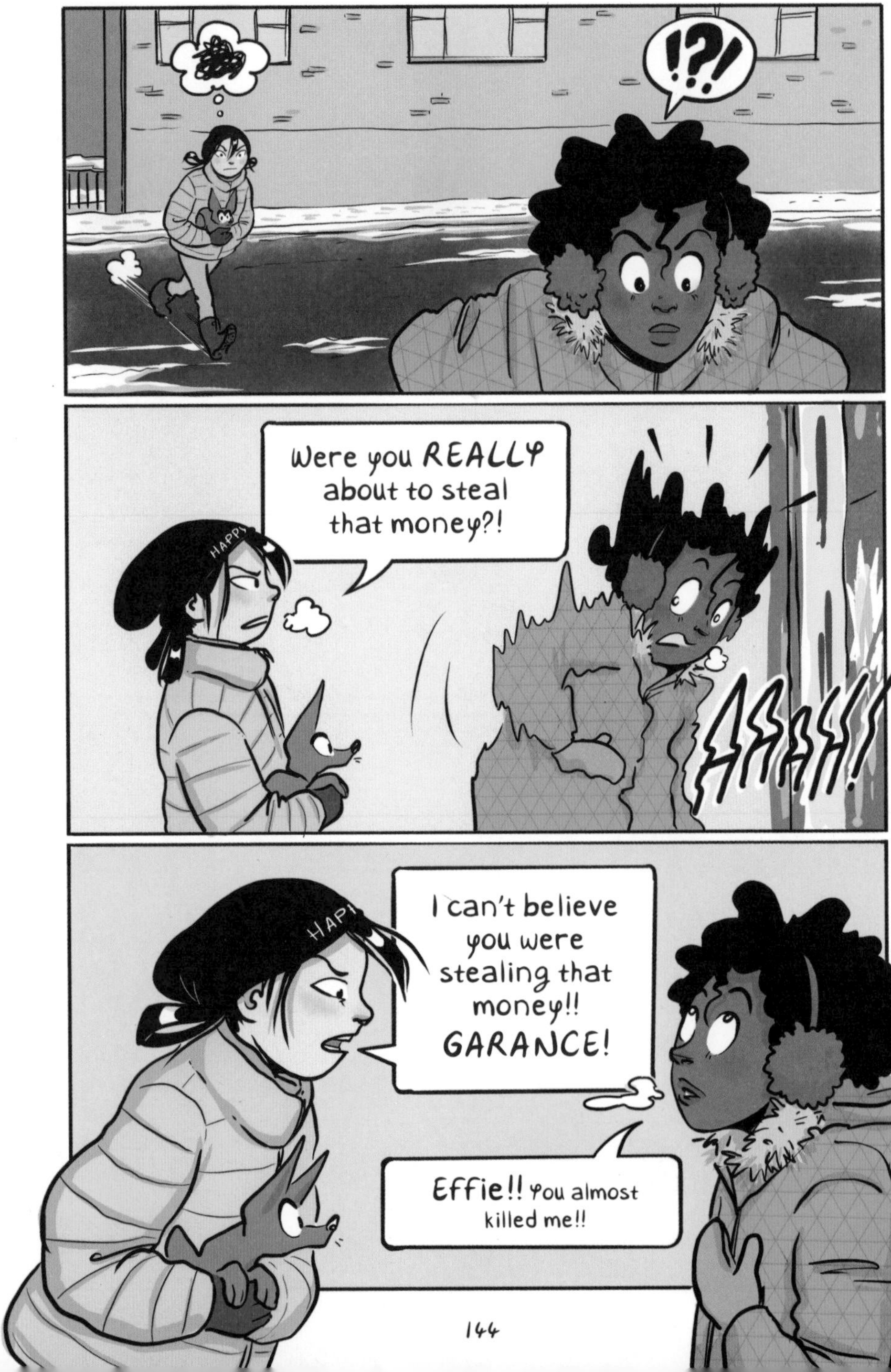
!?!
Were you REALLY about to steal that money?!
HAPPY
AAAH!!
I can't believe you were stealing that money!! GARANCE!
Effie!! You almost killed me!!

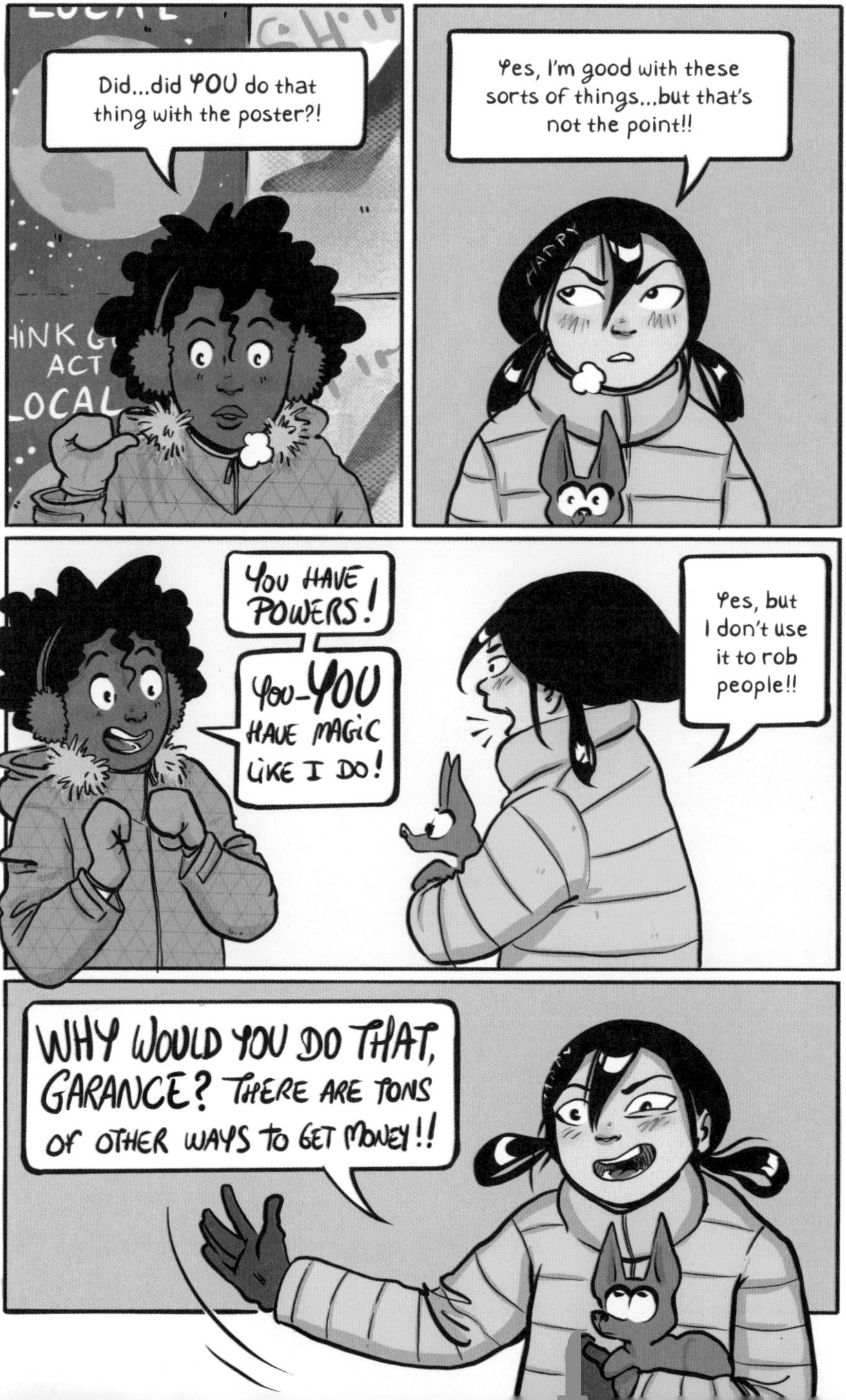
LOCAL
THINK G
ACT
LOCAL
Did...did YOU do that thing with the poster?!
Yes, I'm good with these sorts of things...but that's not the point!!
HAPPY
YOU HAVE POWERS!
YOU-YOU HAVE MAGIC LIKE I DO!
Yes, but I don't use it to rob people!!
WHY WOULD YOU DO THAT, GARANCE? THERE ARE TONS OF OTHER WAYS TO GET MONEY!!

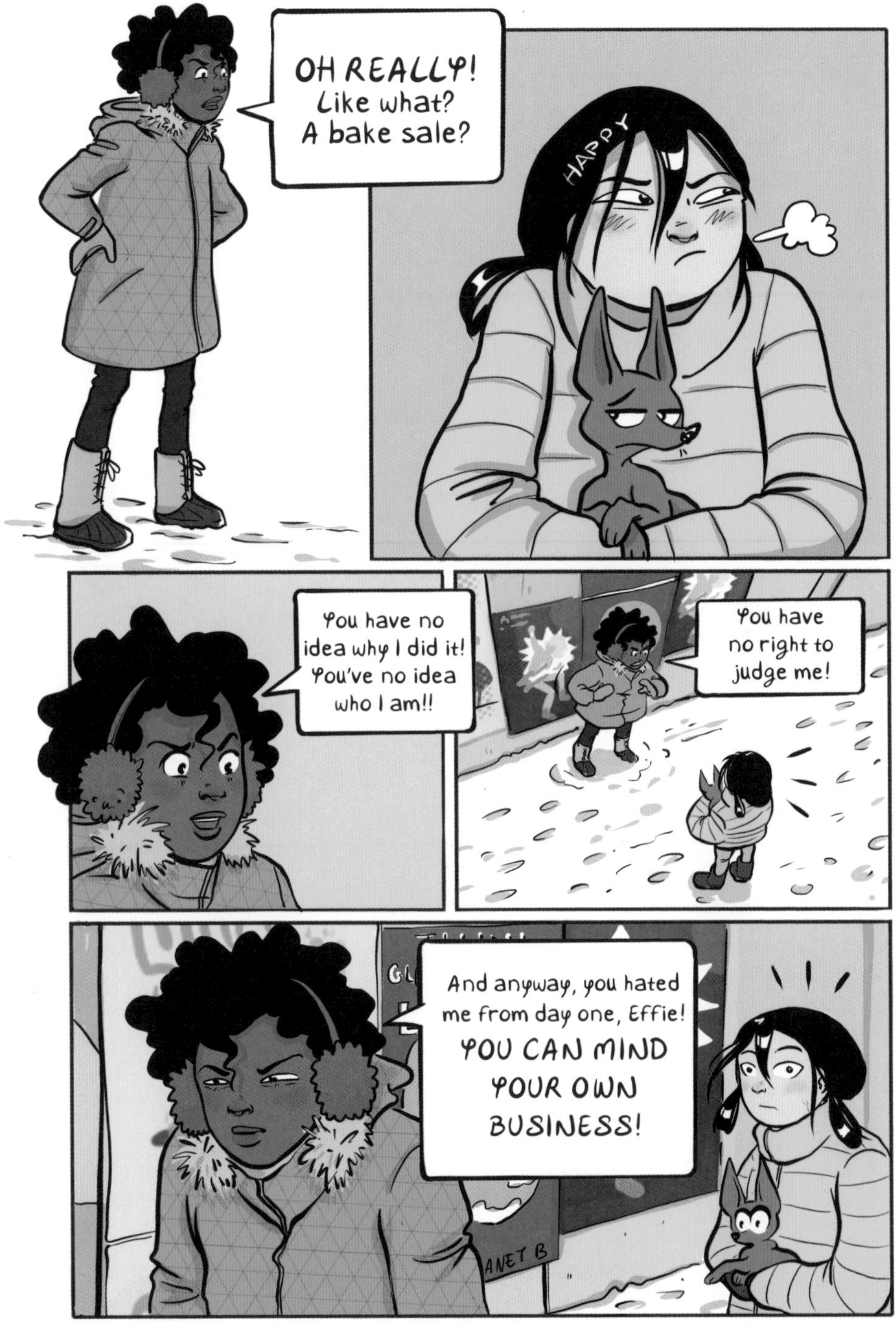
OH REALLY! Like what? A bake sale?
HAPPY
You have no idea why I did it! You've no idea who I am!!
You have no right to judge me!
And anyway, you hated me from day one, Effie! YOU CAN MIND YOUR OWN BUSINESS!
ANET B

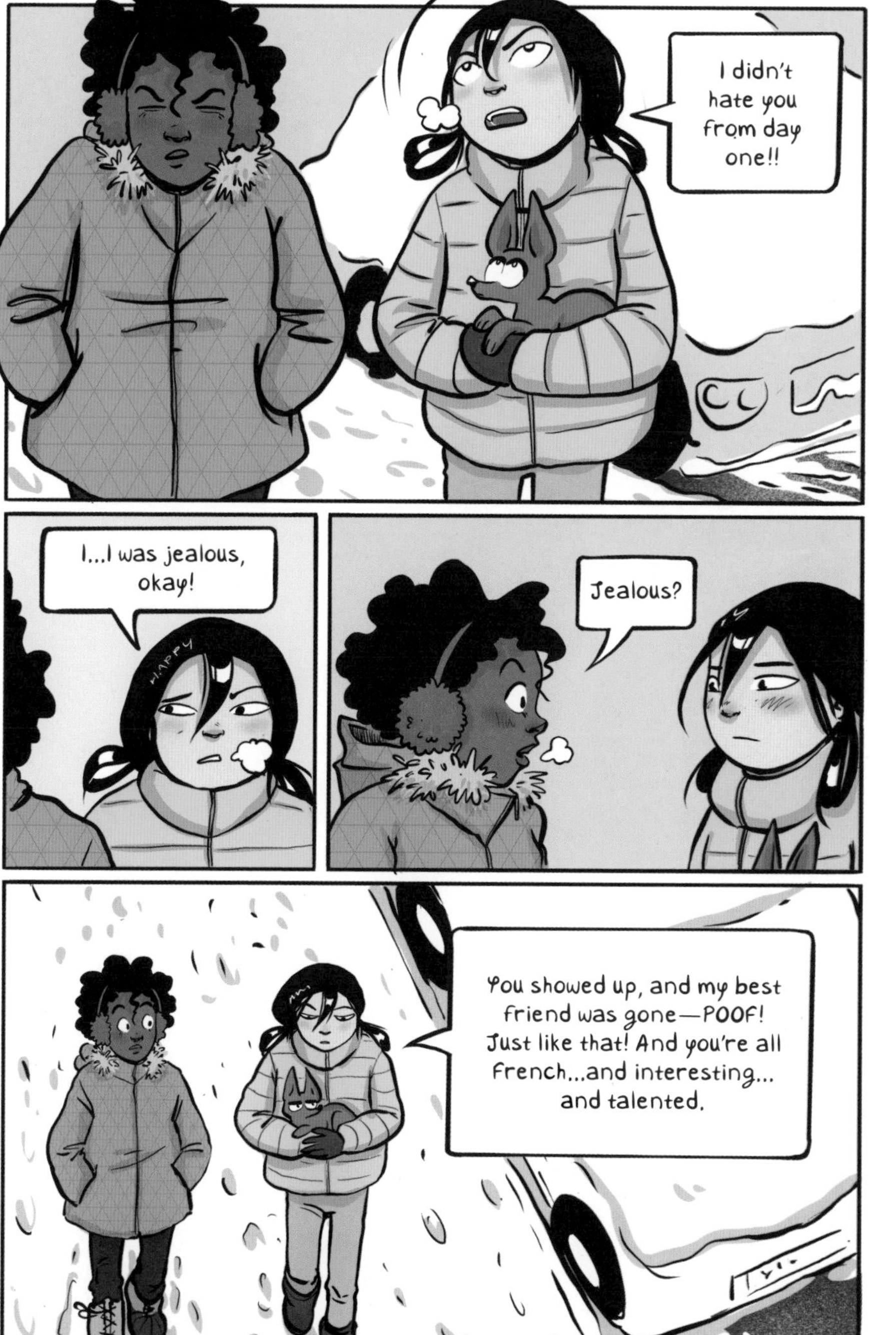
I didn't hate you from day one!!
I...I was jealous, okay!
Jealous?
You showed up, and my best friend was gone—POOF! Just like that! And you're all French...and interesting... and talented.

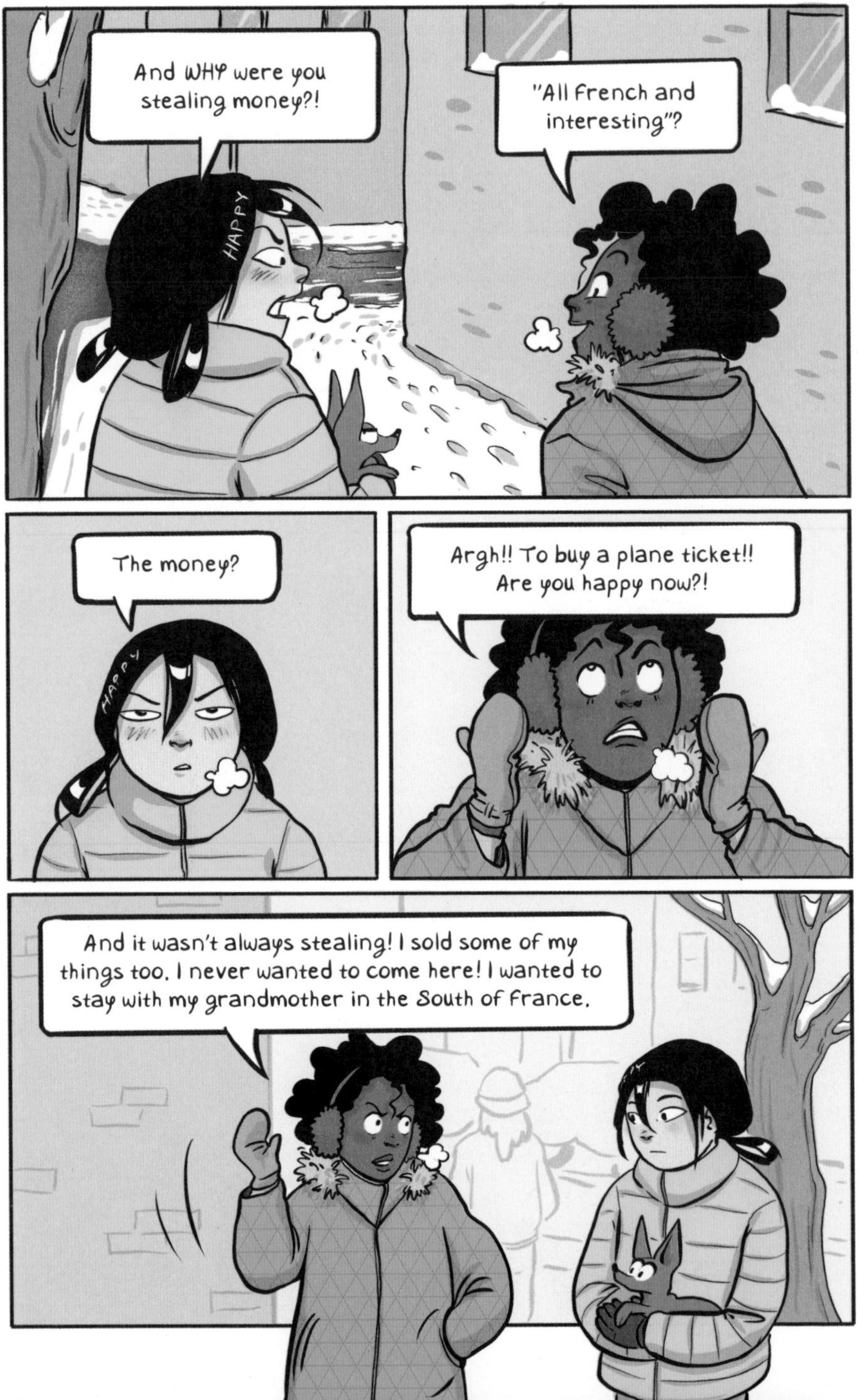
And WHY were you stealing money?!
"All french and interesting"?
The money?
Argh!! To buy a plane ticket!! Are you happy now?!
And it wasn't always stealing! I sold some of my things too. I never wanted to come here! I wanted to stay with my grandmother in the South of France.
HAPPY

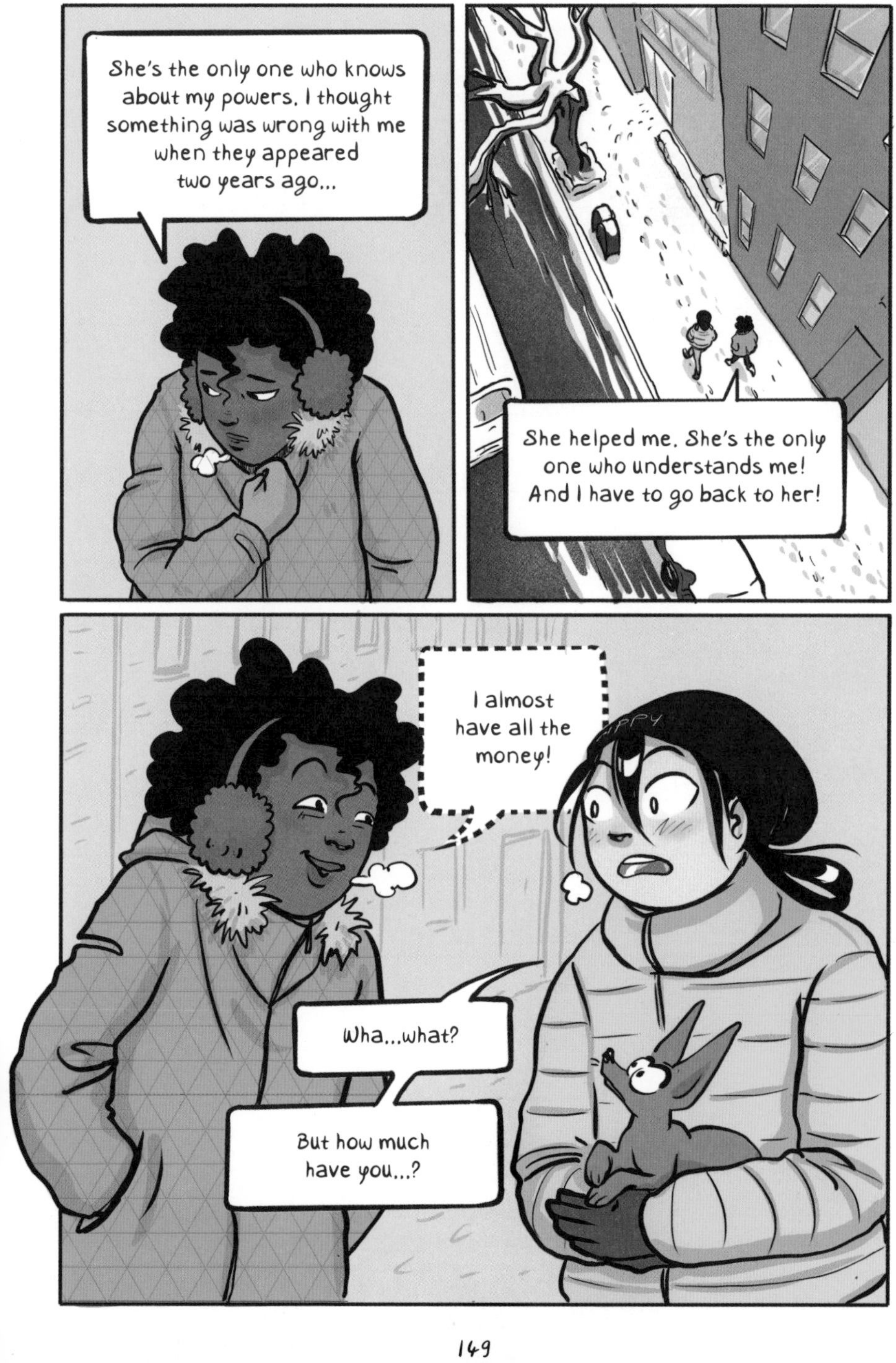
She's the only one who knows about my powers. I thought something was wrong with me when they appeared two years ago...
She helped me. She's the only one who understands me! And I have to go back to her!
I almost have all the money!
Wha...what?
But how much have you...?

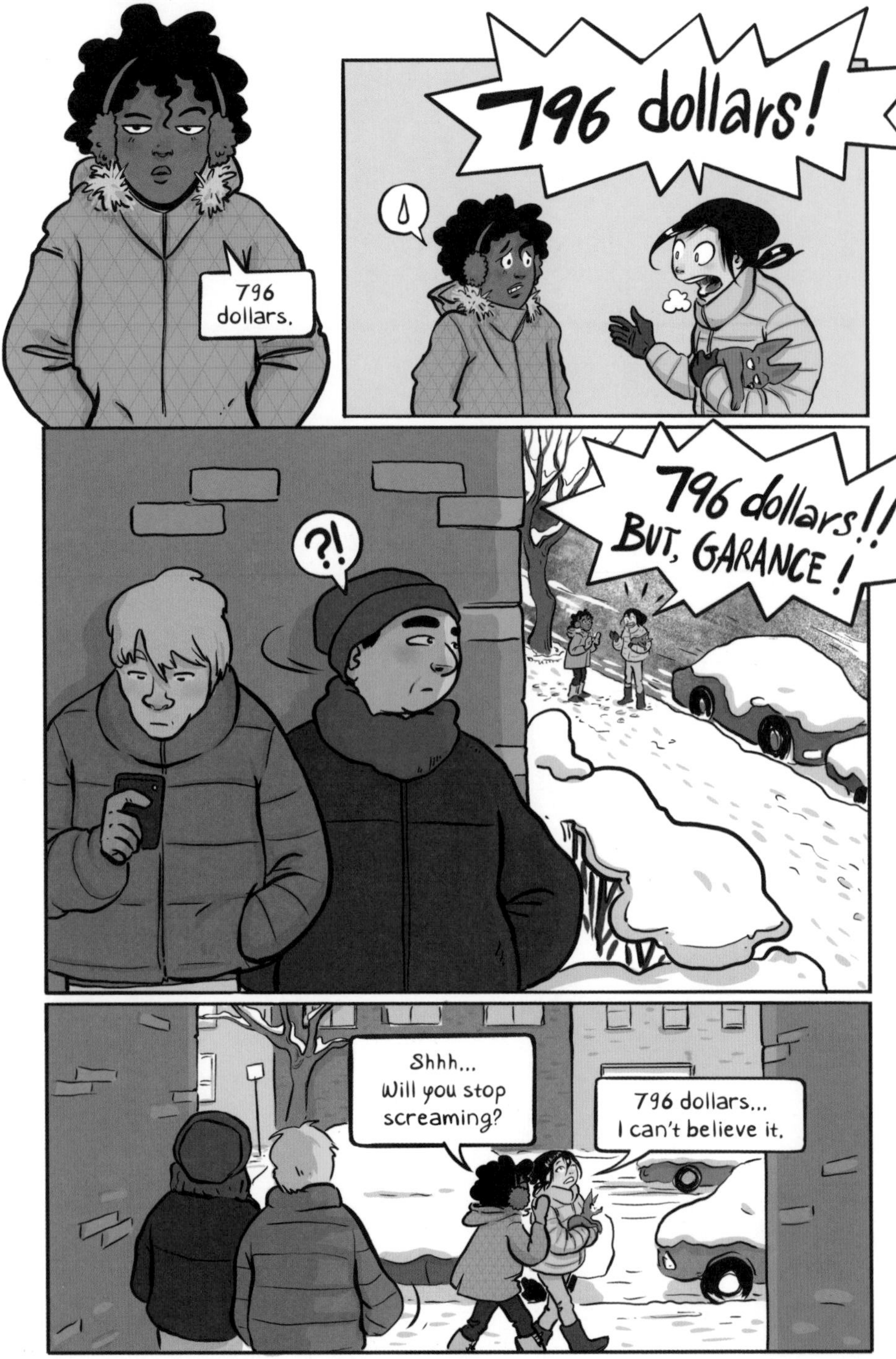

796 dollars.
796 dollars!
!
796 dollars!!
BUT, GARANCE!
?!
Shhh...
Will you stop screaming?
796 dollars...
I can't believe it.

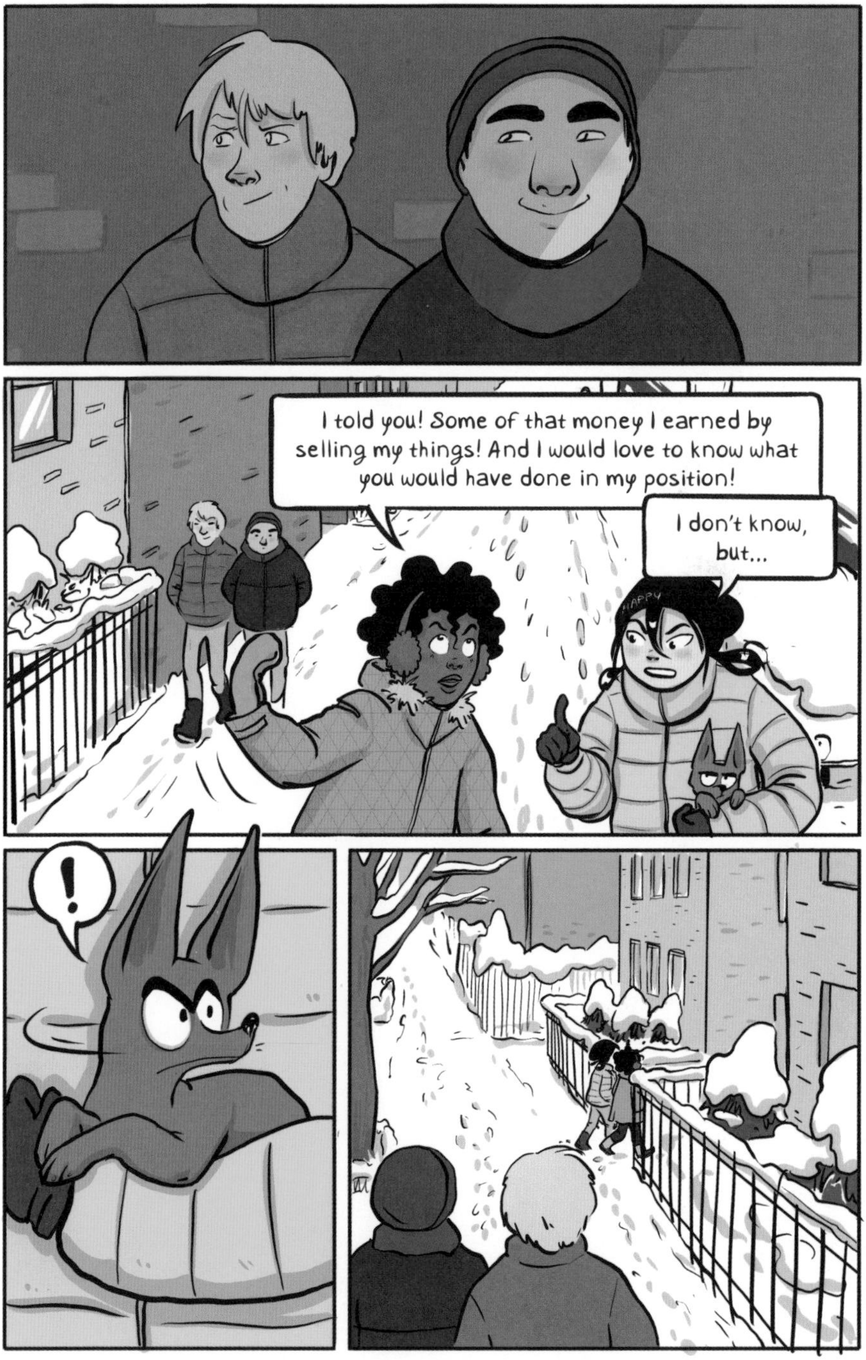
I told you! Some of that money I earned by selling my things! And I would love to know what you would have done in my position!
I don't know, but...
HAPPY
!

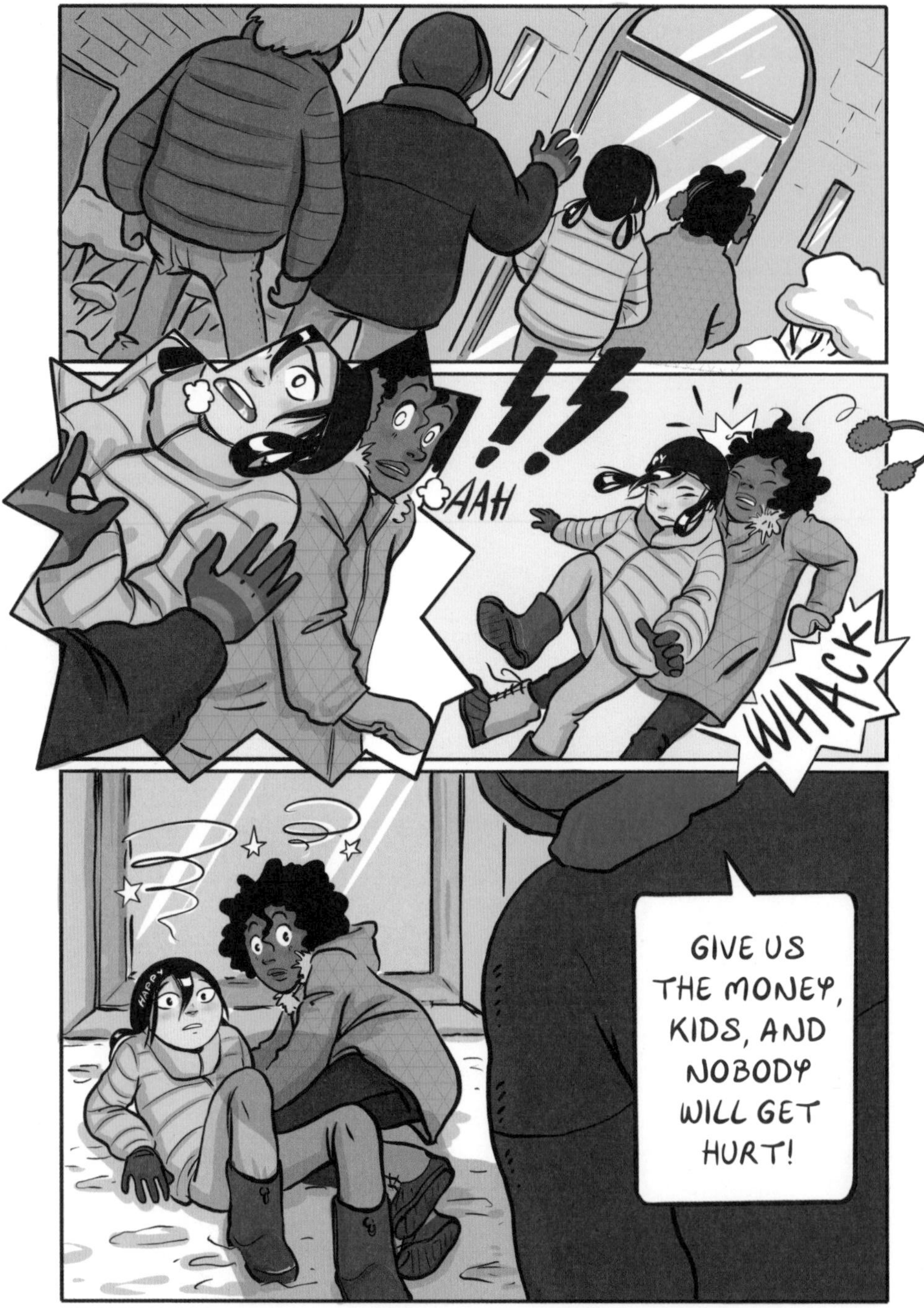
AAH
WHACK
GIVE US THE MONEY, KIDS, AND NOBODY WILL GET HURT!

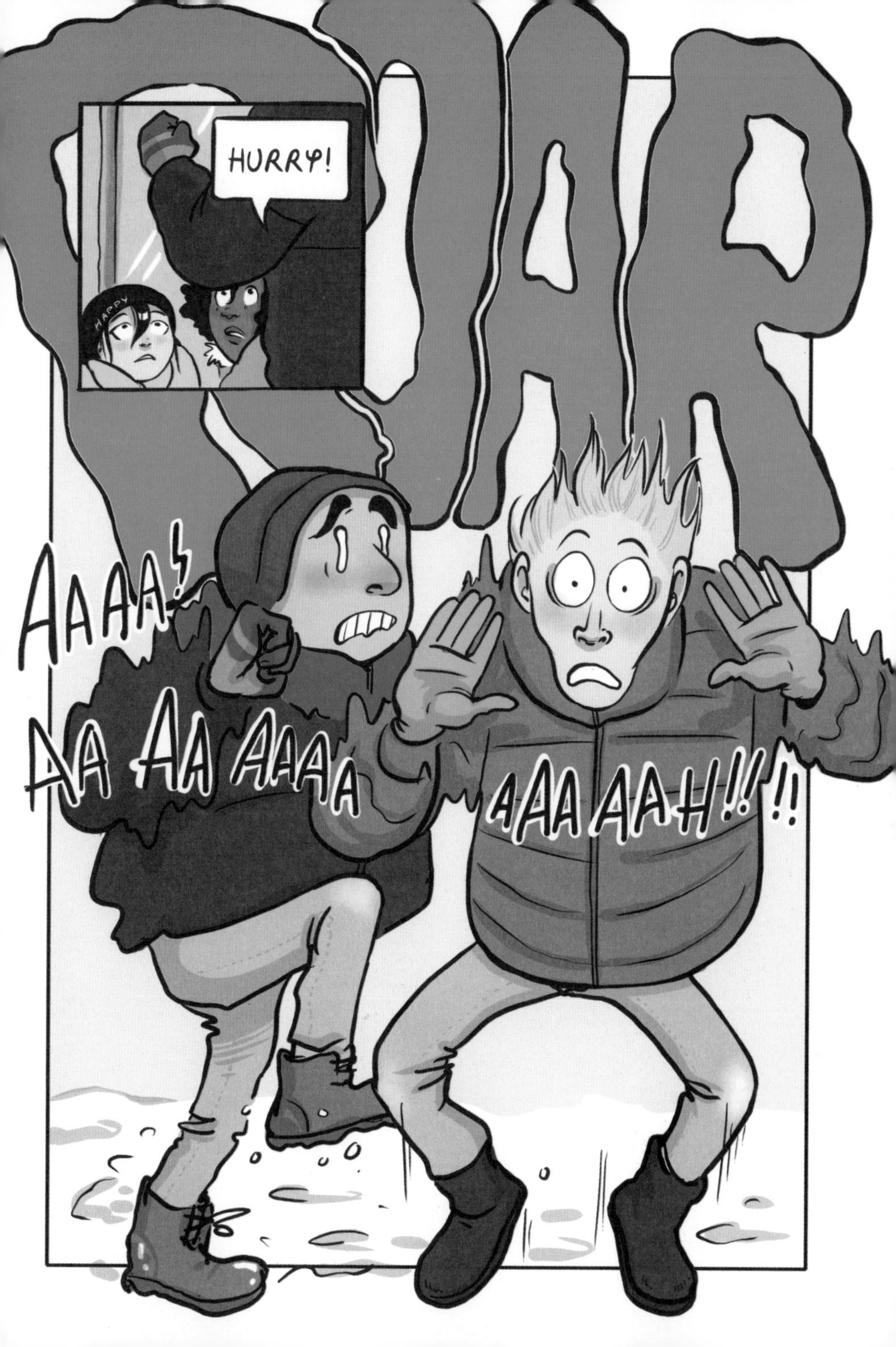
HURRY!
AAAA!
AA AA AAAAA
AAAAAAH!!!!

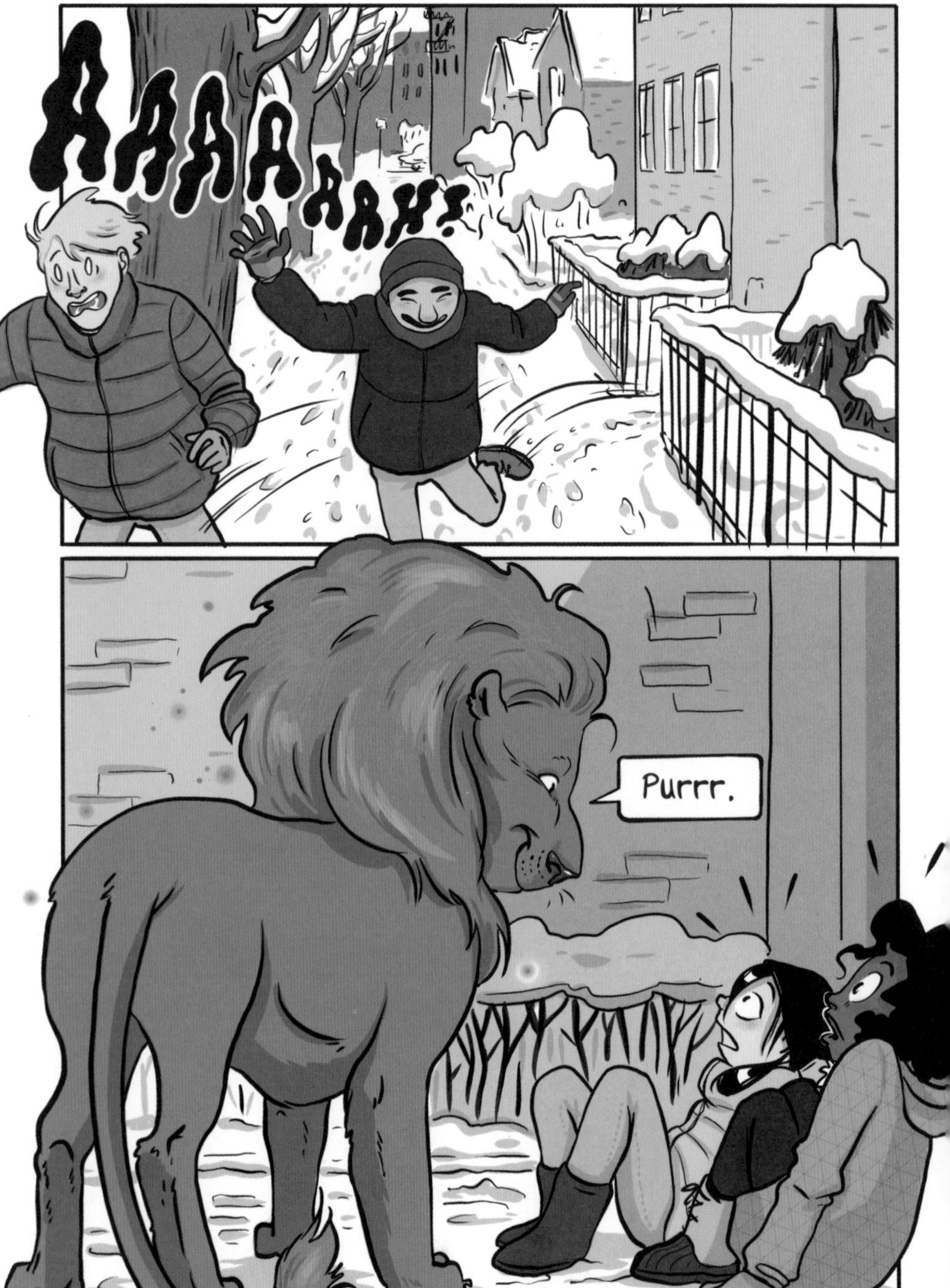
AAAAAAAH!
Purrr.

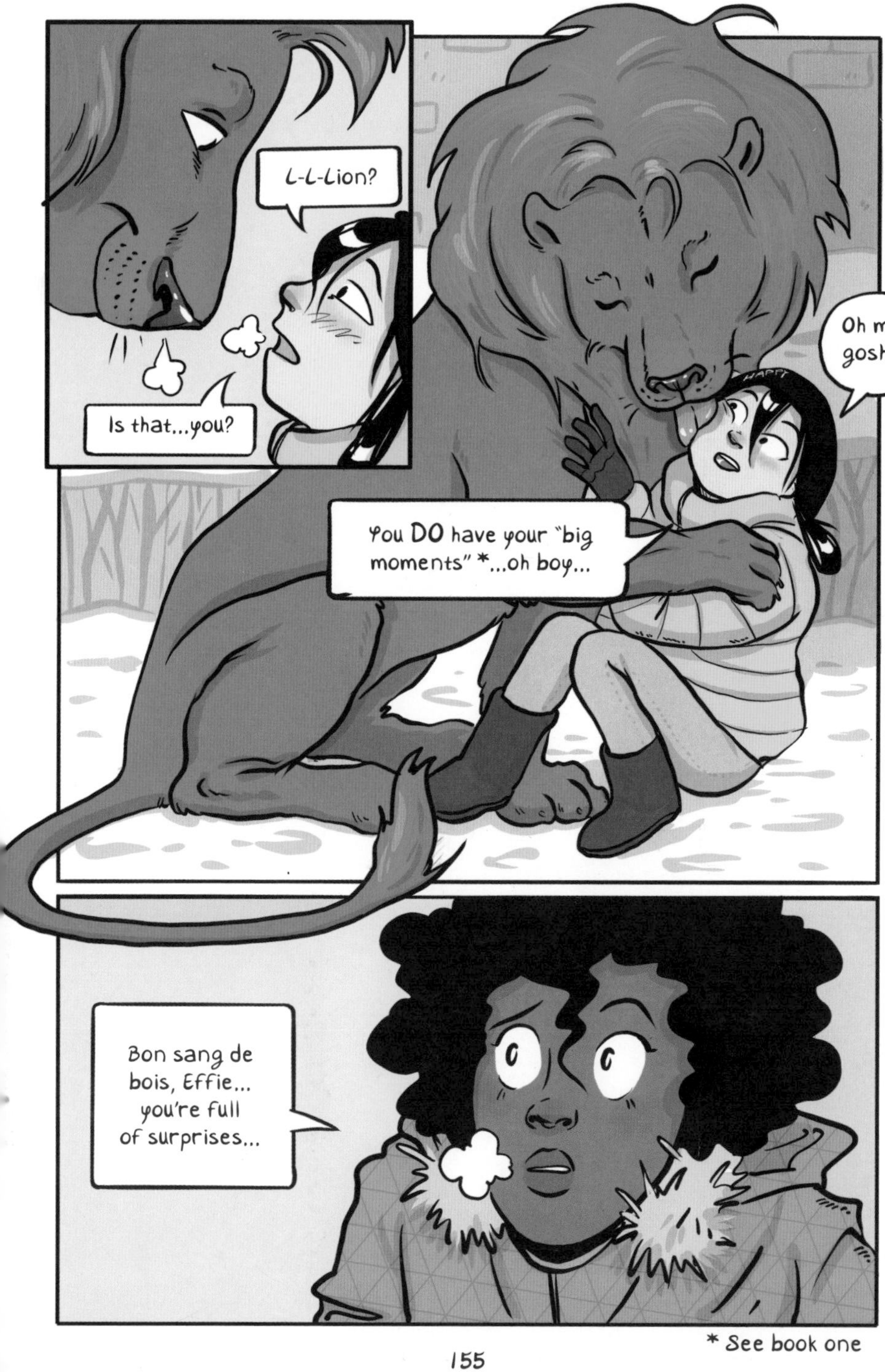

L-L-Lion?
Is that...you?
Oh my gosh!!
You DO have your "big moments" *...oh boy...
Bon sang de bois, Effie... you're full of surprises...

* See book one

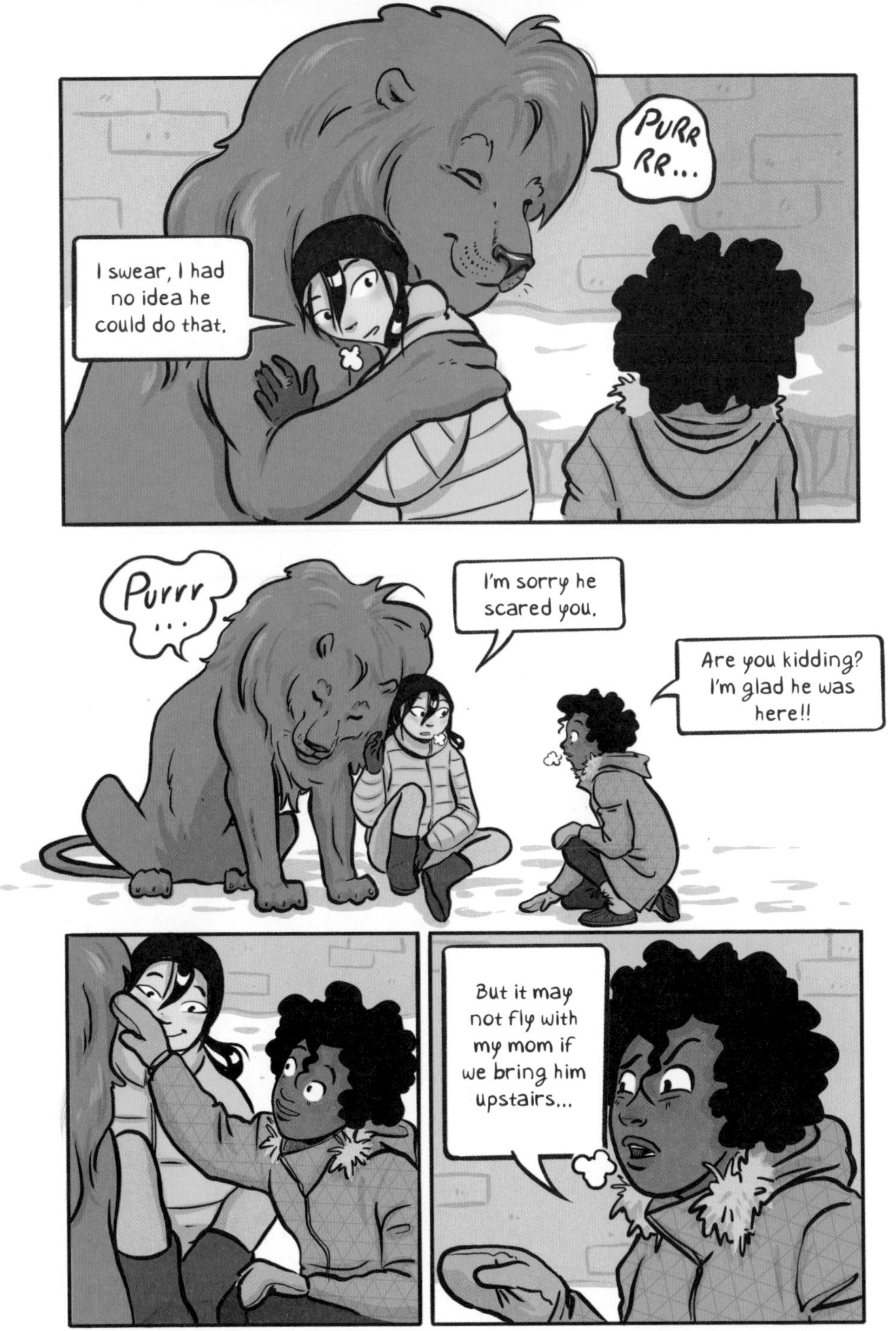
PURR
RR...
I swear, I had no idea he could do that.
Purrr ...
I'm sorry he scared you.
Are you kidding? I'm glad he was here!!
But it may not fly with my mom if we bring him upstairs...

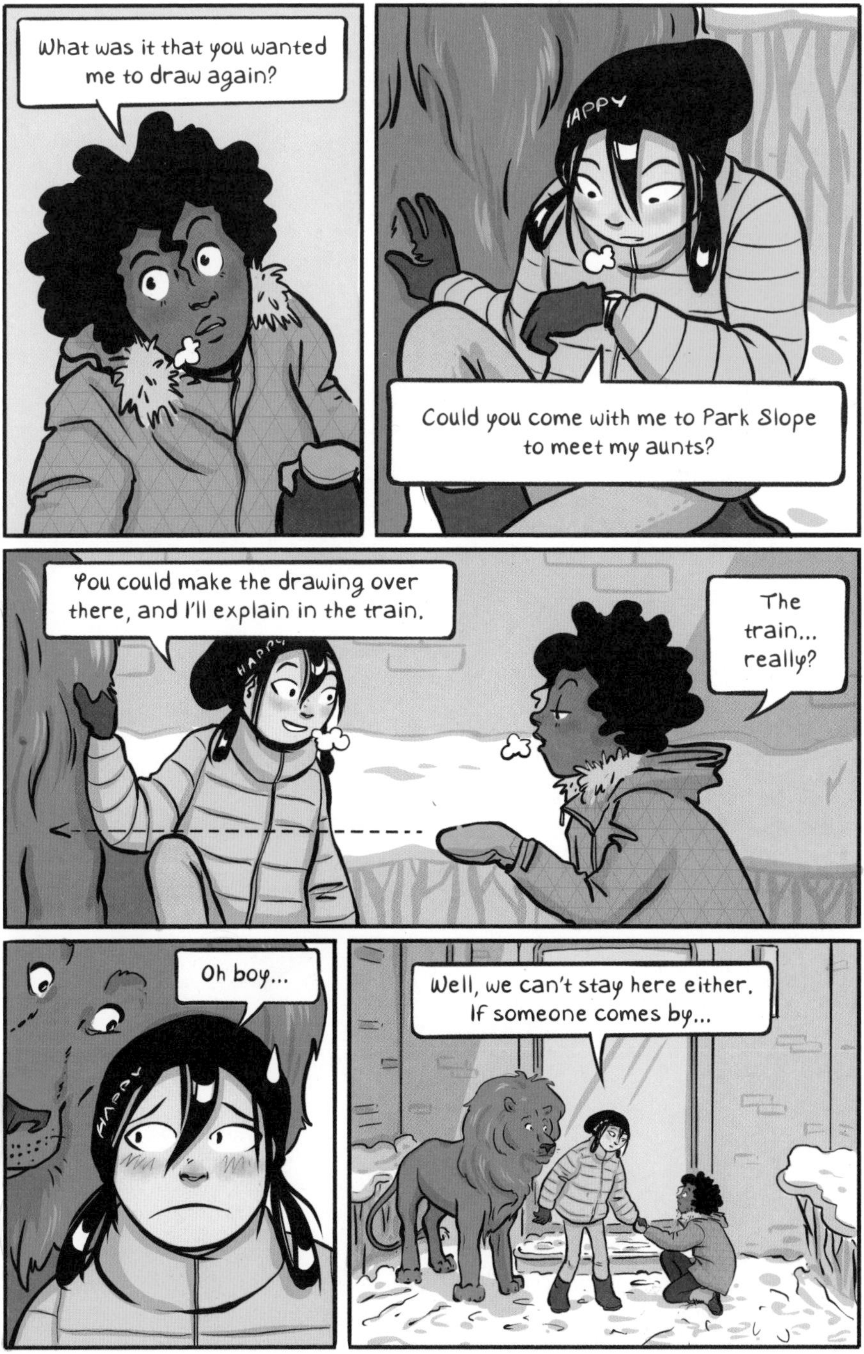
What was it that you wanted me to draw again?
HAPPY
Could you come with me to Park Slope to meet my aunts?
You could make the drawing over there, and I'll explain in the train.
The train... really?
Oh boy...
Well, we can't stay here either. If someone comes by...

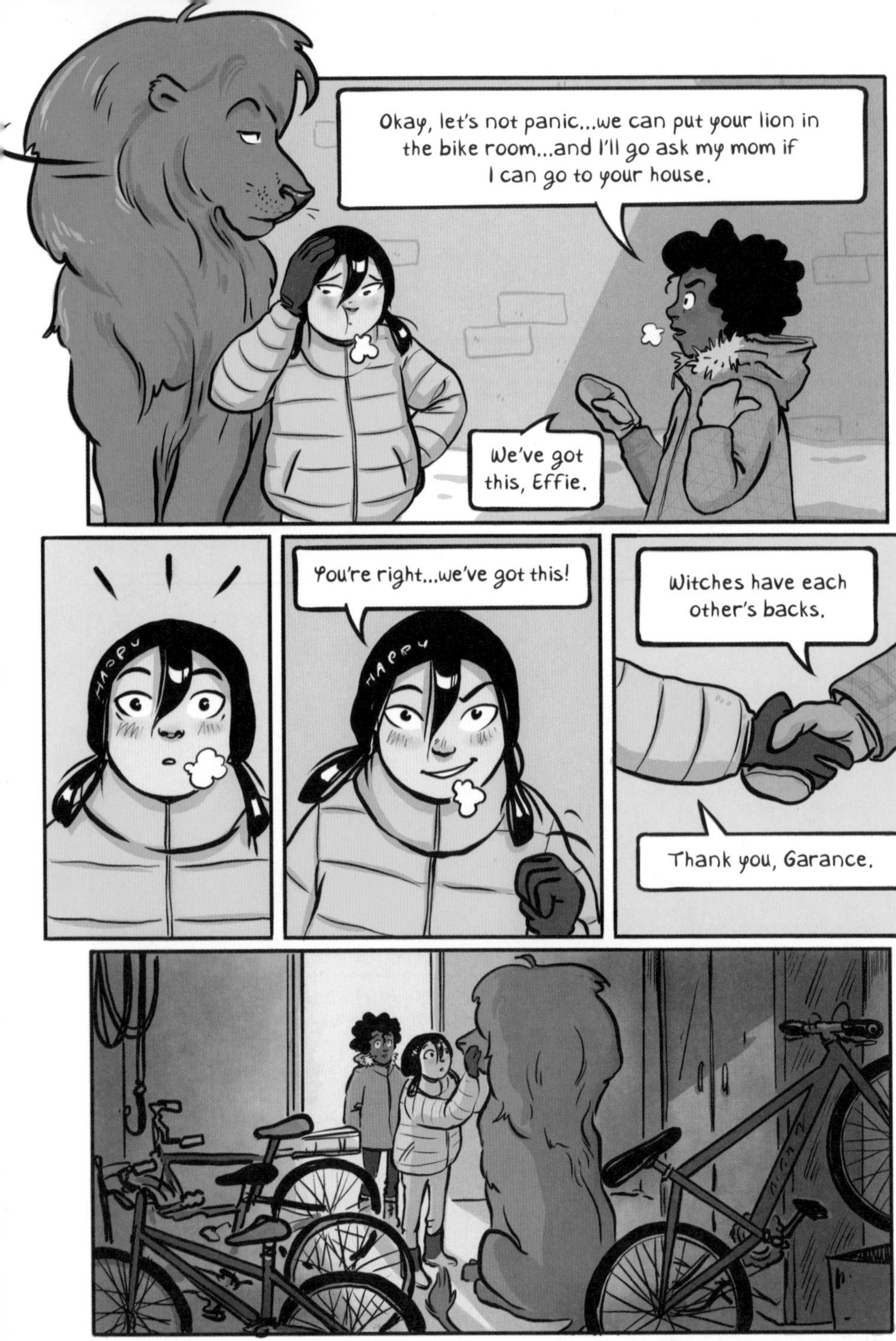
Okay, let's not panic...we can put your lion in the bike room...and I'll go ask my mom if I can go to your house.
We've got this, Effie.
You're right...we've got this!
Witches have each other's backs.
Thank you, Garance.

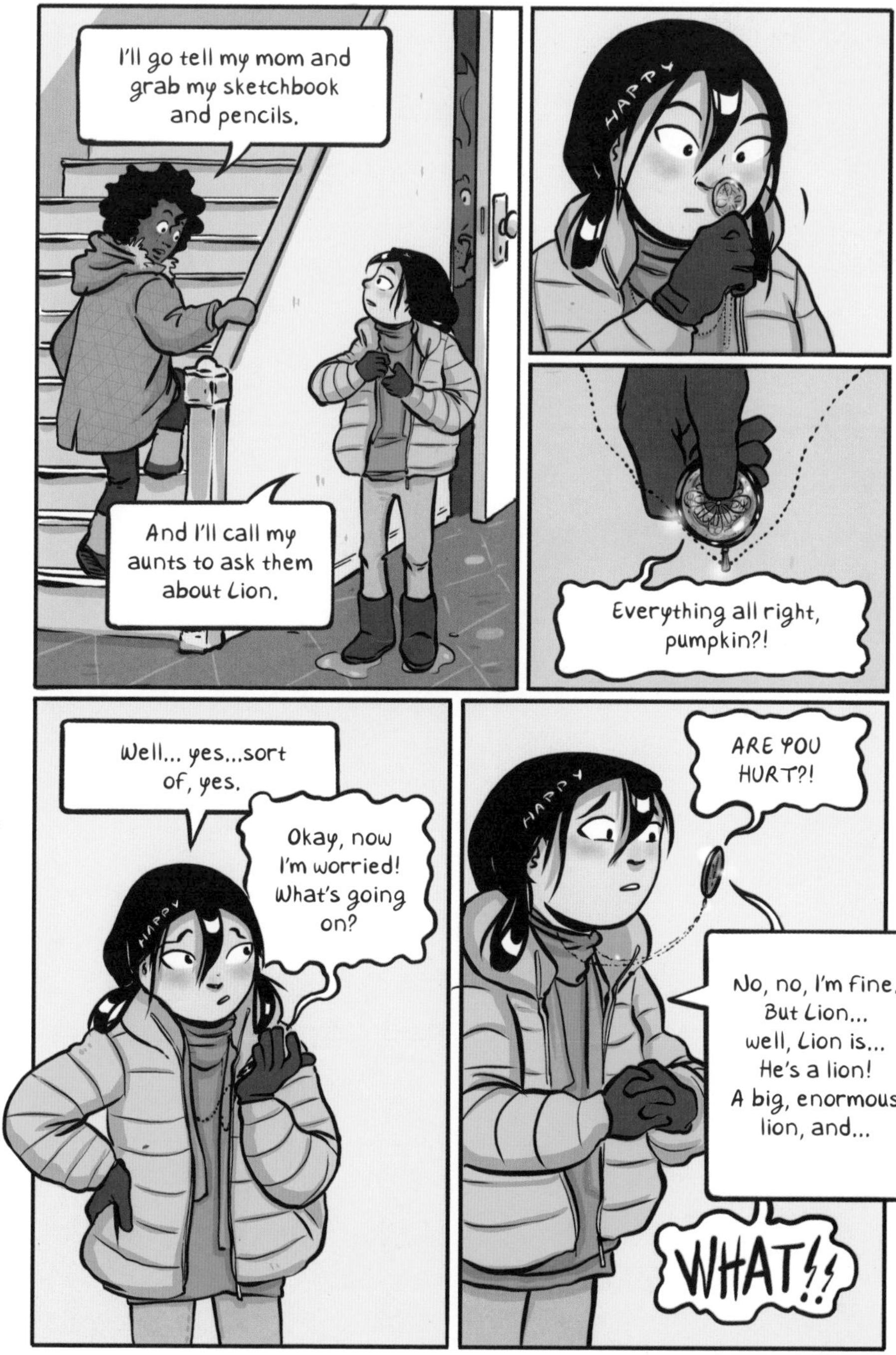
I'll go tell my mom and grab my sketchbook and pencils.
And I'll call my aunts to ask them about Lion.
Everything all right, pumpkin?!
Well... yes...sort of, yes.
Okay, now I'm worried! What's going on?
ARE YOU HURT?!
No, no, I'm fine. But Lion... well, Lion is... He's a lion! A big, enormous lion, and...
WHAT!?

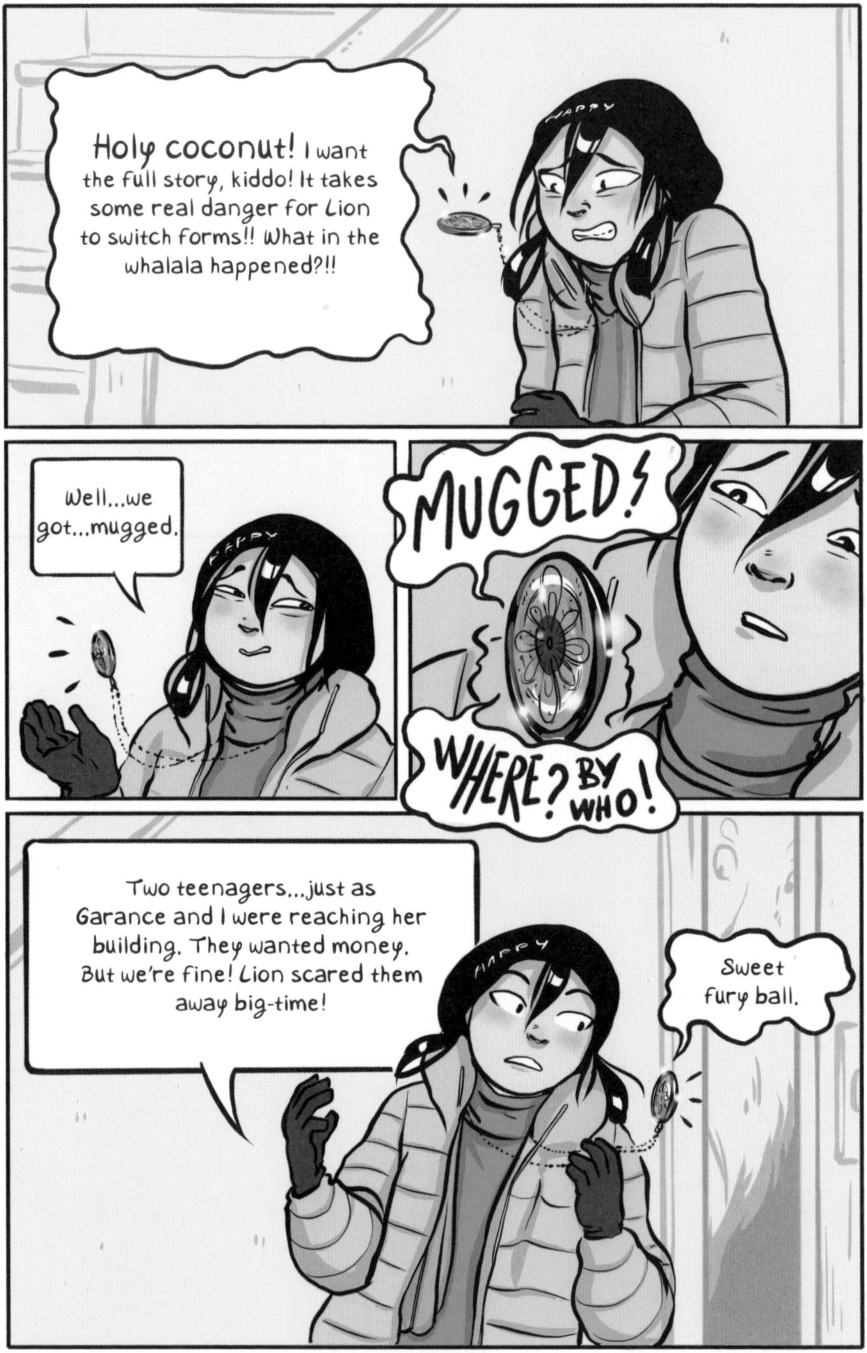
Holy coconut! I want the full story, kiddo! It takes some real danger for Lion to switch forms!! What in the whalala happened?!!
Well...we got...mugged.
MUGGED!
WHERE? BY WHO!
Two teenagers...just as Garance and I were reaching her building. They wanted money. But we're fine! Lion scared them away big-time!
Sweet fury ball.

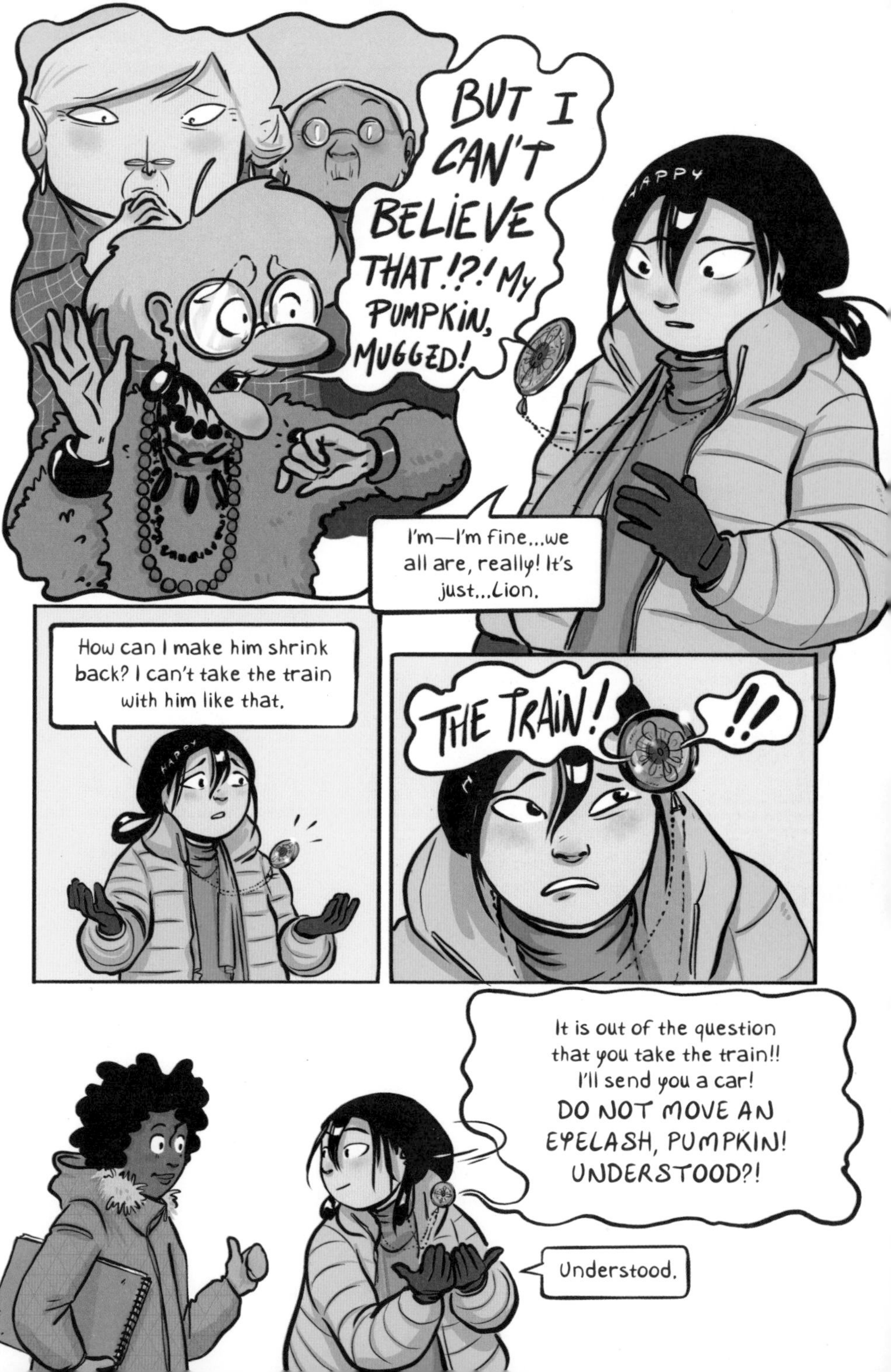
BUT I CAN'T BELIEVE THAT!?! MY PUMPKIN, MUGGED!
I'm—I'm fine...we all are, really! It's just...Lion.
How can I make him shrink back? I can't take the train with him like that.
THE TRAIN!
!!
It is out of the question that you take the train!! I'll send you a car! DO NOT MOVE AN EYELASH, PUMPKIN! UNDERSTOOD?!
Understood.

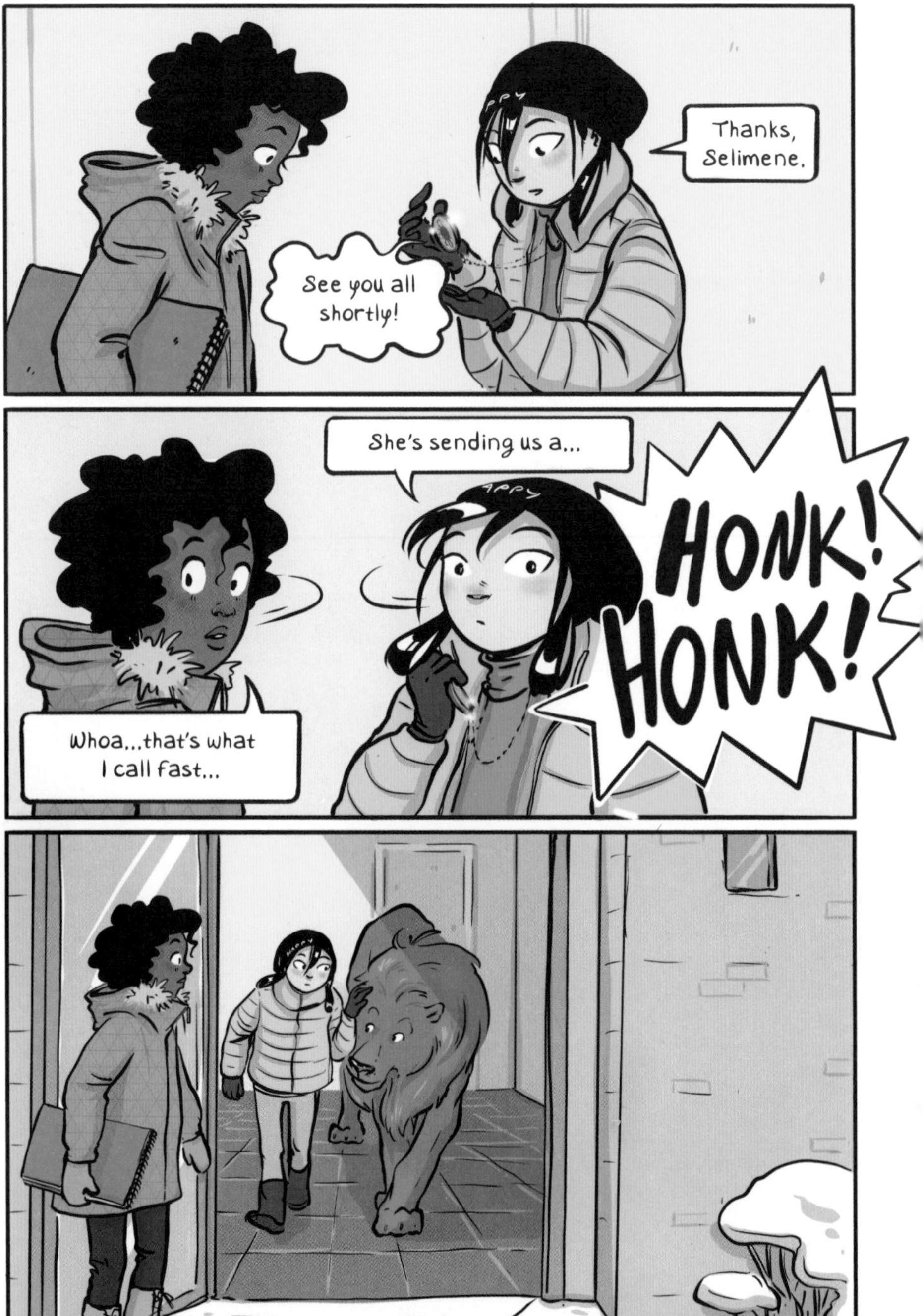
Thanks, Selimene.
See you all shortly!
She's sending us a...
HONK! HONK!
Whoa...that's what I call fast...

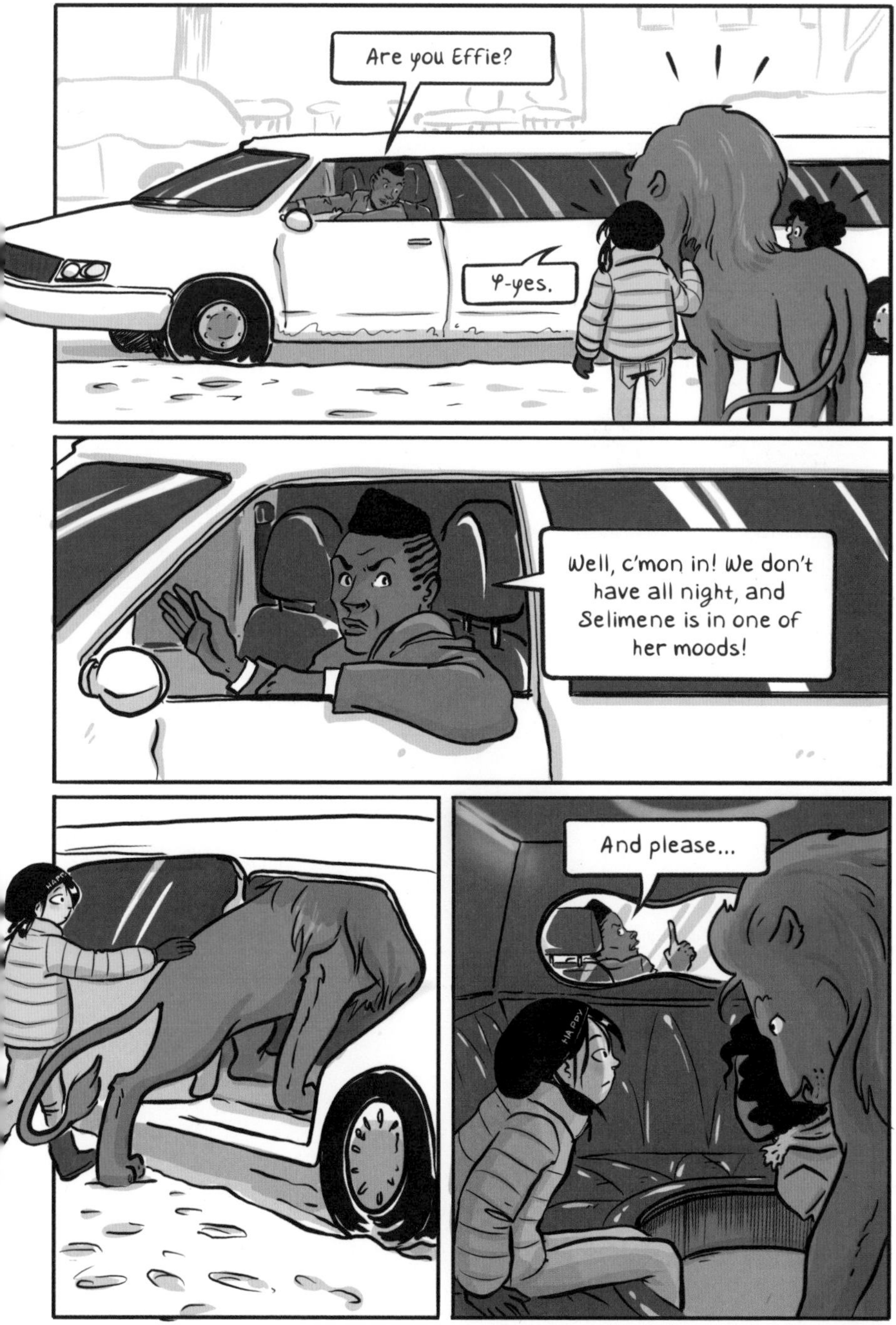
Are you Effie?
Y-yes.
Well, c'mon in! We don't have all night, and Selimene is in one of her moods!
HAPPY
And please...
HAPPY

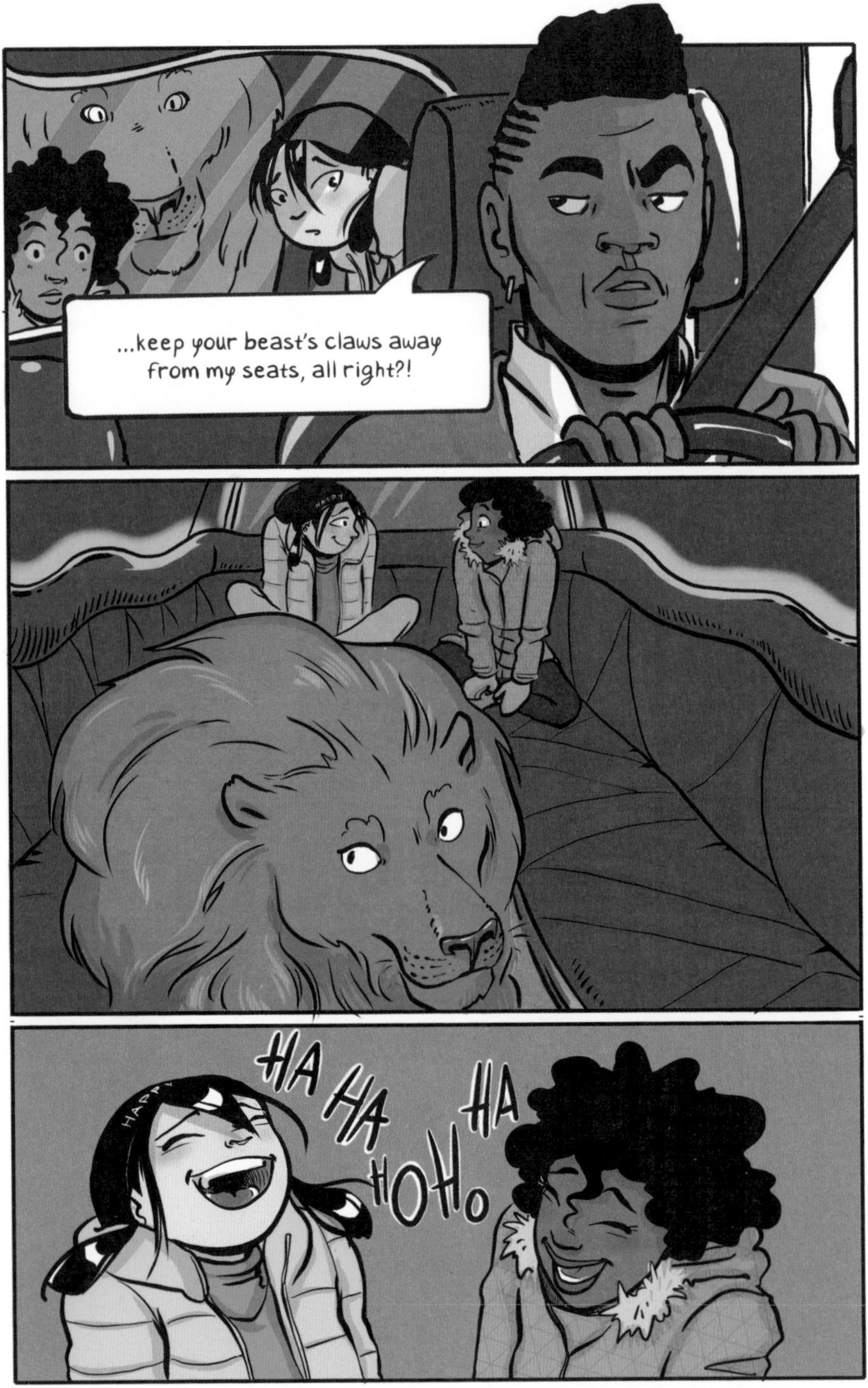
...keep your beast's claws away from my seats, all right?!
HA HA
HA HA
HOHO

Chapter 5

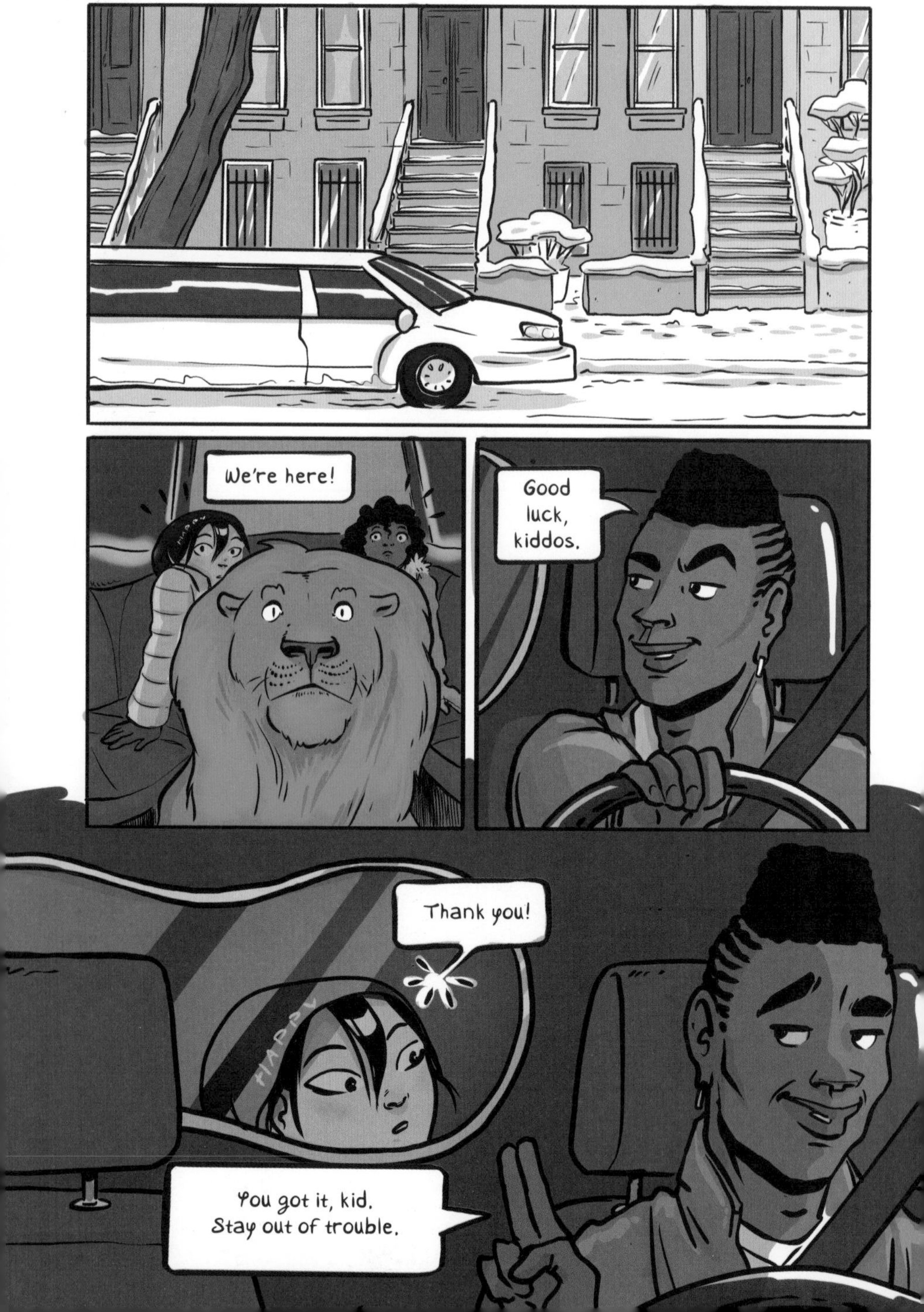
We're here!
Good luck, kiddos.
Thank you!
You got it, kid. Stay out of trouble.

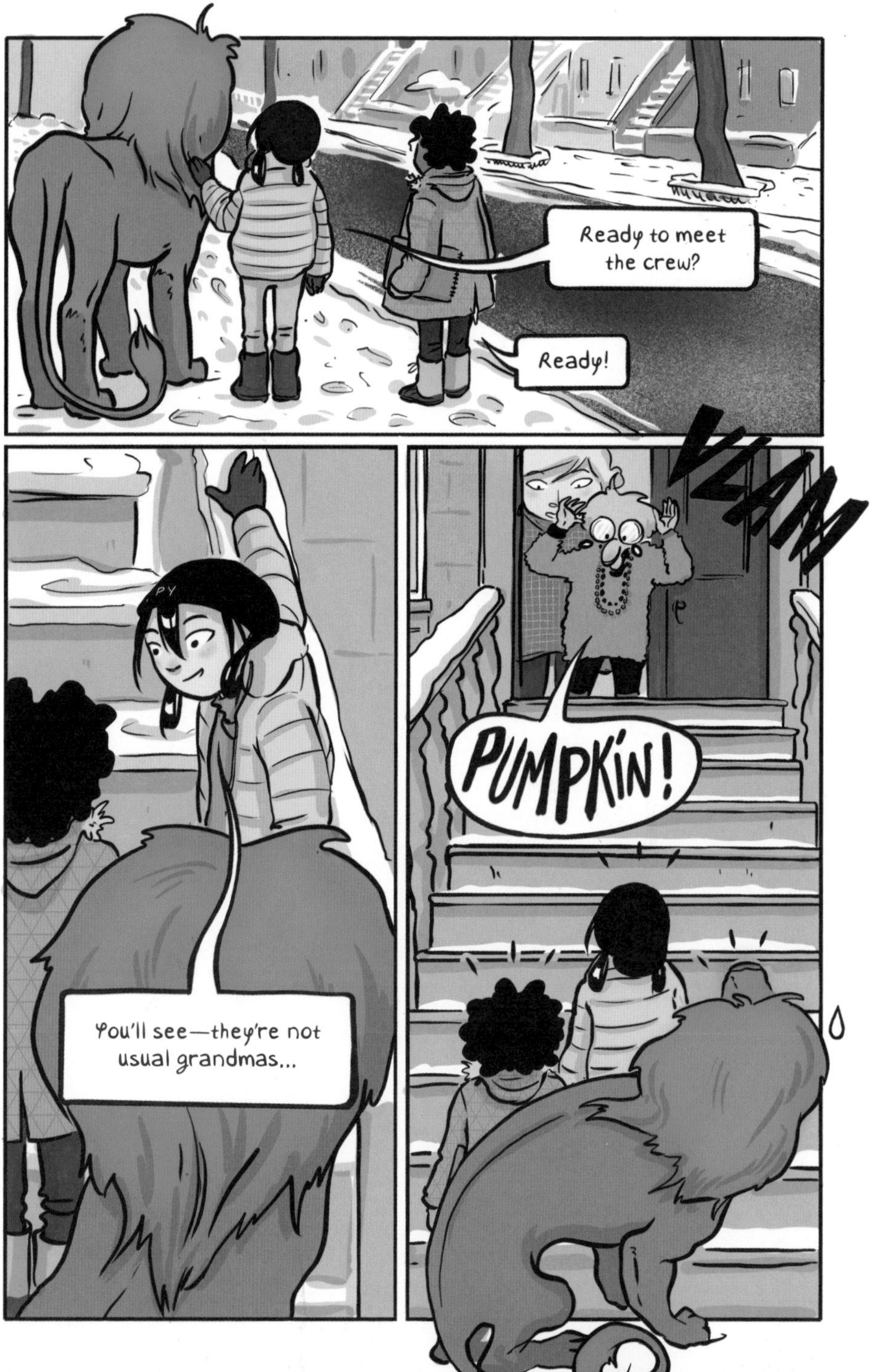
Ready to meet the crew?
Ready!
You'll see—they're not usual grandmas...
VLAM
PUMPKIN!

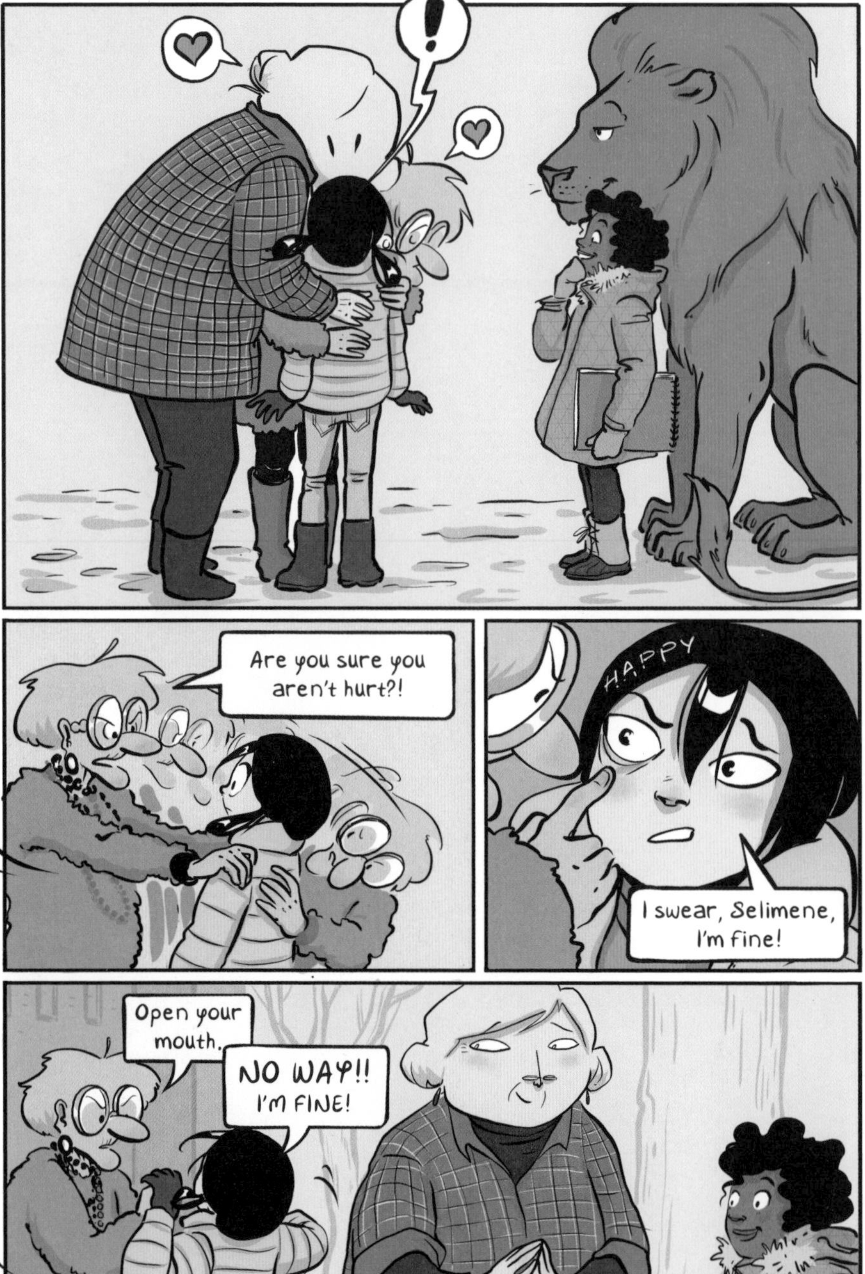
!
Are you sure you aren't hurt?!
HAPPY
I swear, Selimene, I'm fine!
Open your mouth.
NO WAY!! I'M FINE!

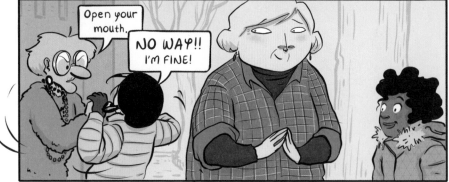

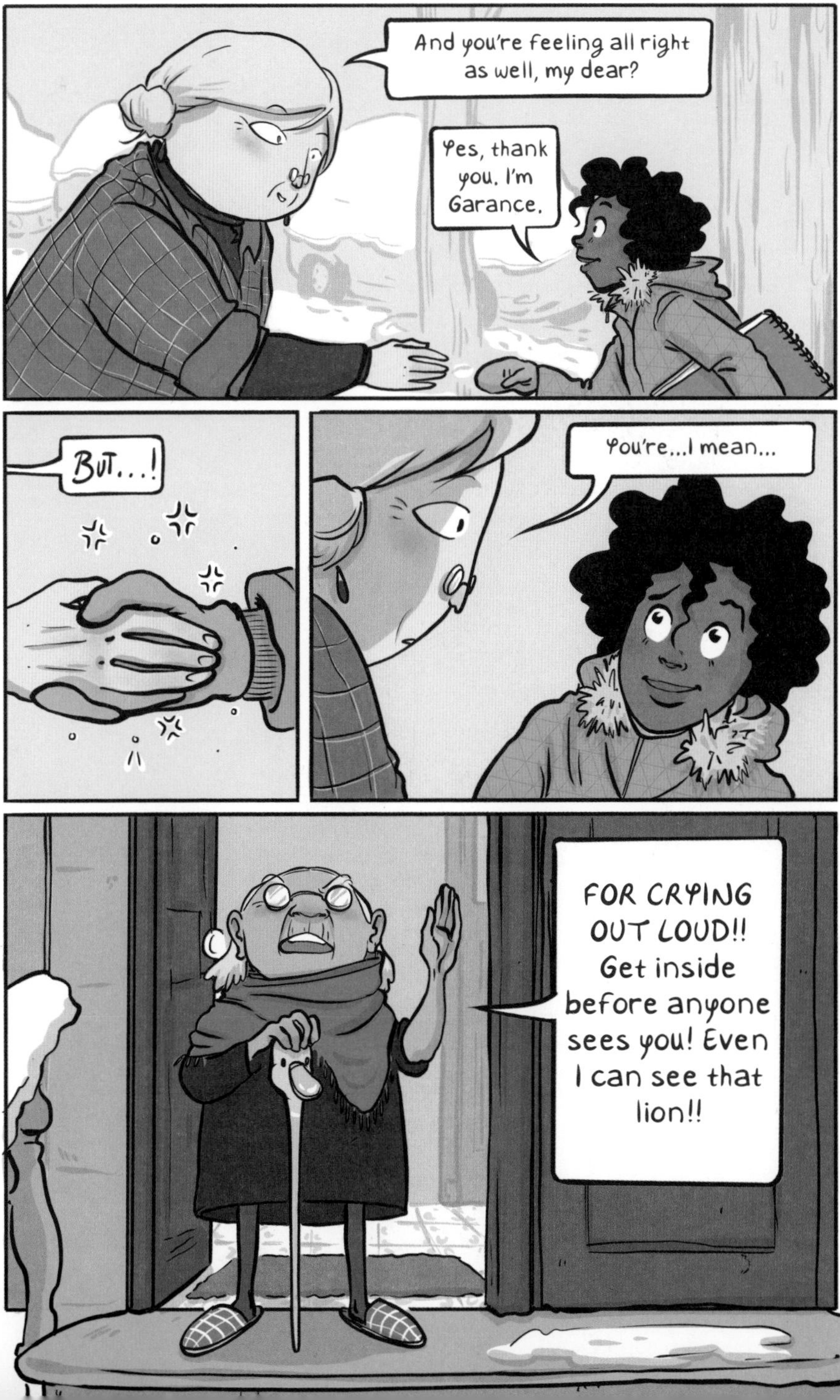
And you're feeling all right as well, my dear?
Yes, thank you. I'm Garance.
BUT...!
You're...I mean...
FOR CRYING OUT LOUD!! Get inside before anyone sees you! Even I can see that lion!!

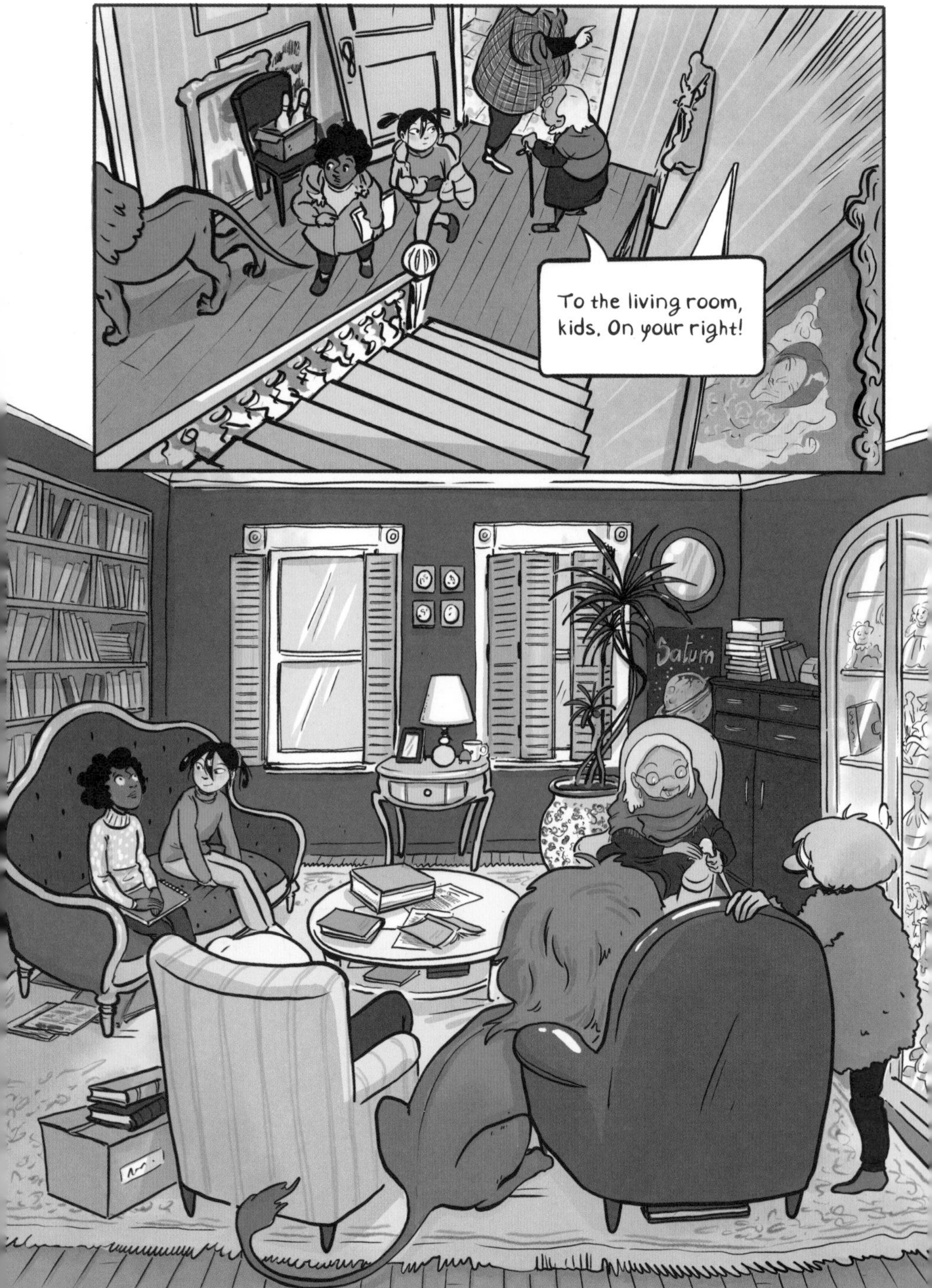
To the living room, kids. On your right!
Saturn

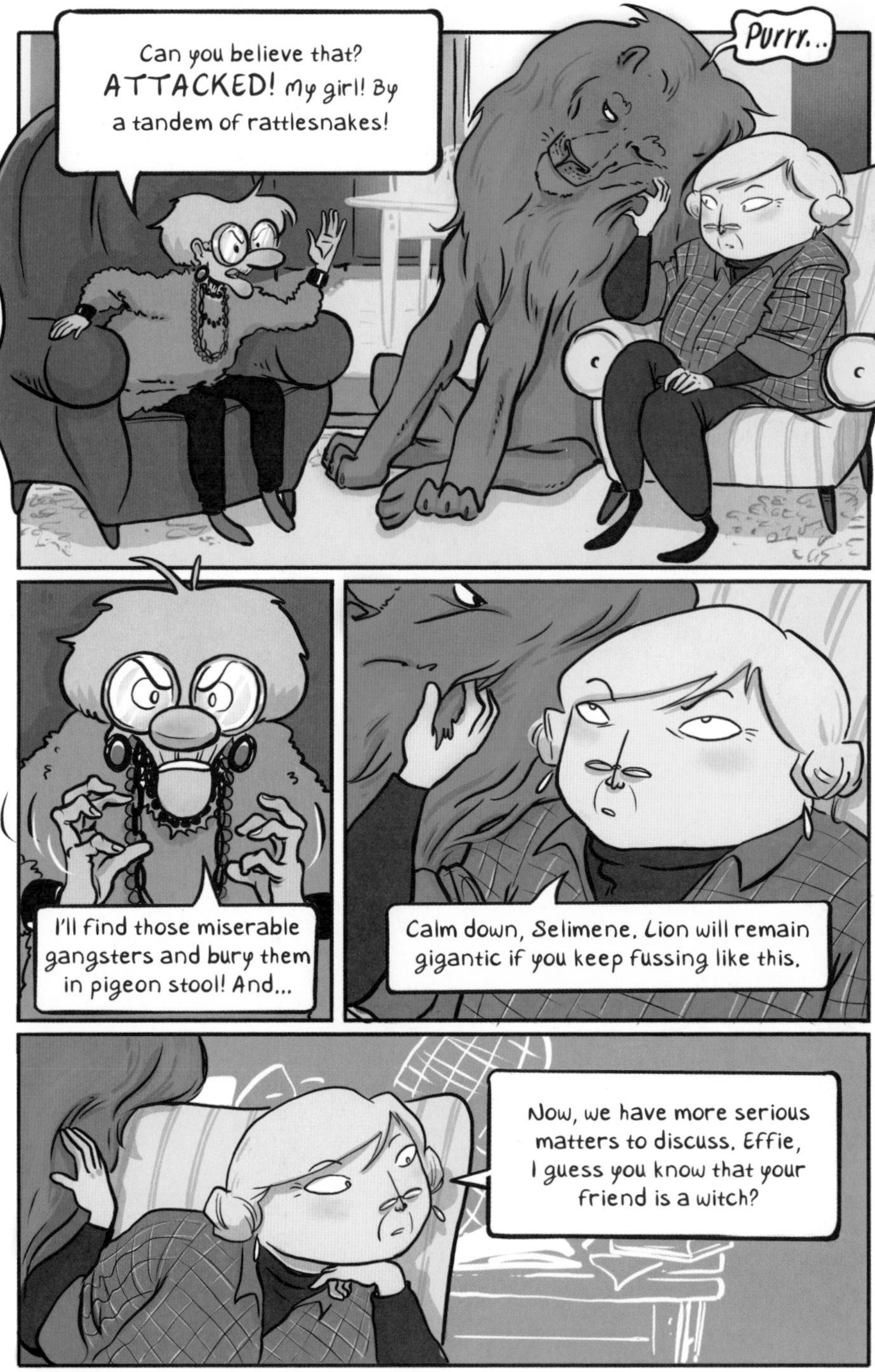
Can you believe that? ATTACKED! My girl! By a tandem of rattlesnakes!
Purrr...
I'll find those miserable gangsters and bury them in pigeon stool! And...
Calm down, Selimene. Lion will remain gigantic if you keep fussing like this.
Now, we have more serious matters to discuss. Effie, I guess you know that your friend is a witch?

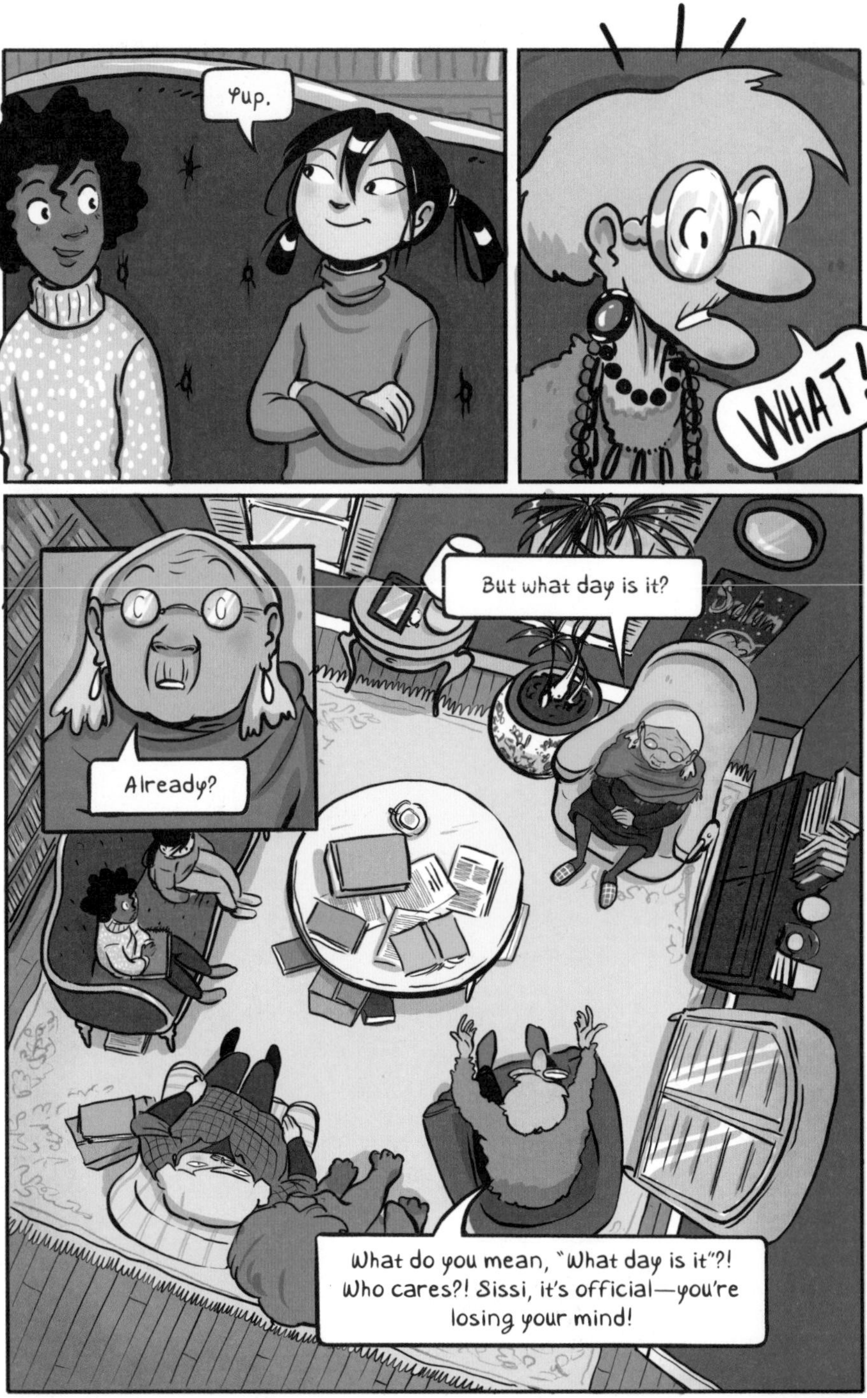
Yup.
WHAT!
But what day is it?
Already?
What do you mean, "What day is it"?! Who cares?! Sissi, it's official—you're losing your mind!

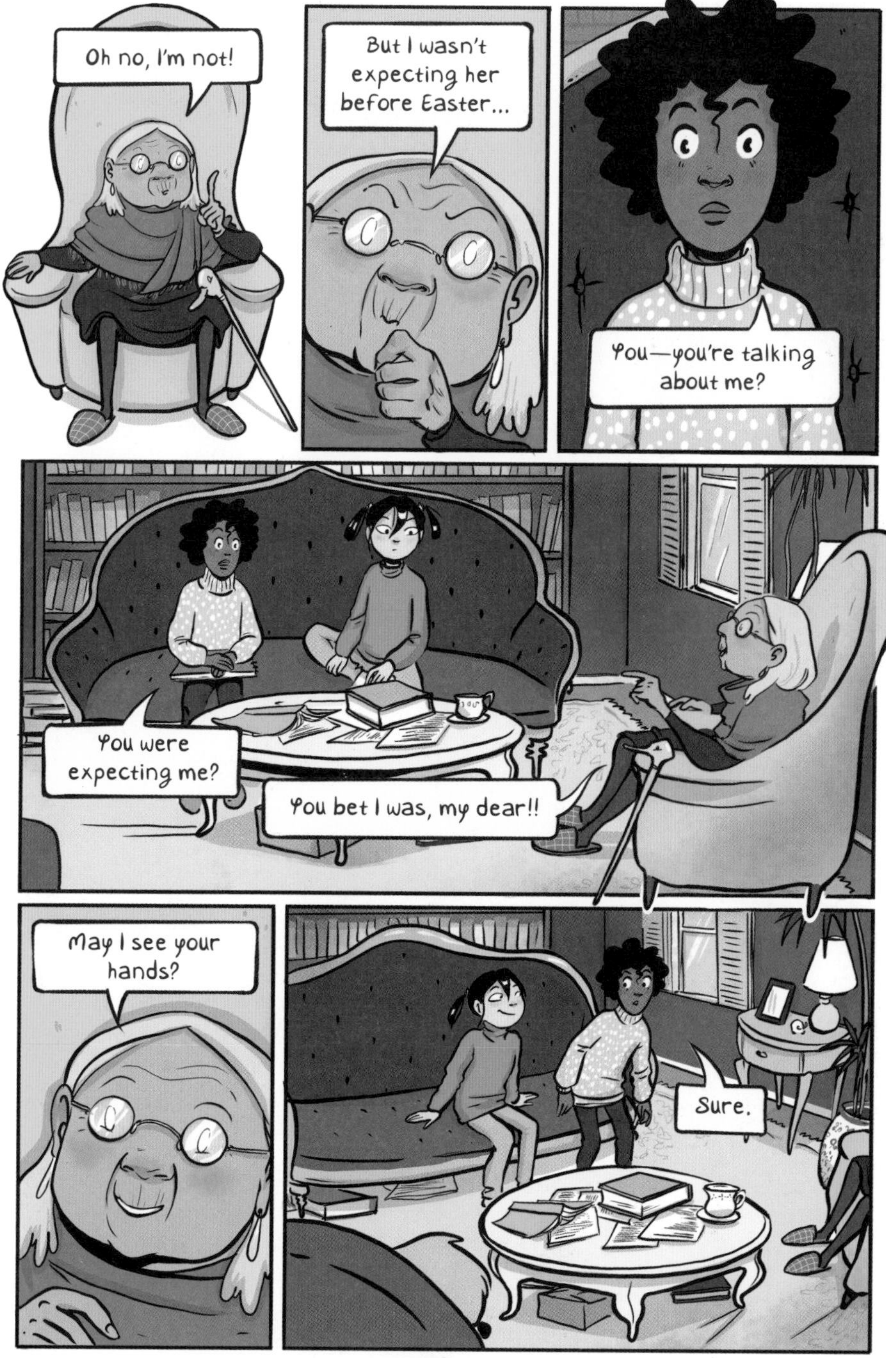
Oh no, I'm not!
But I wasn't expecting her before Easter...
You—you're talking about me?
You were expecting me?
You bet I was, my dear!!
May I see your hands?
Sure.

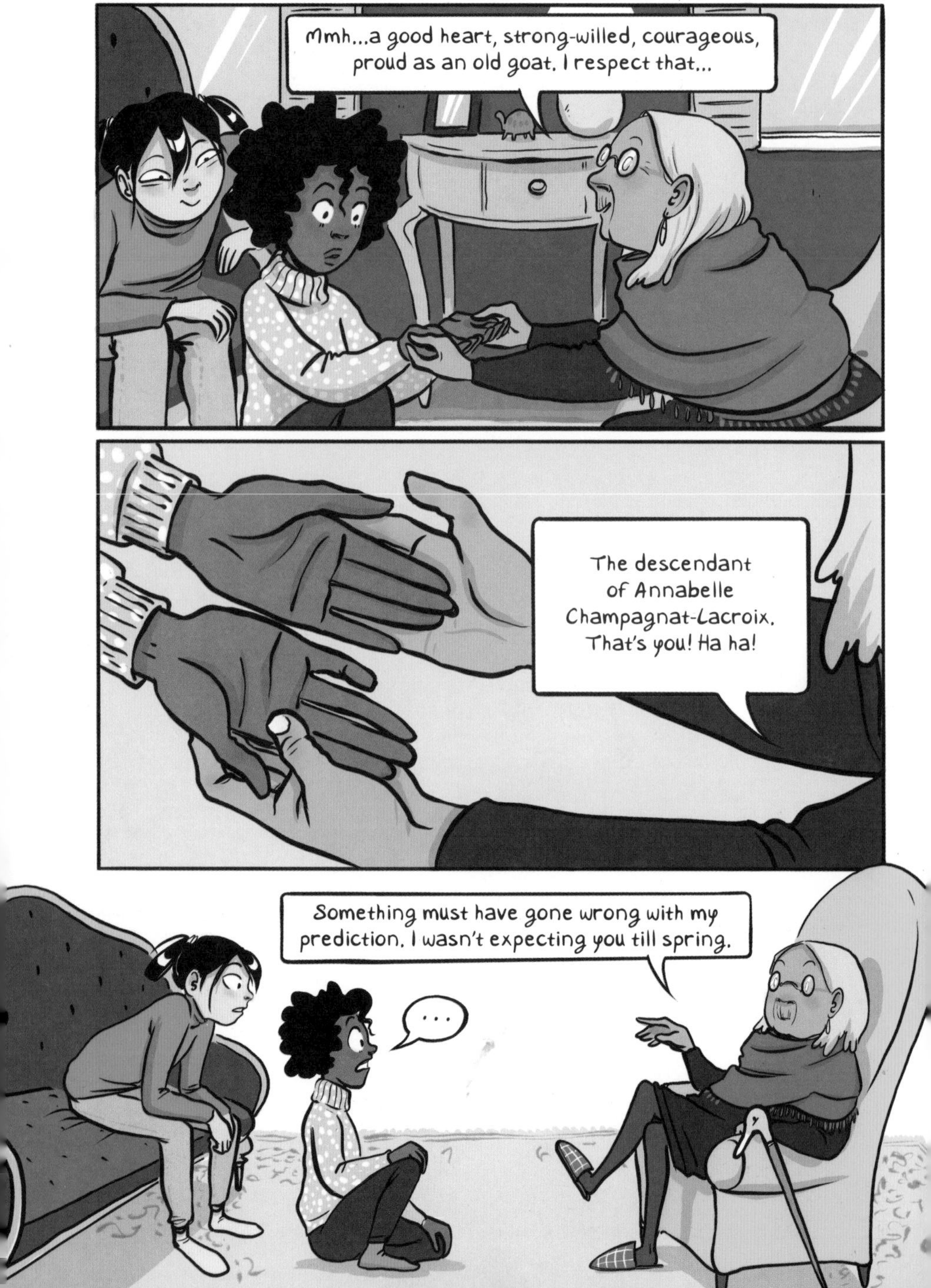
Mmh...a good heart, strong-willed, courageous, proud as an old goat. I respect that...
The descendant of Annabelle Champagnat-Lacroix. That's you! Ha ha!
Something must have gone wrong with my prediction. I wasn't expecting you till spring.
...

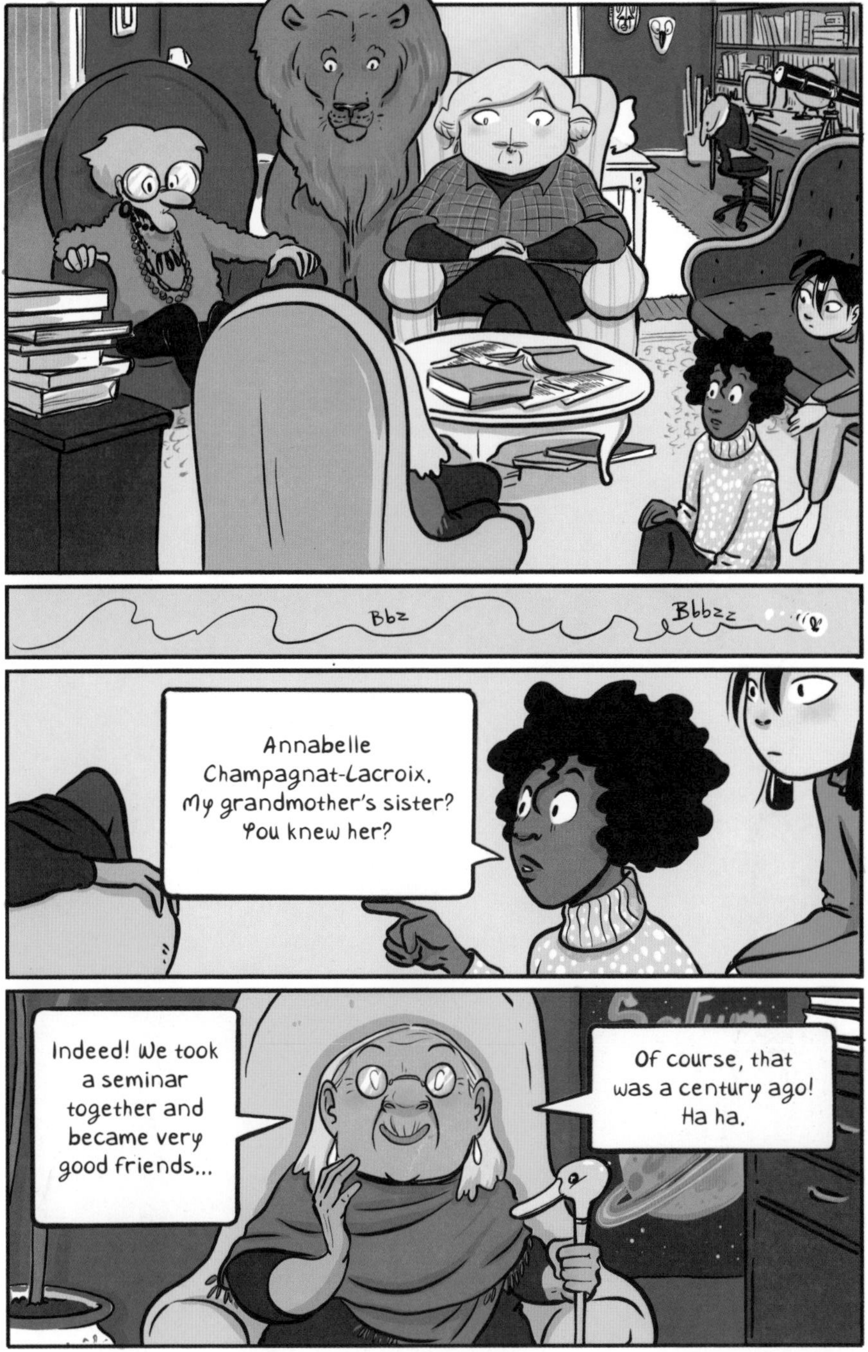
Bbz
Bbbzz
Annabelle Champagnat-Lacroix. My grandmother's sister? You knew her?
Indeed! We took a seminar together and became very good friends...
Of course, that was a century ago! Ha ha.

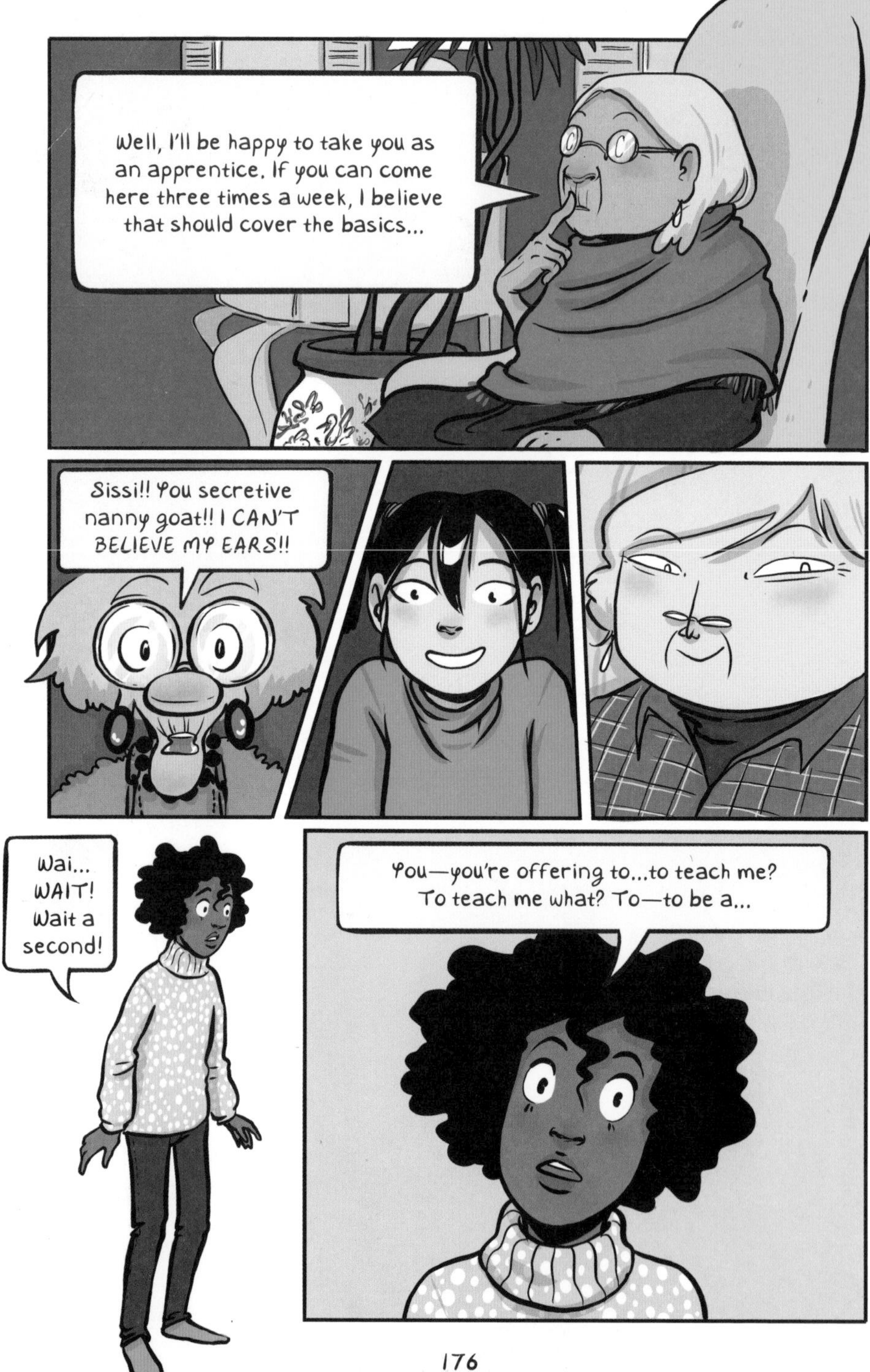
Well, I'll be happy to take you as an apprentice. If you can come here three times a week, I believe that should cover the basics...
Sissi!! You secretive nanny goat!! I CAN'T BELIEVE MY EARS!!
Wai... WAIT! Wait a second!
You—you're offering to...to teach me? To teach me what? To—to be a...

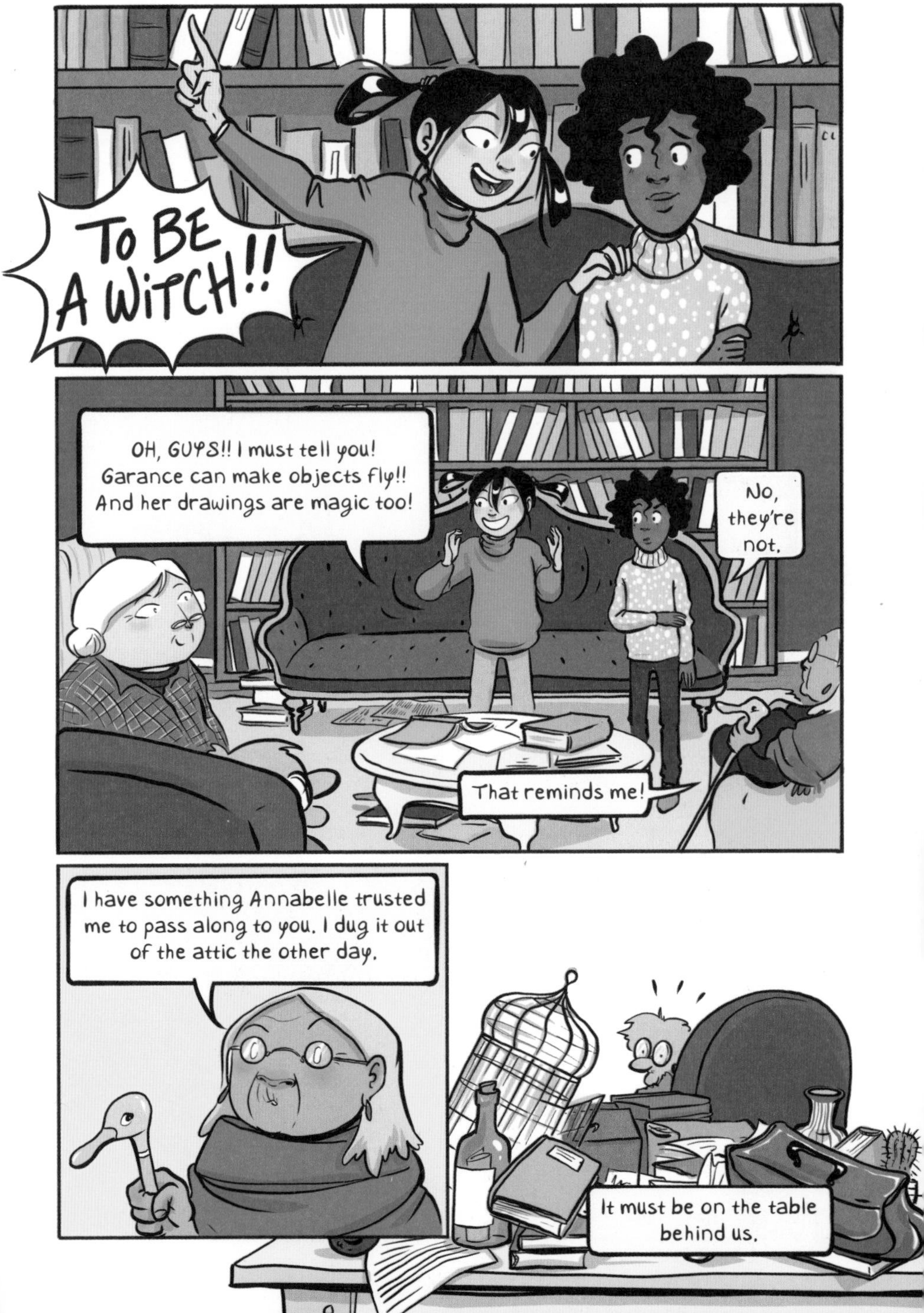
TO BE A WITCH!!
OH, GUYS!! I must tell you! Garance can make objects fly!! And her drawings are magic too!
No, they're not.
That reminds me!
I have something Annabelle trusted me to pass along to you. I dug it out of the attic the other day.
It must be on the table behind us.

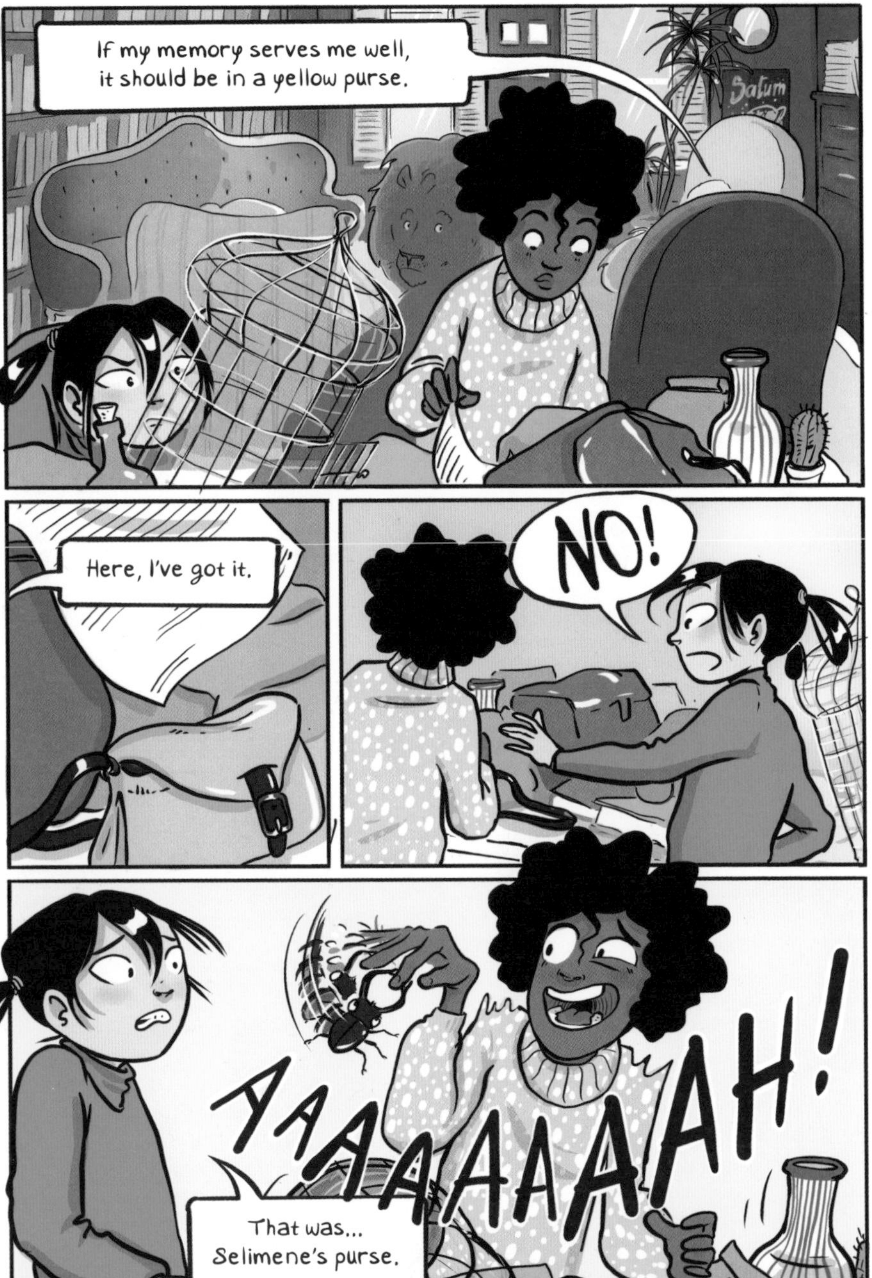
If my memory serves me well, it should be in a yellow purse.
Here, I've got it.
NO!
AAAAAAAAAH!
That was... Selimene's purse.

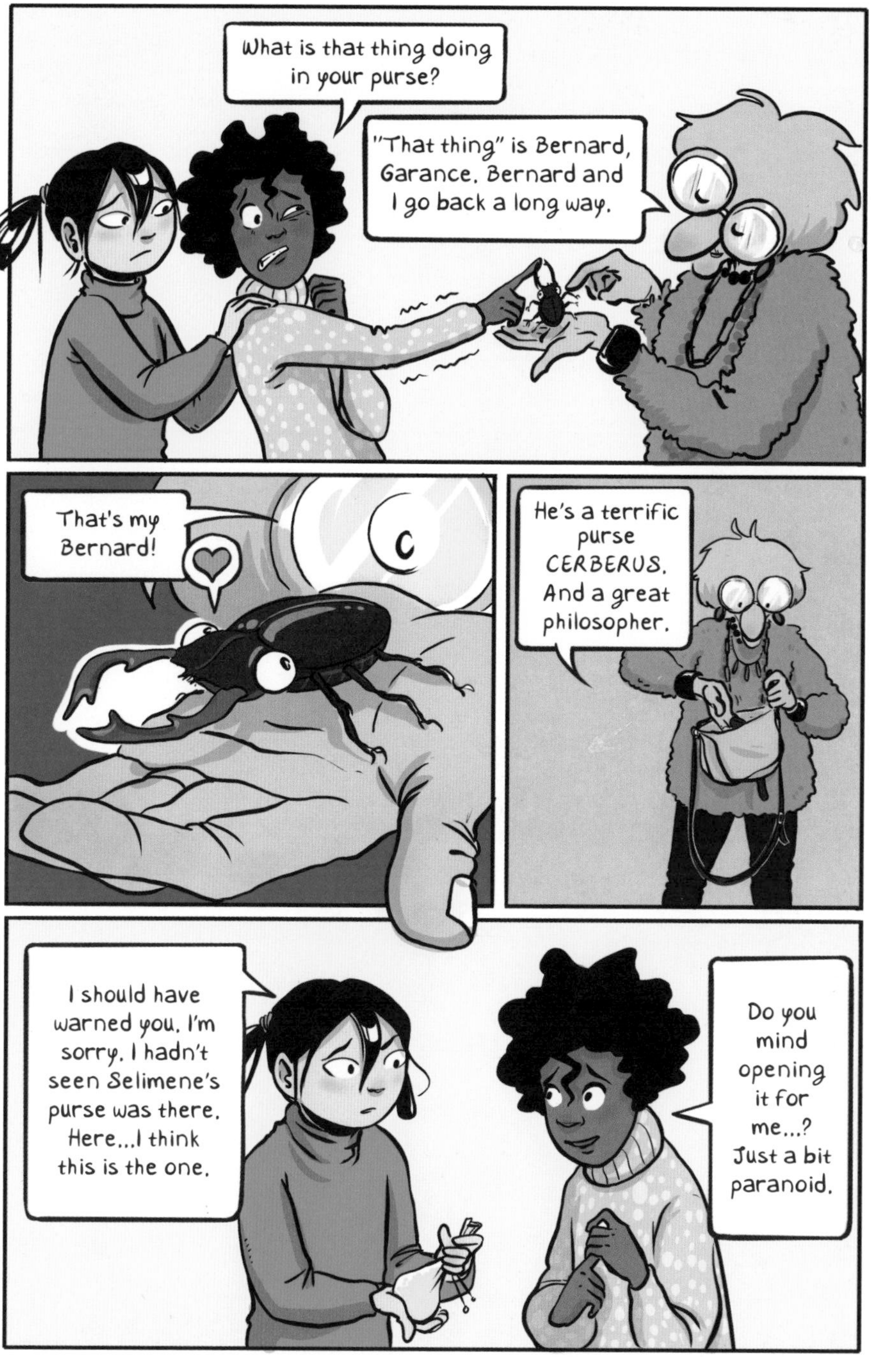
What is that thing doing in your purse?
"That thing" is Bernard, Garance. Bernard and I go back a long way.
That's my Bernard!
He's a terrific purse CERBERUS. And a great philosopher.
I should have warned you. I'm sorry. I hadn't seen Selimene's purse was there. Here...I think this is the one.
Do you mind opening it for me...? Just a bit paranoid.

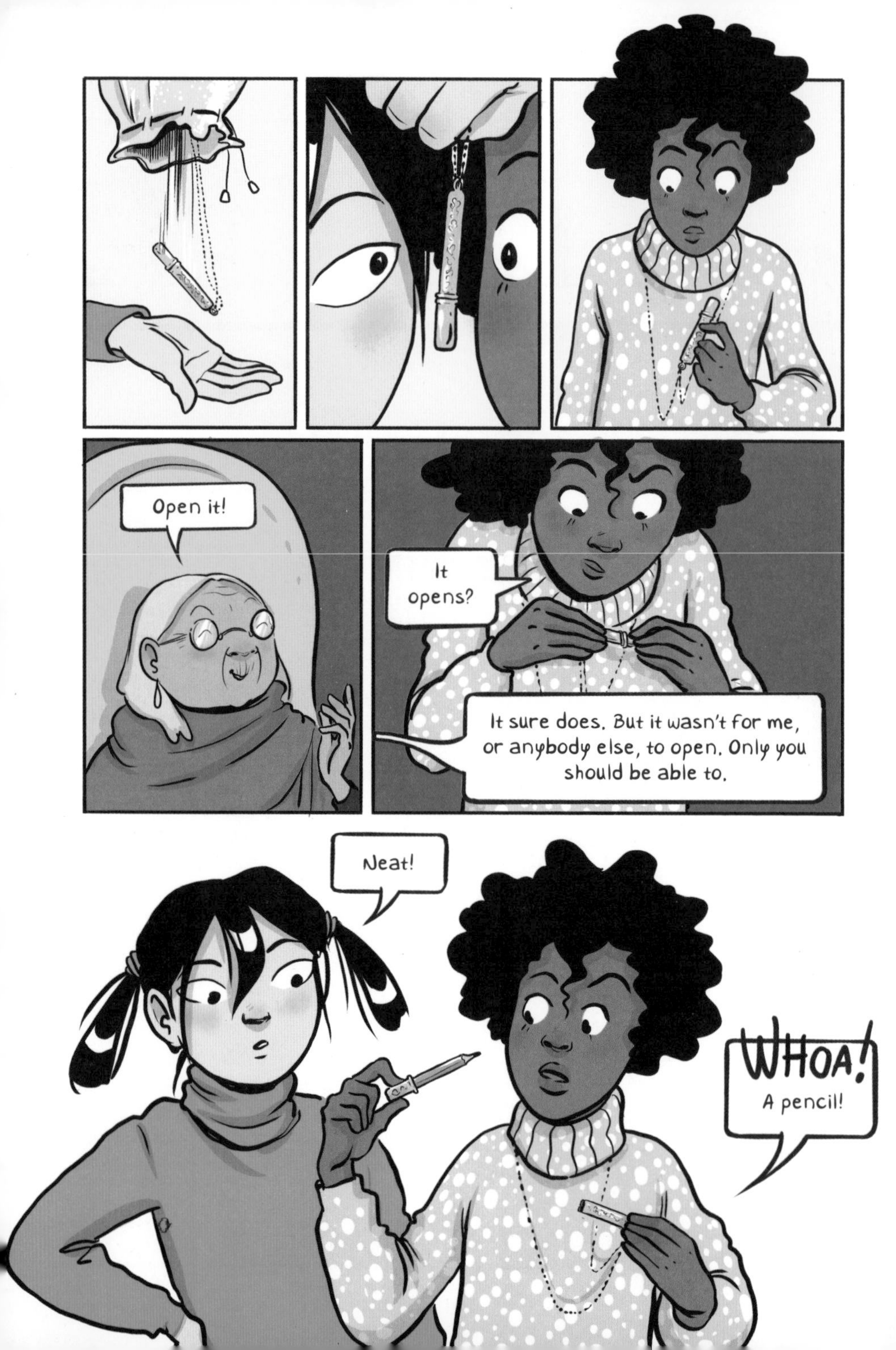
Open it!
It opens?
It sure does. But it wasn't for me, or anybody else, to open. Only you should be able to.
Neat!
WHOA! A pencil!

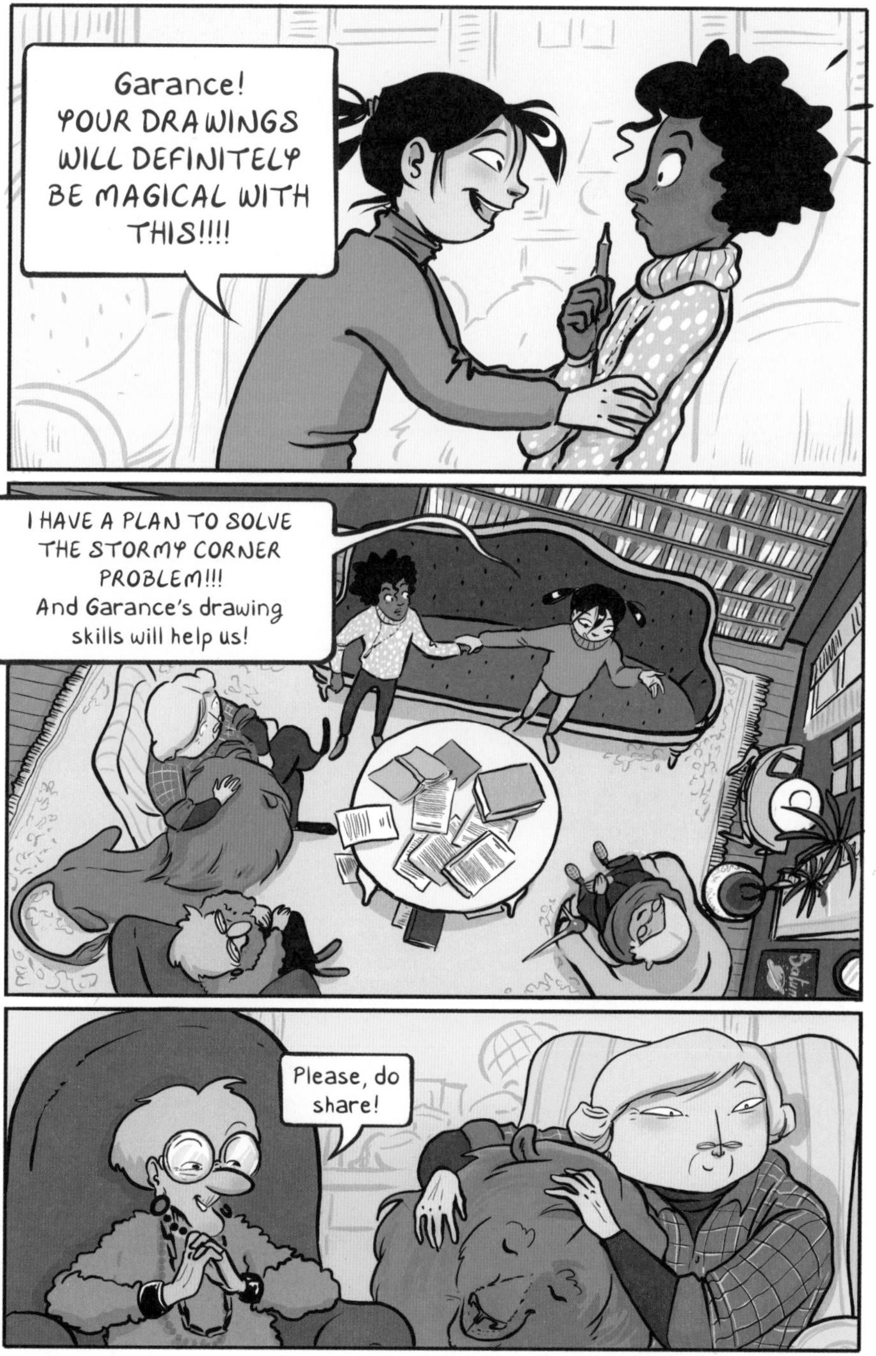

Garance! YOUR DRAWINGS WILL DEFINITELY BE MAGICAL WITH THIS!!!!
I HAVE A PLAN TO SOLVE THE STORMY CORNER PROBLEM!!! And Garance's drawing skills will help us!
Please, do share!

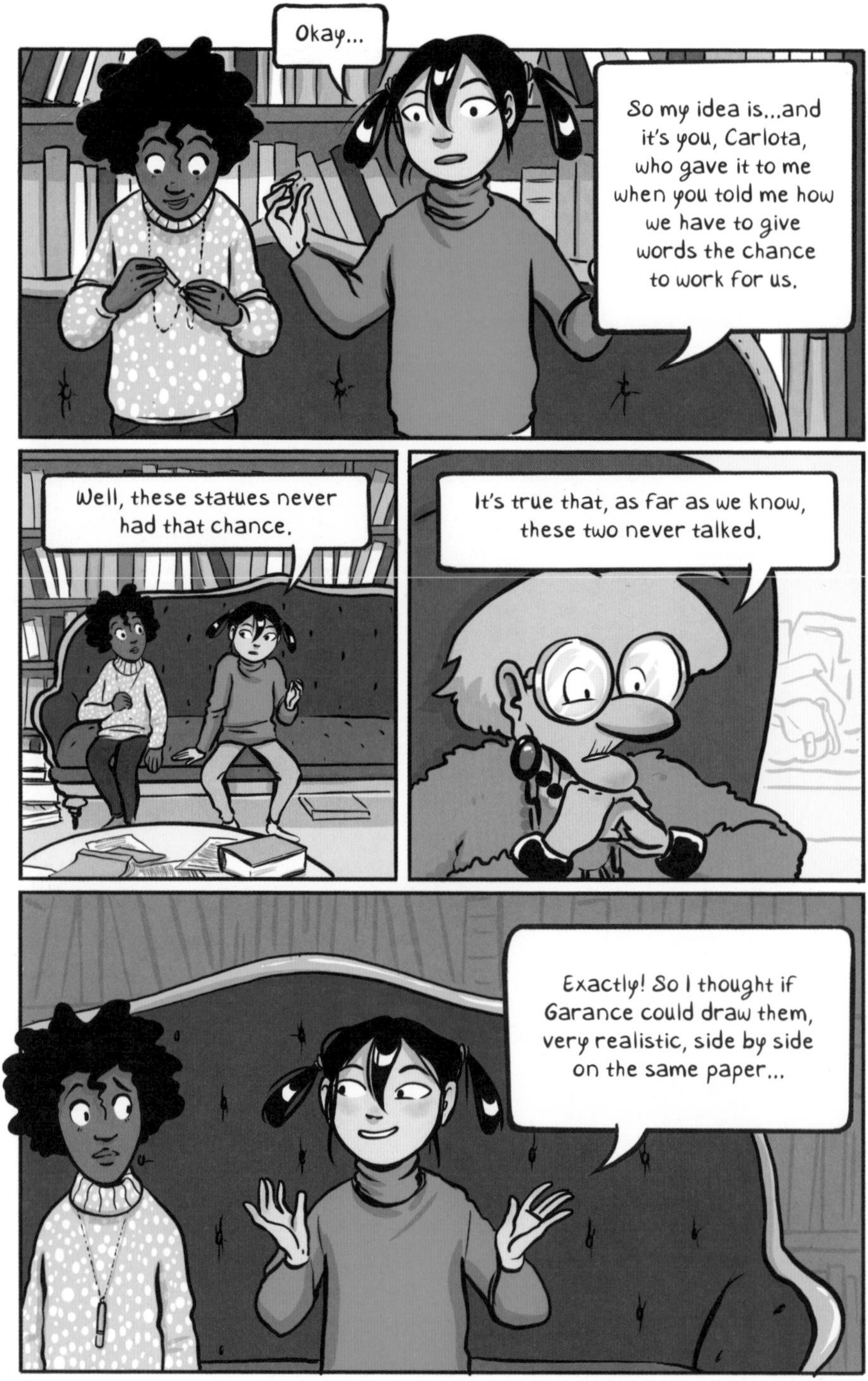

Okay...
So my idea is...and it's you, Carlota, who gave it to me when you told me how we have to give words the chance to work for us.
Well, these statues never had that chance.
It's true that, as far as we know, these two never talked.
Exactly! So I thought if Garance could draw them, very realistic, side by side on the same paper...

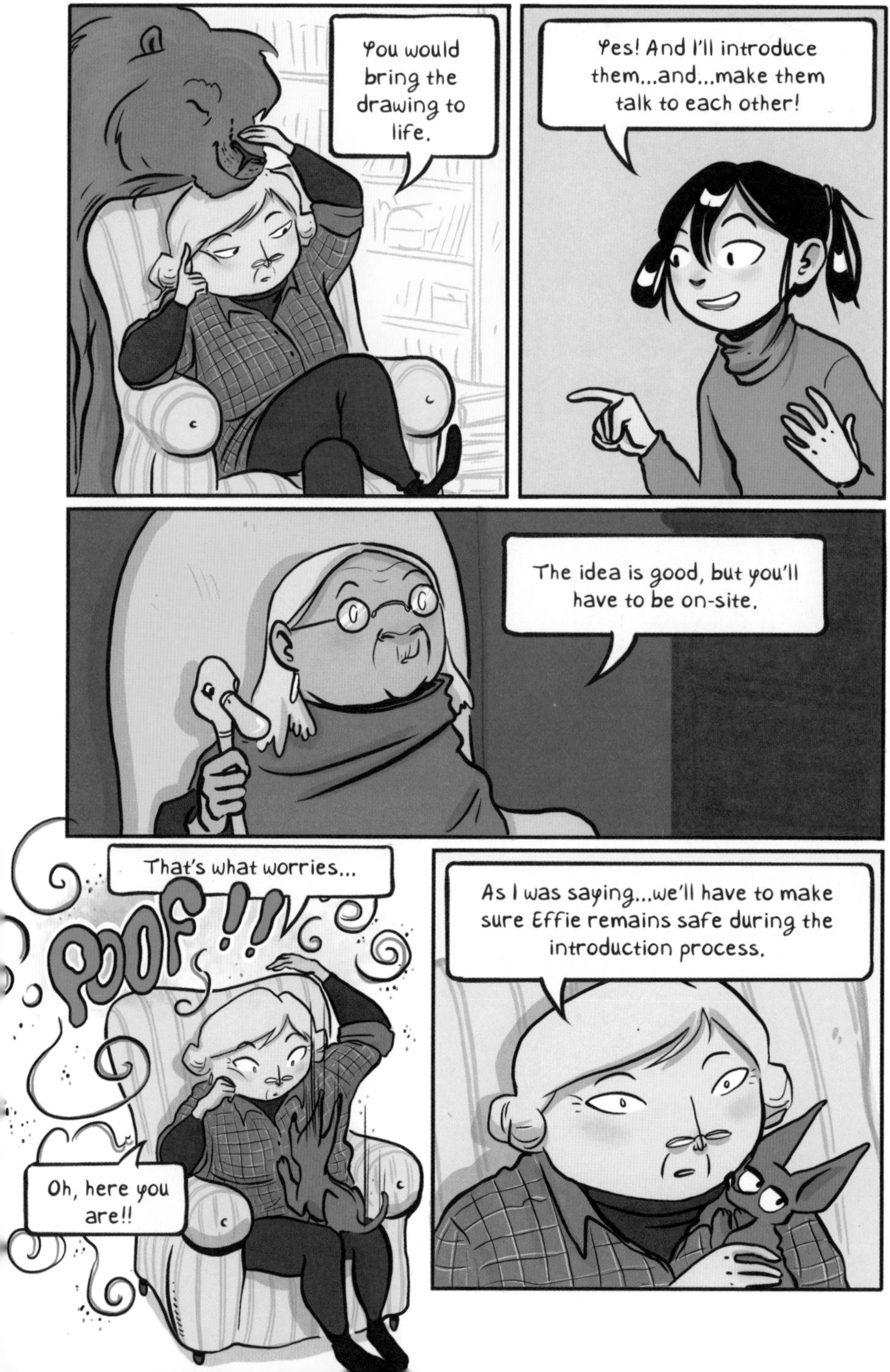
You would bring the drawing to life.
Yes! And I'll introduce them...and...make them talk to each other!
The idea is good, but you'll have to be on-site.
That's what worries...
POOF!!!
Oh, here you are!!
As I was saying...we'll have to make sure Effie remains safe during the introduction process.

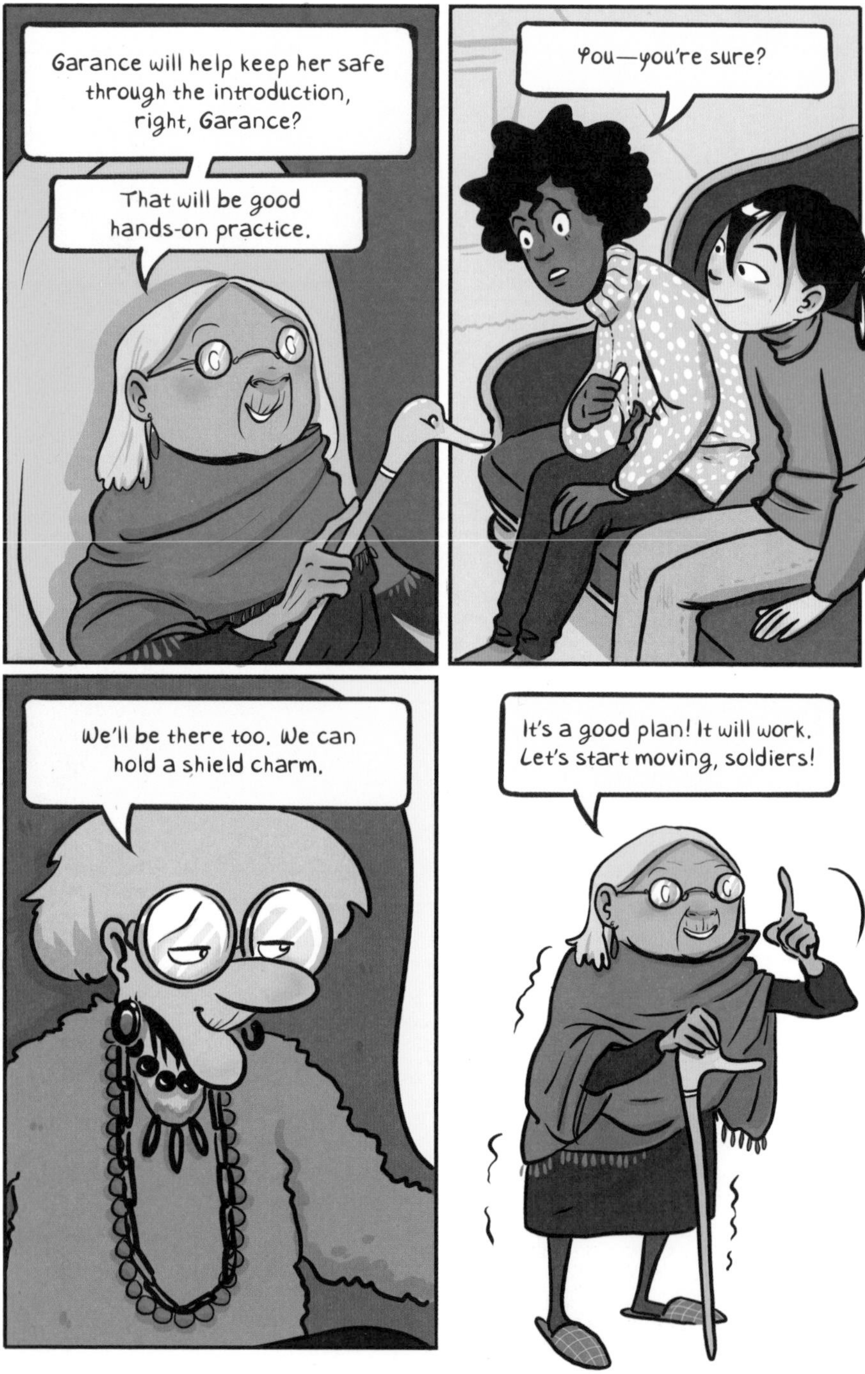
Garance will help keep her safe through the introduction, right, Garance?
That will be good hands-on practice.
You—you're sure?
We'll be there too. We can hold a shield charm.
It's a good plan! It will work. Let's start moving, soldiers!

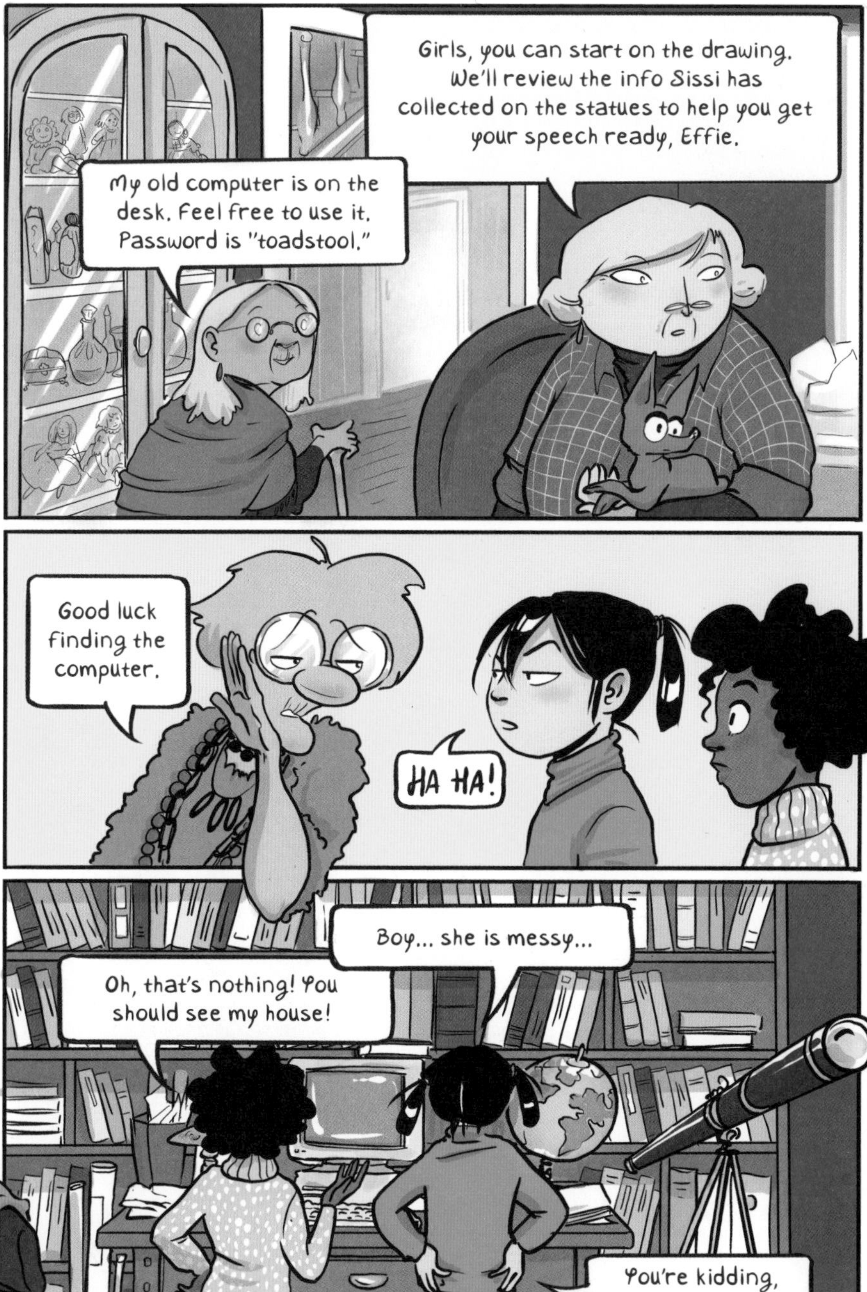

Girls, you can start on the drawing. We'll review the info Sissi has collected on the statues to help you get your speech ready, Effie.
My old computer is on the desk. Feel free to use it. Password is "toadstool."
Good luck finding the computer.
HA HA!
Boy... she is messy...
Oh, that's nothing! You should see my house!
You're kidding, right?

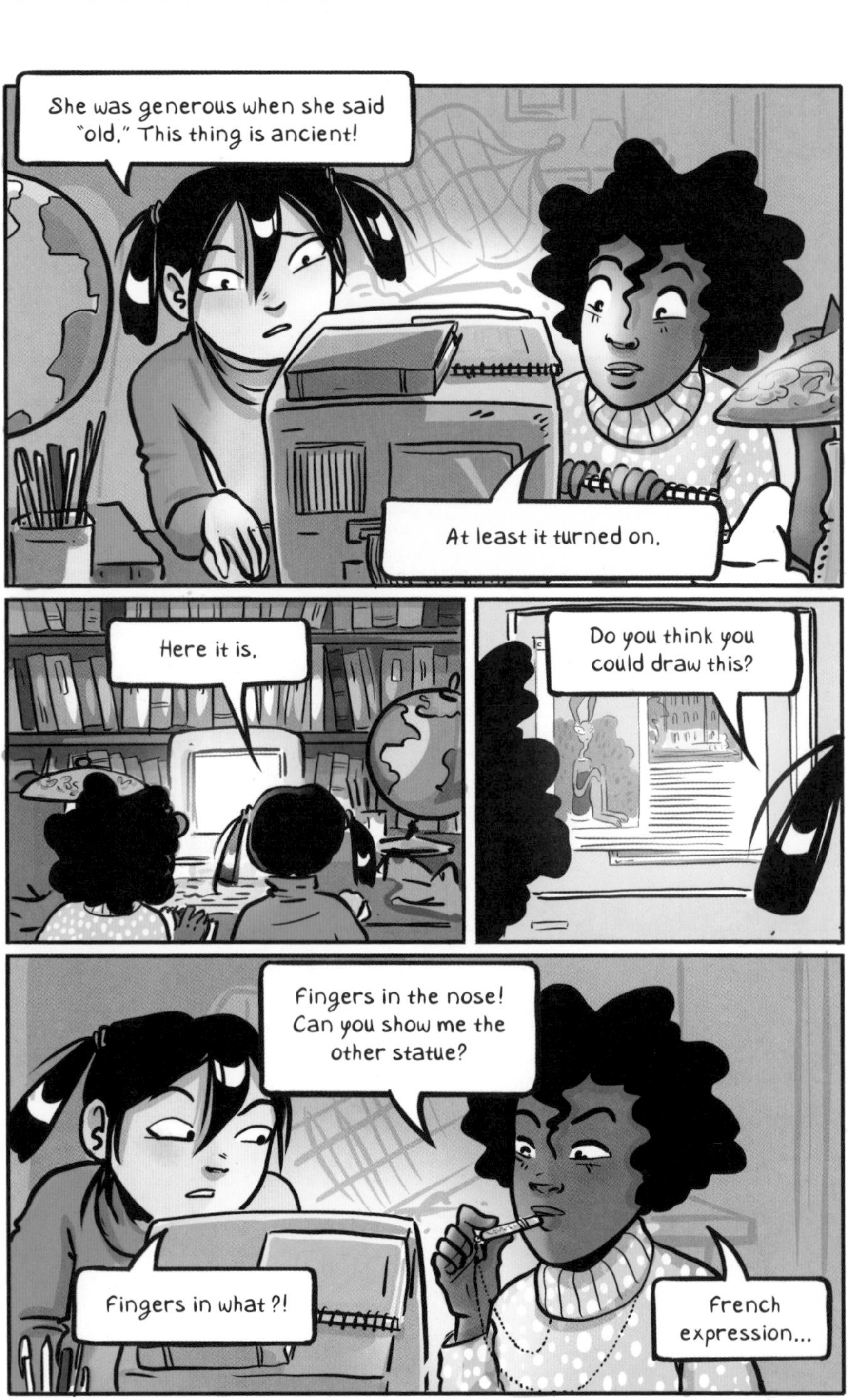
She was generous when she said "old." This thing is ancient!
At least it turned on.
Here it is.
Do you think you could draw this?
Fingers in the nose! Can you show me the other statue?
Fingers in what?!
French expression...

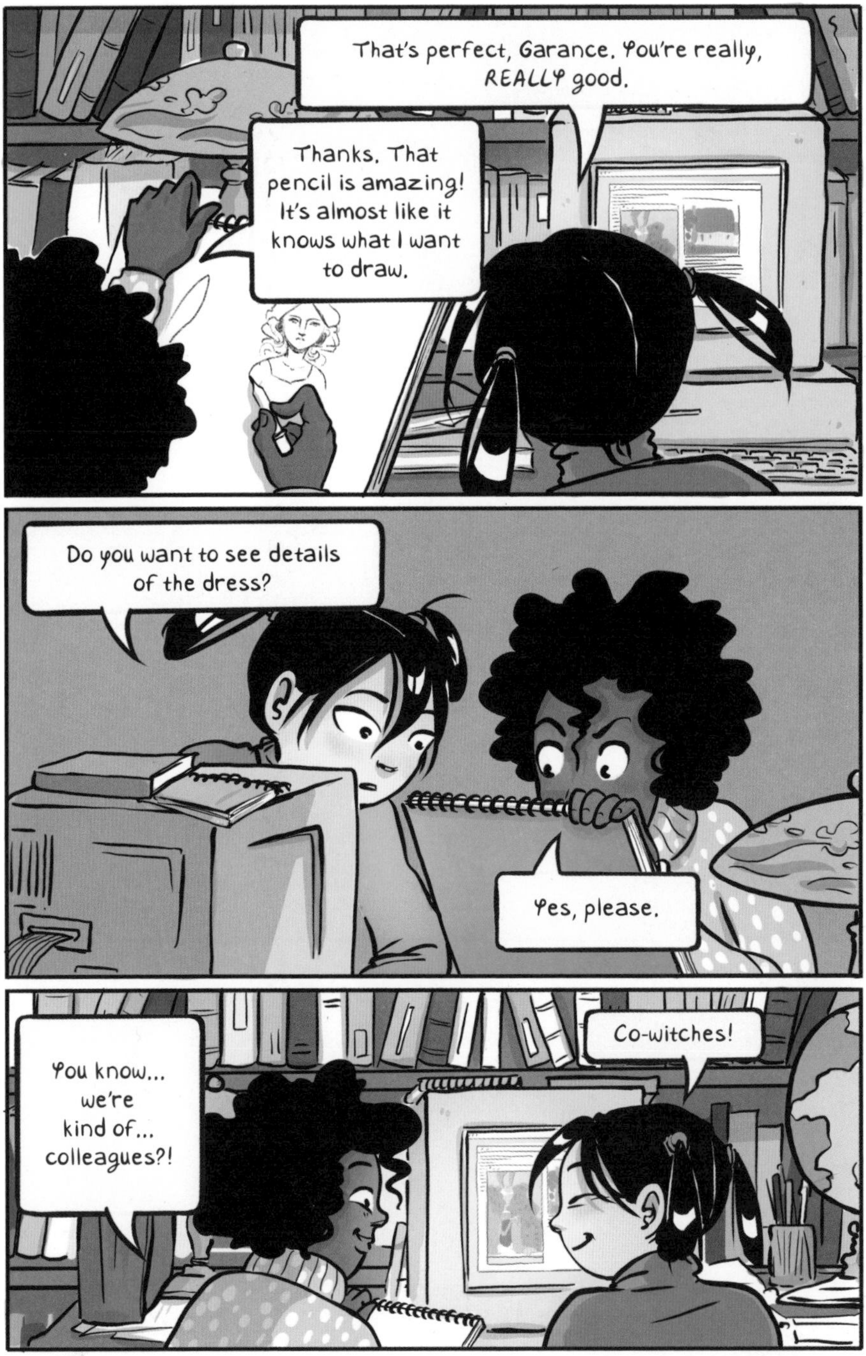
That's perfect, Garance. You're really, REALLY good.
Thanks. That pencil is amazing! It's almost like it knows what I want to draw.
Do you want to see details of the dress?
Yes, please.
You know... we're kind of... colleagues?!
Co-witches!

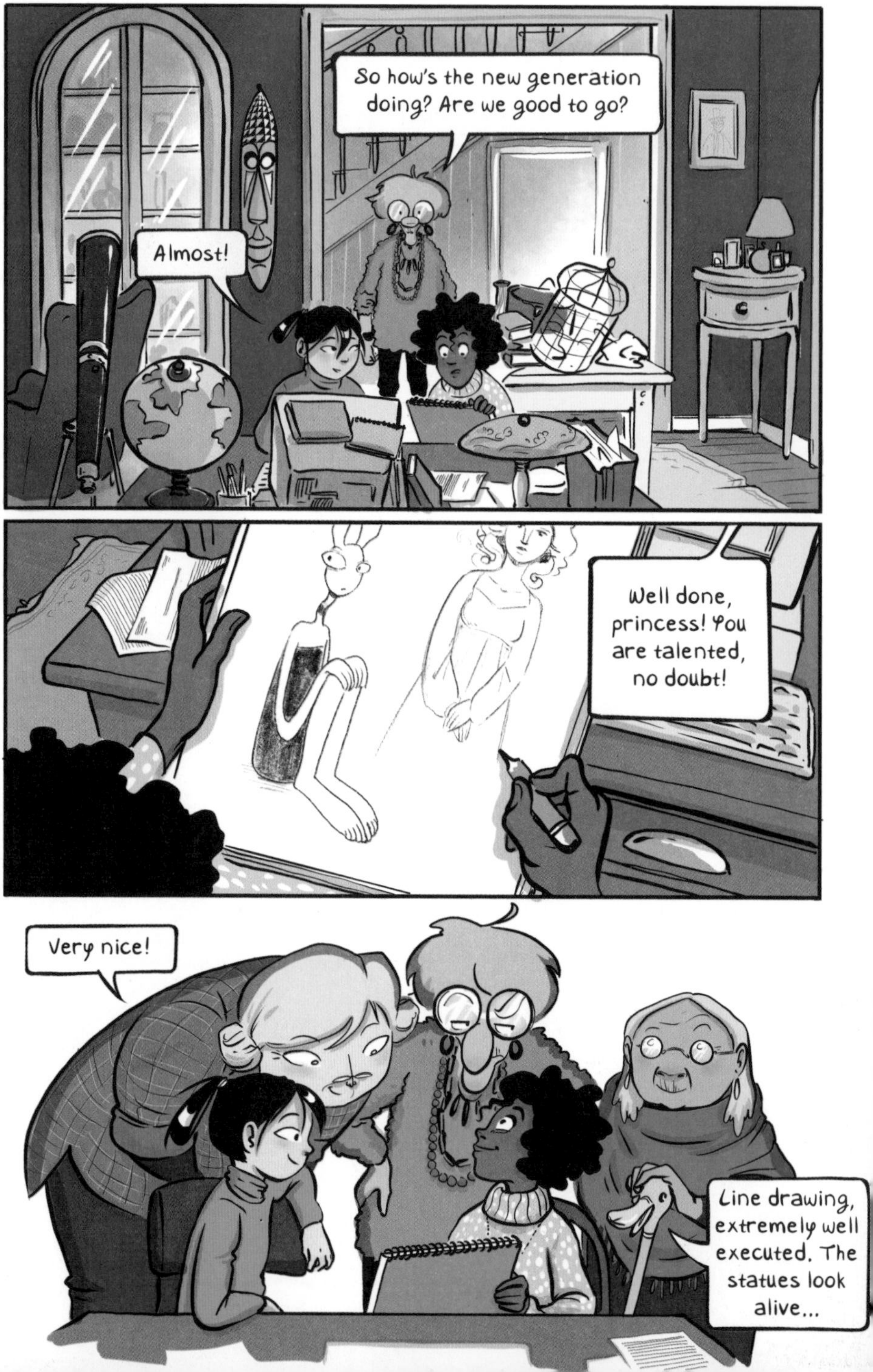
So how's the new generation doing? Are we good to go?
Almost!
Well done, princess! You are talented, no doubt!
Very nice!
Line drawing, extremely well executed. The statues look alive...

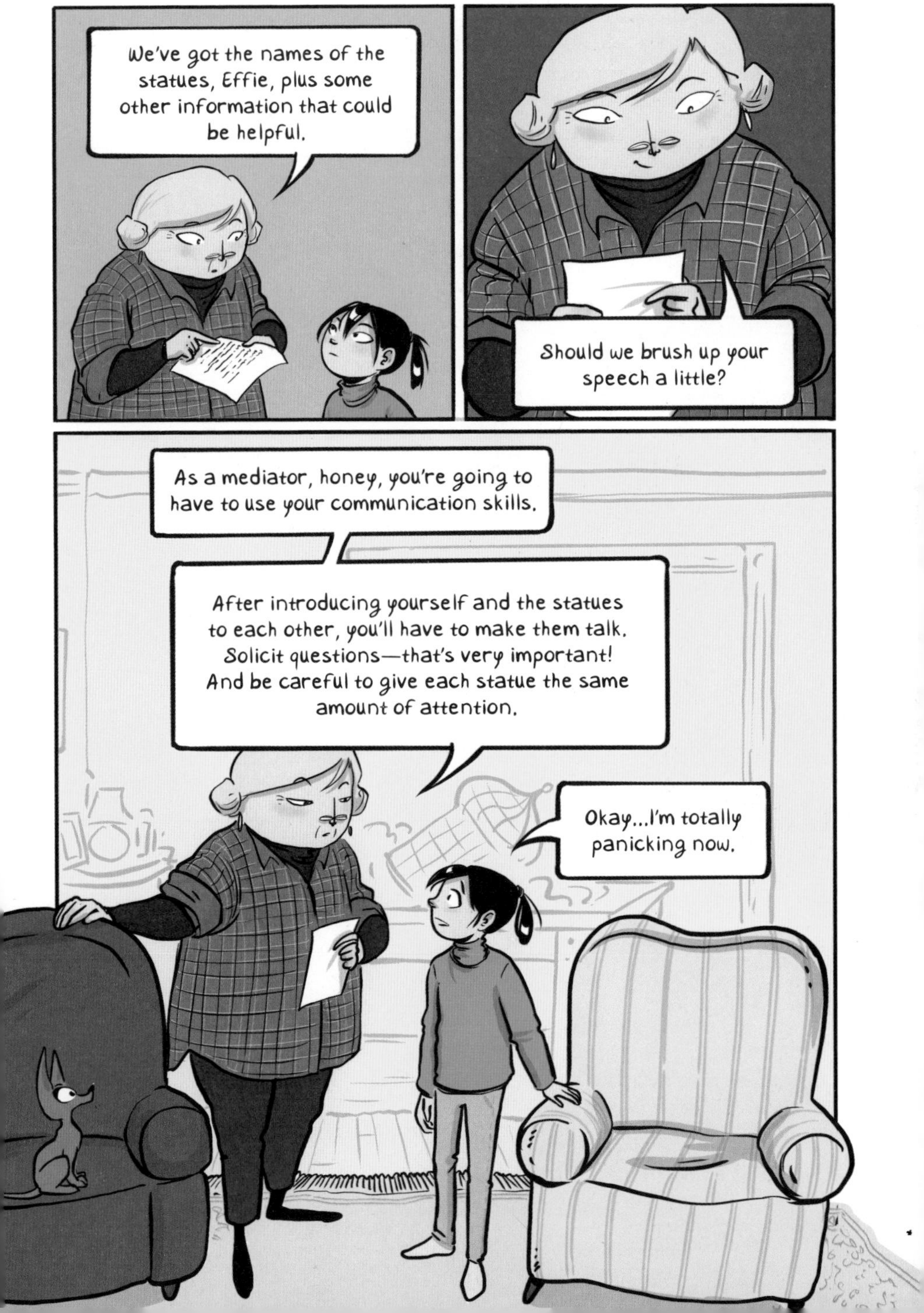
We've got the names of the statues, Effie, plus some other information that could be helpful.
Should we brush up your speech a little?
As a mediator, honey, you're going to have to use your communication skills.
After introducing yourself and the statues to each other, you'll have to make them talk. Solicit questions—that's very important! And be careful to give each statue the same amount of attention.
Okay...I'm totally panicking now.

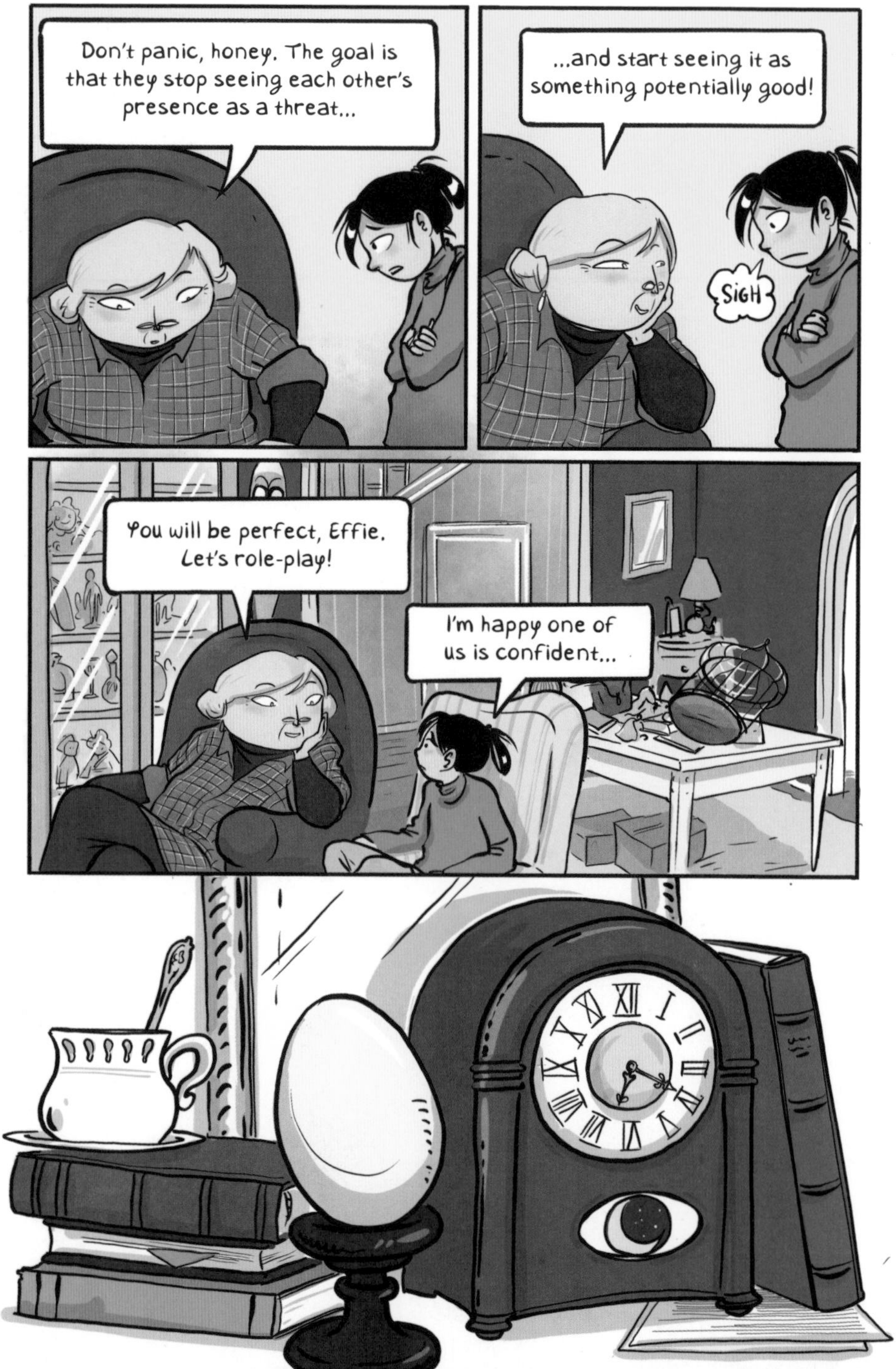
Don't panic, honey. The goal is that they stop seeing each other's presence as a threat...
...and start seeing it as something potentially good!
SIGH
You will be perfect, Effie. Let's role-play!
I'm happy one of us is confident...

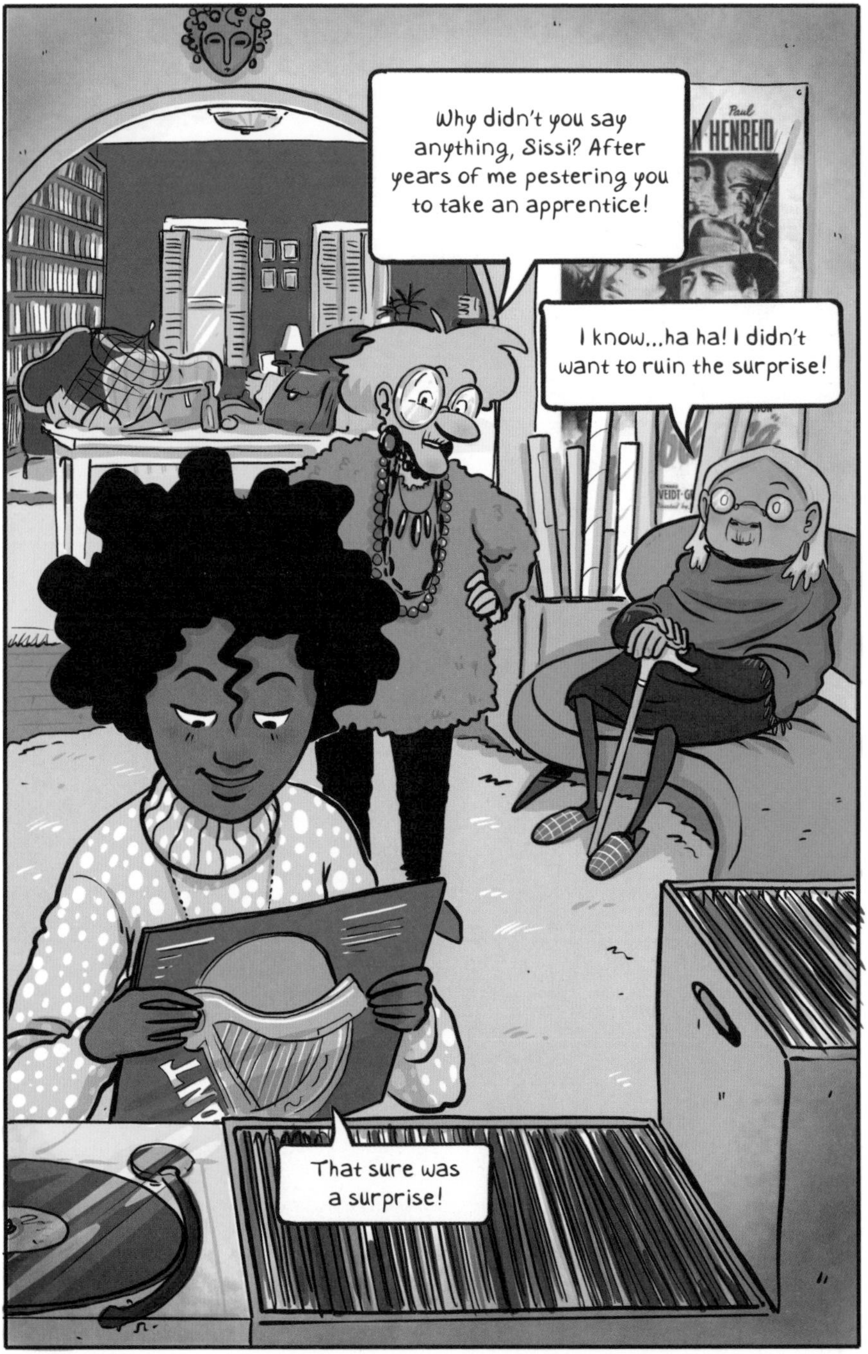
Why didn't you say anything, Sissi? After years of me pestering you to take an apprentice!
I know...ha ha! I didn't want to ruin the surprise!
That sure was a surprise!

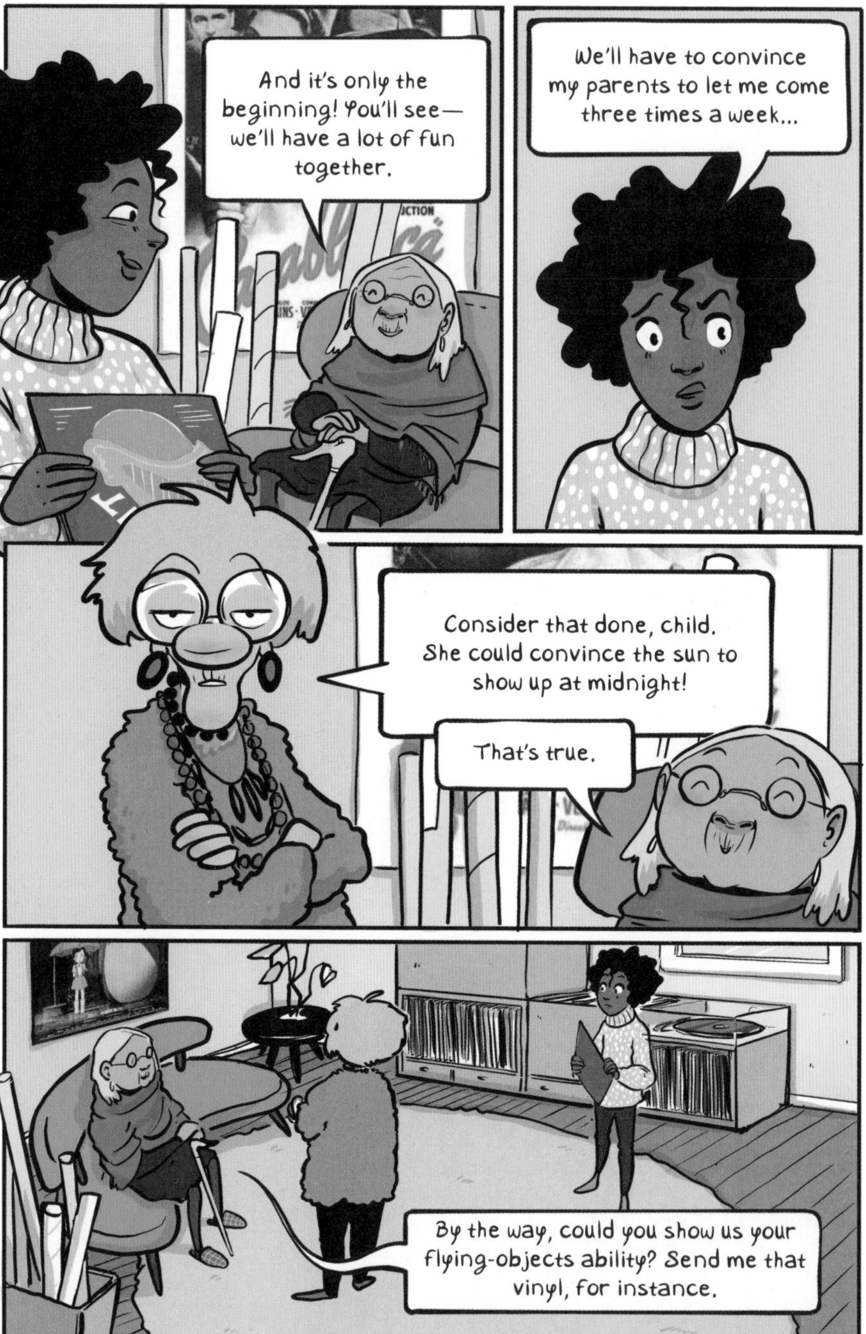
And it's only the beginning! You'll see—we'll have a lot of fun together.
We'll have to convince my parents to let me come three times a week...
Consider that done, child. She could convince the sun to show up at midnight!
That's true.
By the way, could you show us your flying-objects ability? Send me that vinyl, for instance.

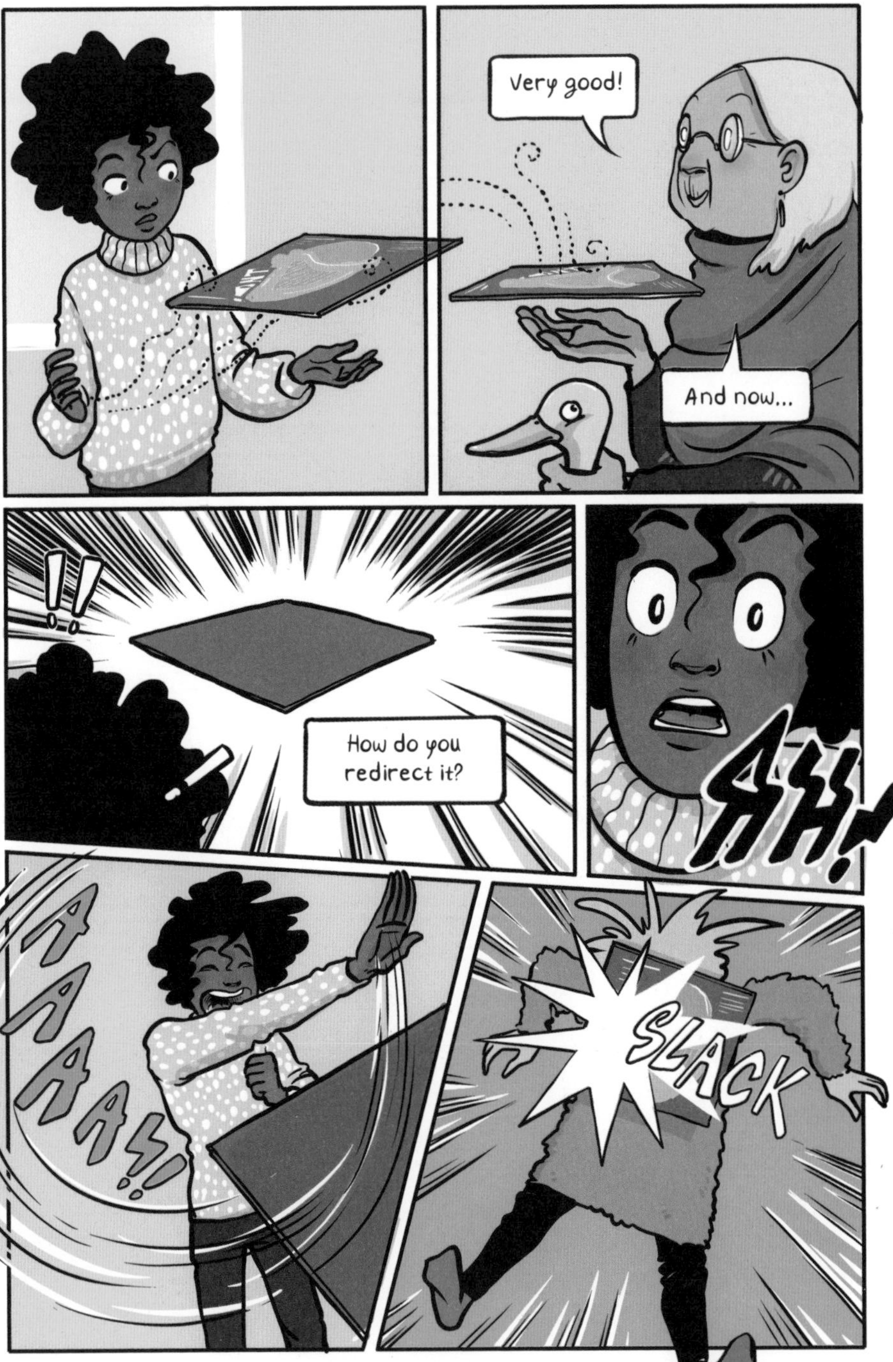
Very good!
And now...
!!
How do you redirect it?
AH!
AAAA!!
SLACK

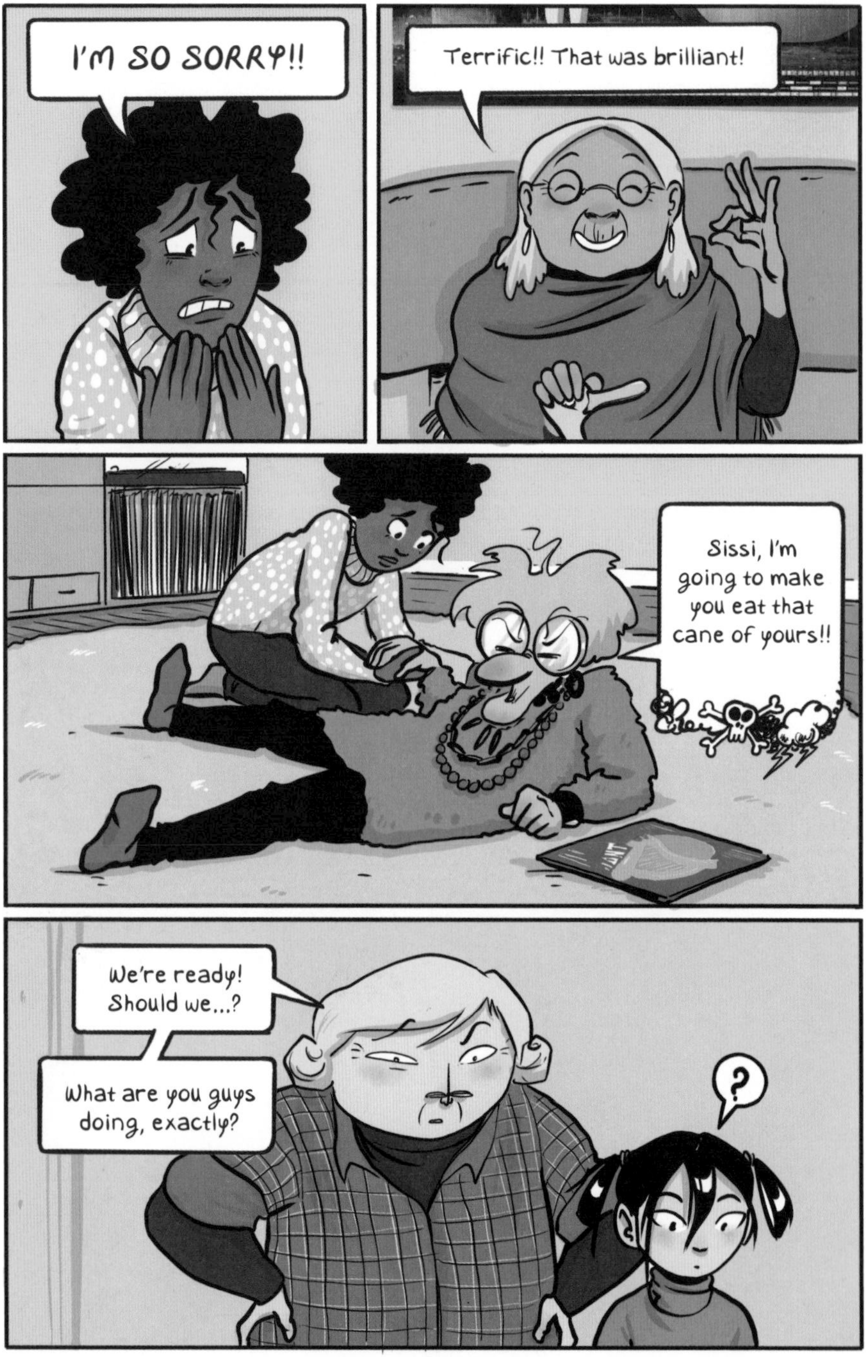
I'M SO SORRY!!
Terrific!! That was brilliant!
Sissi, I'm going to make you eat that cane of yours!!
We're ready! Should we...?
What are you guys doing, exactly?
?

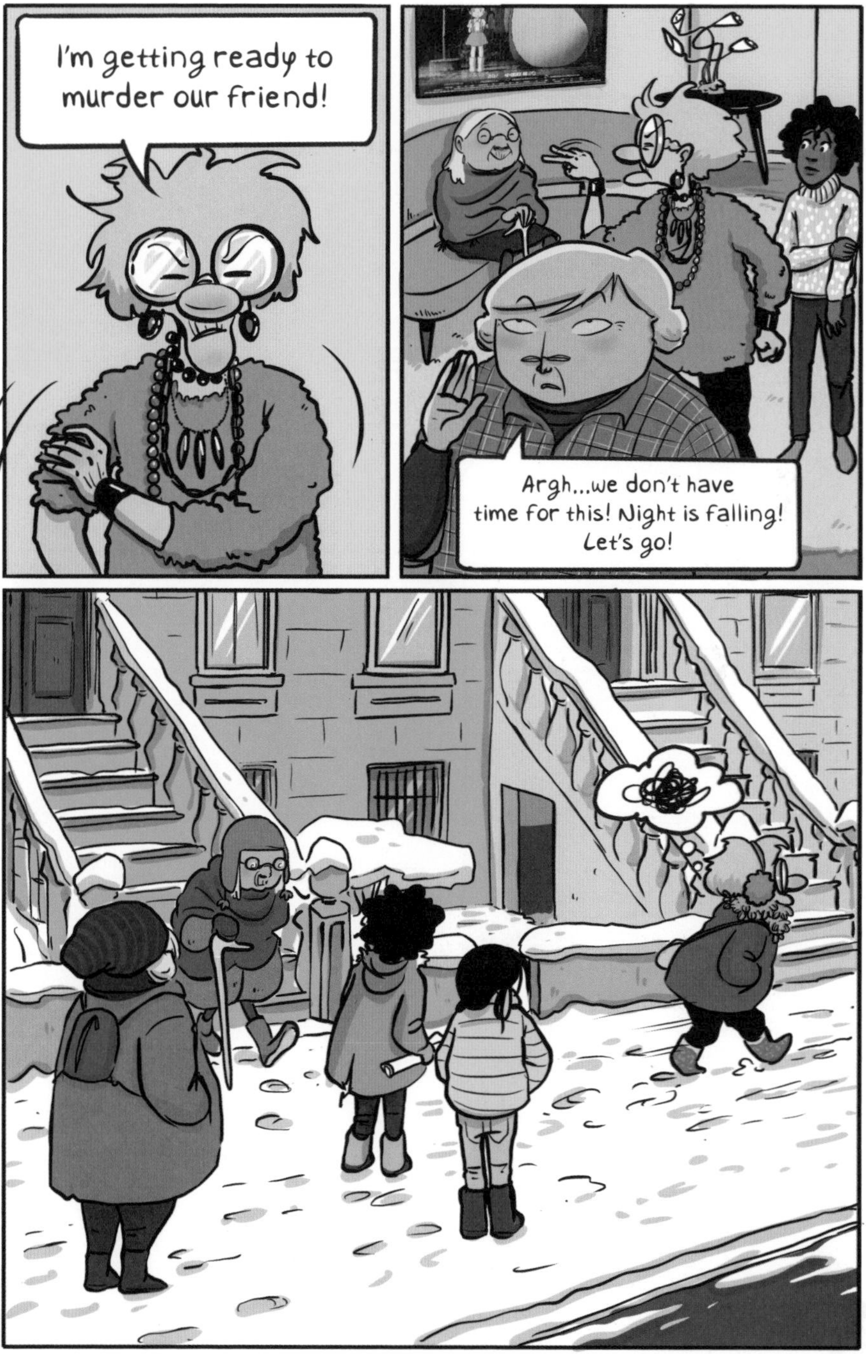
I'm getting ready to murder our friend!
Argh...we don't have time for this! Night is falling! Let's go!

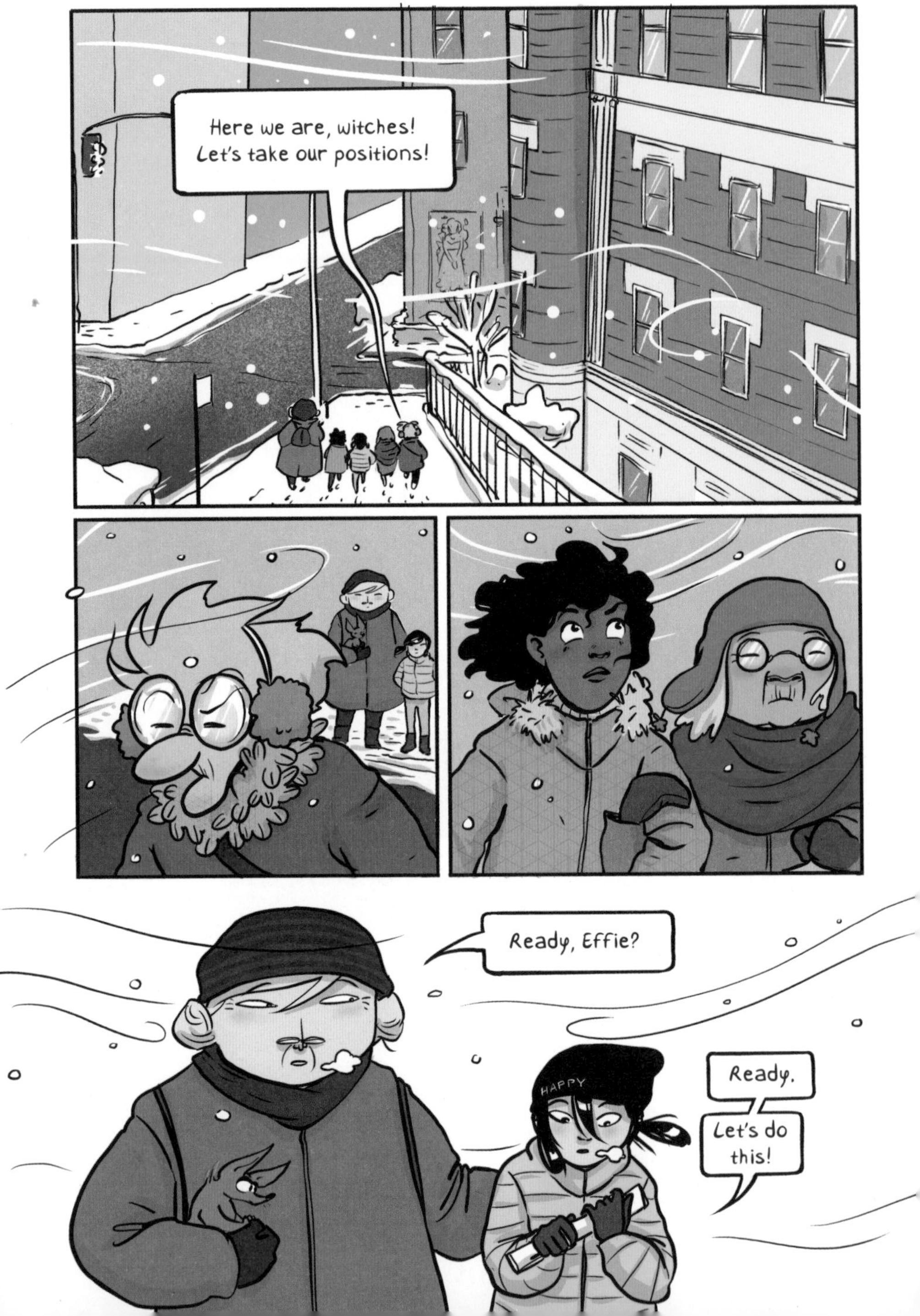

Here we are, witches!
Let's take our positions!
Ready, Effie?
HAPPY
Ready.
Let's do this!

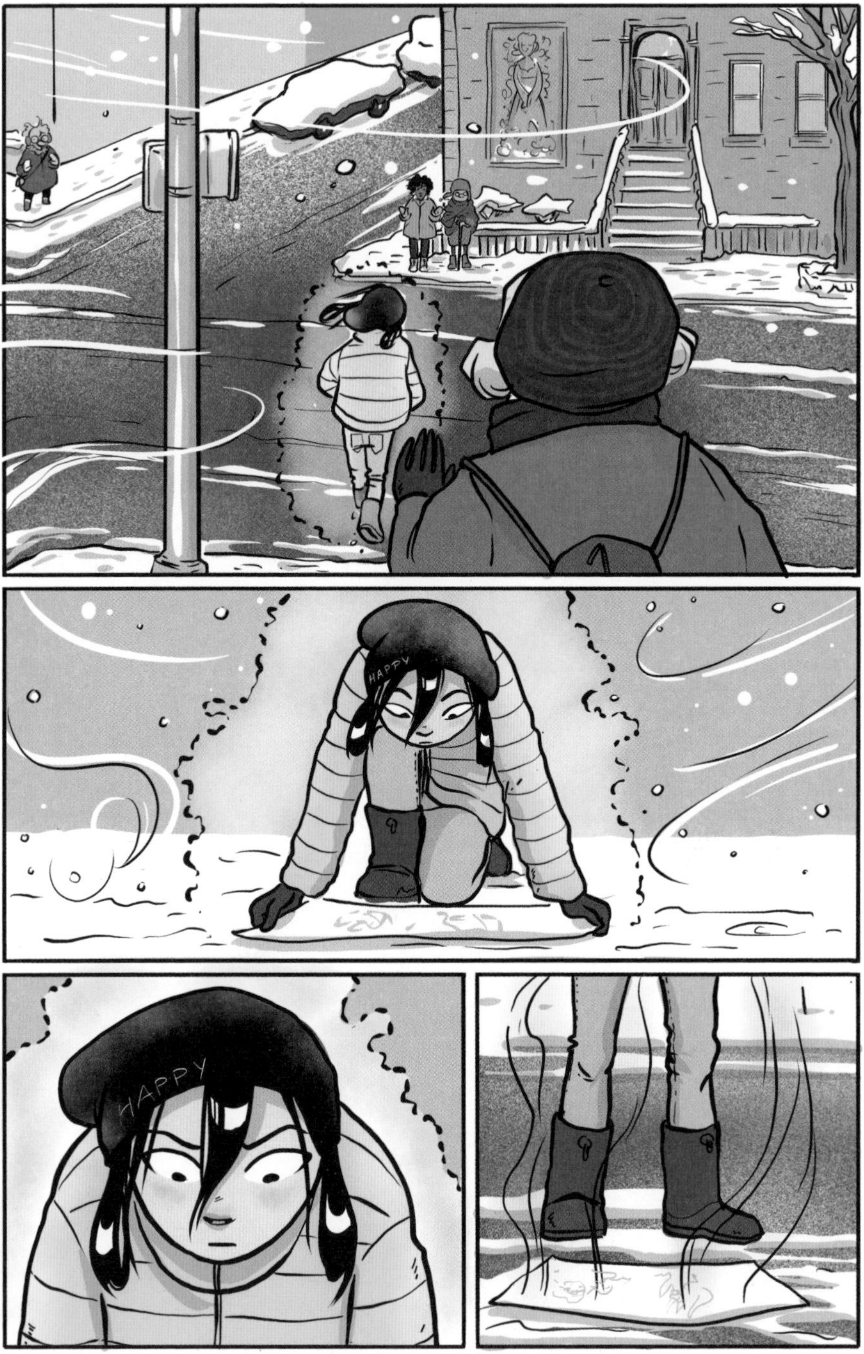
HAPPY
HAPPY

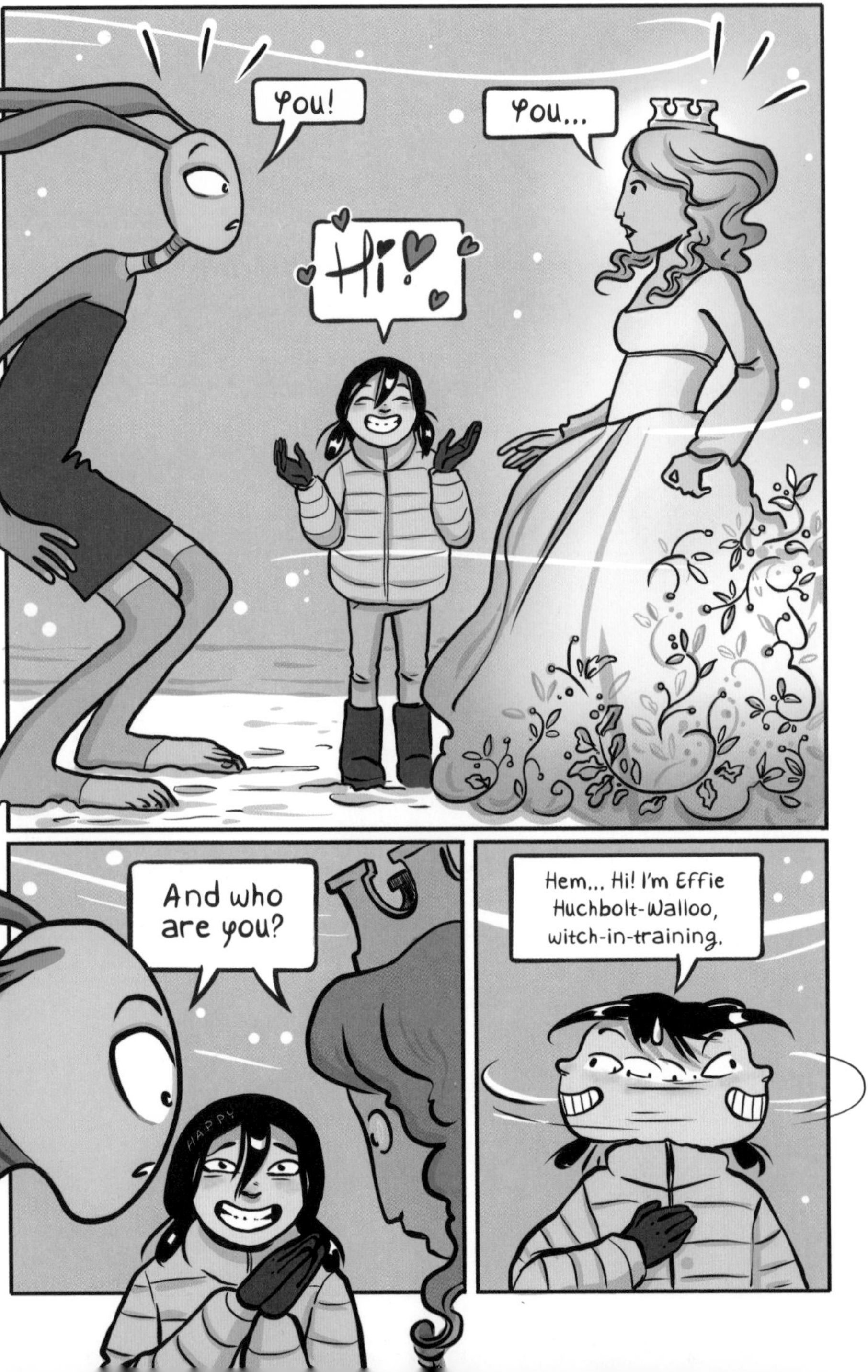
You!
You...
Hi!
And who are you?
Hem... Hi! I'm Effie Huchbolt-Walloo, witch-in-training.
HAPPY

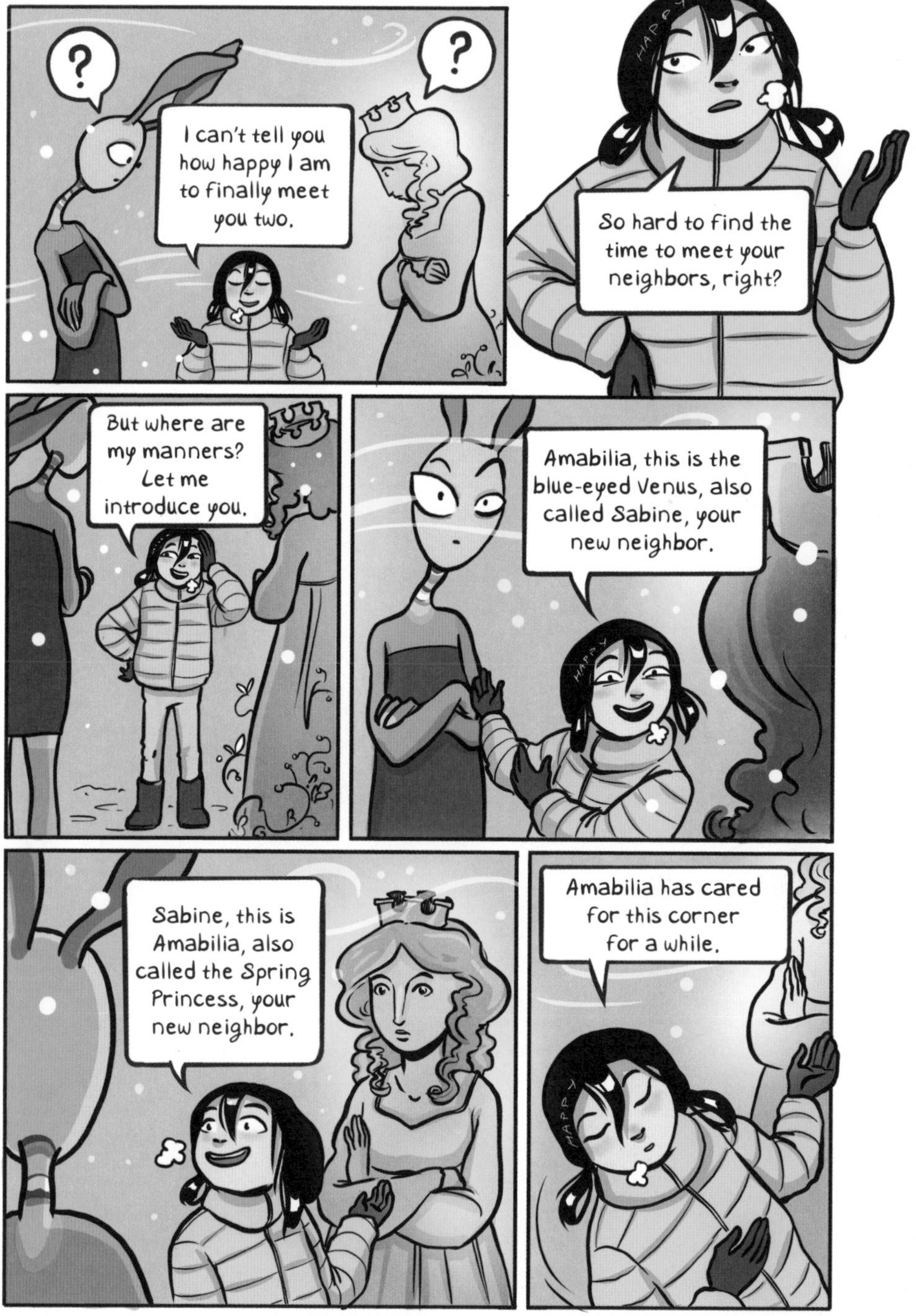
?
?
I can't tell you how happy I am to finally meet you two.
HAPPY
So hard to find the time to meet your neighbors, right?
But where are my manners? Let me introduce you.
Amabilia, this is the blue-eyed Venus, also called Sabine, your new neighbor.
HAPPY
Sabine, this is Amabilia, also called the Spring Princess, your new neighbor.
Amabilia has cared for this corner for a while.
HAPPY

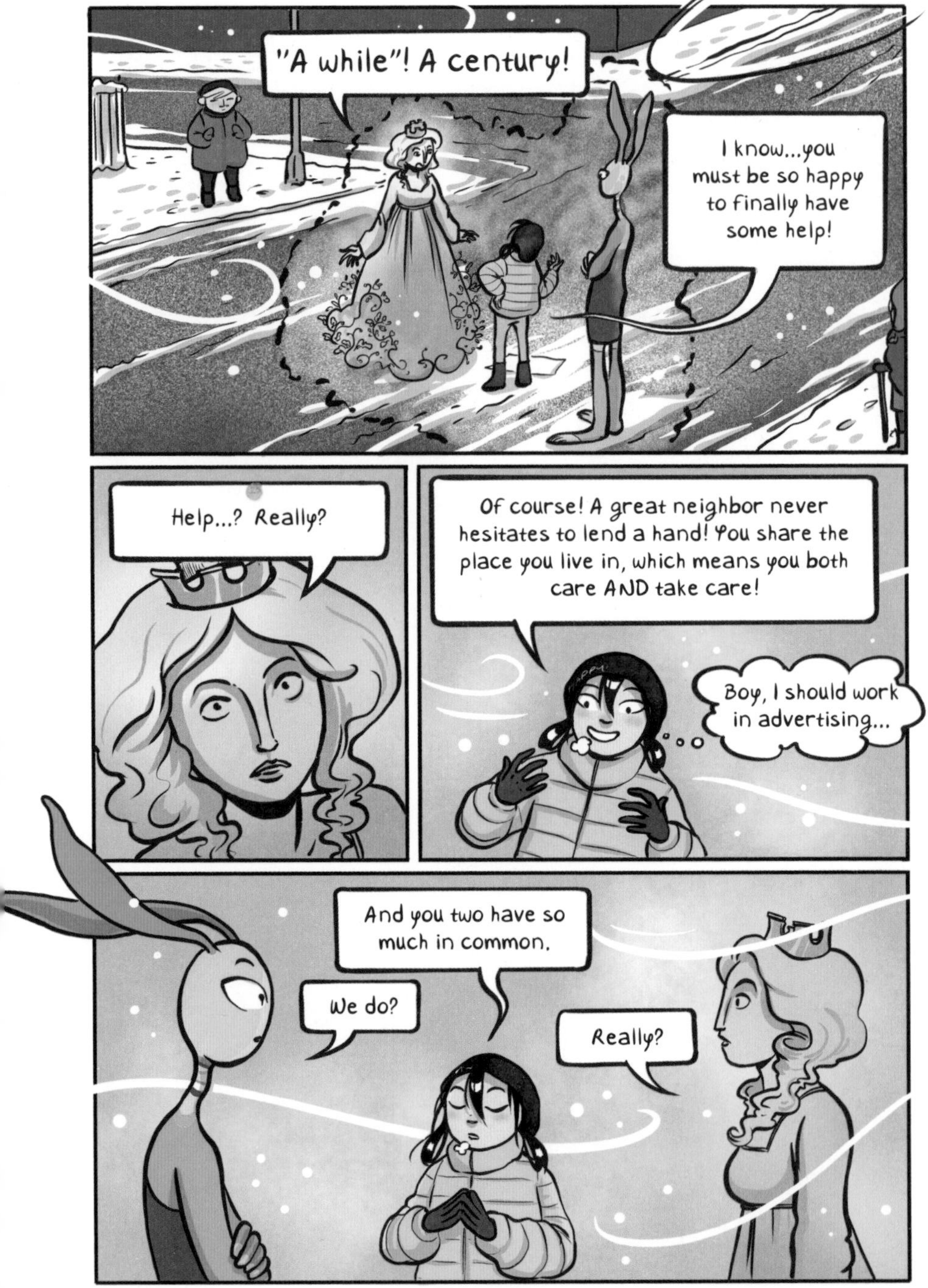
"A while"! A century!
I know...you must be so happy to finally have some help!
Help...? Really?
Of course! A great neighbor never hesitates to lend a hand! You share the place you live in, which means you both care AND take care!
Boy, I should work in advertising...
And you two have so much in common.
We do?
Really?

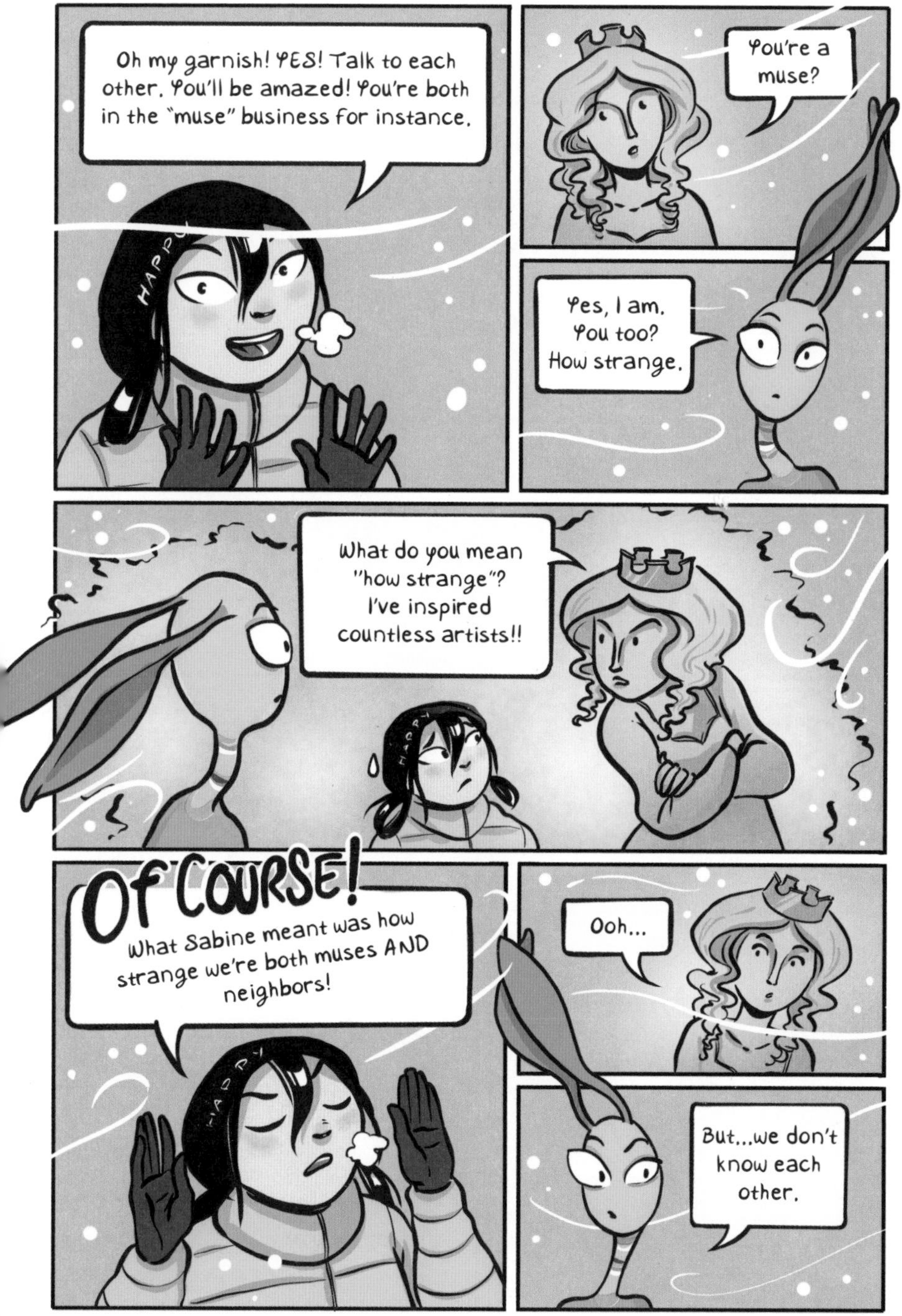
Oh my garnish! YES! Talk to each other. You'll be amazed! You're both in the "muse" business for instance.
You're a muse?
Yes, I am. You too? How strange.
HAPPY
What do you mean "how strange"? I've inspired countless artists!!
OF COURSE!
What Sabine meant was how strange we're both muses AND neighbors!
Ooh...
But...we don't know each other.

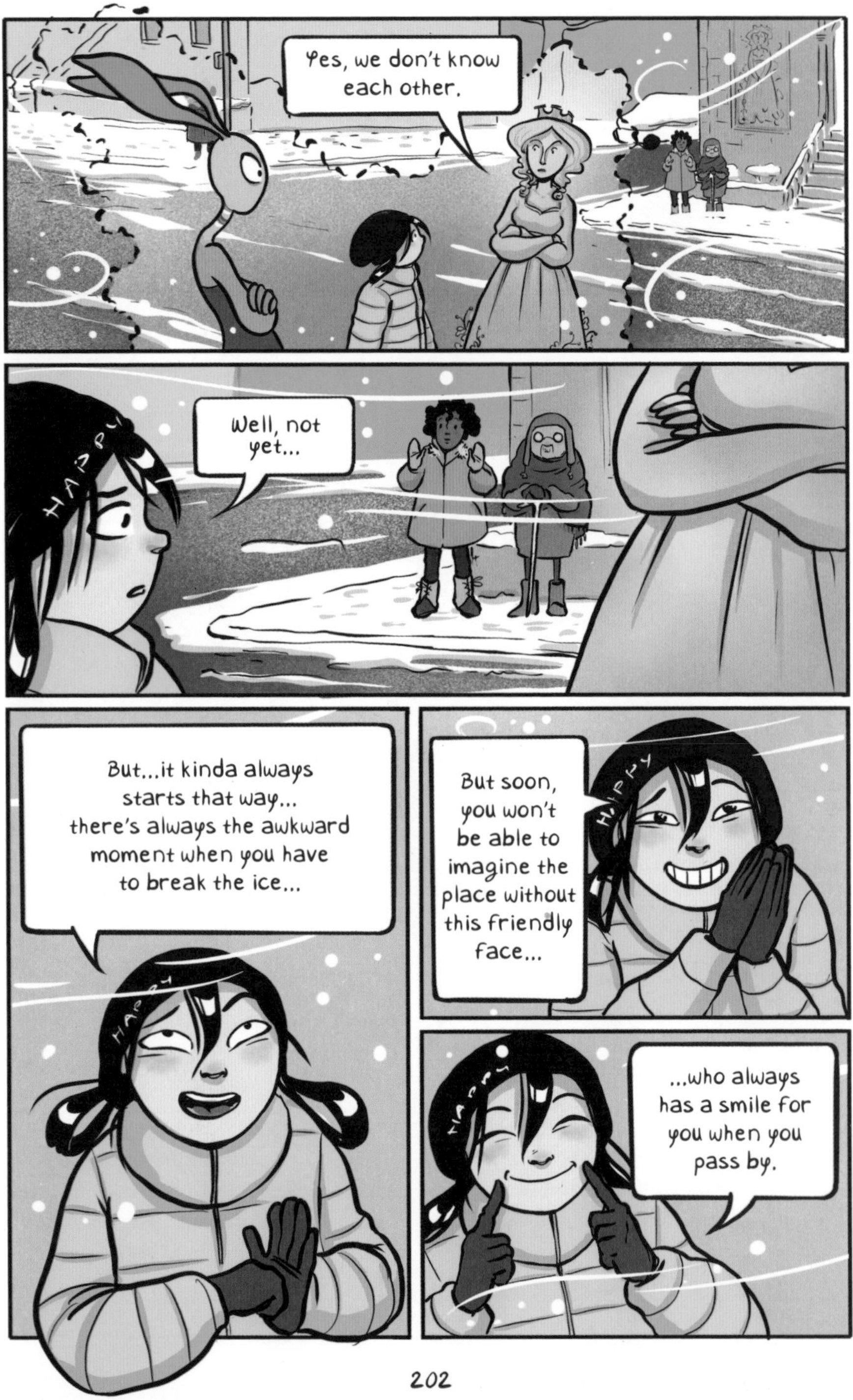
Yes, we don't know each other.
Well, not yet...
But...it kinda always starts that way... there's always the awkward moment when you have to break the ice...
But soon, you won't be able to imagine the place without this friendly face...
...who always has a smile for you when you pass by.

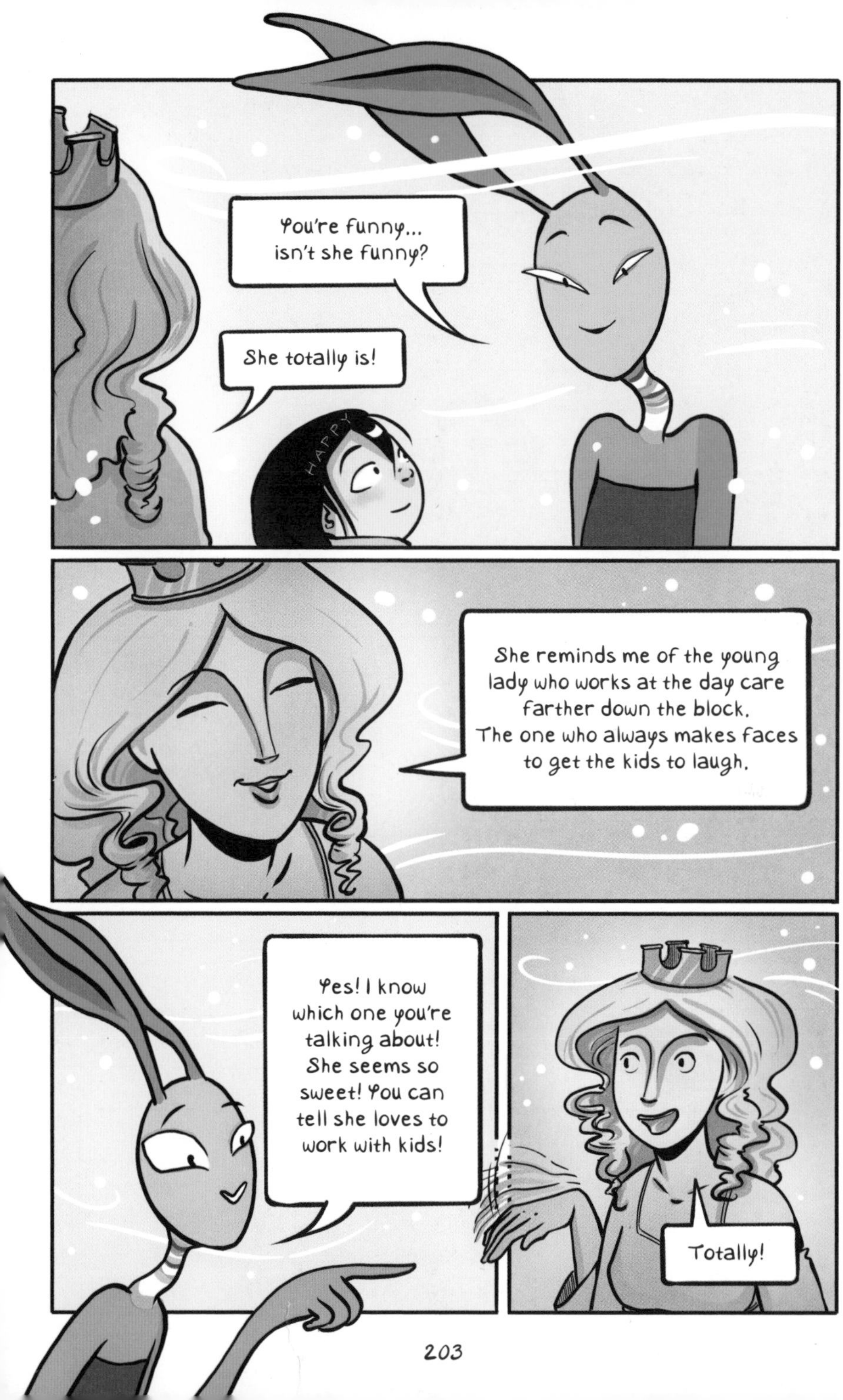
You're funny... isn't she funny?
She totally is!
HAPPY
She reminds me of the young lady who works at the day care farther down the block. The one who always makes faces to get the kids to laugh.
Yes! I know which one you're talking about! She seems so sweet! You can tell she loves to work with kids!
Totally!

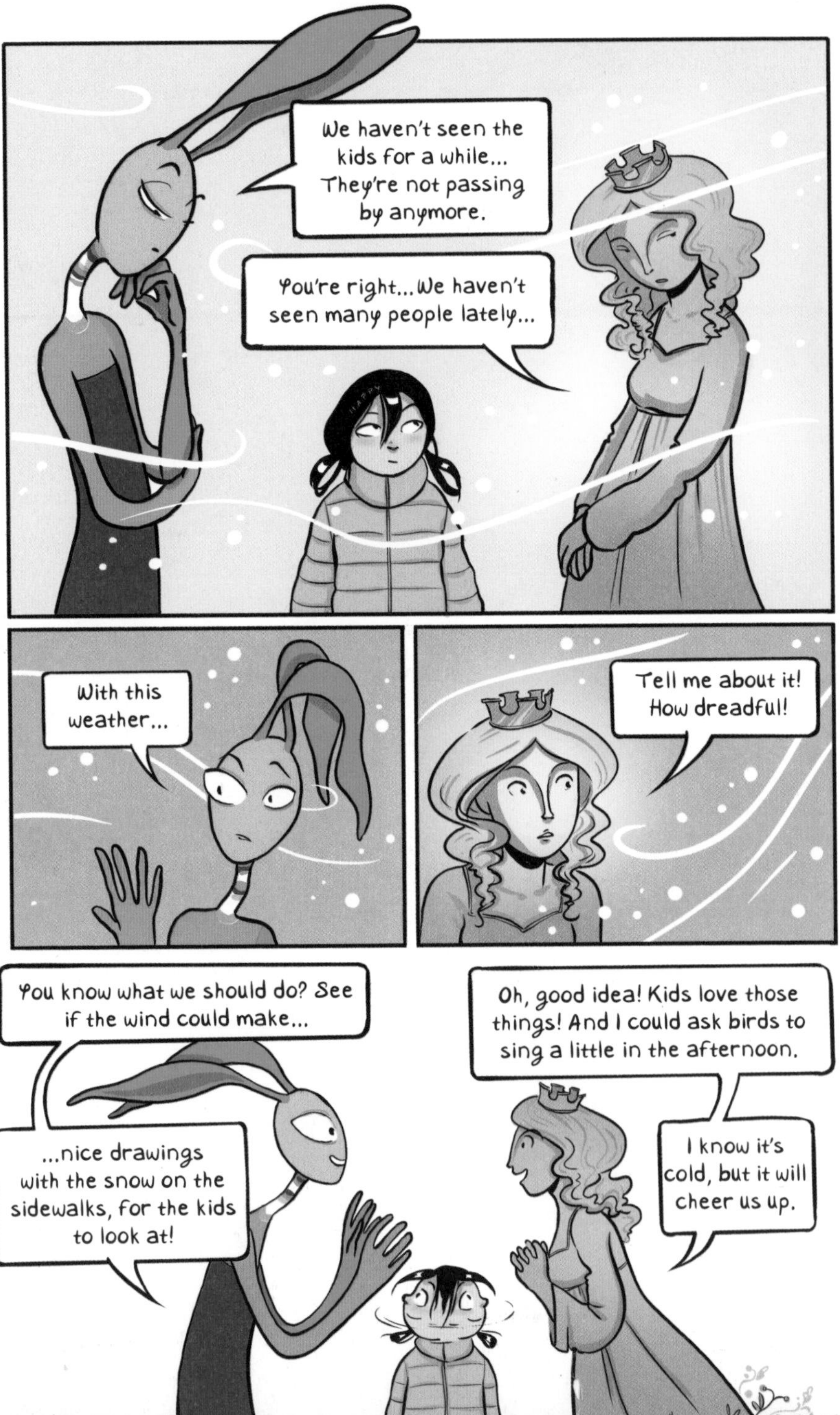
We haven't seen the kids for a while... They're not passing by anymore.
You're right... We haven't seen many people lately...
With this weather...
Tell me about it! How dreadful!
You know what we should do? See if the wind could make...
...nice drawings with the snow on the sidewalks, for the kids to look at!
Oh, good idea! Kids love those things! And I could ask birds to sing a little in the afternoon.
I know it's cold, but it will cheer us up.

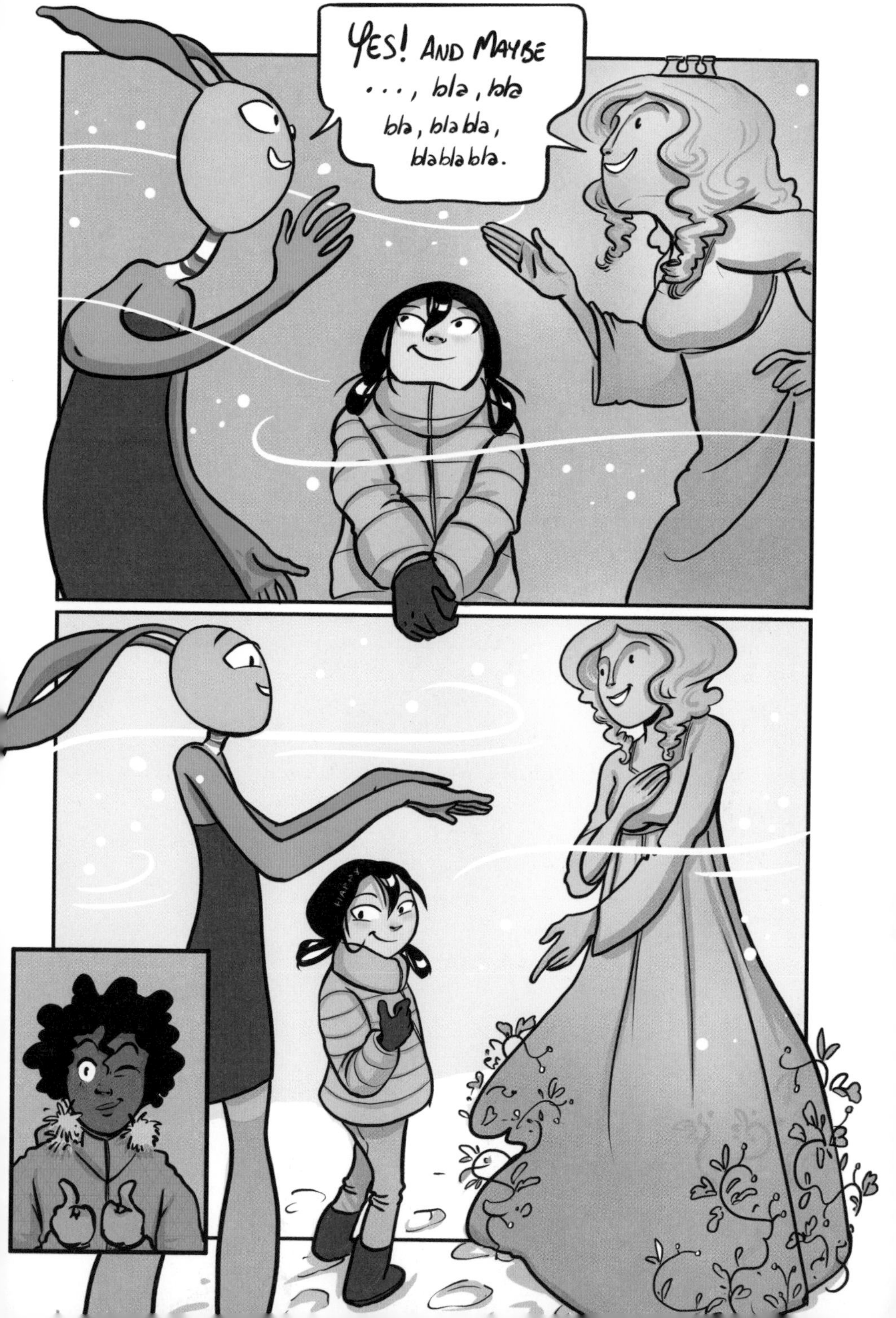
YES! AND MAYBE . . . , bla, bla bla, blabla, blablabla.

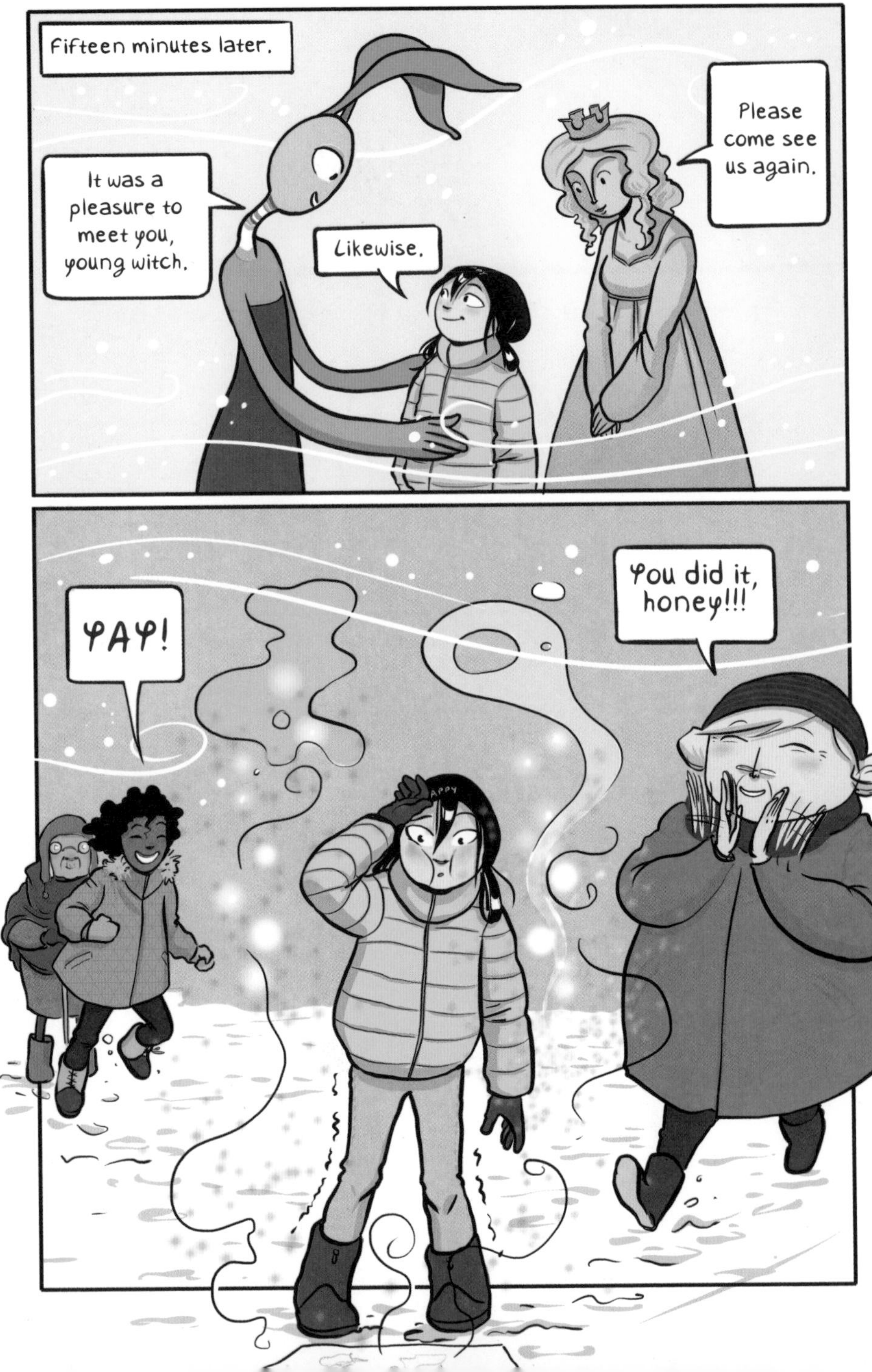
Fifteen minutes later.
It was a pleasure to meet you, young witch.
Likewise.
Please come see us again.
YAY!
You did it, honey!!!

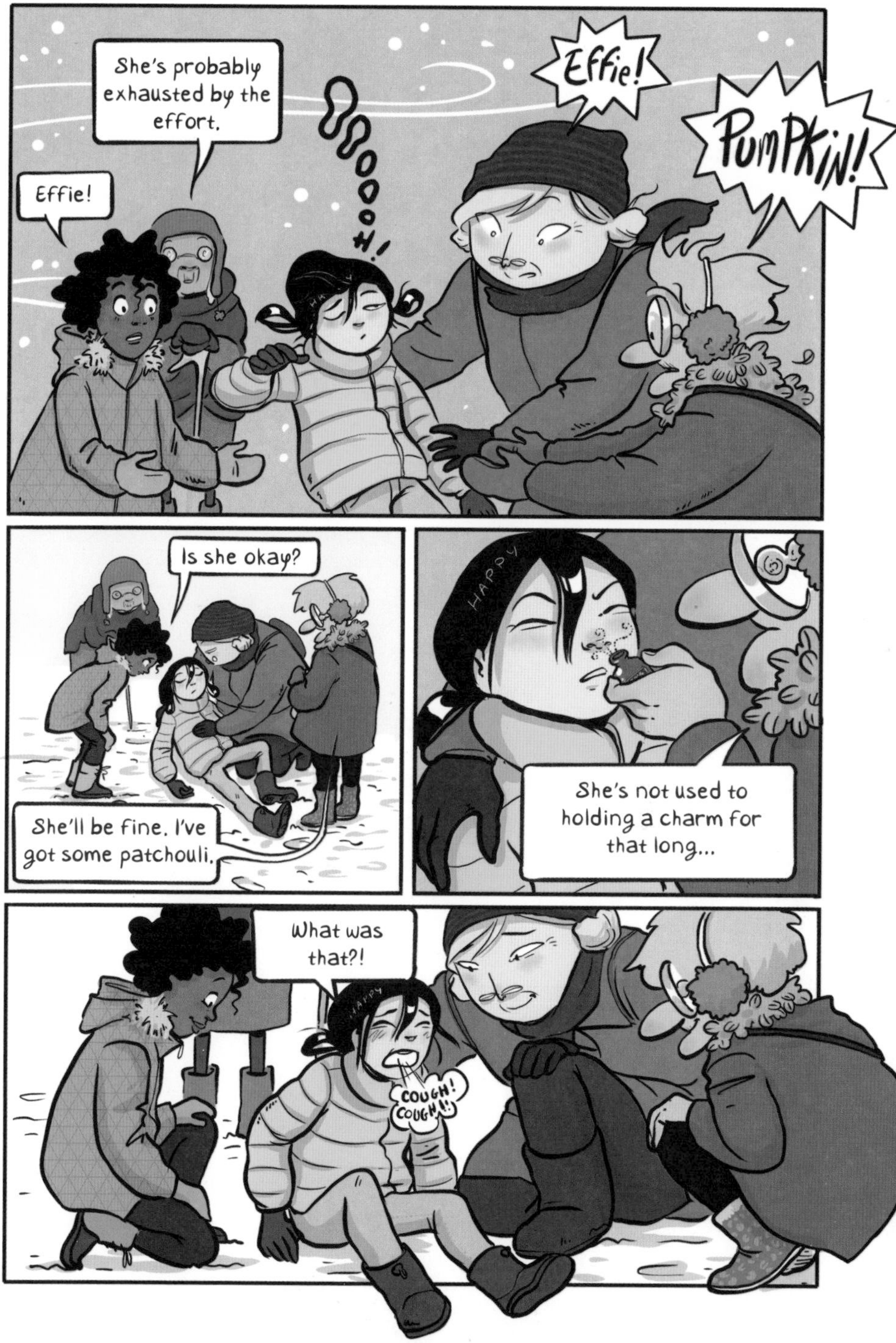
She's probably exhausted by the effort.
Effie!
OOOOOOH!
Effie!
PUMPKIN!
Is she okay?
She'll be fine. I've got some patchouli.
HAPPY
She's not used to holding a charm for that long...
What was that?!
HAPPY
COUGH! COUGH!

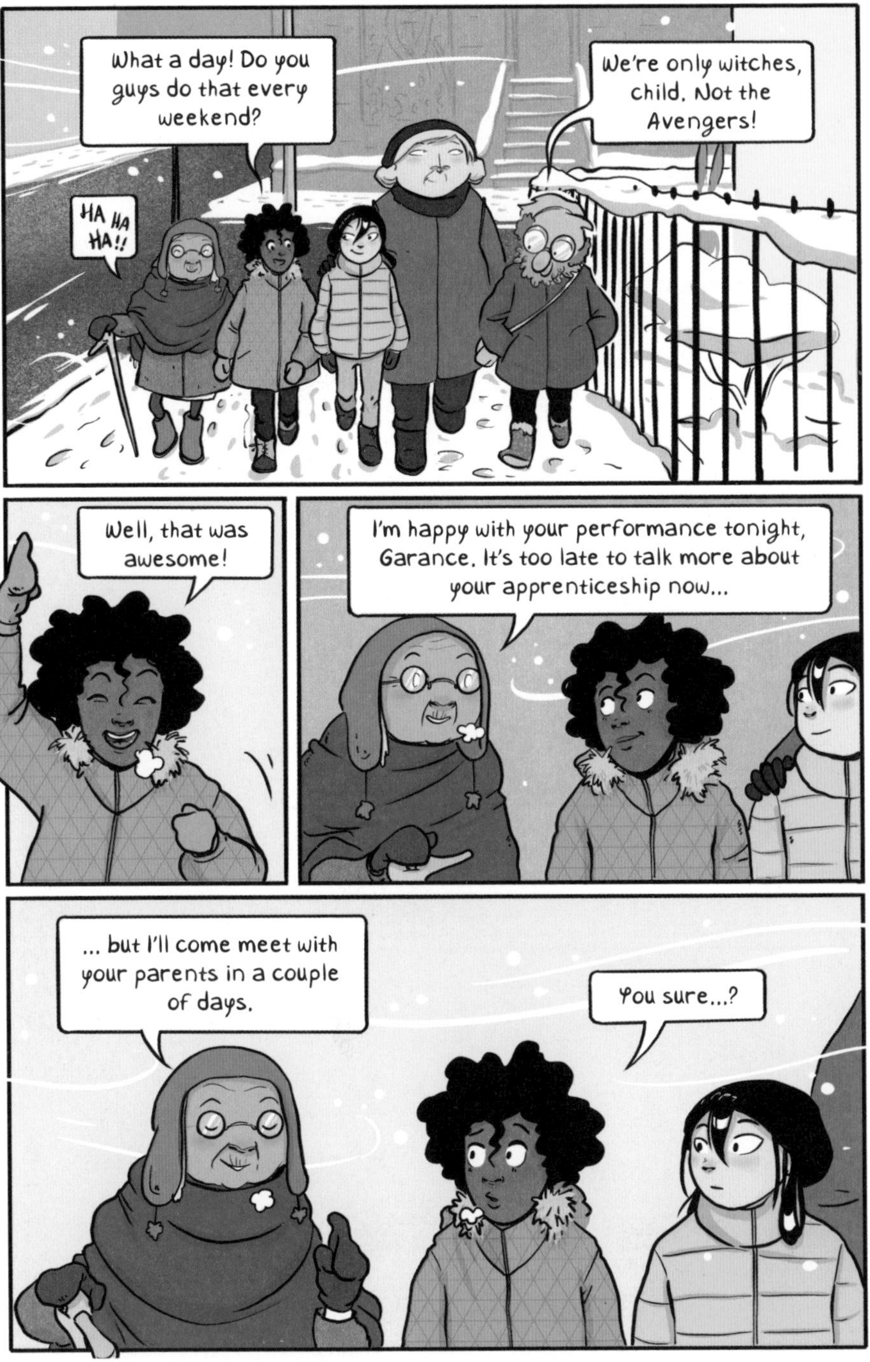
What a day! Do you guys do that every weekend?
We're only witches, child. Not the Avengers!
HA HA HA!!
Well, that was awesome!
I'm happy with your performance tonight, Garance. It's too late to talk more about your apprenticeship now...
... but I'll come meet with your parents in a couple of days.
You sure...?

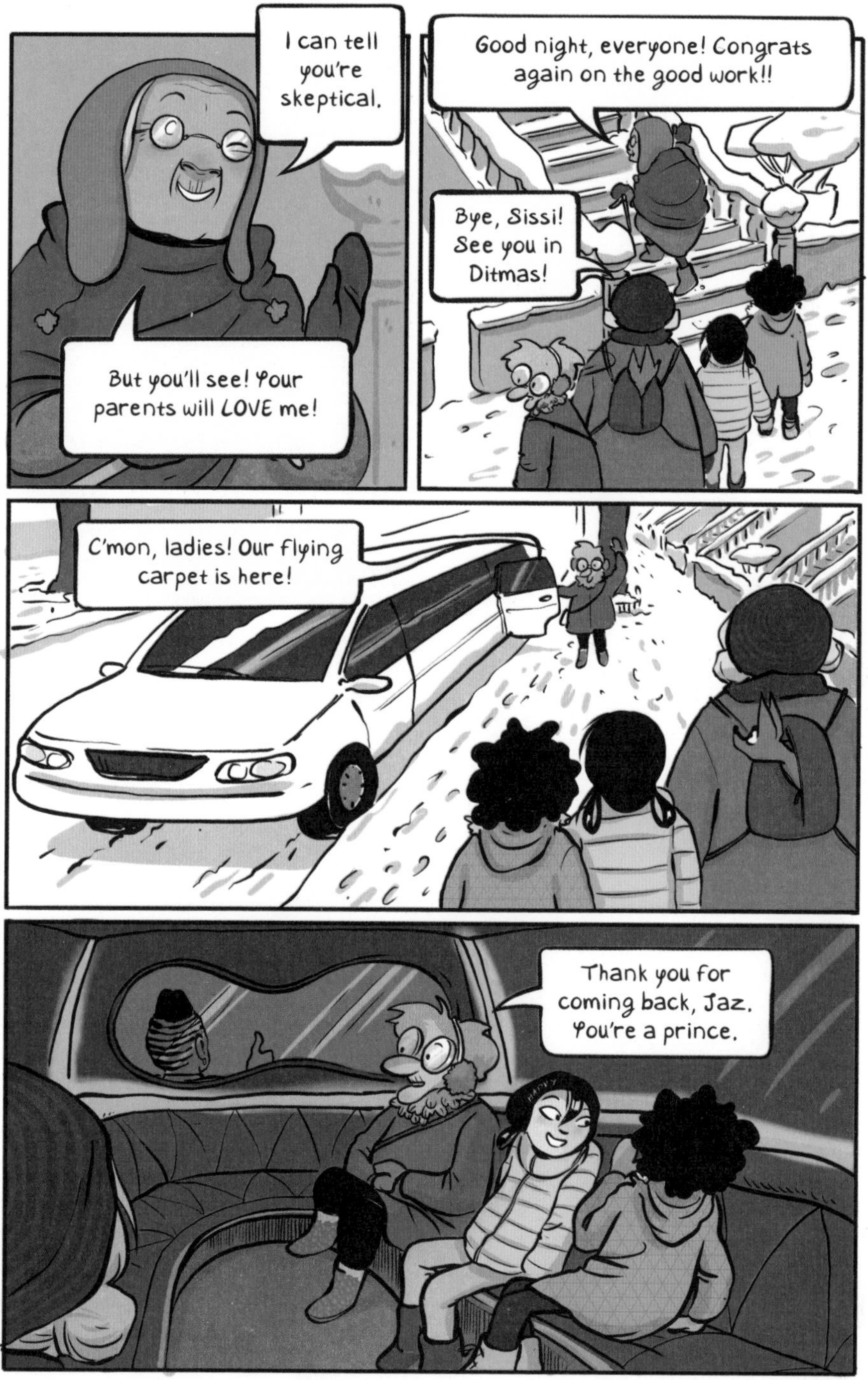
I can tell you're skeptical.
But you'll see! Your parents will LOVE me!
Good night, everyone! Congrats again on the good work!!
Bye, Sissi! See you in Ditmas!
C'mon, ladies! Our flying carpet is here!
Thank you for coming back, Jaz. You're a prince.

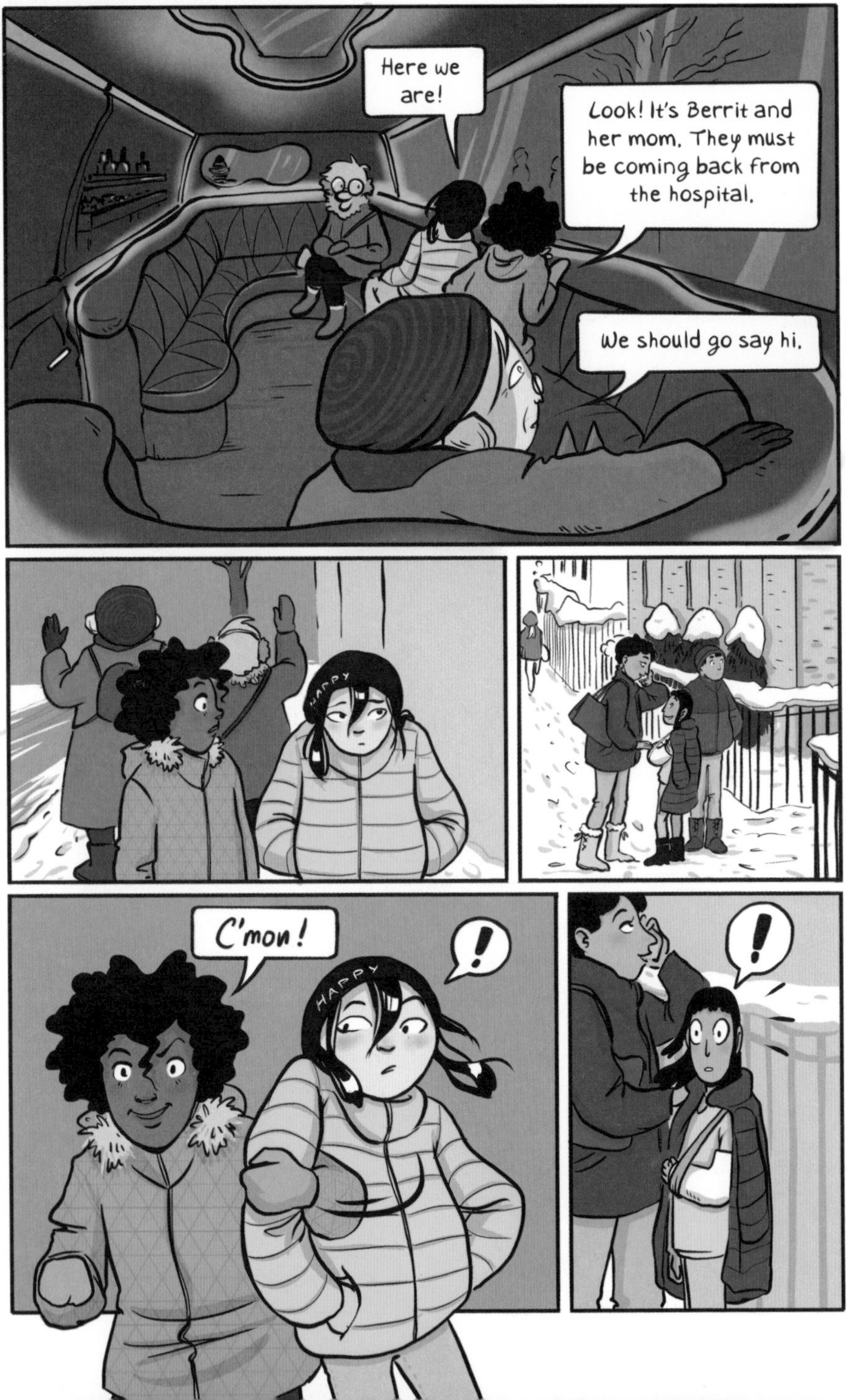
Here we are!
Look! It's Berrit and her mom. They must be coming back from the hospital.
We should go say hi.
C'mon!
!
!

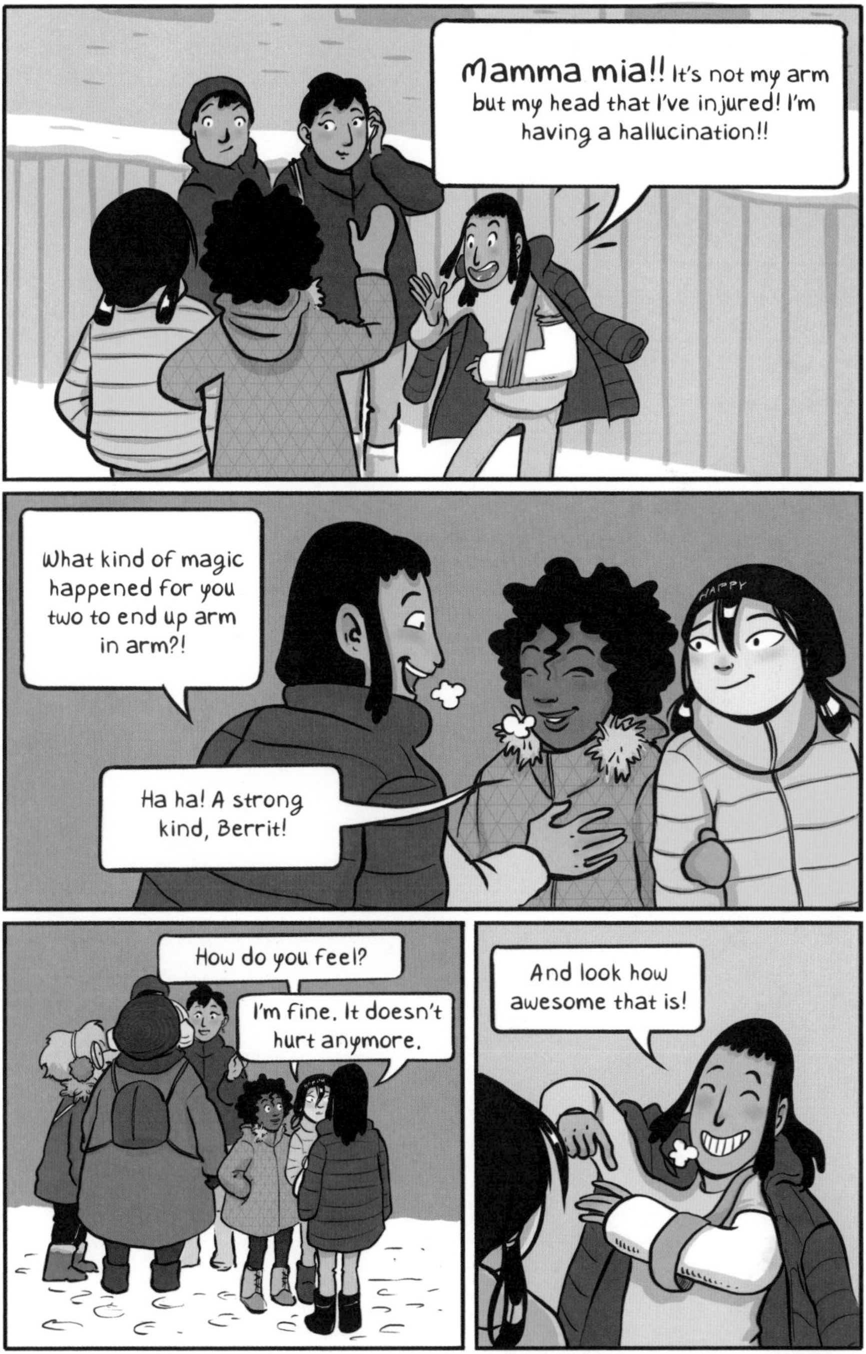
Mamma mia!! It's not my arm but my head that I've injured! I'm having a hallucination!!
What kind of magic happened for you two to end up arm in arm?!
HAPPY
Ha ha! A strong kind, Berrit!
How do you feel?
I'm fine. It doesn't hurt anymore.
And look how awesome that is!

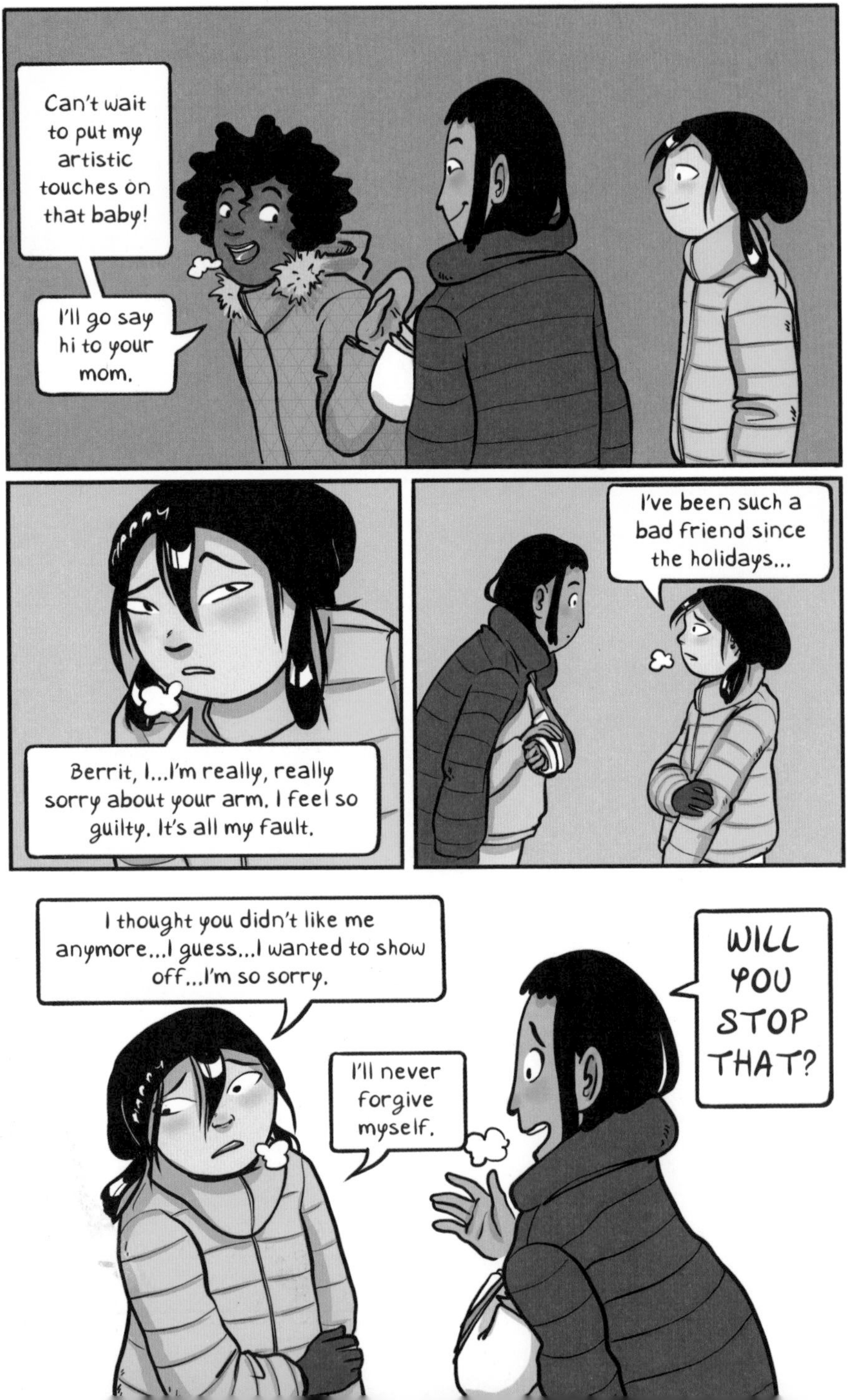
Can't wait to put my artistic touches on that baby!
I'll go say hi to your mom.
Berrit, I...I'm really, really sorry about your arm. I feel so guilty. It's all my fault.
I've been such a bad friend since the holidays...
I thought you didn't like me anymore...I guess...I wanted to show off...I'm so sorry.
I'll never forgive myself.
WILL YOU STOP THAT?

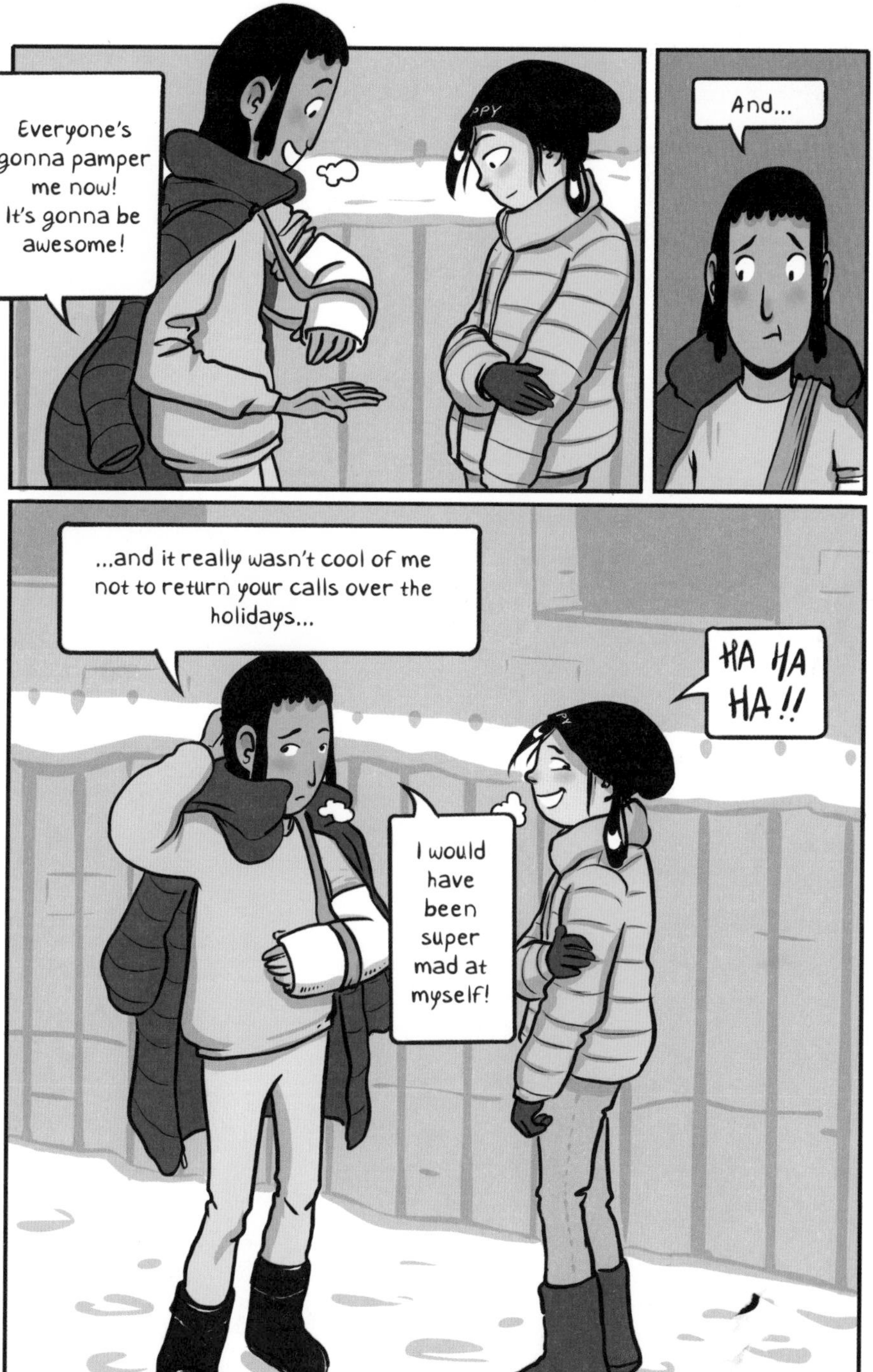
Everyone's gonna pamper me now! It's gonna be awesome!
And...
...and it really wasn't cool of me not to return your calls over the holidays...
HA HA HA !!
I would have been super mad at myself!

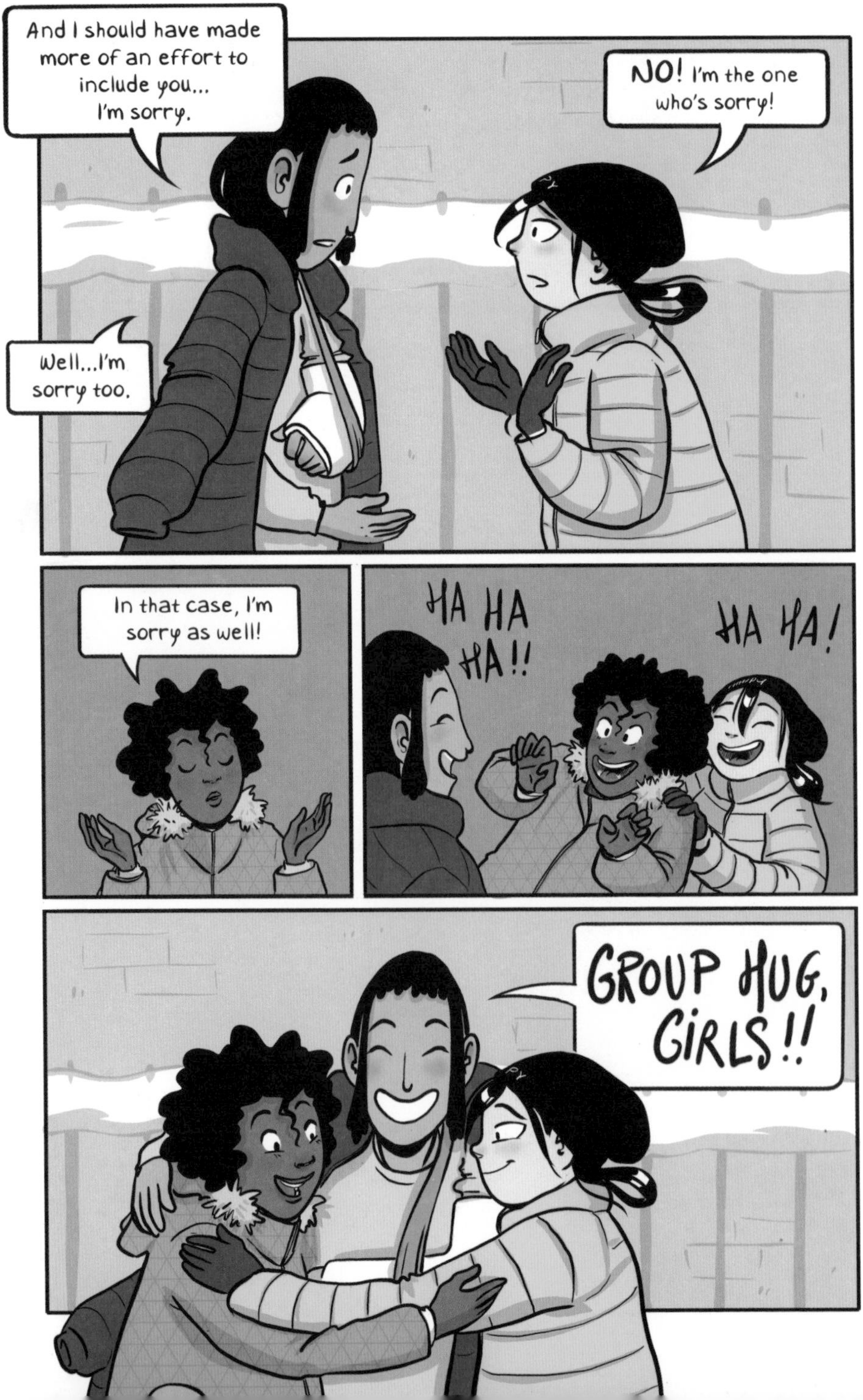
And I should have made more of an effort to include you... I'm sorry.
NO! I'm the one who's sorry!
Well...I'm sorry too.
In that case, I'm sorry as well!
HA HA HA!!
HA HA!
GROUP HUG, GIRLS!!

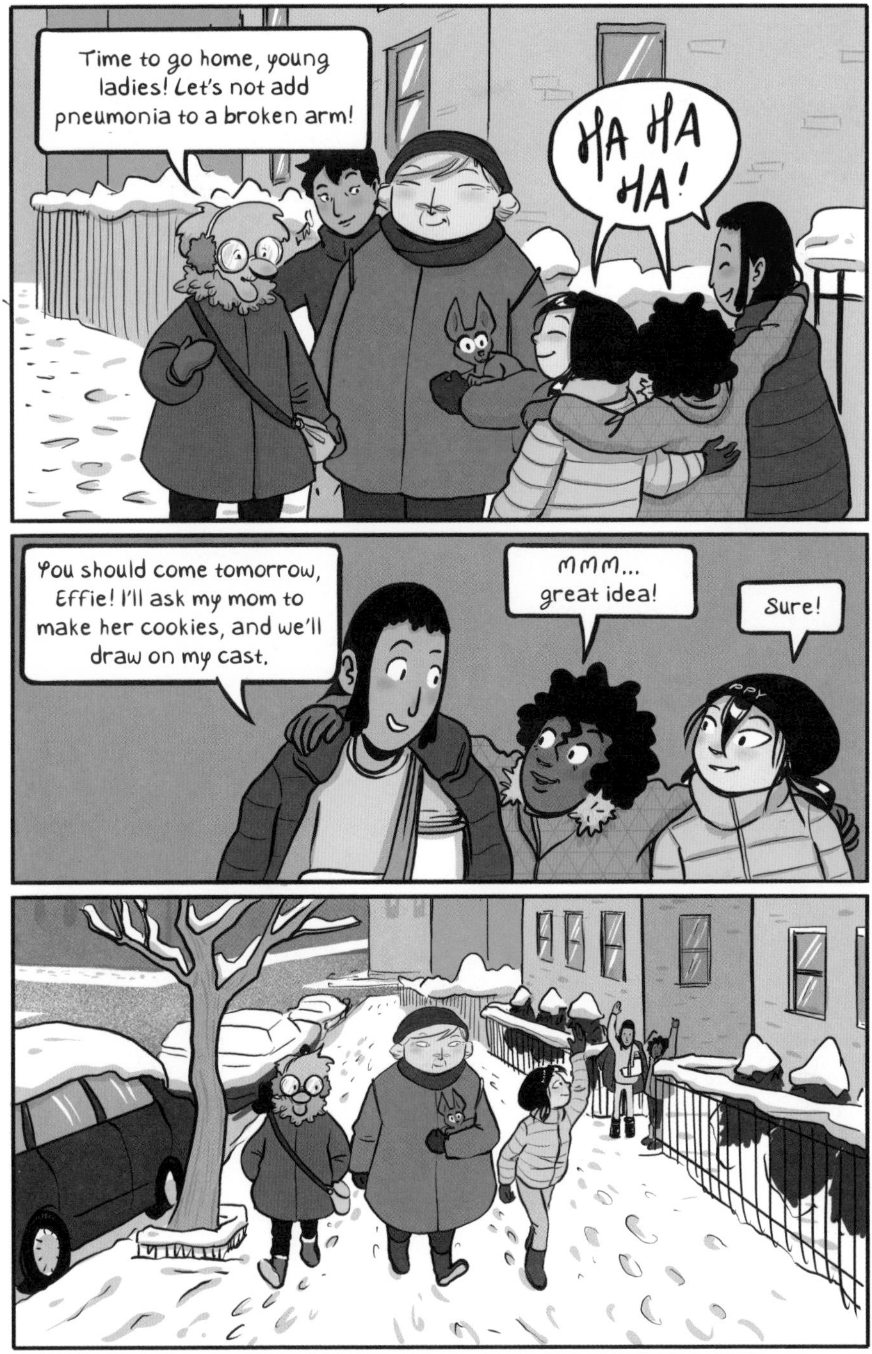
Time to go home, young ladies! Let's not add pneumonia to a broken arm!
HA HA HA!
You should come tomorrow, Effie! I'll ask my mom to make her cookies, and we'll draw on my cast.
MMM... great idea!
Sure!

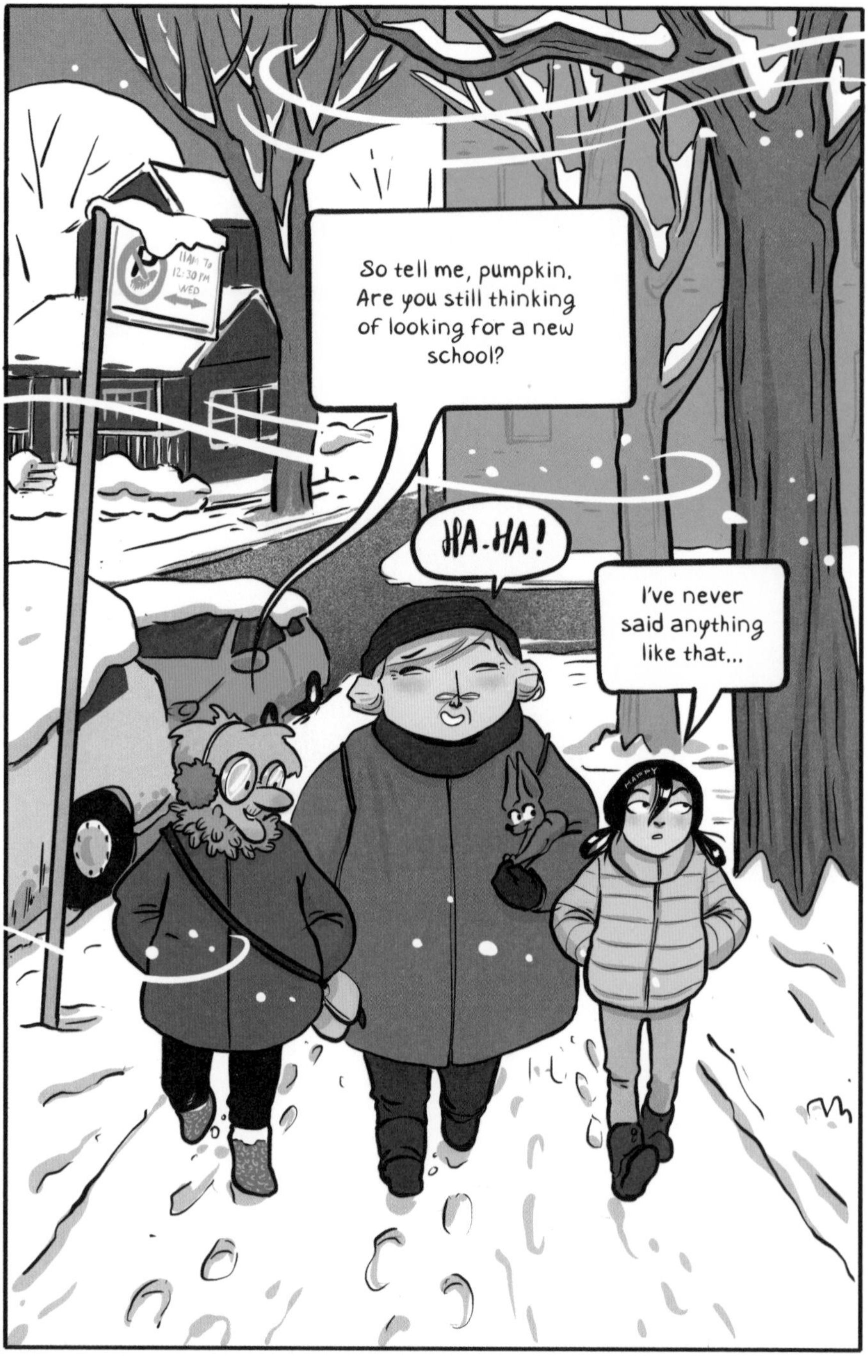
11AM To 12:30 PM WED
So tell me, pumpkin. Are you still thinking of looking for a new school?
HA-HA!
I've never said anything like that...
HAPPY

Epilogue

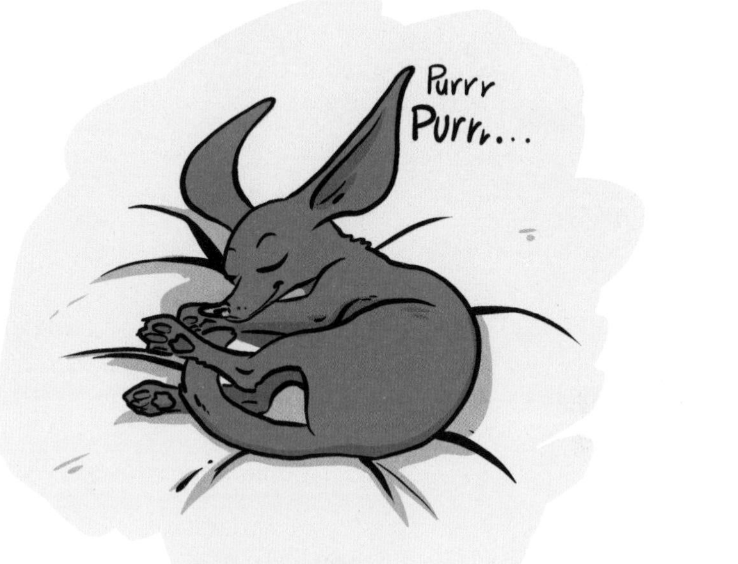
Purrr
Purrr...

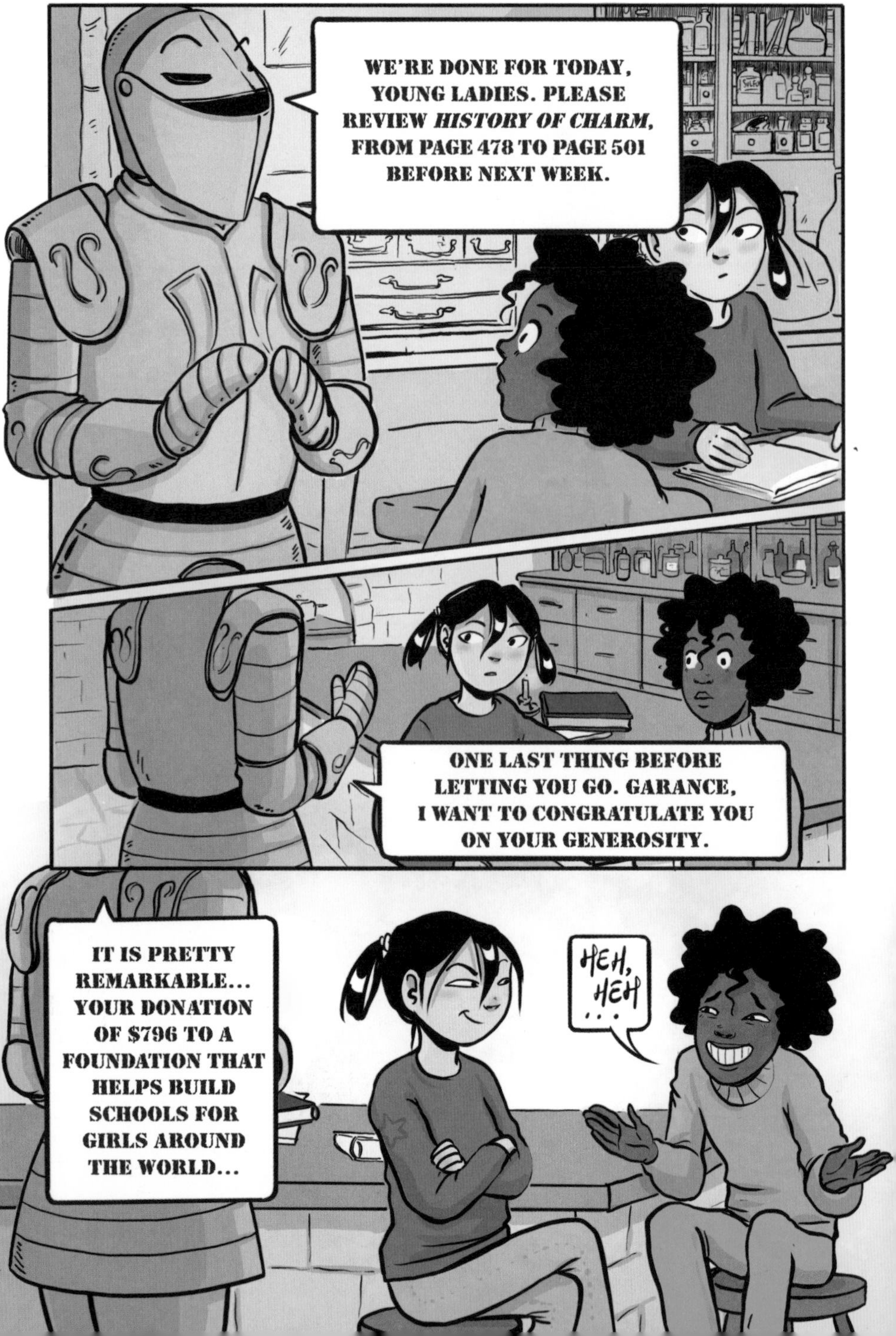
WE'RE DONE FOR TODAY, YOUNG LADIES. PLEASE REVIEW *HISTORY OF CHARM*, FROM PAGE 478 TO PAGE 501 BEFORE NEXT WEEK.
ONE LAST THING BEFORE LETTING YOU GO. GARANCE, I WANT TO CONGRATULATE YOU ON YOUR GENEROSITY.
IT IS PRETTY REMARKABLE... YOUR DONATION OF $796 TO A FOUNDATION THAT HELPS BUILD SCHOOLS FOR GIRLS AROUND THE WORLD...
HEH, HEH...

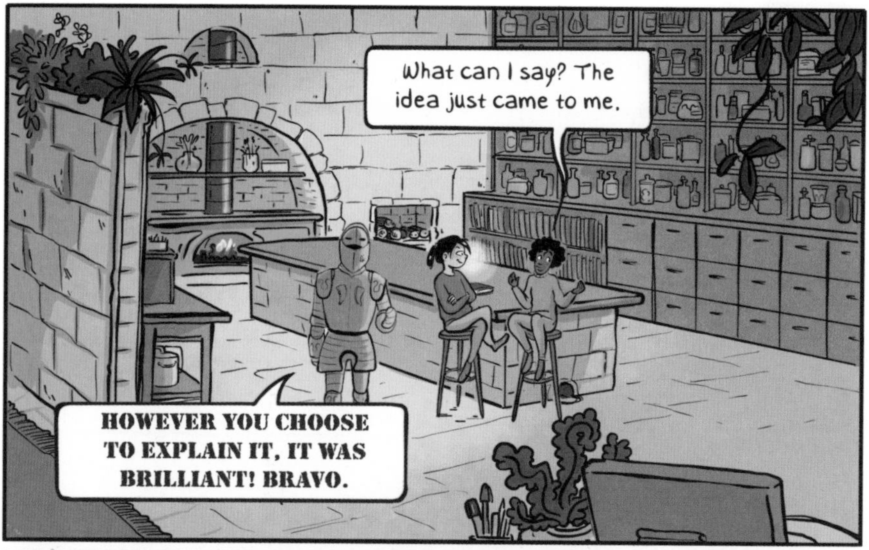
What can I say? The idea just came to me.
HOWEVER YOU CHOOSE TO EXPLAIN IT, IT WAS BRILLIANT! BRAVO.

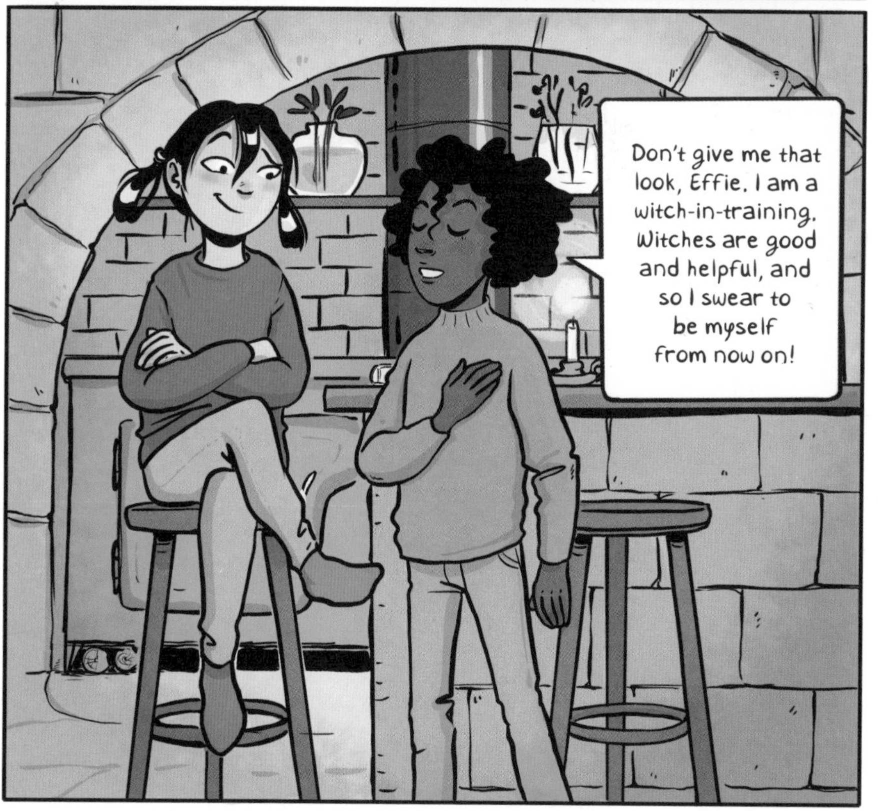
Don't give me that look, Effie. I am a witch-in-training. Witches are good and helpful, and so I swear to be myself from now on!

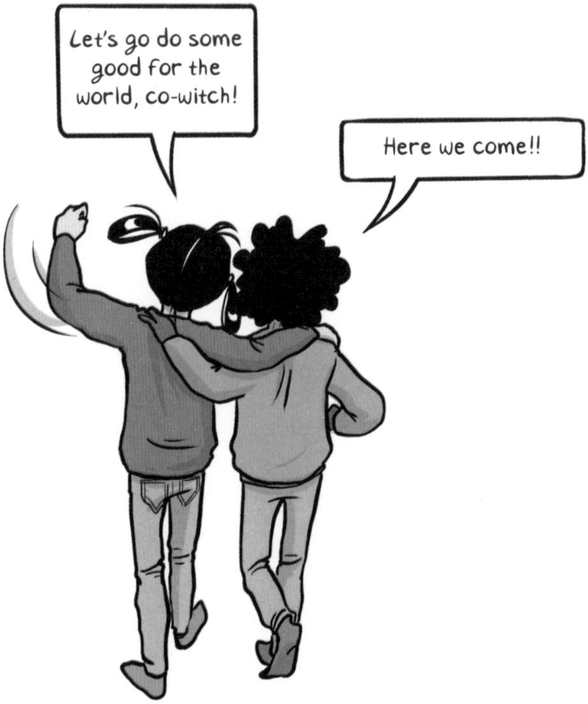
Let's go do some good for the world, co-witch!
Here we come!!

Acknowledgments

Again and again, I want to thank Kelly Sonnack, my extraordinary agent. Thank you for being such an exceptional woman and always standing by my side (rain or shine, worldwide pandemic or not). I am so grateful to be on this adventure with you.

Shout-out to the incredible Random House team, without whom this book wouldn't exist: Gina Gagliano, my editor Whitney Leopard, my designer Patrick Crotty, and Nicole Valdez. Thank you for your hard work shaping today's graphic novel landscape. I am very proud that the Witches of Brooklyn are Random House books, and I can't wait to discover the next graphic novels that'll come out of your magical hats!

Extra-special thanks to my husband, Patrick Flynn, and our children, Ella, Josephine, and Arthur, for being so supportive and enthusiastic about my work.

A BIG thank-you to Ariane for sticking with my crazy family during all the challenges that 2020 threw at us. Choupette, your work with the raccoons made this book possible.

Thank you to my family in France, who showed me so much support and sent me tons of love vibes over the ocean.

Thank you to all the readers who enjoyed *Witches of Brooklyn*. Your nice words brought butterflies to my stomach and made my pencils fly real high!

Finally, thank you to the magical booksellers and librarians who helped and supported the witches. ♡

Sophie Escabasse is a french-born illustrator and comic artist. A Brooklynite at heart, she's now living in Montreal with her husband, their three children, and her old black cat.

Originally trained as a graphic designer, she worked in advertising in Paris and New York City before fully embracing illustration as her career. Her work has appeared in the Derby Daredevils series by Kit Rosewater. Hailing from a family of graphic novel lovers, Sophie has been enjoying comics since she could read. Becoming a graphic novel author has been her lifelong dream, and today she's happily juggling being a mother of three and a comic artist of a new trilogy.

It's a lot of sweat but a lot of fun!

esofii.com
🅞 esofiii

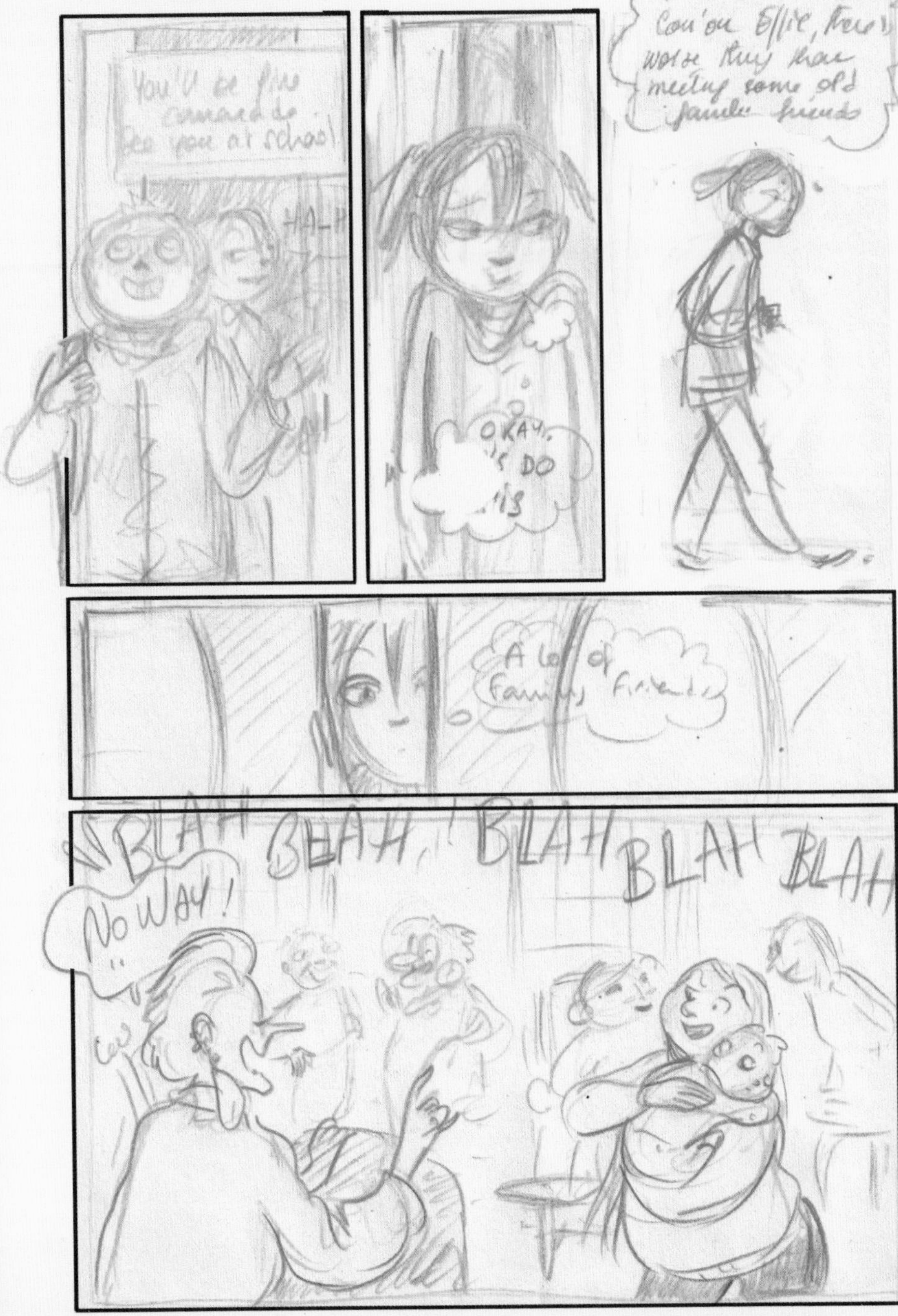

A lot of family friends
BLAH BLAH BLAH BLAH BLAH
NO WAY!

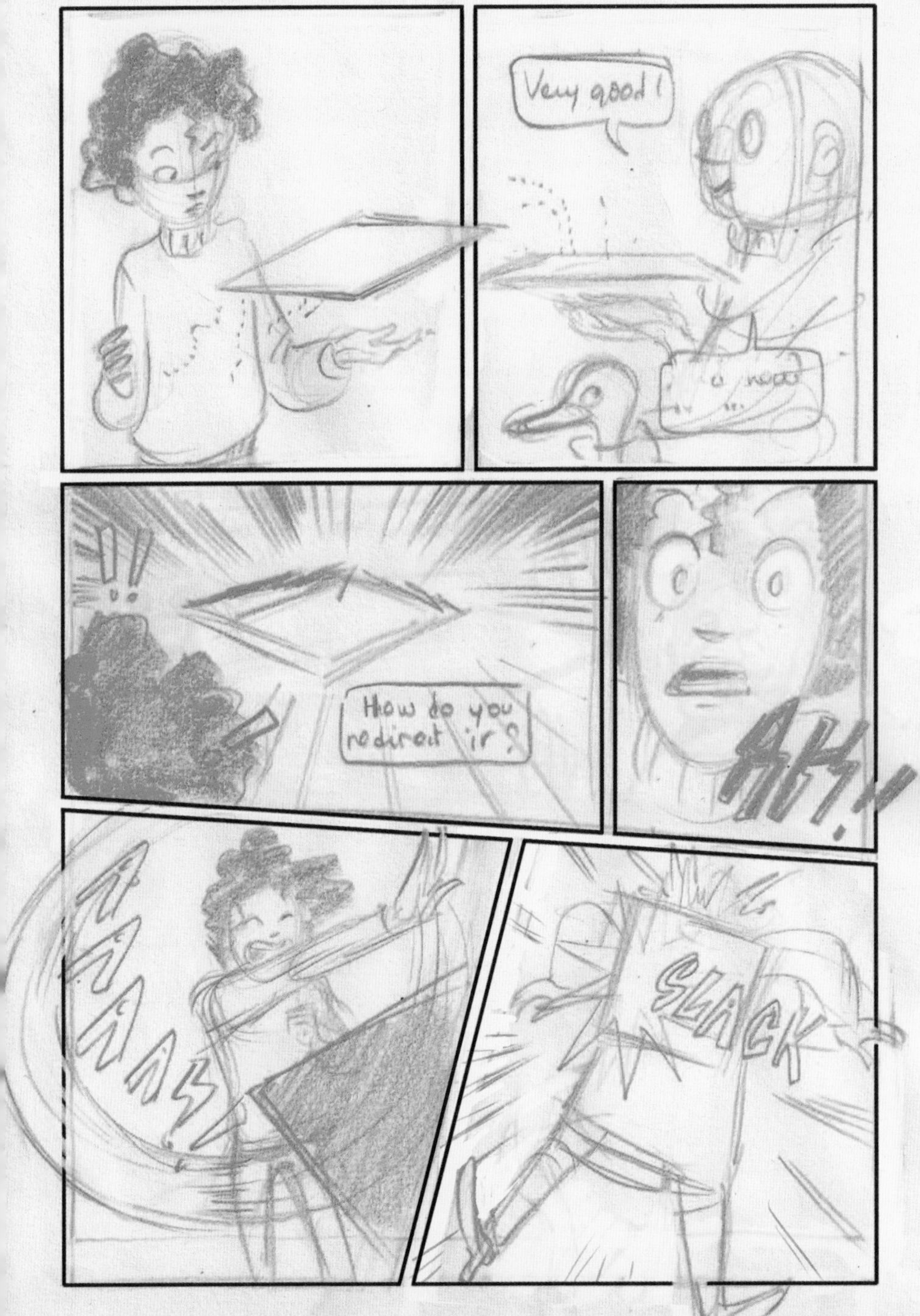
Very good!
!!
How do you redirect it?
AH!!
SLACK

Sophie's Sketchbook

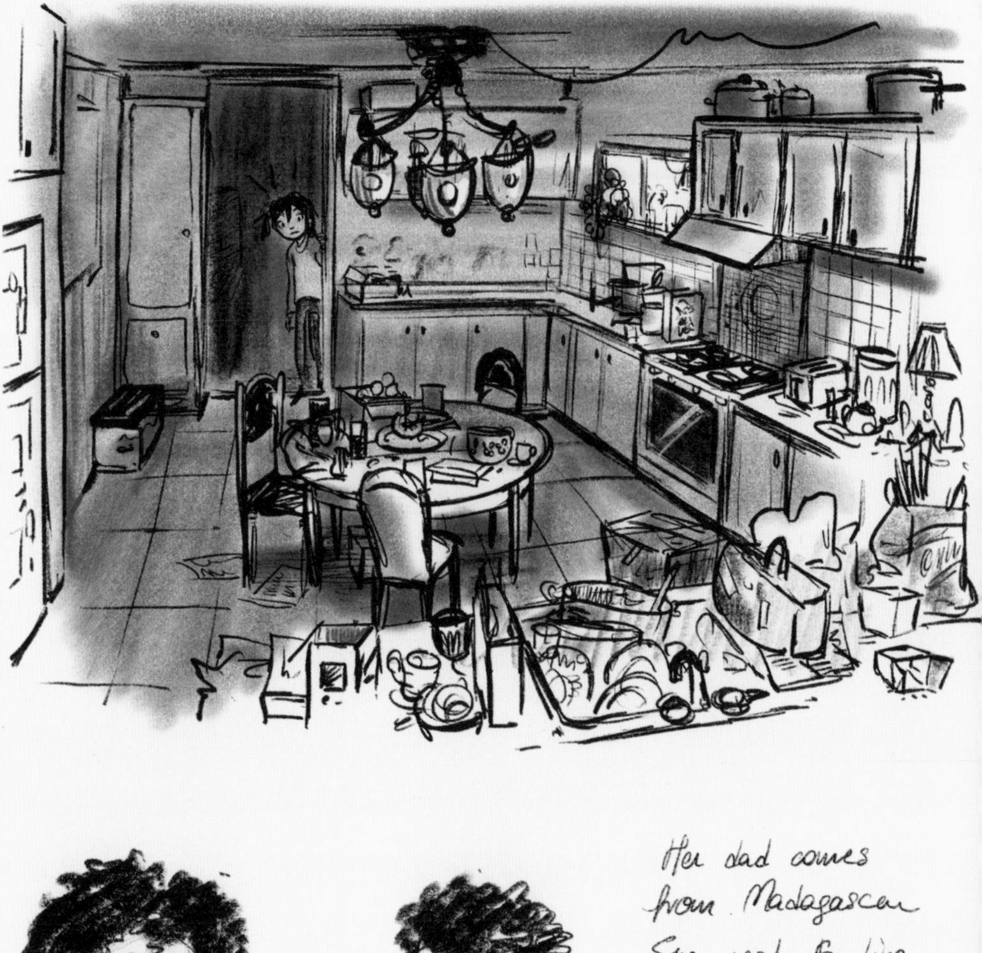

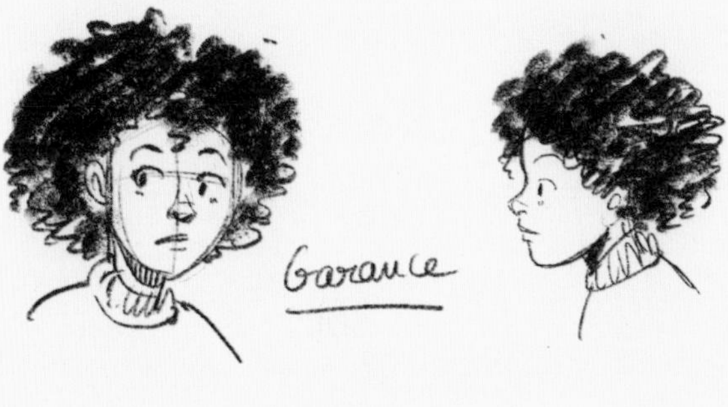
Garance

Her dad comes from Madagascar
She used to live in Marseille.
Then Paris- before moving to Brooklyn

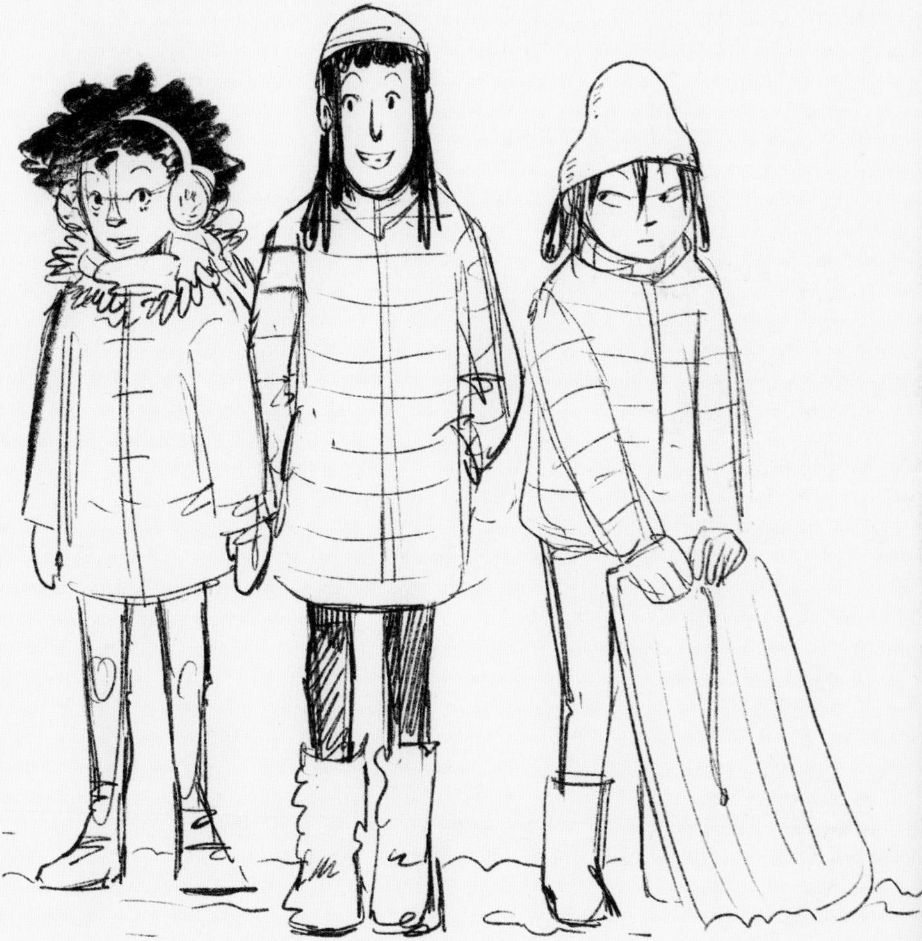

Sophie's Sketchbook

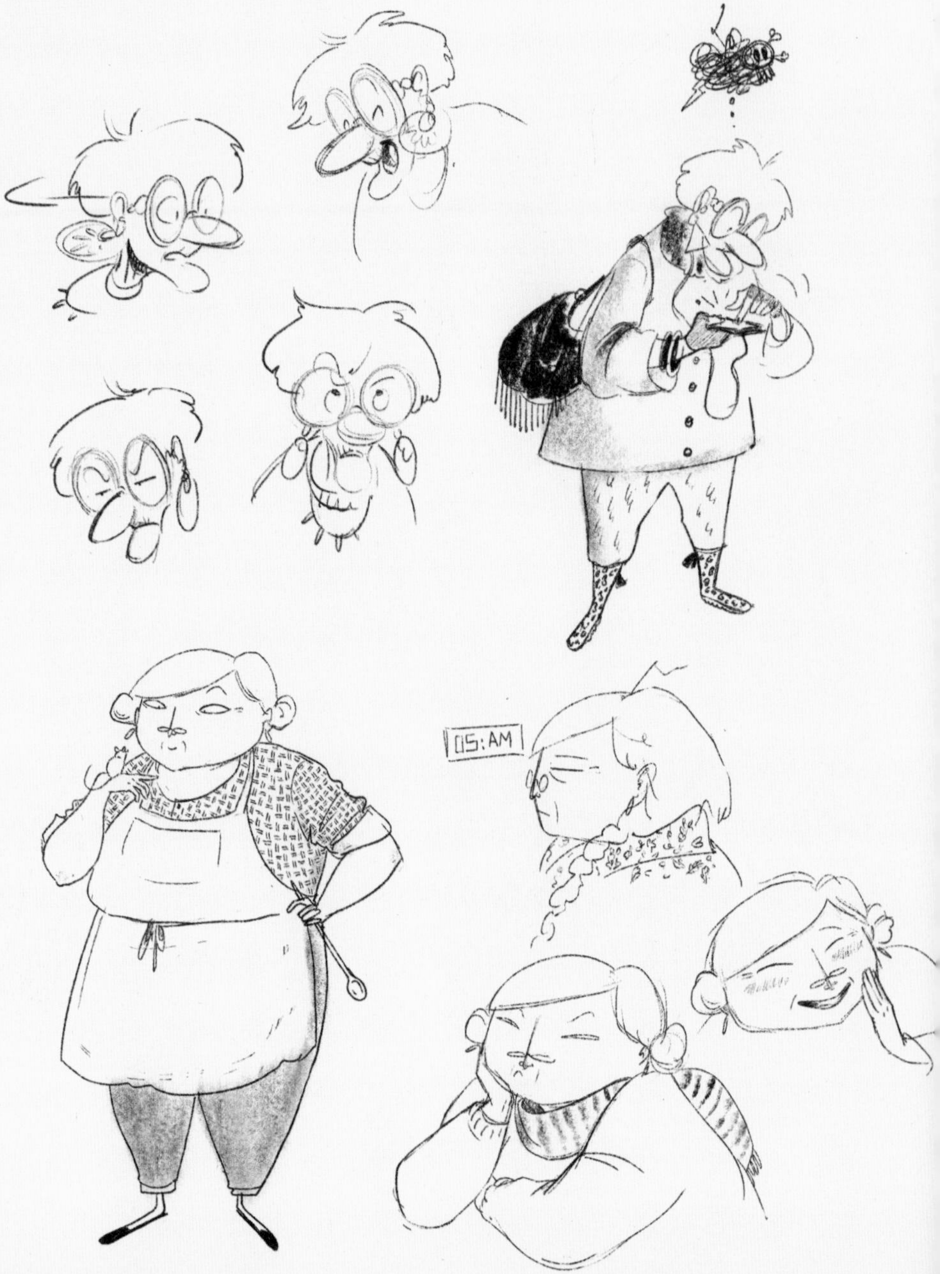
05:AM

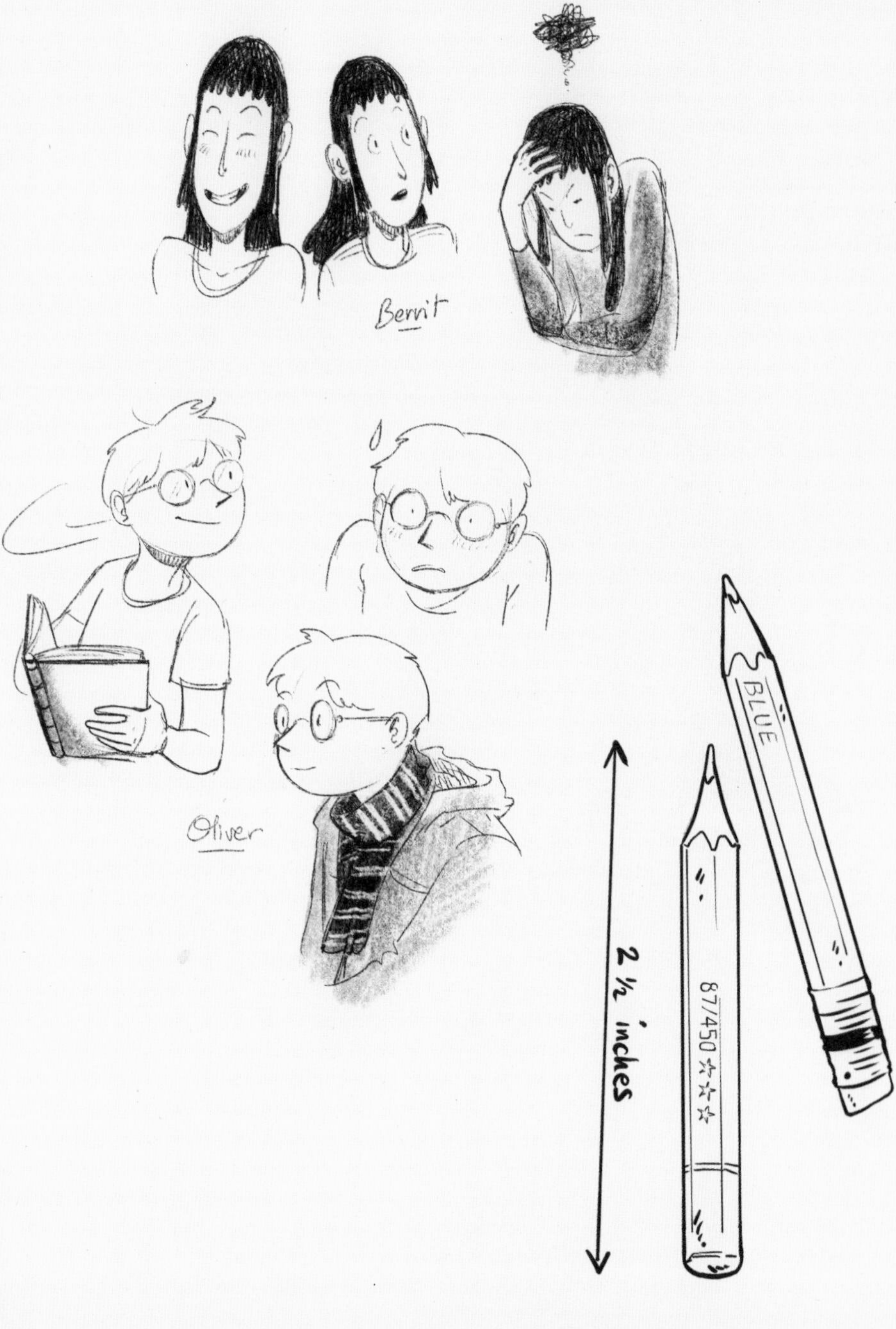
Berrit
Oliver
BLUE
87/450 ☆☆☆
2 ½ inches

Sophie's Sketchbook

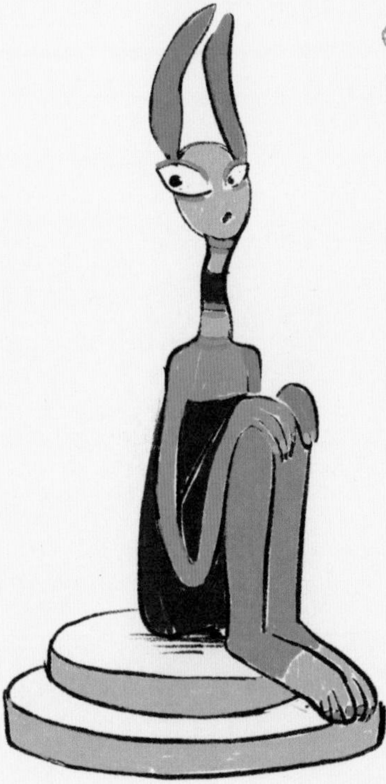

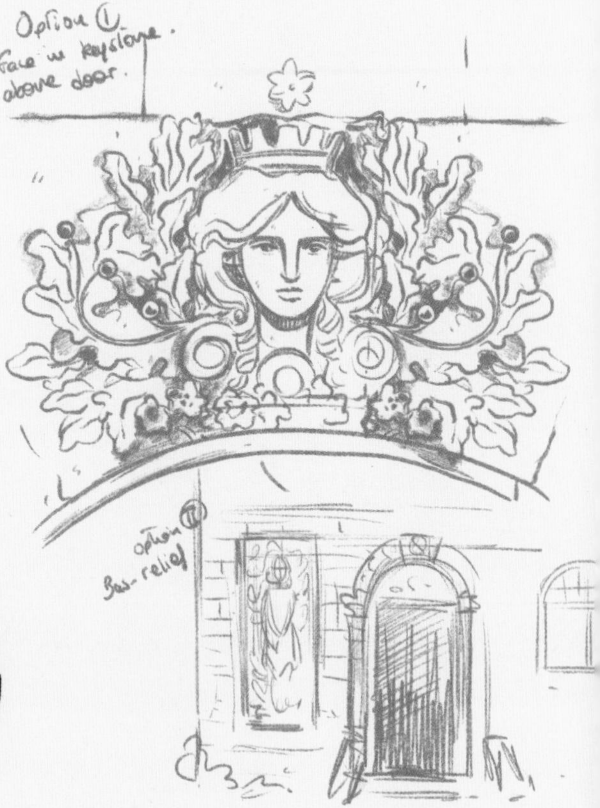
Option ①
Face in keystone
above door.
option ②
Bas-relief

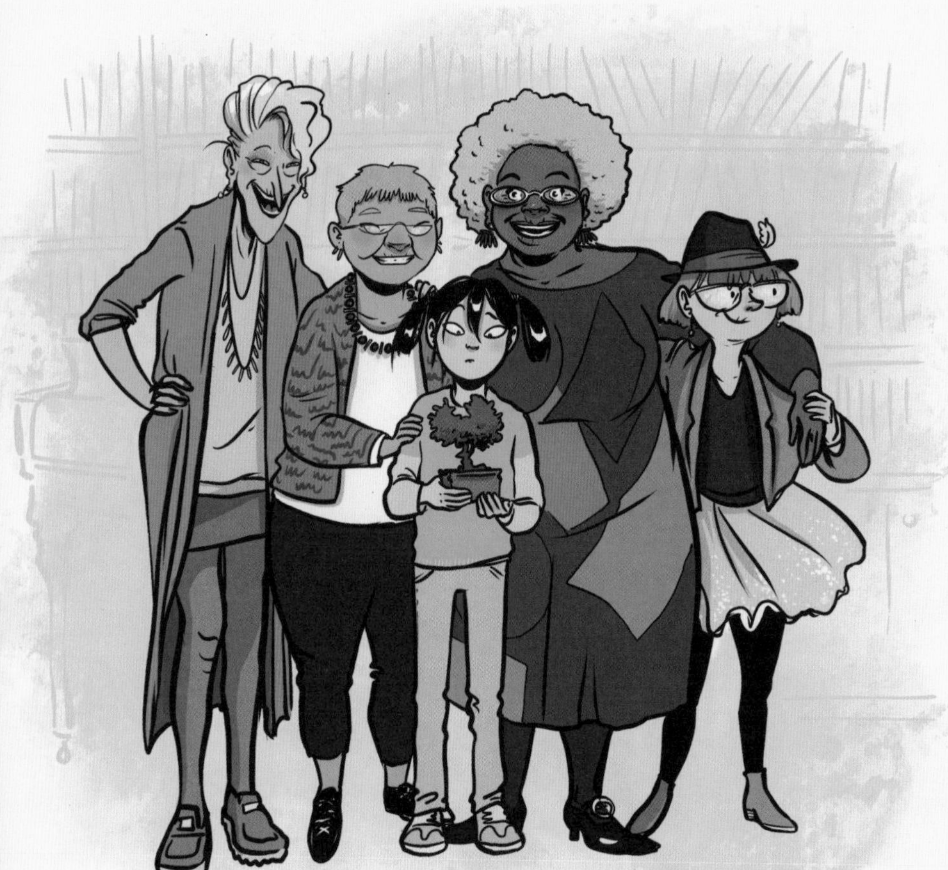

Sophie Escabasse
Witches of Brooklyn

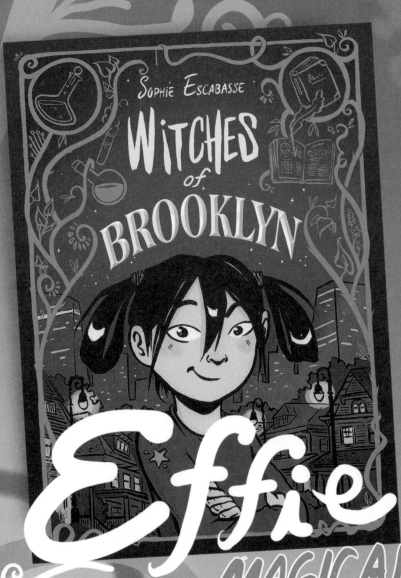

Effie

and her MAGICAL adventures continue in 2022!

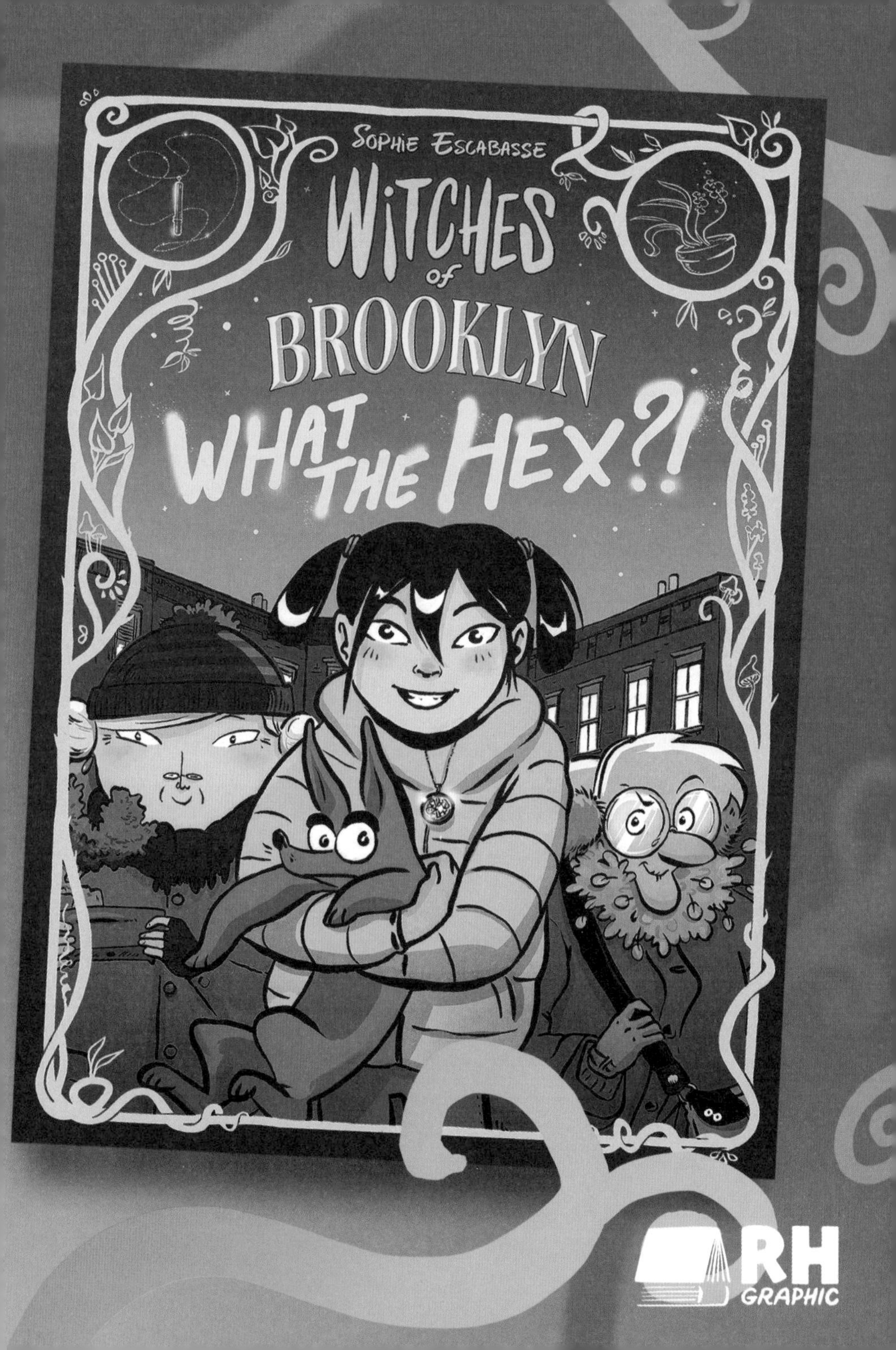
SOPHIE ESCABASSE
WITCHES of BROOKLYN
WHAT THE HEX?!
RH GRAPHIC

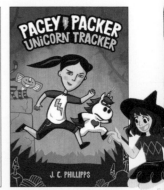